Misty Dreams

A NOVEL

BY

JOSEPHINE STRAND

ISBN: 978-0-578-90092-6

Edited by Magnifico Manuscripts
www.magnificomanuscripts.com

Cover design by Mind The Margins
www.mindthemargins.com

Cover art by Josephine Strand
Josephinestrand78@gmail.com
Josephinestrand.com

PRINTED IN THE UNITED STATES OF AMERICA

DEDICATION

For my husband, Tony, who had all but given up on me ever finishing this book, and for my daughter and best friend Laura. Thank you both for your enduring patience, love and encouragement through this long journey.

ACKNOWLEDGMENTS

Special thanks to Lorraine Fico-White and Nick White for believing in me. This book would not have been possible without your wisdom and expertise.

PROLOGUE

Clare huddled in her dark, stuffy hiding place, her knees pulled up against her chest. Her heart pounded so fast she had trouble breathing. She didn't know where she was, except that they'd been on the road for a long time. She'd tried to look out the window, but it was too dark to see anything.

Sobs gathered in her throat and she pressed her mouth to her knees to stifle them. She was afraid of what would happen if they heard her.

Perhaps it's all just a bad dream, she told herself. Soon I'll wake up and I'll be back at Aunt Lizzie's getting ready to celebrate Christmas Eve and wait for Santa. But she knew it wasn't. She'd bumped her head when she'd sat up to look out the window, and it still hurt. It wouldn't hurt if she was dreaming.

Someone had stuck bubble gum to the upholstery directly in front of her. The ugly green blob stared at her, and she wanted to scrape it off with her fingernail, but she was afraid to move, to make the slightest noise.

She squeezed her eyes shut and prayed like Mom had told her to do when Papa had gone to the hospital and she had been afraid he'd die. It had worked, then, and his heart had healed.

But she hadn't been alone, then, and miles and miles away from home.

PART 1

Richard

CHAPTER 1

St. Isabel Island, South Florida

Under the ruthless tropical sun, heat rose in shimmering waves from the tarmac, much like heat ripples dancing over a burning hotplate, and Richard guessed, just as unforgiving.

The only sounds impinging on the peaceful surroundings as he prepared to descend from the small Learjet were the distant humming of aircraft motors on the far side of the airstrip and the unrelenting buzz of the mosquitoes. The pesky creatures had congregated in voracious swarms around the newly landed aircraft, having perhaps sniffed the arrival of fresh prey.

Slipping on his sunglasses to shield his eyes from the blinding glare, he steeled himself against the inevitable shock of the Deep South heat and descended onto the runway. Summer had come early to southern Florida, and he already regretted the moment of rash impulsiveness that had brought him to this godforsaken place.

Curbing a foul mood that showed no will or inclination to let up, he paused halfway down the rollaway stairs and gazed around what appeared to be a small but busy commercial airport. About two hundred yards to the left of the landing strip, several small cargo crafts were lined up in military precision in front of a row of hangars, some sitting idle, some in different stages of the loading and unloading process. All bore the logo *ElliotAir* painted on the fuselage in bold red lettering. Men in navy uniforms operated forklifts and provided a steady flow of activity in and around the loading dock.

Above the smell of fuel and tar rose a subtle flowery scent which intrigued him, considering there was little or no vegetation in the immediate vicinity of the airfield. It was reminiscent of the fragrance from the jasmine bush growing outside the window at the villa in Capri where he and Erica had spent their honeymoon. Being reminded of his honeymoon tarnished his mood even further.

While he waited for the pilot to unload his luggage, the light cotton shirt he'd judged sensible enough for island wear clung to his body like a damp second skin. He wondered if he hadn't made a colossal mistake in choosing a tropical island on which to spend his—he didn't even know what to call it—sabbatical? Spiritual retreat? Escape from impending insanity?

It was more like the island had picked him. From the moment he'd learned of its existence, he'd experienced an irresistible urge to find it, to see where it led. And why not? At this stage in his life, he had nothing left to lose.

As if sensing his discomfort, the pilot said, "This heat must come as a shock after New York."

The man, who'd introduced himself as Philippe Girard, had flown all the way to Miami to meet him and had gone out of his way to be friendly and hospitable during the flight back. He'd chatted amicably and pointed out features of interest about their final destination, ignoring Richard's obnoxious reserve.

Philippe was around Richard's age and was dressed impeccably. From his gold-embossed aviator's hat over a mop of almost shoulder-length blond curls to the tip of his navy canvas loafers, he appeared relaxed and composed as if he'd just taken a leisurely stroll along Miami's beachfront. Richard wondered, not without a little resentment, if the man ever broke a sweat or lost his cool.

Philippe picked up the suitcase he'd unloaded from the plane and pointed him toward an oversized stucco building with a terra cotta-shingled roof. Looking forward to the promise of a cool shelter, Richard shouldered his backpack containing his laptop and little else, and flanking the pilot, set off in the direction of the main office building.

"How long are you planning on staying on St. Isabel?" Philippe asked.

Richard wiped his brow with the back of his free hand. "It depends on how long I can last before the heat and bugs start getting to me," he replied. He took in the other man's relaxed façade. "How do you do it? I mean, live here, day-in, day-out."

"I couldn't see myself living anywhere else," Philippe replied with the confidence of one who is exactly where he wants to be. But then, being an islander, he'd most likely developed a natural resistance to both the steamy climate and rapacious insect population. "On St. Isabel, island life gets in your blood after a while, which is why we don't encourage mass tourism. Visitors bring more visitors, and before you know it, it's another Key West." He grinned crookedly at him. "No offense."

"None taken."

"So, what do you do in the big city?" Philippe asked.

"I'm . . . in the health care business," Richard replied evasively, making an impromptu decision he'd be traveling incognito. At least for a while he wanted to forget who he was, pretend Richard Jonathan Kelly MD didn't exist. He pushed back the familiar bitter taste of failure and forced himself to focus on the present. He hadn't come all the way here to dwell on the past.

If the other man noticed his deliberate caginess, he didn't let it show. "I'll get the Jeep while you check in with the boss," he said as they approached the office building, and he took off in the opposite direction.

On stepping into the shade of the building's wraparound veranda a young woman came out with a welcoming smile on her striking face. A more-than-striking figure complemented the face, Richard noted.

"Hi, I'm Courtney Elliot. Welcome to St. Isabel Island," she said holding out her hand. He took it, her grip feeling cool and strong in his clammy one.

So this was "the boss" Philippe had been referring to, and probably the same person who had signed the receipt for the advance payment on his temporary lodgings. Even as he associated the name with the logo imprinted on the aircraft, his heart skipped a beat. Courtney Elliot. Surely not the mysterious C.E. indirectly responsible for his traveling halfway across the country on some crazy-ass jaunt?

He told himself it was most likely a coincidence. C.E. were just two common initials. They could belong to anyone, even on an island this small.

"Richard Kelly," he said. "I have to admit you don't fit my preconceived expectations of a buxom, gray-haired, elderly innkeeper."

Her laugh was spontaneous and judging by the way she held on to his hand a tad longer than necessary, openly flirtatious. "That would be my mother, Sonia Elliot. She runs Serena. I have to warn you, though. She may be gray-haired but she would hate to be described as buxom—or elderly, for that matter." Vivid, dark-speckled green eyes swept over him, lingering unabashedly, which only contributed to his discomfort.

"Did you have a pleasant flight?" she asked.

"Yes, thank you," he replied, then added, "Nice perk, by the way."

She smiled. "Glad you enjoyed it. ElliotAir is largely a freight business. Our planes fly on a daily basis transporting merchandise from the mainland to the neighboring islands, so it's no hardship for our pilots to make a short detour to pick up a guest from time to time." She gestured him to a chair. "Can I offer you a cold drink?"

"Sure, the colder the better," he accepted readily.

As she turned, her long mane of jet-black curls swung out gracefully, settling back onto her smooth-tanned shoulders in a soft cloud. Richard followed her into the air-conditioned interior as she led the way through a small reception area and into a modernly equipped office. He removed his mirrored sunglasses, allowing his vision to adjust to the light streaming through the wide picture windows overlooking the airfield. The room was pleasantly cool and spacious, its subtly exotic décor contributing to enhance the tropical ambience. His eyes were drawn to the young woman as she walked over to a small refrigerator behind the desk. As he silently admired the slender curves in skintight white denim, he was surprised to feel a flush of embarrassment rise to his face. He supposed he should be thankful his male impulses hadn't died with the rest of him.

He quickly averted his gaze and focused, instead, on the surroundings. Holographic prints of vintage commercial airplanes, all except one, a giant oil portrait of a tawny-haired, distinguished-looking man hung on the wall above the desk. His eyes automatically searched for the artist's signature and discovered it wasn't the one he'd hoped to find. It was impossible to ignore the twinge of disappointment that came with the discovery, even as he told himself if he'd come to St. Isabel expecting to find signs of the elusive C.E. lurking in every corner of the island, he was more messed up than he'd thought. For all he knew, this person—this faceless, sexless image that had taken up residence in his brain—wasn't necessarily an inhabitant. He or she could be anyone, even a passing tourist.

"My father, Edward Elliot Junior," Courtney said noticing his interest. "He founded ElliotAir almost thirty years ago." He caught a shadow passing over her expression for a second, and he surmised her father was no longer living. "Please, have a seat, Mr. Kelly. Beer or soda?"

"Richard, and I'll have a soda," he said.

Courtney returned with a can, then sat across from him, crossing one elegant leg over the other. "So, what brings you to St. Isabel?"

He avoided her gaze and undid another button on the front of his shirt. "Just taking a break from city life," he replied vaguely. "I'll be using the time to finish a book I'm working on."

"A book." She sounded surprised. "We've had guests with some interesting backgrounds staying at Serena but never a writer. Let me guess. Adventure? Suspense? No, wait, you strike me as the type who revels in the apocalyptic. Science fiction, perhaps?"

He wondered how she'd come to that striking conclusion after only a few minutes of having met him. He considered telling her the truth, but that would defeat the purpose of maintaining his anonymity. "A bit of all three," he replied. It was close enough to the truth if one considered the still-relative obscurity and complexities of the workings of the human brain.

She appeared perplexed as she tried to make sense of his response, then she said, "I'm sure General Morris will find you an interesting addition to the household. He's a thriller aficionado himself."

"General Morris?"

"Serena's oldest returning guest and a voracious reader," she explained. "He's a retired NASA officer and confirmed bachelor and has a standing reservation on a suite three months out of every year. He's a bit of a grouch but you can't help liking him."

Richard had no particular interest in meeting General Morris, nor did he have any plans to mingle with his fellow guests while staying at Serena. All he wanted to do was keep to himself and work off his funk in peace.

The door swung open and Philippe bounded into the room. With long, purposeful strides the pilot headed to the refrigerator where he helped himself to a beer. Then he dropped his gangly form in Courtney's executive chair, propping his feet up on the desk as if he owned the place.

"Damn," he said fanning himself with his aviator's hat. "I can't remember it being this humid in April."

Hah, not so immune, after all, Richard thought with perverse satisfaction.

The man's total lack of respect for his boss's workspace appeared to annoy Courtney Elliot, who fired him a scathing look. "If you're ready, you should take Mr. Kelly up to the house," she said in a crisp tone. "I'm sure he'll want to settle in."

A corner of Philippe's mouth lifted in a lazy smirk. "Yes, ma'am," he drawled lifting two fingers to his brow in mock salute. He took another swig of the beer, then swung his legs off the desk. "Shall we go?" he said to Richard.

By the time they were back outside, Courtney had regained her composure. "Come back to the airfield one of these days. I'll treat you to an aerial tour of the island," she told him. "On the house, of course."

"You fly?"

She narrowed her eyes at him. "Do you have a problem with female pilots?"

"Not at all," he said, realizing he'd struck a nerve without meaning to.

Her eyes danced with humor at his evident discomfort. "I promise I won't crash us both to the ground," she said.

He saw the derisive twinkle in her eyes. "In that case . . . thank you," he said.

During the short drive to the resort his escort kept up a steady stream of chatter during which Richard learned a few interesting facts about the Elliots' plantation home/turned guest house. Courtney's grandfather, the senior Edward Elliot, had purchased the plantation house and had converted it into a vacation home for his family. Later, when they'd moved to the island on a permanent basis, it had become their principal abode. Only about a decade or so earlier had it been converted into an exclusive guest residence.

"The house was originally built around 1857 by a rich sugar farmer, then passed along to his descendants who lived in it until the mid-1950s," Philippe told him. "The story goes that the last owner, who was a bit of a high roller, had experienced a stroke of bad luck at the gambling tables and was letting the property go to ruin. When a few years later his pineapple plantation suffered severe damage during a powerful hurricane, he'd had no choice but to sell. The late Edward Elliot Senior purchased it for a song and restored the house to its original splendor."

"What became of Edward Elliot Junior?" Richard asked.

The man's jaunty demeanor dwindled a little. "He died several years ago of heart failure. A true gentleman, as well as a savvy businessman," he said. "He built up the air freight business from the ground up when still in his thirties, and within a few years put together a sizeable fleet. Sonia ran the company for a while after he passed, until she decided to dedicate herself entirely to the guest house."

"So now Courtney's at the helm," Richard said.

Philippe nodded and grinned. "Runs it like a drill sergeant."

There was no mistaking the pride transpiring from the man's tone, which Richard found intriguing for someone who minutes earlier had been openly rude toward the very same employer. He wondered what it was about Philippe Girard that irritated Courtney. Could it be Courtney Elliot was a snob?

"Been working long for the Elliots?" he asked.

"Going on twenty years now," Philippe replied. "I came here from Quebec City on a brief island adventure and ended up staying."

It explained the unmistakable trace of a French accent Richard had detected.

Switching gears in the conversation Philippe asked, "Do you sail?"

"I do," Richard said, before he remembered his sailing days were a remote part of his life, the life he'd left behind. "Used to, that is. Had a small boat out on Long Island for a while."

"Come down to the marina one of these days. You can do some great sailing around St. Isabel."

HIS FIRST THOUGHT, when they turned off a wide, palmetto-bordered driveway and drew up in front of a sprawling Greek revival mansion, was that the place was nothing like he'd expected, but then, he hadn't known what to expect. His assistant had made the reservation; his only requirements were peace and quiet, and a space where to park his laptop in the dubious event his pre-depression enthusiasm for the book he was supposed to have finished months ago returned. The former plantation home was an impressive two-story, pre-Civil War construction built on a luxuriantly green rise facing a spectacular view of the Atlantic Ocean. Its grand yet demure exterior exuded an aura of tranquility that did justice to its name.

Philippe dropped him off in the wide Spanish-style courtyard and continued to Richard's new lodgings with his luggage. An olive-skinned young man came to meet him and relieved him of his backpack. His long dreadlocks wobbled as he introduced himself as Juan in a clipped and colorful accent, and motioned to follow him inside the house, leaving Richard staring after him in bemusement. He'd half expected to be met by the stereotypical stiff-lipped liveried servant, the type one usually saw in those antebellum-era movies. Certainly not a Bermuda shorts-clad, sandal-footed young man with a friendly smile.

As he crossed the threshold of the old mansion, he was taken aback by the grandeur and richness of the interior. He'd rubbed elbows with the elite long enough to recognize everything in this house was authentic and priceless, down to the carved moldings and Italian marble floors. Wide, heavy oak doors opened onto an airy hallway complete with crystal chandeliers and sweeping double staircase, though without the overstated opulence one would expect to find in a rich plantation owner's home. The décor was Victorian, from the antique furniture and peer mirrors to the silk wall coverings and inlaid sideboards. He had the impression he'd stepped back a couple of centuries. Any minute now a plump housekeeper in a white apron would sweep her long black skirts through the side door and usher him inside.

The woman who crossed the hall and met him with a welcoming smile was far from the lace and crinoline type, though she blended in nicely with the dignity and serenity of the house. She was petite and delicately built, with gentle blue eyes that reached disturbingly deep inside him. A cap of premature snow-white hair framed the delicate oval of her face in a short, sleek bob. The tiny jolt he experienced at the sight of her had nothing to do with his momentary loss of touch with the present but, rather, with a strange sense of recognition, as though he'd unexpectedly come face-to-face with an old acquaintance. But he was sure he'd never seen this woman before.

"Mr. Kelly, welcome to Serena." She took his hand in a surprisingly strong grip. "I'm Sonia Elliot. I trust you had a comfortable trip from New York?"

"I did, thank you," he replied. "I appreciate you accommodating me on such short notice."

"I'm glad to have had the opportunity, considering we are always at full capacity this time of the year. I don't usually rent out the beach cabin, but your assistant sounded so . . . determined."

He met her smile and saw the twitch of amusement. "I understood you were willing to forgo a few premium comforts in exchange for absolute privacy. How about I take you there right away and you can freshen up?"

"I'd appreciate that."

Shouldering his backpack, he followed his host through whitewashed French doors onto a side gallery. "There's a paved pathway to the beach, but everyone prefers to cut through the garden. It's faster and much cooler this way," she said.

The garden was more like a steamy hothouse than the refreshing haven his host had alluded to, though he had to concede it beat a trek on a sun-drenched walkway. The place was a maze of towering trees over a thick undergrowth of palmetto shrubs, giant ferns and indeterminate species of exotic plants teeming with colorful birds. The luxuriant, untamed landscape made him think of Molly. His pet Capuchin would have been at home in this natural habitat. Not that the primate had ever seen anything remotely close to a tropical forest in its too-brief lifetime, but no doubt her natural instinct would have kicked in had she been given the opportunity.

Hell of a time to get maudlin, he scoffed at himself, and trudged after his host along the narrow path. When they finally reemerged into the open, they were standing before a nondescript, pastel-painted bungalow with lattice trim and a wraparound deck. It was built on stilts, like most beachfront constructions in the South. It wasn't much bigger than a cabana, but it was sturdy and well-maintained, and most importantly, it was tucked back far enough into the dense shrubbery to be shielded from potential prying eyes. Two Adirondack chairs were arranged next to a wooden table, promising long hours of blissful solitude. Not far from the cabin a hammock hung between two palm trees swaying in the gentle breeze rising from the ocean.

"It used to be the groundskeeper's lodge," Sonia explained leading him into the air-conditioned interior, "but my father-in-law had it converted to a beach house. It's a little cramped but I was still able to fit a desk into the corner. You did mention in the paperwork you were working on a book." She indicated where the small desk stood, ready to accommodate his laptop and research materials. The place was small and spartanly furnished, but it would more than adequately serve its purpose. He intended to do nothing more than write, swim, and sleep, though he might have to work on the latter.

He turned to find a pair of charismatic eyes studying him. Eyes as intensely blue as the sky above their heads.

April skies.

The thought popped into his head unexpectedly, and a stab of pain cut off his breath momentarily. Suddenly he knew why Sonia Elliot had made such a startling impression on him.

Misty. The name blazed before his eyes like a blinding neon sign, and he was helpless to stop his thoughts from hurtling back to the past as a blurry vision of a blond-haired blue-eyed little girl emerged from its murky depths.

He immediately pushed the image and everything else with it aside. He wasn't in any state of mind to be digging up old ghosts. "It's perfect," he said, more brusquely than he'd intended.

Juan deposited his backpack on the floor, graciously accepted the generous tip Richard handed him, and quietly faded out of sight into the leafy background.

Sonia didn't notice his momentary lapse in concentration. "We had an early lunch today, but if you're hungry I could have a snack sent down," she offered as they stepped out onto the deck.

"No, thank you, I had something in Miami," he said.

"I know you've asked to have your meals served in the cabin, but should you change your mind you're welcome to join me and the other guests at the house later this evening. Dinner will be served at six."

He didn't think he'd take her up on the offer but thanked her anyway.

She hesitated in the doorway. "I hope you enjoy your stay with us, Richard. You don't mind me calling you by your first name, do you?"

He made an effort to smile. "No, of course not."

"And I expect you to do likewise. Please don't hesitate to call the house should you require anything."

CHAPTER 2

"Is this your first visit to the island, Mr. Kelly?" a sprightly middle-aged woman seated next to Richard asked. Louise Van Patten, he'd learned, was a retired school principal from Atlanta, who for the past decade had celebrated her wedding anniversary on the island, despite the fact her third and last husband had been dead for the latter half of that time.

Not wanting to appear uncouth on his first day at Serena, Richard had finally decided to accept his host's invitation to dine at the mansion, but he was fast regretting it. "Please, call me Richard. And, yes, it is," he replied.

"What made you choose St. Isabel?" Courtney Elliot asked.

The daughter of Serena's owner sat across from him at the dinner table, and he was uncomfortably aware of her unwavering attention.

"I wanted to get away from the city for a while and it seemed like the ideal place," he replied, not wanting to admit his had been a completely random choice.

"Well, if it's quiet and solitude you need, you've come to the right place," another guest who's name Richard had missed declared. "There's not a lot of hustle and bustle here, unlike on the more popular islands."

"St. Isabel could do with a little hustle and bustle, if you ask me," Courtney put in dryly. "Nothing much ever happens here."

"Don't mind her," Sonia said, glancing at her daughter with obvious disapproval. "Fortunately for us, our local administrators don't share her craving for excitement."

Her attention reverting to Richard, Louise asked, "But tell me, why would a handsome young fellow like you want to vacation all alone on an out-of-the-way island?"

Before he could point out this wasn't exactly a vacation, Courtney intervened on his behalf. "Richard is working on a novel," she announced to her table companions.

All eyes focused on him with varying degrees of surprise.

"That so?" a lean, older man with sharp, piercing blue eyes and a pencil-thin mustache asked. He was General Morris, the guest Courtney had described as a thriller aficionado. "Can't say your name rings a bell. Do you publish under a pseudonym?"

A bite of the succulent grouper stuck in Richard's throat and he coughed discreetly into his napkin before answering. "No. It's my first, actually. So far I've only published a few short pieces." He refrained from mentioning they'd been mostly reports on biomedical studies.

Louise saved him from having to elaborate further, once again jumping in on the conversation. "I'm glad you chose St. Isabel to find your muse. There's nothing better than island living to get your creative juices flowing. Hemingway wrote some of his best work in Key West," she pointed out.

The general snorted. "I don't know about Mr. Kelly, but I for one wouldn't want to be characterized as someone whose literary career was marred by poor health and weak-mindedness—great novelist though he was."

Louise launched him a withering look. "Are you implying being compared intellectually to Hemingway may be conducive to bad luck?"

"I meant nothing of the sort. Just stating the facts, is all. No need to get your panties in a twist," the man responded gruffly.

"Louise, why don't you try some of Celeste's ginger-marinated asparagus? Our chef would feel insulted if you don't try her new experimental dish." Sonia cut in with the obvious intent of diverting the woman's unyielding attention from Richard's persona.

"I sense that you don't like to talk about your work. Something tells me you're a Virgo."

Richard turned to the woman who had spoken, making an attempt to appear impressed. "As a matter of fact, I am, Ms . . ."

The woman flushed like a schoolgirl. "Hathaway. But please call me Rosemary. I dabble a little in astrology and palmistry," she explained. "Virgos are a reserved lot, as well as extremely observant, which I imagine is a good trait in your line of work. I'd love to read your hand one of these days."

Richard conjured up a weak smile. "That's . . . very kind of you."

He managed to get through the rest of the dinner without succumbing to the temptation of drinking himself into a stupor—something he'd become quite adept at lately—but kept it down to two glasses of wine, just to give him enough of a buzz to sustain the pressure of the relentless probing. When his host suggested they convene in the parlor for a drink he declined, claiming fatigue.

Stepping out into the balmy night, he filled his lungs with the salty breeze and the ever-present fragrance of jasmine, which, he'd learned, grew profusely on the island. Despite the overzealous display of curiosity in his regard, the company had been pleasant enough. He just wasn't in the right frame of mind to socialize. Not that he'd ever been the social type. Not long ago, his life had been a constant merry-go-round of dinner parties and cocktails, golf meetings, and business lunches. But it hadn't been his life. It had been his ex-wife's, and the life of Dr. Richard Kelly, esteemed neurosurgeon and reluctant member of New York's upper crust, and he was done with that. He'd come to St. Isabel to evade from a trap of apathy of his own making. Becoming part of an eclectic group of strangers wasn't exactly his idea of evasion. What he craved most was a good night's rest, one not haunted by dreams that woke him up drowning in his own sweat.

He breathed air into his lungs as he looked up at the picture-perfect sky. It made him think back with nostalgia to the early stages of his career, to the many months spent bringing medical relief to war-torn countries, fighting a hopeless battle against malaria and famine, when despite the widespread misery and despair, everything he'd done had seemed meaningful and right. His life had purpose, then.

He released a shaky breath. Where had it all gone wrong? Twenty-four years striving to build a creditable self-image, and what did he have to show for it? A medical career in shambles, a miserably failed marriage behind him, and a bleak future to look forward to. His existence was no more meaningful now than it had been when he'd been growing up a lonely, derelict kid no one wanted—a social misfit. In some ways he'd reverted to being that unhappy, introvert twelve-year-old. Except this time, he was on his own. No charitable system to back him up, no Good Samaritan to lend him a helping hand. No second chances. He'd had his, and he'd blown it.

He thrust his hands deep inside the pockets of his Chinos and balled them into tight fists. What would they say, all those high-society snobs in his wife's exclusive circle of friends if they knew the hands that had earned him innumerable awards and worldwide acclamation had become ineffective and useless? But then, knowing Erica, the news had already spread. He wouldn't put it past her to find a way to plant the last nail on the coffin of his career. After what she'd done, nothing would surprise him anymore.

He'd had big dreams when he'd met Erica, dreams of success and noble accomplishments, but also of one day having a family of his own. Since he'd entered the medical profession, he'd focused on making the best of himself and had been amply rewarded with a successful and fulfilling career. Erica had been the cherry to top off that success. Or so he'd believed.

She was all he thought a wife of a prominent career man should be: smart, beautiful, witty, and charming, but all those appealing qualities had been on the surface. Underneath she was self-centered and ambitious. A successful attorney and the daughter of a state politician, she'd been raised in ease and luxury. She'd considered his hard-earned position as Chief Surgeon of the Neurology Department at Mercy General Hospital too humble a means of making a living and had cunningly coerced him into abandoning a self-gratifying career to pursue a more financially rewarding one. As President and CEO of Minerva, Inc., a neuroscience biotech research company, he'd been offered a multimillion-dollar endowment and a new research department. His reputation had soared and so had the corporation's profits. But he'd soon realized it wasn't glamour and fame he sought. No matter how noble the cause, he'd found little satisfaction in what he did, no real sense of fulfillment. The thrill of the day-to-day challenge of the OR was gone, the invigorating sense of gratification and conquest he'd felt coming home at the end of a long day of saving lives. Medical research was a wonderful and vitally important field of study, but it wasn't for him; he needed to live the hands-on, day-to-day scurry of hospital life. He needed the human contact, the adrenaline-driven teamwork; he needed all of this to know he was *alive*.

When he'd finally decided to quit with Minerva, Erica had been furious.

"Are you insane?" she'd shouted when he'd confronted her with the news of his impending resignation. "Only a fool would throw away such a prestigious position for a post in an inner-city hospital."

He'd bristled at her reaction, but he'd held his ground. "I'll be chief surgeon of a major hospital, and it's not without its rewards. I may not make as much money, but we'll be far from destitute. Besides, I wasn't much more than that when we met. I didn't hear you complain then."

"Things are different now. We have a position to uphold—a reputation."

He'd scoffed. "You, perhaps. I'm just an accessory, an ornament for you to parade around to your rich friends. It's not how I envisioned my future."

Erica's eyes had flashed threateningly as she'd delivered her ultimatum. "If you leave Minerva, we're done."

He'd known for a while their three-year marriage wasn't going anywhere and that their lives were headed in different directions, but her words had stung. "If that's the way you want it."

She'd been strangely subdued afterward—perhaps too subdued—which should have tipped him off. Instead, he'd mistaken her silence for acquiescence. He'd convinced himself she was willing to make an effort to save their marriage, to accept him for who he was. He'd believed it so fervently it had come as a shock when, soon after his resignation from Minerva, Erica had moved his belongings in the guest wing of the house and begun divorce proceedings. It was a quick, uncomplicated divorce. There had been no mudslinging at each other from across the expensive conference table in her high-power attorney's office, no lavish demands on her part. She hadn't even asked for alimony or a settlement agreement, with the exception of their Hamptons home. She'd been very civil about the whole thing. When it was over, he'd felt sad and empty but immensely relieved. Except, he hadn't known she was pregnant with his child.

He realized he'd been standing in the shadows of the grand mansion for a while, simply staring up at the sky, but it felt good—soothing somehow. Perhaps it was the quiet, he thought. Or the grim anticipation of another restless night. He doubted this getaway to Paradise would grant him the relief he needed, which made this impromptu trip all the more pointless. Working on the book might just do the trick, but then what? Sooner or later he'd crash and then that sickening pain would hit him again, resurrecting the utter sense of loss for the child that, unbeknownst to him, had been growing inside Erica's womb.

The child he'd never know.

CHAPTER 3

Something was off. The peculiar structure looming in front of him hadn't been there before. He'd have remembered if he'd come across it the previous two times he'd taken the shortcut through the grounds. Somehow, he'd become distracted and lost his way.

As he came closer, he realized it was some kind of gazebo—a greenhouse, perhaps, or an oversized garden shed—but in the waning light it was hard to tell. Creepers and vines covered most of its domed roof and glass walls, making it barely distinguishable through the dense foliage.

The place was as dark and silent as the fast-approaching night, but he noticed the door was slightly ajar, as if someone had forgotten to close it. A slight shiver ran down his spine. Not that he believed in ghosts, but for some reason he was reminded that at least four generations of families had lived and died on the property.

He stepped inside and found a switch next to the entrance. The room flooded with light. The unmistakable odor of turpentine lingering in the slightly musty air and the painting paraphernalia scattered about told him it was an artist's studio. An oil painting sat on an easel—a work in progress. Several more unframed canvasses were stacked along the walls on the dusty floorboards, mostly seascapes and landscapes, some still lifes. He wasn't enough of an art connoisseur to judge the quality of the craftsmanship, but all were certainly eye-catching. He moved to another stack and singled out a watercolor. It portrayed a toddler, a boy with huge chocolate-brown eyes brimming with tears. One small fist was swiping at his tear-streaked face. It was startling to see how the artist had managed to capture the child's distress, bringing it to life with a clever play of light and shadows.

His eyes cut to the signature on the bottom righthand corner. One simple name. *Clare.*

Clare. Not C.E. Another member of the Elliot household? he asked himself. A long-term guest?

He scanned the interior for possible clues. A broken-in velour sofa stood against the heavy ivory drapery, a paint-smeared smock abandoned negligently on its cushioned seat. Next to the sofa stood a small bamboo bookcase holding a few well-worn classics and an extensive collection of historical novels. If he'd discovered nothing of the mysterious Clare, he at least knew she was a romantic at heart. It also reminded him he was trespassing on private property, and it was time to head back before it got too dark.

Then something else caught his attention, something that produced an eerie tingling at the back of his neck. More paintings, partially hidden between the folds of the drapes. Before he even pulled back the heavy fabric, he knew what he'd find, and his pulse quickened. There was no mistaking the stark, dramatic flair, the odd indistinguishable shapes, and in the midst of the undecipherable clutter, what appeared to be the unmistakable outline of a dog. He knew, even before seeing the signature, they had been crafted by the same hand. The mysterious C.E.

It had been a week since he'd made the discovery at a sidewalk display of a SoHo gallery, a small place sandwiched between a used bookstore and a busy coffee shop. He wasn't particularly drawn to abstracts, but something about this one called to him in a peculiar way. All he could make out were vague suggestions of modern architecture juxtaposed with ghostly human shapes. It was as if someone had taken a completed jigsaw puzzle of a cityscape and scrambled it in a burst of anger or frustration. The artist's initials, barely distinguishable within the erratic swirls of color, were as mystifying as the subject itself, but a label on the dust cover had caught his eye. *Island Art and Hobby Supplies, St. Isabel Island, FL.*

He'd turned his back on the painting that day, but he hadn't been able to get it out of his mind. Two days later he'd gone back, only to discover it had been sold. That's when the idea to trace the origins of the painting had come to him. He'd seen it as a sign, a means to pull himself out of the dark bottomless pit he'd stumbled into after discovering Erica's betrayal. For weeks he'd been floundering, hoping for a foothold, and in a coincidental and indirect way, the painting had provided it to him.

He rolled back on his heels. Something told him the artist was a woman, not anything in the painting itself, but in the elegant precision of the inscribed initials. Had his first instincts been right? Was the attractive CEO of ElliotAir the mysterious C.E.? If so, who was Clare?

He couldn't place the glamorous, stylish Courtney in the musty, dust-ridden place among the trees. But women seldom were what they appeared to be. A poor judge of character like himself knew it.

Later, stretched out on the hammock on his secluded beach, he folded his arms under his head and let the breeze wash over him. His inability to unwind told him he was no closer to regaining his peace than he'd been a week ago. He should have known there wasn't a place on Earth far enough to outrun his demons—and maybe, just maybe, he didn't want to. Perhaps he clung to a subconscious death wish and needed a way to speed up the process.

He tried to focus on the smattering of stars up above. He'd never seen them shine so brightly—or maybe he'd never cared enough to notice. Stargazing wasn't something a busy surgeon had time for. How many of the meaningful things had he forgotten how to do, like listening to music or reading a good book? Simply living.

One of the more prominent stars blinked down at him more brightly than the rest.

"Did you know Sirius is the biggest and brightest star in the sky?"

A child's voice he'd thought forgotten spoke to him from the past. It was Misty who'd pronounced those words. It had been almost seventeen years since he'd last seen her or thought of her. He didn't know why her memory surfaced now. It had to have something to do with that star.

Spurred by a sudden impulse, he rolled off the hammock and went into the cabin to rummage through his things for his wallet. The small photograph was still there, tucked inside one of the hidden folds. It was the only memento of Misty he'd held on to—no doubt more as a subconscious reminder of having failed her than as a sentimental keepsake.

His fingers shook as he held it. It had faded a little with time, but the image of the little girl with a white-faced monkey perched on her left shoulder was still achingly familiar, and he wasn't prepared for the flood of memories that swept over him.

CHAPTER 4

Manhattan, Christmas Eve, seventeen years earlier

Richard Kelly had never been a believer. At least, not since he was five years old and still believed Santa Claus was a kindhearted old man from the North Pole who traveled the world bringing gifts to children. Angels, to him, were mythical creatures, artists' figments of imagination, like the ones painted on the ceiling of Holy Trinity Church in the South Bronx. He remembered them well because as a child he'd sat counting them and studying their mesmeric features, Sunday after Sunday, while waiting for the sermon to be over. He'd never expected to actually come face-to-face with a live one someday. Certainly not in a noisy, overcrowded department store.

He saw himself sitting on a pew, too small to see much more than the vast vaulted ceiling beyond the sea of adult heads, as clear and unwelcomingly familiar as if it were yesterday.

"Don't forget to pray for the cleansing of your soul," his grandmother would always tell him before the beginning of Mass.

Whatever that meant. He'd never heard of a soul needing cleansing, as if it were a dirty face. Still, he'd prayed to those pretty angels whose clean faces looked benevolently down on him, asking for the purification of his wicked soul. With some luck they'd take pity on him and bring his mother home. Back when he was still a gullible kid, that is, until he'd developed some semblance of a brain and realized it was all a waste of time and energy.

He blinked to clear his vision, but the angel didn't dissipate in a flash of heavenly light.

He was hallucinating, he thought. The stress of juggling college and two part-time jobs had finally gotten to him.

From the crowd of kids and adults, she—*the creature*—blinked in response, then continued to stare in muted fascination. Her eyes were so blue and bright they made him think of the sky on a clear day in April.

Get a grip, he told himself.

This was no angel. It was just another awestruck kid captivated by his pet capuchin monkey's antics. Perched on the back of Santa's gilded throne, Molly was putting on the act of a lifetime for the children lining up to meet Santa, and Molly knew how to work the crowds. She fancied herself a comedian and reveled in all the attention she could get, the pesky little show-off.

He handed his last visitor—a fidgety five-year-old with a Christmas wish list as long as the Long Island Expressway—to her waiting mother and tugged at his collar. He couldn't wait to get out of the ridiculous outfit. He was perspiring underneath it and the artificial mustache tickled his nostrils, making his eyes water. He imagined his nose rivaling old Rudolph's up there, suspended from the ceiling. Why had he agreed to take this job? He could think of a dozen places he'd rather be on Christmas Eve than sitting in a velvet chair, bouncing obnoxious children on his knee and asking them dumb questions.

Having Molly along as a sidekick helped ease some of the pressure, especially when it came to distracting the more restless kids. A primate was the animal least emblematic of Christmas, and Molly didn't have the docility of a reindeer, but it didn't bother the children. Kids were a weird species. Give them some novel entertainment, toss them a handful of lollipops, and they'd turn into docile little lambs—for a while, anyway.

It had been Mr. Murphy, his supervisor, to foist the job on him after Richard had dared to question the soundness of the holiday display.

He still heard the sound of Mr. Murphy's pompous, nasally response reverberating in his ears, after Richard had pointed out the display was a safety hazard.

"Thank you, Mr. Kelly. If in the unlikely event I'll ever need your advice on how to do my job, I'll ask for it."

Richard had been tempted to tell him he'd rather be stocking shelves on double shifts than spending five hours entertaining a bunch of spoiled brats, but he'd known better than to insist. It was either take it or be out of a job.

"Can I at least bring my pet monkey along?" he'd asked the supervisor. "She's good with kids and I have a hunch she'll help bring in more business."

To his surprise, Murphy hadn't been opposed to the idea. Obviously the prospect of increased profits represented an opportunity to ingratiate himself to his superiors and a possible career boost.

"I'll check with management, but it shouldn't be a problem. Make sure she's kept on a short leash and out of the reach of the children."

There was a break in what was probably the 999th replay of "Jingle Bell Rock," as the overhead speakers announced ten minutes to closing.

"Sorry folks, Santa's closing shop for the night," the photographer called out to the disappointed crowd and began to gather his equipment.

At last, Richard thought, lifting himself off the chair and stretching. One more screaming toddler to bounce on my knee and I'll be screaming, too.

He'd promised his pals he'd join them at Charlie's Bar and Grill for a Christmas Eve snack and a smuggled beer, but now he wondered if he'd even have the energy to do anything other than drag his feet to bed.

A chorus of complaints rose from the still lingering crowd.

"Sorry, kids, no more pictures tonight. You'll have to come back next year," he said in his best Grinch voice.

To hell with jolly and nice. Next year, Murphy could find himself another willing schmuck to do the job.

Molly let out a series of obnoxious shrieks, not ready for the fun to be over. He threw the monkey an incinerating glare designed to shock her into submission, but she only shrieked louder, causing people to stop and stare.

His nervousness mounted. All he needed was for the supervisor to show up and he'd be in big trouble.

Then he remembered the candy canes. Molly was a glutton for candy and had discovered a new weakness for the peppermint kind. He reached for his bag and found to his dismay it was empty. He swung around to a suspicious shuffling sound behind him and saw a gloating Molly clutching the remaining candy canes to her hairy chest.

"Bad girl. Give those back. They don't belong to you," he reprimanded the insubordinate primate. He moved to take the candy from her, but his movements were hindered by the padded suit. His co-workers and the handful of bystanders howled with laughter, assuming it was part of the act. Molly let out a mutinous screech and flung the candy canes high in the air in the general direction of the crowd. Children lunged for the flying candy while Molly continued to squeal, this time in obvious delight.

Richard was already envisioning the pink slip materialize before his eyes. He might as well start emptying his locker and hand in the key.

The angel look-alike's big, blue eyes were still staring. He noticed there were no adults with her. She looked alone and strangely out of place. He rummaged through the sack, hoping to find a stray candy cane or a lollipop to give to her, but only came up with a fake holly branch—some decorative stuff that had somehow gotten mixed up with the candy.

He handed her the holly. "Sorry, I'm clear out of candy."

He was surprised when she took it, her eyes lighting up. "Thank you," she murmured, sounding as if he'd given her a priceless piece of jewelry.

Richard's heart did a funny little flip, but he didn't have time to explore the peculiar phenomenon.

Above the din of the music, he heard a series of popping sounds coming from overhead. "What the—?"

His head jerked toward the ceiling where the fiberglass sleigh and reindeer apparatus hung by thin nylon cables, the same that were now snapping off the ceiling in rapid succession, as if in rebellion for the extensive amount of strain to which they'd been subjected. All eyes turned upward in alarm as everyone realized what was happening.

"Watch out, it's coming down!" someone yelled.

More screams rose from the crowd but before Richard could spring into action, the girl propelled toward him like a mini tornado. He fell backward, his arms flailing as he struggled to maintain his balance on the edge of the platform, but he lost his footing and stumbled backward, hitting his head against one of the brass posts. The next instant, stunned and hurting, he heard a loud crash.

As his vision cleared, he saw the girl sprawled on the carpeted platform, partially buried by the debris.

AN UNNATURAL SILENCE had fallen over the crowd of late holiday shoppers, a silence so deafening Richard thought the blow to his head had damaged his hearing. But then everyone spoke at once, sharp, incredulous gasps and agitated voices, topped by Molly's terrified shrieks. People began to gather around the podium.

"Heavens, did you see that? The entire apparatus came down!"

"The poor girl—"

"Call management, quick!"

Suddenly alert, Richard bounced to his feet and raced toward the child, his trained instincts as aspiring medical caregiver on alert. "Never mind management. Call freaking 9-1-1!" he yelled to the gaping security guard.

The man snapped out of his momentary daze and pulled out his radio. Within an instant Richard had yanked off the beard and hat and dug through the debris.

The girl lay on her side, one arm stretched out in front of her, the other partially folded beneath her. Only a few tendrils of hair were visible from underneath the rubble covering her head. He very carefully removed as many fragments of the wreckage as possible without causing her further harm. It was a painstaking business made more dramatic by the tense hush around him. Then her face reappeared, grotesquely covered with blood, so that he couldn't see where her face ended and her hairline began. He was almost sure she wasn't breathing.

He took a deep steadying breath. The advanced first-aid courses he'd taken would come in handy—if he could avoid freaking out.

He thought he'd mastered the drill for trauma emergency intervention to perfection. They'd even had the students memorize a mnemonic device to help them remember the various steps to follow, but his mind drew a total blank.

A bigger crowd had gathered around them and he wiped the sweat off his forehead with his sleeve.

Come on . . . Come on, think, he said to himself. What's the first step? Something about emotional first aid . . . Reach out. Reach out physically. That's it.

He touched her. She was warm, but deathly still. Victim nonresponsive, he thought. Check. What next? Reach out emotionally. Protect and reassure. Sure, like she can hear me. The kid is out cold.

It was painful trying to get his vocal cords to function. Something he refused to identify as panic had dried up every drop of saliva in his mouth and throat. He put his lips close to her ear. "Hang on, kid. You'll be fine. The medics'll be here any minute."

He tried to visualize the check list in the casualty assessment instructions manual. *Assess the damage.* Yeah, that he could do. *Check for possible trauma to the cervical spine.* Finally, it was coming back to him.

There was no way to tell if her skull was fractured or if there were other broken bones or internal bleeding. He held his cheek next to her open lips. At least she was breathing. Keeping his palm on her forehead, he put two fingers of the other hand on her Adam's apple. Sliding the fingers down the side of her neck, he searched for a pulse on the carotid. He counted one, two, three, four, five . . . ten seconds.

Good, he thought, as he detected a slow but steady pulse.

A male voice delivered the final store-closing announcement through the speakers, cool and courteous as usual, as if an innocent little girl hadn't just been knocked out senseless setting the grounds for a major lawsuit. He gritted his teeth. What did they think this was, business as usual? Didn't they realize there was a serious emergency here?

A familiar figure emerged from the crowd. "Rick, what the hell happened?"

It was his friend, Tony Valenti. He recalled having arranged to meet him at closing time.

"The whole darn Christmas show came down and knocked the kid out. The weasel. I warned him something like this was bound to happen!"

"Warned who? What are you talking about?" his friend asked.

Richard didn't bother to answer. He pulled at the Velcro straps of his jacket, ripping it off. "Give me a hand. We have to get her into the safety position."

Tony looked at him blankly for a moment, then sprang into action. "Safety position. Right."

"Don't move her!" someone admonished.

"It's cool, pal. My friend here's practically a med student and knows his stuff," Tony said to the concerned salesclerk.

"Get a hold of both her ankles and make sure you hold them together," Richard instructed. Tony nodded and positioned himself at the child's feet. "Now, while I take her shoulders, very carefully turn her sideways towards you . . . that's it."

"What's going on here?"

Hearing the supervisor's voice Richard sprang instantly to his feet, hands balled into fists. Tony put a restraining hand on his shoulder while holding a frightened Molly with the other. "Chill, man, everything will be fine," he said.

The supervisor pushed his way through the crowd. "Stand back, please, stand back!"

At his commanding tone Richard's strained nerves snapped and he lunged for the man. Tony and the security guard had to restrain him.

"This is your fault!" he shouted as he struggled to break free.

Fury flashed in the supervisor's eyes, but he retained his composure. "Relax, my boy. It's nobody's fault," he said calmly.

"I'm not your boy," Richard snapped. "Those cables weren't sturdy enough to bear the weight of the props. I told you it was an accident waiting to happen, but you couldn't care less. You wanted to top every holiday display in the city. 'Give Macy's a run for its money', you said. If I were you, I'd find myself a lawyer real fast."

Tony tugged on his arm. "What are you doing?" he hissed in Richard's ear. "Keep this up and he'll have you out on your ass in no time."

"Who cares? It's a crappy job, anyway," Richard said.

He'd never cared much for the man and he'd have knocked that condescending expression off his scrawny face if he didn't have two pairs of arms restraining him.

The supervisor's face turned beet red. He grabbed a handful of Richard's shirt. "How dare you threaten me!"

"Get your hands off me!" Richard shouted, shrugging him off.

"You're fired. I'll make sure you don't get a job in this store again."

"You can't fire me. You don't have the authority to."

"We'll see about that," the man replied with an arrogant sneer.

"Murphy, what's going on here?"

Harold George Lancey Jr., owner of Lancey's Superstore, strode up to them as the guards carved a channel through the crowd for him. The flustered Murphy took a step back and straightened his impeccable pin-striped suit.

"An accident, sir. It was all an unfortunate accident," the man hastened to explain to his boss.

"It's all his fault. It wouldn't have happened if he hadn't insisted on hanging those props from the ceiling."

Ignoring the supervisor, Mr. Lancey turned to Richard. "Tell me what happened," he demanded briskly but not unkindly.

Richard gave him a detailed account of the incident. When he was done, Lancey turned around. "Where are the girl's parents?" When no one came forward he asked, "Does someone know this girl?" But he was met with only shrugs and bewildered expressions.

The paramedics arrived and Richard was relieved to see the name tags bearing the Mercy General logo on their breast pockets.

Good, friendly territory, he thought.

While the paramedics attended to the girl, he gave them a brief but detailed report of what had occurred, then added a professional nuance to his tone as he explained, "I was able to assess the victim's breathing and pulse are slow but steady. Her cuts appear to be severe, although there's no sign of arterial bleeding."

One of the two paramedics, a brawny, dark-skinned man, looked at him in an assessing manner. "And who might you be?"

"Richard Kelly, sir. I work here. Part-time, that is. I have a day job at Mercy General." He didn't bother to specify his day job consisted essentially in emptying out trays in the hospital cafeteria.

"Well, Richard Kelly, you did a fine job," the man said.

Richard stood by as the medics intubated the girl and administered oxygen, getting her ready for transportation, experiencing almost a feeling of belonging and camaraderie through the entire process. He may be a long way from taking the Hippocratic Oath, but it made him feel one step closer.

CHAPTER 5

*C*oma. The dreadful diagnosis was whispered behind closed doors and in the hallways of Mercy General's ICU, where the unidentified little girl lay surrounded by tubes, IVs, and monitors.

"Sir, how bad is it?" Richard asked Dr. Maxwell Mallory, chief of surgery at Mercy General. If his former guardian and mentor was surprised to see him, he didn't show signs of it. He gestured him to a chair and pushed aside some papers he'd been looking at.

In the small corner office overlooking the East River, the man gazed at him over the top of his reading glasses, his expression stern. "You know I can't discuss a patient's condition with a nonfamily member," he said.

Richard tamped down his annoyance. "I realize that, sir, but I thought, you know, given my almost premed status and given my personal involvement in the matter—not to mention being the primary witness . . ."

"That's a lot of givens," Dr. Mallory observed, sounding more amused than annoyed.

"Please, sir. The kid wouldn't be here if it weren't for me. She got hurt trying to push me out of the way."

The man's eyebrows drew together in a contemplative frown. "Well, I suppose you're entitled, if only for the fact you were there to provide assistance, very likely saving her life," he said.

"Thank you, sir," Richard said.

He waited nervously while the older man went through the laborious task of cleaning out his pipe and refilling it. The ritual was as familiar to Richard as the man's unfashionably thick mustache, his collar-length salt-and-pepper hair, and rumpled scholarly appearance. This time, however, his motions were slower than usual, leaving Richard wondering if he should take it as a bad omen.

The doctor finished what he was doing and set aside the pipe, then looked at Richard. "She's still in a deep coma and so far we have seen no improvement of her cognitive functions. Fortunately, there were no internal injuries or broken bones, but the violent blow to her head has caused severe trauma to the brain."

A sickly feeling settled in the pit of Richard's stomach. It wasn't fair. He should be the one lying in a coma, all cut and bruised. He would have been better able to sustain the impact.

"What are the chances of her regaining consciousness?" he asked.

The doctor shrugged. "It's difficult to say at this stage. The results of the initial tests have shown no change. She's in a state of extreme unresponsiveness and doesn't react to pain stimulation."

"In other words, there's a good chance she may never wake up. Or that she may die."

"I wouldn't make that drastic an assumption. In these situations, we have no recourse but to wait and see how she reacts to the therapy. In most cases, spontaneous and complete recovery may occur in a short period of time but sometimes it can take months—even years. Dr. Burnstein, the neurosurgeon assigned to her care, will be able to make a better assessment once all the test results are in."

Richard couldn't sit still any longer and sprang from his seat. No matter how hard he tried, he couldn't eradicate the girl's swollen and bloodied face from his memory. "What about the rest? I mean, she looked pretty banged up last time I saw her."

"A few bruises and skin lacerations. Might require some minor surgical repair. Nothing that won't fade with time." The doctor raised his eyebrows at him. "For heaven's sake, sit down or are you planning on wearing out a path on my rug?"

Richard hadn't realized he'd been pacing nervously and stopped. "What do you make of the fact no one has shown up to claim her?" he asked. "Surely someone must be looking for her by now, what with all the media coverage and police involvement. How can someone not realize their kid is missing after almost forty-eight hours?"

Dr. Mallory shook his head. "I really don't know what to tell you, son, except this is New York, where stranger things have been known to happen."

"They're saying there've been no reports of missing children matching the girl's characteristics," Richard said. "It's like they don't even know she's missing."

As a material witness Richard had been interrogated multiple times about the night of the accident. He'd been asked the same questions over and over again until he'd wanted to lash out in frustration. When had he first noticed the girl? How long had she been standing there? Did anyone talk to her? Did she look lost or worried? Who did they take him for, a pervert? He'd only been doing his job, not scoping out the toy department for an easy catch.

It was really himself he was mad at. He should have said something. Why hadn't he gotten her name instead of giving her a stupid holly twig?

Murphy had been fired and the storeowners were now facing charges for child endangerment due to aggravated negligence. Not that it changed anything for the girl, and it sure didn't make Richard feel any less responsible.

The doctor pushed his glasses farther up his nose and reached for his papers again. "I'm sure it's just a matter of time before someone shows up. In the meantime, it's possible she may regain consciousness, in which case we'll know more."

While the chief was being so magnanimous Richard asked him whether he minded if he checked in on the girl from time to time, see how she was progressing.

"Of course. Just as long as you don't make a nuisance of yourself and keep that rampant curiosity of yours under control."

CHAPTER 6

When on New Year's Day the comatose patient miraculously regained consciousness, the entire hospital staff was in a clamor.

"What do you mean she doesn't remember who she is? Are you saying she's lost her memory?"

"I'm afraid so," Dr. Mallory said. "The MRI shows damage to the left temporal lobe, which can—though it's extremely rare—cause autobiographic memory loss."

Richard stuck to the man's side following him into the elevator. He'd deliberately waited for his former guardian to end his shift so he could get firsthand information on the child's condition. "Does she remember the accident?" he asked.

Dr. Mallory shook his head solemnly. "Not only doesn't our young patient remember being involved in the accident, she seems to have forgotten everything preceding it. Not her name, not where she comes from, nada. It's as if her history's been completely erased. Only time will tell if it's of a temporary or permanent nature. Fact is," he concluded on an ominous sigh, "at least for the time being she can be of absolutely no help to us in tracing her family."

Permanent amnesia. Where had he heard that before? It had to have been in one of those tear-jerker soaps his landlady couldn't get enough of, one of those corny tricks script writers used to prolong the plots when they ran out of fresh ideas. Problem was, this wasn't Hollywood and Dr.

Mallory—or Dr. Max, like Richard liked to call him—wasn't in the habit of endorsing whimsical prognoses.

"She doesn't fully understand what's happening to her and she's scared, as is to be expected."

IN THE SMALL private room where the girl had been relocated, the drapes had been pulled back to let in the bleak wintry light. Pillows had been stacked behind her back to keep her elevated. She sat with her face toward the window, beyond which thick snowflakes accumulated on the wide concrete ledge. Someone had brushed her hair to a glossy shine, parting it on either side of her face. Richard's fists clenched inside the pocket of his borrowed scrubs and in doing so, came in contact with the fake holly the girl had dropped in her fall. He barely remembered having picked it up from the floor and pocketing it after attending to her. With some luck, seeing it again would stimulate her memory.

When she turned her head toward him, Richard's initial impression was she couldn't be the same person he'd seen on Christmas Eve. This was no starry-eyed angel look-alike, not this hideous-looking monster with a mummy face and sunken, lifeless eyes. It was all he could do not to rush out yelling there'd been a terrible mistake, a body switch.

Through the slits in the bandages, the girl continued to look at him, showing no signs of recognition.

No surprise there, he thought. There's no chance she'd recognize in me the klutz masquerading as Santa Claus.

"Hi." His voice came out squeaky, sounding like a stylus sliding swiftly over one of those vinyl music records Tony collected. He hadn't heard it sounding like that since puberty.

He cleared his voice and tried again. "Hi. My name's Richard."

There was a glimmer of apprehension in her eyes as her gaze swept over the green scrubs. "Don't worry, I'm not a doctor," he hastened to reassure her. "I had to wear this stuff so I could sneak in to see you. I work in this hospital. I help serve all that yucky hospital food that makes you want to throw up—that is, when I'm not mopping up the throw-up." She said nothing but kept on staring at him with her creepy, vacant expression.

He leaned his hip on the edge of the bed. "I'm sorry about what happened to you in Lancey's. I was there when old Rudolph and his buddies fell on you. I was older-looking then, and a little . . . chubbier, you could say. It'd be pretty hard for you to recognize me."

He couldn't remember a time when he'd sweated so much, except under the Santa suit. The fake smile he'd pasted on his face was starting to make his jaw cramp. "I remember you quite well, though. You were standing near Santa's platform soaking up my pet monkey's antics like it was a circus act." No reaction. "You don't remember any of that, huh?"

He pulled out the fake holly twig and held it out. "Do you recognize this?" he asked. The girl threw a quick glance at the ornament then continued to stare at him blankly.

This isn't working, he thought.

"I should go. If they catch me here, I'll be in trouble," he said. As he stepped away, he saw a jar on the wheel-in cart the nurse had left behind and an idea hit him. It was probably stupid, but he thought, What could it hurt?

He pulled the privacy curtain so it hid him from her line of vision, fiddled a little with the jar's contents, then opened the curtain. "Et—voilá!" He wiggled his eyebrows the way he'd seen Dr. Mallory do countless times to distract young patients.

The girl recoiled, her eyes resembling those of a startled doe.

"Whoa—it's okay," he said and quickly tore off the makeshift cotton wool beard he'd stuck to his face with surgical tape. "I know, I suck at the Santa thing. Seems you're the only one who notices it," he said, making a poor attempt at humor.

He was wasting his time. He may as well give it up and leave her to her oblivious little world. Then a strange thing happened. Like a sudden break in a cloudy sky, the wariness in the girl's eyes receded, unveiling the incandescent blue that had held him spellbound on Christmas Eve. The effect was so startling, he was speechless for a while.

Her lips moved, and he could have sworn he heard a tiny bubble of laughter escape from them, so soft he wondered if he'd imagined it.

Relax, he told himself. No need to get excited about a measly reaction.

He scrunched up his face in mock reproach. "You aren't by any chance laughing at me, are you?" he asked.

She began to shake her head in denial but uttered a moan of pain. "No," she murmured. Her voice was scratchy, as if she hadn't used it in a long time.

At last, some real progress. Letting out his breath slowly, he settled more comfortably onto the bed. "So tell me," he asked in a serious tone worthy of Barnaby Jones, "what were you doing at Lancey's on Christmas Eve?"

OF COURSE, THE girl didn't remember. As far as she was concerned, she was born on New Year's Day. No matter how many brain stimulation techniques they subjected her to, she couldn't remember a single detail about herself or her life prior to waking up in a hospital bed. According to her psychoanalysts, it wasn't necessarily a negative thing. It would ensure her mental stability while her body healed. The theory was she couldn't miss what she didn't remember. As the last person to have spoken to her that night in Lancey's it was Richard's moral obligation to provide her with a new identity. He'd had enough of her being referred to as Jane Doe. Each time he heard someone refer to her in that way, he'd been tempted to point out she wasn't a damn corpse. He decided she'd be called Misty, short for mysterious. It suited her current status, and it sounded cute at the same time.

After that initial encounter in the ICU, he no longer wanted to run when he saw her. The cherubic façade that had spooked him Christmas Eve was—at least for the time being—camouflaged by the unflattering dressings. He found if he didn't look too closely into her unsettling blue eyes, he could almost pretend she was just another patient.

As each day passed and her physical and emotional distress became less evident, the gentle disposition he'd picked up on in Lancey's resurfaced. She was quick and smart, with an IQ well above average for one her age— estimated at being around nine or ten. No particular abilities stood out other than a certain aptitude for drawing. As she grew stronger, she spent hours sketching anything and everything around her, including the familiar faces of the nurses who fussed and watched over her.

Richard found it peculiar that although she seemed to have forgotten everything related to her past, she was quite adept at a skill she had obviously developed at an earlier time.

"The patient's memory loss appears to be of a retrograde nature," he'd heard Dr. Burnstein explain to his panel of students, "a rare condition where events directly preceding the injury are deleted from the patient's memory, whereas certain actions—like moving, walking, breathing, that is, everything one learns while growing up—are not forgotten. Once the psychological trauma of her injuries wears off, she's likely to regain her full memory."

Since she was an abandoned child, Dr. Burnstein's optimistic expectations served little to ease Richard's mind. Soon her bandages would be removed, and he'd have to see her scarred and battered face. He'd heard the nurses whisper among themselves about reconstructive surgery, laser applications, and skin grafts, and just the thought of her being subjected to more suffering made his insides turn over.

Though he told himself repeatedly the little foundling wasn't any concern of his, that she had the care of some of the best specialists in the field, an irresistible compulsion had him coming back to see her at every opportunity he could get, hoping to see some change that might indicate an initial return of her memory. Besides, it wasn't as if friends and relatives were lining up to see her. She needed to know she wasn't alone. Misty herself didn't seem to mind him dropping in at odd hours of the day; in fact, she looked forward to his visits. She no longer scrutinized him as if he were a hostile alien, which helped ease his guilt a little. Each time he walked in and saw her eyes light up with pleasure, a peculiar sensation stirred in his gut.

"Richard, I thought you'd never come," she said a couple of weeks later.

"What, miss me already? It hasn't been that long since I sneaked in a slice of chocolate mousse cake."

"That was *hours* ago, and I'm so bored," she grumbled.

He couldn't blame her; it had to be tiresome being confined to a hospital bed, with nothing better to do but sleep and watch TV. Bored or not, it was gratifying to know his company was appreciated.

"Tell you what. One of these days I'll sneak in Molly and introduce her to you."

She clapped her hands with excitement. "Promise?"

He crossed two fingers across his heart, then brought them to his lips, like he'd seen one of his foster sisters do. "You bet."

CHAPTER 7

"No way am I giving up my Saturday afternoon to visit a sick kid in a hospital," Jake said to Richard, pushing his wire-rimmed glasses farther up his nose.

"Yeah, it's bad enough the holidays were ruined, what with you going nuts over a freak accident—which, incidentally, you had no hand in," Tony added, idly picking at the crumbs left in the empty bowl of potato chips. Mozart, the stray cat he'd rescued and named after his favorite composer took over the bowl and slowly and methodically began to lick it clean.

"Come on, guys, one hour of your time, that's all I ask," Richard pleaded. "She saved my life. The least I can do is help her get her memory back."

Tony rolled his eyes. "Just because some kid you don't even know happened to be in the wrong place at the wrong time doesn't mean you're forever indebted to her for sparing you a concussion. What—suddenly you're a believer of the Confucius moral principles or something?"

"She came at me like a twenty-ton steamroller, all forty pounds of her. She saw it coming even before I had time to realize it was happening. It's almost as if she were . . ."

"As if she were what? Psychic? Supernatural? Surely you don't believe in that metaphysical crap?"

Jake, who was struggling to keep a restless Molly from chewing off the buttons of the leather jacket he'd picked up at a flea market for a bargain price said, "Dude, if we get caught smuggling a monkey into a hospital we'll be in big trouble and you could lose your job."

"No one would know. I'd do it myself if I weren't on duty until eight-thirty; I can't very well hide her inside my uniform until then. Besides, I promised Misty I'd bring her."

"Yeah, yeah. Tell that to the judge when you're trying to bail us out of the slammer," Tony said. He rubbed his eyes wearily and pushed out of his chair. "What the heck, let's go see this baby miracle worker and get it over with. But thirty minutes, tops. I have dynamite plans for tonight and I don't intend to be late just 'cos some kid needs babysitting." He shook his head as if he couldn't believe he was being suckered into doing something he didn't want to do. "Jeez, for weeks I work on this first-class babe till I'm blue in the face and when I finally manage to snag a date, you come up with some humanitarian aid plan. What a guy's gotta do for a bro."

Jake was still hesitant. "But I promised the guys I'd join them for band practice."

Tony cut him a withering look. "They can wait a few minutes, can't they?" Then he pointed a finger at Richard. "You better remember this next time your sportscaster pal offers you tickets to the Rangers game."

"Yeah," echoed Jake.

WHEN RICHARD POPPED his head inside Misty's room shortly before nine, he couldn't believe his eyes. Not only wasn't Misty quietly propped up in bed watching cartoon videos as he'd expected, but Tony and Jake were still there. The cozy little group sat around a small table seemingly engrossed in a game of poker while a moving lump underneath the bed covers told him Molly was entertaining herself, playing hide and seek with the hospital linen. They were all apparently oblivious that it was well past visiting hours.

Tony shot up like lightening at his approach. "Jeez, you scared the sh—heck out of me. I thought it was Nurse-zilla. She almost caught Molly once already."

Hearing the nickname for the department's most feared nurse sent a nervous tingle down Richard's spine.

Misty jumped up in glee. "I won three games out of four," she announced proudly, waving her cards triumphantly.

"Is that right?" Richard asked. Contrary to all expectations, his friends seemed to have fared quite well in Misty's company.

So much for the half-hour concession, he thought.

"Yeah. Two straights and a full house. Cost me my Don Mattingly card," Jake said.

"And a stick of bubblegum and two whole dollars," Misty added triumphantly.

Richard stared at his friend. Jake cherished and safeguarded his prized autographed baseball cards jealously as if they were priceless artifacts. He couldn't imagine him relinquishing a single one of them, not even for the sake of goodwill.

Tony gave Misty a reproachful look but his eyes danced with amusement. "Serves us right for teaching a kid a grownup's game."

Before Richard could fully recover from the shock, the unmistakable squeaking of wheels sounded in the hallway, signaling the imminent arrival of the medicine cart. "Uh, guys, I'm afraid you've overextended your visit. You don't want Nurse Roberts catching you here."

"Uh-oh. Nurse Roberts can be really strict," Misty said in a grave tone.

Richard peered at Tony. "Correct me if I'm wrong, but didn't you mention a hot date?"

His friend looked sheepish. "Oh . . . right." He glanced at his watch. "Jeez, I hadn't realized how late it was." He sprung up quickly and chucked a worn brown leather jacket over his white T-shirt with the phrase "I don't give a shirt" written on the front. He took out a fine-tooth comb from his inside pocket and smoothed it over his thick mahogany hair. "Forgive me, Misty-mine, but I really need to hit the road. Thanks for a great time," he said.

Misty-mine?

Misty flashed Tony one of her engaging smiles under the unbecoming dressings. "Thank you for coming to visit," she said.

"Any time, sugar."

"I'll take Molly home," Jake offered as he slipped the recalcitrant primate inside his jacket and pulled up the zipper around it.

Richard thought he had stumbled into the Twilight Zone. "What happened to band practice?" he asked him.

"It . . . kind of got postponed. It's not that we had a gig to prepare for or anything."

"Hey, look, I really appreciate what you both did," Richard said as his friends prepared to leave.

"Don't mention it," Tony said easily, causing Richard's brows to rise even farther into his forehead.

"Come see me again soon," Misty called after them like the perfect little host.

"Count on it, babe," Tony called back, and Jake seconded that with a thumbs-up.

"Looks like you had a good time," Richard said to Misty, as soon as his friends had left.

"Oh, yes. Tony and Jake are so much fun. Tony makes me laugh," she said with a giggle. Her eyes misted over as she added, "He said your friends are his friends and since I'm your friend, I'm also their friend and that's why they came to visit me."

"He did?"

Wait till they try to cash in on that bribe, he thought perversely.

"And Molly's a sweetheart. Did she get separated from her parents, like me?"

He was taken aback by the question, and he realized for the first time how much Misty and Molly had in common. "She was a little more than a baby when I bought her three years ago. Two or three years old, I think. I don't know who her parents were or where she came from; I rescued her from a homeless man who mistreated her, exposing her to the damp and cold to beg for money. I gave him one hundred dollars for her."

"Poor baby," Misty said sympathetically.

Surprisingly she'd had no problem making friends with Molly the mischief-maker, when most kids were usually a little afraid of her. He shot her a speculative glance. "Do you remember Molly from that night in Lancey's?"

She shook her head in denial. "I'm sorry," she said somberly.

"Hey, no sweat," he said offhandedly, even as his morale dropped a notch. Not that he'd had much faith in the experiment, anyway.

He helped pick up the cards and put them back in their box. "Better get into bed before Nurse Roberts gets here."

When the nurse rolled in the cart moments later, Misty was already under the covers, the picture of innocence. "Will you come again tomorrow?" she asked him.

"You bet, funny face," he said, chucking her playfully under the chin.

She giggled. He'd taken to calling her funny face since he'd caught her looking at herself for the first time in the bathroom mirror, her eyes wide with shock and her bandaged face soaking up her tears. It had been a tough few minutes before he'd been able to convince her she didn't have the face of a monster, and that it would just look a little funny until the bandages came off.

Deep inside he knew his guilt wasn't the only reason he kept coming back; it was a feeling of obligation to look out for Misty, of responsibility toward a lost, defenseless human being like he had once been. As much as he enjoyed her company, he hated what she symbolized—a stage in his life when he'd depended on strangers for survival. For that, he envied Misty her amnesia.

Nurse Roberts, as the tag pinned to her prominent bosom said, gave him a reproving look. "Disturbing my patient again, Kelly? May I remind you hospital rules apply to everyone, *including* the service personnel?" She pronounced the last words with tight lips, manifesting her disdain for the nonmedical staff. "I thought I told you not to come here after hours. You'll end up getting me into trouble."

"Please, Nurse Roberts, let him stay a little while longer," Misty pleaded.

"Sorry, young lady. Rules are rules and must be obeyed."

Misty exchanged a conspiratorial smirk with Richard, rolling her eyes comically at him over the nurse's back as the woman expertly and efficiently tucked in her blanket. "Tomorrow you'll be moved to a larger room so you can be together with other children. That means absolutely *no* after-hours visits," Nurse Roberts said, throwing a meaningful glance in Richard's direction.

The witch. Richard bet the new arrangements were all her doing. It didn't take much to figure out her hostile attitude toward him had more to do with his having an association with the chief than with hospital rules. It was all over the hospital the acerbic nurse had a thing for Dr. Max, and the more the chief ignored her, the more acerbic she became.

"I have Dr. Mallory's permission to visit Misty," he said. It wasn't entirely true, but he couldn't resist the urge to rub his personal connection with the chief of surgery in her face.

She pierced him with a chilling stare. "I don't care if the Surgeon General of the United States himself gave you permission. The patient is my responsibility, and I take my orders from the head of the department. Now, I'm afraid you have to leave."

"Yes, ma'am," Richard said, suppressing the urge to stuff her prim little starched cap down her prissy throat. He expected she'd have an apoplectic fit if she were to discover a wild beast had been smuggled into her precious department. He found the thought quite amusing.

He made a gagging gesture behind the nurse's back that made Misty stifle a giggle, then said in his best Schwarzenegger impersonation, "I'll be back."

CHAPTER 8

Richard watched Philippe Girard as the pilot, elbows deep in black grease, expertly worked a wrench around a bolt on a boat's engine. The grimy, mind-absorbing manual labor reminded him of his youth, when tinkering with his foster parents' malfunctioning vehicles was usually one way to vent his restless energy, and he almost envied him.

"I thought your job was to fly planes."

Philippe looked up, squinting against the sun's glare. He was bare-chested and wore a pair of cut-off jeans and the typical nonskid shoes trained skippers wore. His shaggy sun-bleached hair hung loose on his shoulders and held at bay by a red bandanna, giving him the air of a modern-day pirate.

"Flying's just a part-time occupation, something to feed my adventurous spirit," he said. "This here's my real baby, my own little chartering service."

Richard glanced around the marina, where a number of fishing boats and pleasure crafts were moored snugly on either side of the narrow wooden slip.

Philippe gave the wrench one last tug, then pulled a soiled rag from his back pocket to wipe his hands. "Glad to see you've resurfaced," he said, hopping onto the dock. "I was starting to think you'd changed your mind about going sailing."

"Been covering a lot of ground on my book," Richard explained.

Philippe's grin widened, his white teeth a stark contrast with the deep tan of his face. "Lost your momentum or something?"

"Just needing to decompress."

It was true, though he'd been better after his first night at Serena, when seeing Misty's picture again had unleashed a storm of emotions that had torn through him like a powerful tsunami. He'd woken up in the hammock the next morning to the tinkling sound of empty beer bottles knocking against each other on the sand as the breeze rolled them about. The turmoil inside him had subsided, leaving him nauseated and beaten, like a wrecked boat drifting aimlessly on the ocean, yet suffused with a mild sense of peace he hadn't experienced in a long time.

"Well, then, you've come to the right place," Philippe said. He gestured to the vessel he'd been working on, an elegant cruiser Richard calculated to be at least forty feet long. "This is the Camèlie, the pearl among pearls of my modest fleet. Had to replace the pan gasket for an oil leak. Want to try her out?"

This was the first time Richard had ventured this far from the cabin. He'd had no actual plans of going sailing, not until the hubbub of a busy marina and its smells had penetrated his senses, stirring a passion long dormant. "No, thanks. I think I'll play it low-key and start off with something smaller, do a little sightseeing close to shore. It's been a while since my boating days. I need to regain my sea legs."

"In that case, I have just the thing for you," Philippe said, and gestured Richard to follow him. He stopped in front of a small single-sailboat sandwiched between a handsome schooner and a twenty-something-foot sloop. "I just filled the tank of her outboard motor, though I doubt you'll need it. Stay downwind and you'll have enough in your sail to keep you going."

Richard studied the freshly painted dinghy rocking lazily in the sun. "It'll do," he said, his hands already itching to feel the familiar trappings of a sailboat once more.

Minutes later Philippe helped him raise the sail and untie the mooring line. "Currents tend to be a little strong around these parts, but once you're on the other side, it should be smooth sailing all the way. There's an onboard radio in case you run into any trouble."

Richard nodded and thanked him for the tip.

"One more word of advice," Philippe said. "Don't hug the shore too closely or you'll risk grounding. Some inlets and lagoons are quite shallow around here. Keep an eye on the seabed. A brown area is an indication the coral formations are close to the surface. You don't want to risk damaging the reefs."

Richard found the man's cautionary lecture mildly irritating, though he had to concede making clients aware of the risks to the island's ecosystem was an important part of a charter boat owner's job. "I'll make sure to remember that."

He threw his backpack containing sunscreen and a bottle of water into the boat, then hopped in. "Should I settle now or when I bring her back?"

"No need. First time's on the house," Philippe replied.

The generous gesture took Richard by surprise. "Thanks."

Minutes later he was out in open water, tiller in one hand, the other controlling the mainsail, rediscovering the thrill of being one with the ocean. As Philippe had warned, the currents were stronger out in the open ocean and he had to keep a tight grip on the tiller and mainsail to avoid being pulled adrift. Once he sailed past the merging streams of currents, it began to glide on an even keel again.

He passed small keys no bigger than a tennis court, and hidden inlets so rife with the sights and sounds of marine life it was like traversing into a strange and primitive world.

Mangroves and seagrass lined the rocky shore in water so clear he could see the brightly colored fish moving among the corals on the seabed. Richard understood why Philippe felt the need to dispense warnings. This was nature in its purest form. It would be a shame for anything or anyone to spoil it.

He stood with his face to the wind, soaking up the view and breathing in the pungent salty air. The roar of the wind in his ears had always given him an exhilarating sense of freedom and control. When he closed his eyes, he pretended he was on the *Kelly's Folly* again, plowing through the waves in blissful solitude. He'd enjoyed going out on his boat in the Hamptons, but Erica had never taken to sailing. She was always careful not to ruffle her elaborately coiffed hair or expose her flawless skin to the harshness of the sun's rays. There'd been a lot of things he and Erica hadn't shared a passion for.

His hand slackened on the tiller as he rounded an outcropping of rocks in the ever-changing coastline, and he was immediately captivated by the feral beauty of the landscape. The terrain, this side of the island, grew dramatically in elevation, rising from the depths of a crystal-clear lagoon, culminating in a verdant rise. At the summit stood an imposing limestone construction—a castle of some sort. As the boat drifted farther into the cove, he realized it wasn't a castle but a religious structure. A convent, perhaps, or a monastery. A domed turret towered over the edifice, topped by a crucifix. It appeared old, most likely a vestige of the Spanish colonization era.

He was drawn in by the area's air of disconnect from civilization. It was almost surreal. There were no boats anchored in the cove, but on a narrow strip of white sandy beach at the base of the rocky rise, there were noticeable signs of human activity.

Hit by a sudden impulse, he repositioned the boat, bow against the wind, preparing to lower the anchor. Diving into the water, he emerged from the lagoon minutes later, surprised to find several pairs of suspicious eyes fixed on him. Shaking droplets from his face, he waded out onto the beach. Five or six children scrambled to their feet, clearly frightened by the presence of a stranger.

"Who are you?" one of the older boys demanded, his gaze dark with diffidence.

Richard suppressed a grin at the boy's boldness. "My name is Richard Kelly. And who are you?"

"Tommy," the boy replied after a slight hesitation.

"Awesome castle," Richard said, gesturing to the elaborate sand structure they'd been so intent on modeling, they hadn't noticed the boat enter the cove.

One of the older girls in the group took a step forward, planting her feet between him and the younger ones in a protective stance. "You aren't supposed to be here. This is private property," she said.

"Is that right?" Richard asked, not so amused this time.

"It belongs to the nuns and strangers are not allowed here. If Ms. El—"

The rest of her sentence was drowned out by a chorus of loud voices approaching from behind the shrubbery at the foot of the rock wall. Before Richard had a chance to grasp what was happening, a noisy stream of children materialized from the underbrush as if by magic. Sandals and hats flew in every direction as the rowdy mob spilled onto the beach in a wild, disorderly fashion. Play tools and items of clothing were abandoned haphazardly in a race to the water. Amidst whoops of excitement and squeals of protest as some bullied their way to the advantage line, an older girl shouted orders.

"Remember, keep to the shallow end of the lagoon, and when I say out, I mean *out*, and that means no more than twenty minutes in the water. The last one to stall will be sent back to clean out the chicken coop."

She had her back to the lagoon and was gamboling backward, shouting at the top of her lungs in a futile attempt to make herself heard. Before Richard could step out of the way, the girl swung around and barreled chest-first into him, sending them both sprawling into the surf in a tangle of arms and legs.

The breath was knocked from Richard's lungs, and he gulped in salt water. Coughing and sputtering, he struggled to sit up, his arms still around the young girl, only vaguely conscious of a dull ache throbbing in his left rump where it had hit a jagged rock. Then the girl raised her head to look at him through eyes the color of April skies, sending his mind into a tailspin.

Misty?

CHAPTER 9

"I'm so sorry. Are you all right?"

He blinked several times to clear his vision. The human tornado he'd collided with—a decidedly more mature person than he'd initially thought—leaned over him with a worried frown on her face. Her long blond braid fell over one shoulder, the wet end of which grazed his belly, reassuring him she wasn't an apparition.

He managed to raise himself into a sitting position but was hit by a dizzying spell, one he suspected had very little to do with the bodily impact and more with the fact that for a moment—for one crazy, incredible instant—he'd believed to have seen Misty's eyes staring back at him.

She scrambled to her feet and held out a hand to him. "I'm terribly sorry. I didn't see you. You're not hurt, are you?"

"No, not at all," he replied with as much dignity as he could muster. To be mowed down by a small, willowy wisp of a girl was a crushing blow to his manhood, and he was sure his humiliation showed.

He accepted her hand and stood, feeling like a gawky, fumbling ninth grader, dripping seawater all over her already soaked blouse and shorts. She smiled up at him, revealing a perfect set of teeth framed by full, slightly sun-chapped lips. Even wet and bedraggled, she was exquisite.

She exhaled with obvious relief. "For a moment I was afraid you'd suffered a concussion or something."

Definitely something, he thought.

Her face grew suddenly alarmed. "Oh, no," she cried out.

He followed the direction of her gaze and saw a multitude of what appeared to be colored eggs floating in the lagoon. She immediately began to scoop up the objects, dropping them into a basket. The children rushed to help her, and after a great deal of splashing and squealing, rescued most of the plastic eggs.

His brain still swaddled in a daze, Richard followed the activity until something bright, shiny, and half-buried in the sand between his feet caught his attention. He stooped to pick up the stray egg and placed it in the basket with the others.

"Oh, good, you rescued the golden egg," the young woman said with an embarrassed smile. "I dropped the basket when I bumped into you and didn't realize the eggs had fallen out. They're for the Easter egg hunt we're having right after playtime, and . . ."

She stopped and regarded him with earnest curiosity, as if only then fully cognizant of his presence. "You know this is a private beach, right?" she asked.

"So I'm told," he replied, sheepishly. As if on cue, some of the older children gathered protectively around the young woman. "I'm sorry, I didn't realize I was trespassing."

She angled her head and tapped the tip of a finger on her lips. "Let me guess. You missed the big no-trespassing sign at the entrance to the cove."

He slid his gaze across the narrow expanse of water, and sure enough, there it was, a large and conspicuous signpost jutting out from the rocks, not far from where he'd dropped anchor. Hard to miss, but evidently the same irresistible force that had attracted him to the place had made him oblivious to everything else.

"Guilty as charged," he admitted, feeling like a chastised teenager who'd committed an infraction.

She gave him an earnest look. "That's too bad. You realize I have to report you, don't you?" she asked.

Report me? he thought. What is she, the beach police? The sign stated, "Trespassers Will Be Prosecuted," but it wasn't as if he'd planted a beach umbrella and rolled out the cooler box.

"Look, I can explain—" He caught the twinkle of mischief in her eyes and knew he'd been played.

"On second thought," she said, "maybe I should hand you over to my fearless Lilliputians, here." She assumed an authoritative stance. "What do you say, o' citizens of Lilliput?" she asked, addressing her brood of miniature bodyguards. "Should Captain Gulliver, here, be punished for his infraction or should he be shown clemency?"

Then she leaned over to him, warning in a hushed tone, "We've recently finished reading *Gulliver's Travels* and I fear they could easily relate."

Before he could think of a suitable comeback, the newly appointed jury exploded in a chorus of blood-curdling propositions.

"Tie him up!"

"Take him prisoner!"

"Let's carry him back to his boat and sink the boat!"

"No, no, don't want to!"

The discordant protest came from a little curly redhead, whose eyes brimmed with tears of empathy. "I don't want to tie him up," she said, lips trembling.

The young woman gave Richard a resigned look. "It's your lucky day. Sherri is against prosecution, and since she's the group's official spokesperson we have no choice but to pardon you."

Richard winked at the child. "A woman after my own heart," he said.

"On condition, of course, that you properly identify yourself. We aren't in the habit of welcoming just any stranger into the Country of Lilliput."

He promptly held out his hand. "Richard Kelly, from New York. I'm lodged at Serena, on the other side of the island.

You're welcome to call the resort and check out my credentials," he added for good measure.

She shook his hand and didn't pull back when he held hers a moment longer than was ethically necessary, while he marveled at the cool, soft feel of it.

"Pleased to meet you, Richard Kelly, and welcome to Monks' Cove. I'm Clare Elliot. Clare without the 'i'," she specified. "I teach Pre-K up at the monastery. My mother, Sonia Elliot, owns Serena."

She was his host's daughter, Courtney's sister. She didn't resemble either, but something about her eyes struck a deep inner chord in him, same as her mother's had.

Then his mind did a quick double-take. Clare, he realized, was the name signed on the glasshouse paintings. Was it possible she, and not Courtney, was the artist behind the reflected sensibility and passion in the soft pastels of seascapes and children's portraits?

Clare Elliot. C.E.

What was even more bizarre was the possibility she could also be the person whose initials he'd seen on the strange painting he'd traced all the way to this island.

He struggled to find his voice while he grappled with the electrifying thought. "Glad to make your acquaintance, Clare without an 'I'. Sorry for showing up like this—and for getting you all wet."

She looked down at her T-shirt, now plastered to her skin in a revealing way. "Oh, it's nothing," she said laughing, but her face had turned a rosy shade.

There was something uniquely refreshing about her. She wasn't a raving beauty, not in the classical sense of the word, but she had a sparkle and a wholesomeness about her that added to her appeal.

Relieved the children had lost interest in him, he glanced toward the rise. There was no visible outlet beyond a smattering of trees and overgrown shrubs, just a solid rock wall bordering the entire perimeter of the beach.

"Is there a secret passage back there or are you all expert rock climbers?" he asked.

Her lips curved upward in a grin. "Come, I'll show you."

He followed her to the base of the rocky wall. "It's a very ancient staircase," she explained, gesturing to the entrance of a narrow tunnel carved into the rock. "It was excavated by the Franciscan monks who occupied the monastery in the eighteenth century for easy access to the beach. Monks' Cove got its name from them."

"A smuggling tunnel. Impressive." He noticed the small square openings cut into the face, no doubt to allow the light and air into the passage. He had to admire the ingenuity and resourcefulness of those monks. A complex structure like this had to have been quite an undertaking, requiring strength and technical skills.

Her chin tipped upward. "Monks didn't smuggle," she said, and he suppressed a smile at her defensive stance.

"You can't know that for sure. In British colonial times, people would do anything to avoid paying custom duties," he couldn't help taunting.

"In British colonial times," Clare said, mimicking his tone, "monks lived simply and frugally. Besides, they grew everything they needed right on their own land and didn't suffer famine." She propped her hands on her hips and narrowed her eyes at him. "Is it a New York thing or are you just innately cynical?"

"Probably a bit of both," he admitted, then added, "Sorry, I didn't mean to question your monks' integrity."

His effort at sounding contrite failed to impress her. "We should get back. The children have been taking advantage of my absence far too long," she said.

"I take it the monks no longer inhabit the monastery?" he asked as they retraced their steps.

"Not in the last two centuries. Since then it's been the home of the nuns of the Humility of the Blessed Virgin Mary. They're a very old order founded by St. Isabel of

France in 1259," she explained. "The original building was erected in the fifteenth century, when the first Spanish settlers came to America, but through the centuries it was destroyed numerous times by fires and hurricanes and rebuilt each time. You should drive up and visit the monastery some time."

Again, he was surprised by her open friendliness. "Are you always this trusting of strangers?" he asked.

"No, only when I'm responsible for half drowning them."

Her lopsided smile made his chest tighten. He wanted to tell her she reminded him of someone he'd known a long time ago, but he held back. It would surely send out the wrong vibes. Besides, it was plain crazy. Misty was in the past. Clare Elliot, on the other hand, was very much present, and an enigma that tantalized his curiosity. And damn if she didn't intrigue him.

"Were you born on the island?" he asked.

"Born and bred. Lived here all my life."

"What do you do when you aren't teaching or entertaining trespassers on the beach?"

She didn't seem to mind the probing question. "I paint as a hobby," she replied.

His heart gave a tiny lurch.

"Mostly, though, I tend to the orphans who board at the monastery."

Orphans. The term rudely propelled him back to the past. "I thought orphanages had gone out with the Dickens era."

"Oh, St. Isabel Monastery isn't an orphanage, not in the traditional sense of the word," she said. "It's more like a safe house for a small number of children from particularly difficult backgrounds, and who are struggling with psychological or emotional handicaps. We provide a safe haven for them and help them overcome their difficulties, until they're ready to be adopted or taken into foster care."

Different practices, same system, he was tempted to point out. Instead, he said, "Sounds like quite a workload."

"And you sound like my mother. She's always complaining I work too much. But it's no hardship when you love what you do. Besides, living on Monastery Hill makes it convenient."

"You live at the monastery?"

She laughed at his obvious surprise. "No, I have my own place close by. I'm not a nun, nor aspiring to become one, if that's what you're thinking."

"I wasn't thinking anything," he said, but something in the way she looked at him told him she could see right through his lie.

She sat on a flat rock in the shade of a palm, her vigilant gaze trained on the children "And what do you do when you're not encroaching on people's private property?" she countered, mimicking his earlier tone.

He shrugged. "Nothing much." Besides feeling sorry for myself, he thought. "In another life I was a neurosurgeon."

For some reason he was reluctant to hide his real identity from Clare. Something about her inspired him to be himself.

"A neurosurgeon. As in removing tumors and repairing blood vessels?"

Her lukewarm reaction came as a complete surprise. He was used to women fawning all over him when he stated the nature of his profession, and he didn't know if he should be offended or amused. For a shocking second he imagined wiping that look of mock disbelief from her face with a kiss. The image sobered him instantly.

"Appearances can be deceiving," he said, his voice coming out raspy and awkward.

Amusement sparkled in her eyes. "What a coincidence. Gulliver, too, was a doctor. The children will be tickled silly when I tell them."

"Must be karma."

A lock of her hair had come loose from her braid, its tip grazing the corner of her mouth, and he almost reached out to brush it away. What was it about this girl—this woman, really—that made him gravitate toward her in this irrational and totally inappropriate way?

Fortunately, she didn't pry into the reason he wasn't a neurosurgeon anymore. Instead, she asked, "So, what brings you to St. Isabel?"

He eased down next to her, leaving a safe distance between them. "Just taking a break . . . from a personal situation. I'm using the time to finish up a medical book I've been working on for some time."

Her smile slackened. "I'm sorry. About the personal situation, I mean."

"Thank you."

The sympathy in her eyes prompted him to steer the conversation away from his persona. He had too many questions of his own about her, the most pressing concerning her association with the glass house buried in the forest. He wondered why he hadn't run into her at the mansion, and why her studio seemed as though it hadn't been used in a while. "Do you ever go home to Serena, in between teaching and overseeing needy kids?" he asked.

Her eyes shied away from his. "Not as often as I should. As much as I hate to admit it, my mother's right. I tend to get too wrapped up in my work and let too much time lapse between visits."

The ruefulness in her tone told him her family meant a lot to her but for some reason, she felt obligated to pour her heart and soul into her work.

"How do you like it at Serena?"

From the speed with which she shifted the focus of the conversation back to him he surmised she was just as skittish as he about discussing private matters.

"I like it well enough, though by opting for the seclusion of the groundskeeper's lodge over five-star amenities, I may not be affording it the justice it deserves," he said.

"You're staying at the cabin?" she asked surprised.

He shrugged. "I'm not what you would call the gregarious type."

He told her how he'd mislead his fellow guests into believing he was an aspiring mystery writer, and how his deception had ended up snowballing out of proportion.

"Don't worry, your secret's safe with me," she promised, eyes twinkling with humor. "What kind of medical book are you writing?"

He wondered if her curiosity was genuine or if it was just her way of distracting him from asking her more personal questions. "It's a study of the effects of trauma as a result of brain injury, primarily a collection of experiences and testimonials gathered over the course of my career."

Her wide-eyed expression reflected genuine astonishment. "You must have come across a good many brain injuries to have amassed such a vast baggage of information to fit into a textbook. What are you, seventy-five?"

He didn't know whether to be offended or flattered by her question. Fortunately, he was spared coming up with a suitable response.

"Ms. Elliot, Joey needs to go potty!" The girl who had confronted Richard earlier trundled toward them, towing a sullen-looking toddler by the hand. "But I think it's too late," she announced with a distressed grimace.

Clare slid from the rock, dusting sand off her shorts. "Thank you, Maria. Leave Joey with me and run up to call Sister Adelia," she instructed with the confidence and composure of one accustomed to handling crises on a daily basis. "There, there, don't cry," she crooned gently to the boy. "Sister Adelia will take you up to the monastery to get cleaned up and have you back in no time."

Richard stared at the boy, recognizing in him the child portrayed in the painting he'd seen in the glass house. The resemblance was remarkable, down to the blond bristle-brush haircut and unhappy look on his tear-streaked face.

"This is Joey. He's only three and a half years old," Clare told him, as if to justify the child's physiological mishap.

"He doesn't talk," piped in a childish voice next to Richard, and he glanced down at the little redhead who had so valiantly rushed to his defense earlier.

Richard met Clare's eyes inquiringly and was surprised to see a glimmer of sadness. "Run along, now, Sherri, you're missing all the fun," her teacher said.

"Looks like they keep you on your toes," Richard said, as Maria led the little girl away.

"You have no idea."

Though the response was glib, her eyes remained troubled. It reminded him he was interfering with whatever activity they'd been involved in before he'd crashed their party. "I'm sorry for having taken up so much of your time."

She made a dismissive gesture. "It's just playtime. It does the children good to run wild from time to time."

He smiled. Clearly Clare Elliot had a completely different perspective than any of his former caregivers when it came to dealing with troubled minors.

"Would you like to join us for the Easter egg hunt? We were scheduled to have it tomorrow, Easter Sunday, but they're predicting rain showers, so we decided to have it a day early," she said.

For a moment he was tempted to accept the invitation. There was so much more he wanted to know about Clare Elliot, but the idea of entertaining a bunch of rowdy kids didn't appeal to him. "It's very kind of you to ask, but I should be heading back to the marina and return the boat."

She smiled. "Well, then, enjoy the rest of your stay at Serena," she said.

CHAPTER 10

S ome things were different from the last time Richard had been in the pavilion, indicating someone had been there recently. On the center easel, a new painting had replaced the partially finished seascape. This, too, was a beach scene, one where children holding woven baskets full of colored eggs crept around crevices in the rocks and sneaked beneath the shrubs. He barely made out the tiny dinghy drifting away from an all-too familiar cove, the wind in its sail. The abstract paintings were still there, among the folds of the drapes, as if forgotten or deliberately hidden from sight. The paint-splattered smock was draped over the back of a chair, fresh turquoise and yellow now dominating over stale smudges. An ancient floor fan had been dragged to the center of the room to face the easel to provide some respite from the damp heat.

He peered at the sticky notes stuck to the chipped mirror over the sink. *Urgent! Need more cayenne. Maryvale Bapt. Church Crafts Show Sun. May 12. Remind Juan again for strelitzia bulbs!*

A funny paper clip in the shape of a laughing pig held together other odd scraps of paper. He smiled as he picked up a hairbrush left negligently on the marble counter and fingered the few fine strands of honey-blond hair weaved between its long bristles. If he'd needed tangible proof of Clare Elliot's earthly existence, he'd found it. There was a certain mystical charm about the friendly pre-K teacher that mesmerized him. Days after his visit to Monks' Cove, he still hadn't been able to get her out of his mind, and he'd sometimes wondered if he had imagined her, if his discovery of Monks' Cove wasn't a byproduct of his current condition.

He thought about Courtney and how startlingly different the two sisters were . . . the first, dark, artfully striking and blatantly exuberant, the other fair, unpretentiously pretty and spontaneous. The wild and fiery Amazon and the gentle Aphrodite, born from the foam of the sea. Each mysteriously charismatic in her own way.

"I was wondering where you'd disappeared to."

Sonia Elliot was standing in the open doorway. "The door was unlocked," he said by means of an apology.

If his host was annoyed to find him snooping around her property, she didn't show it. "It used to be my late husband's favorite hideout," she told him. "He spent hours in here growing his prized orchids. Now it's my daughter Clare's art studio; she uses it when she comes to Serena."

"She's very talented."

Pride lit up her face. "Yes, she is."

"Were you looking for me?" he asked.

"Yes. There was a telephone call for you from New York. Someone called Lisa Collins. I tried putting it through to the cabin but you weren't there, so I took a message and came to find you. I saw the light through the trees."

The mention of his assistant's name was like being jerked awake from a pleasant dream. If Lisa had called, it had to be important, and urgent business, which could only mean Erica.

"She asked me to tell you she's sending some important papers from your attorney's office. You're required to sign them and FedEx them back to her."

More documents to sign, he thought. Though the divorce had been finalized weeks ago, the paperwork seemed endless. It probably had to do with his deeding his part of the South Hampton house over to his ex-wife. The sooner the matter was settled the better. He hated the place. Too damn sterile. Too many unpleasant reminders.

"Thank you. I appreciate you going to the trouble of delivering the message in person."

"She also said to tell you the UCLA Neurology Department has been trying to reach you regarding their offer of a fellowship."

He glanced at her sharply, but Sonia's expression remained neutral. "Thank you. I'll call Lisa in the morning." He knew he wouldn't. He wasn't ready to plan for the future and take on new responsibilities. The risk of fading into obscurity grew bigger with each passing day, but he couldn't reconnect with his old life yet.

"Can I interest you in joining me for dinner?" Sonia offered. "Our regulars are dining on the mainland and the rest of the guests had other plans for the evening. I feel I've been neglecting you since your arrival and it seems like a good opportunity to make amends."

He was about to extend the usual polite refusal, then changed his mind. He'd only had to see the intensity in her look to realize he had some explaining to do, and he should get it over with.

IT WASN'T UNTIL after dinner that the topic of his identity came up. He and Sonia lingered on the terrace while a maid went discreetly about her business, rearranging furniture and covering the chaises for the night. A storm brewed and heavy rains were expected for the night hours. The first signs of turbulence had already appeared with sudden gusts of wind ripping through the palms, scaring the birds out of their nests. Far into the distance, brilliant flashes of lightning crackled in the graphite sky, casting a silvery blanket over the water.

"I love it out here at night. There's something to be said about Serena's embracing tranquility."

Sonia's wistful sigh led Richard to suspect his host's very busy schedule didn't allow her too many of these peaceful moments. "Whoever named it probably felt the same way," he said.

"That would be my father-in-law, the first Edward Elliot," she said. "He named it after his mother, who died giving birth to his younger brother. He said the name suited the place, and he was right."

"You aren't originally from St. Isabel, are you?" he asked.

She smiled. "Is it so obvious?"

"Hard to miss those New England vowels."

"I grew up in a small town in Maine and moved here as a young bride. Seems like yesterday, yet it's been thirty-six years."

"Do you miss it?" he asked conversationally.

"Not as much as I used to. I'd get a little nostalgic at times, when I still had family there. They're all gone, now, and I have nothing to go back to but memories. St. Isabel has been my home for as long as I can remember. I can't imagine living anywhere else."

She pulled a light cotton cardigan off the back of a chair and threw it over her shoulders. "And what about you, *Doctor* Kelly? What moved you to come to St. Isabel?"

His fingers tightened on the edge of the marble balustrade at the obvious emphasis on his professional title. He was rattled but not surprised; he'd been anticipating this conversation all evening yet still found himself unprepared.

"I'm sorry I wasn't completely honest," he said.

There was no trace of ill feelings on her face, only understanding. "There's no need to apologize. I'm sure you have your reasons for staying under the radar." She smiled. "Everyone is entitled to their privacy, even absconding talented neurosurgeons."

He smirked. The lady had done her homework. "Do you always make it your business to investigate Serena's guests?" he asked.

She didn't seem offended by his blatant criticism. "Let's say I like to know who I take into my home. When I take a reservation," she explained, "I always follow up with a verification call, and the contact number you left had a recorded message relating to the nature of your business. Your name sounded vaguely familiar, then I remembered having read some articles on minimal invasive brain surgery in the *Family Medical Digest* written by a Dr. Richard J. Kelly, and that's when I made the connection."

Shame prickled his conscience and he wished he could take back his words. "Do you have a particular interest for the workings of the human brain?" he asked, forcing a smile.

She reached out and plucked a wisteria petal from the vine creeping up to the balustrade. The sweet perfume it released mingled with the pungent ocean air as she rolled it between her fingers. "I'm interested in anything that has to do with scientific progress. It comes down to my roots, I suppose. My father was a doctor, and his father before him."

He cocked an eyebrow. "Am I to believe Serena's tireless and capable hostess missed her true calling?"

She laughed softly. "Quite the opposite, actually. I'm too squeamish to so much as dress a wound. Just the sight of my own daughters' scraped knees was enough to make me lightheaded," she admitted sheepishly. "My older sister, on the other hand, turned out to be an excellent pediatrician, just like our father."

He smiled ruefully to himself wondering what she would think if she knew how little talent and fame meant when you let your fear take over your life till it grips your mind, body, and spirit.

"I didn't lie when I said I was here to write," he said. "I really am working on a book—although its subject matter is nowhere near as intriguing as your guests assume."

He described his work and told her of his intention to promote it as educational material in neurosurgical studies.

"Which, given your remarkable success to date, you shouldn't have any trouble marketing," she said.

Her complimentary remark made him slightly uncomfortable. "Thank you. It's been a while since I've written anything worthwhile. I've toyed with this project for so long my publisher's all but given up on me. I guess I needed this time at Serena to get my muse back."

Sonia studied him seriously. "The book isn't the real reason you came to St. Isabel, is it?" she asked candidly.

A powerful clap of thunder shook the foundations of the old house, saving him from having to answer right away. The first drops of rain fell onto his clenched fists, cool but bringing no relief.

"Sorry, I have no right to poke my nose in your private business, but I want you to know I can be a good listener if you feel like talking."

"Thank you," he said, but couldn't help thinking listening to her guest's woes was carrying out her hostess' duties a little too far.

As if reading his mind, she said, "I've had a lot of practice through the years. You aren't the first guest to come to Serena carrying some heavy baggage—and I don't mean the material kind. I try to help them as best I can, even if it means acting as their sounding board."

"And does it work?" he asked trying not to let his skepticism transpire.

"Not always," she admitted. "Sometimes they leave no happier than when they first arrived, and I know I've failed. But at least I know I've tried."

He swallowed the bitter lump in his throat. "Thank you, but a few weeks in paradise won't right all the wrongs in my life."

"Maybe not, but you could learn to accept them and move on."

He was about to form a protest, but the combination of heartfelt concern and empathy in Sonia's eyes stopped him. Something told him she'd known pain and heartbreak in her lifetime.

"I've screwed up once too many times in my life. I don't know how to move on anymore," he surprised himself by saying.

"You will. We all do, eventually. We just have to find it within ourselves," she said softly.

The words were strangely comforting.

There must be something about angel-blue eyes and their hypnotic effect on me, he thought.

Sonia shivered, rubbing her hands over her arms. "It's certainly getting damp out here. What do you say we continue our conversation inside?"

He pulled away from the balustrade. "Thank you, but I should be on my way. I've kept you up long enough."

"You'll get drenched. Let me at least loan you an umbrella."

"No need."

A little bit of rain might help clear his head, he thought. "Well, then, good night."

CHAPTER 11

Richard didn't particularly like flying, even less so when such activity involved a vintage bi-motor and an overly zealous woman at the commands. The nerve-rattling squeaking and shuddering of the plane's old joints as its handler executed one hair-raising trick after another was driving him crazy.

He had only himself to blame. Courtney Elliot had been very persistent in her offer to treat him to a bird's-eye view of the island, and he hadn't wanted to appear uncouth. Of course, he hadn't counted on having to savor the experience on a rickety old plane that looked and functioned like a World War Two relic.

His edginess didn't go unnoticed, and Courtney seized the opportunity to poke fun at him. "Come on, Kelly, loosen up," she shouted over the din of the motors. "Experience the exhilaration of dominating the world from above. Feel the rush."

He grimaced. The only rush he was feeling right now was one of cold dread. "With all those fancy planes of yours, all you could come up with is this old trap?"

She fired an affronted glance at him. "Old trap? I'll have you know this is a 1967 Beechcraft Seneca."

"And that's supposed to reassure me?"

"They're good, solid machines. They don't make them like this anymore."

"Let me guess. You happen to own the last surviving specimen," he said.

Courtney shook her head. "You disappoint me, Kelly. I didn't take you for a wimp."

"I'd rather be a live wimp than a dead daredevil," he said, but the noise drowned out his voice.

He focused on the view. "Looks like most of the island is pure wilderness," he said, observing the vast expanse of green they flew over.

"That's right. Two-thirds of the island is a state-protected nature preserve," she said. "Most of the housing developments are scattered along the coast." She veered again, banking slightly on the passenger side to give him a better perspective of the area. "That's Mermaid Point Keys up ahead," she announced, pointing to a row of small islands off the coast. "Aren't they a spectacular sight?"

Richard craned his neck to see the cape of the island he'd cruised around the week before. From up here, the tiny green specks that formed the keys took the shape of the fractured tail of a giant emerald sea creature.

He saw the familiar shape of the monastery atop the rocky promontory and the tiny strip of white sand directly below.

"That's Monks' Cove," Courtney said, following the direction of his gaze.

"Ah, the nuns' hallowed ground," he said, remembering the narrowly missed ambush by a small army of orphans.

"You know of Monks' Cove?" she asked in surprise.

He told her about his sailing expedition on the dinghy and his confrontation with the monastery children. "Those kids guard it like a nuclear Fort Knox. I might have met with a terrible fate had your sister not bailed me out."

"You've met Clare?" she asked.

"Yes, inadvertently, you might say." At her puzzled glance he explained, "I missed the keep-off sign and swam ashore."

"It's kind of hard to miss, don't you think?"

Her mock-disbelief made him uncomfortable. "I admit I was a bit sidetracked by the rugged beauty of the coast."

"And maybe just a tad curious," she said.

He was tempted to deny her allegation, but he'd be lying. He'd been more than a tad curious and completely ensnared by the magical allure of the place, including that of its resident mermaid.

Later when they were back on the ground and pulling out of the airfield parking lot in the company jeep he said, "You're not at all like your sister."

She gave a little shrug. "No two siblings are ever alike. What makes you think Clare and I should be any different?"

"It was just an observation."

"My, for one who claims to spend most of his time holed up in an isolated cabin, you've been awfully observant," she said, her tone brittle. "Is this some kind of research technique you use for your writing?"

All at once she'd become cold and defensive, and he couldn't understand why.

"No. I just couldn't help noticing your sister didn't inherit the business gene you and your mother share."

"Clare has never been interested in the air freight business," Courtney said. "Teaching is everything to her."

"She certainly seems very committed to her work."

Courtney laughed dryly. "That may be the understatement of the year. She lives for those kids. At her age, she should be taking up other interests, enjoying life. But you have to know Clare to understand why she lives the way she does."

Her tone made it clear she understood but didn't approve of her sister's lifestyle. "What do you mean?" he asked.

Her expression changed, becoming strangely wistful. "There's a reason Clare lives a segregated life, and it's because it hasn't always been an easy one for her. She's overly sensitive, emotionally fragile at times . . ." She trailed off, as if the subject was a difficult one for her.

Then she gave him an embarrassed smile. "I'm sorry, I didn't mean to sound critical. The truth is, I tend to be overly protective where my little sister is concerned."

"No need to apologize," he said.

Courtney's veiled warning to steer clear of her sister had been distinct, and it left him with an unsettling feeling. He wondered if he'd missed something that day on the nuns' beach, and if the anonymous paintings in the glass house were a reflection of Clare's so-called fragility.

Courtney pulled to a stop in Serena's courtyard. "So, how is the book coming along?" she asked in a decidedly cheerier tone.

"It's coming along well. I've covered a lot of ground since arriving."

"Good. Then maybe you can stop playing the hermit crab and enjoy the island a bit more. Ever been parasailing?"

He chuckled. "Nice try." Being segregated in his cabin didn't seem like a bad idea when the alternative was to play along with Ms. Elliot's adventurous schemes.

"How about scuba diving? Don't tell me you're afraid of that, too."

"I'll have you know I'm a fully certified PADI diver."

"Then I'm sure you won't have any trouble accepting the challenge," she said with a smug grin.

CHAPTER 12

She sat cross-legged under the low-lying branches of a solitary palm. Her strong, melodious voice reverberated off the rocky confines of the cove as she read from a book to a semicircle of children. She looked up when the dinghy rolled into the lagoon, and for a moment their gazes locked. Coming back was wrong, he knew, but he hadn't been able to stay away.

By the time he reached shore, the children had gathered at the edge of the lagoon, hailing him boisterously as if he were a war hero returning victorious from a long and bloody battle.

"What, no blood-thirsty warriors out here today?" he asked as he emerged from the surf.

"Nah, you're okay," one of the boys said, revealing a gap in his front teeth.

"Thanks," Richard said. It was heartening to know he'd been upgraded from unwelcome to okay. "You're okay, too," he said.

The sprightly little redhead rushed to greet him effusively, throwing her arms around his legs and almost knocking him off balance. He stood motionless, his instincts telling him he should repay her with a solicitous gesture—like ruffle her hair or tweak her nose, but he was disempowered by his old, misguided grudges. He told himself it wasn't these kids' fault they carried an invisible stigma that messed with his mind and raised barriers.

When he finally managed to disengage himself from the little girl's clinging limbs, he walked over to Clare.

She looked different today. Large, owlish, round-rimmed glasses perched on her nose, and a black tie hung loosely around the neck of her white buttoned-up shirt. No doubt about it, she was the most unconventional schoolteacher he'd ever met. She looked so young . . . a heart-stopping, grown-up version of Misty.

He forced himself to ignore the familiar tightening in his chest. "Would you believe me if I said I missed the signs again?"

She replied with a skeptical grimace.

"Yeah, that's what I thought," he said. "Just say the word and I'll leave."

Her eyes sparkled like blue diamonds through the round spectacles, which, he realized, were lens-less.

"No need," she said, closing the book she'd been reading. She nodded toward the children still huddled around him. "Looks like an amnesty has been declared. They no longer see you as the enemy."

He grinned, then gestured to the book. "Please, don't let my presence distract you."

"Too late for that. As much as they love a good story, a surprise visitor is a far more tempting distraction. Not to mention they get a break from my hawkish supervision."

"Glad to be of help," he said, firing a conspiratorial wink in the children's direction.

He lowered himself to the woven mat she sat on, crossing his legs in imitation of her style. He couldn't imagine there being anything hawkish about her. He thought she looked funny and adorable in the fake glasses and tie. For the first time in his adult life he wished he were five again so he could join these lucky children on this beach every day, listening to her soft voice transport him to faraway and imaginary places.

"Let me guess. Harry Potter." He pointed to her funny attire. "It's a dead giveaway."

She nodded. "*The Chamber of Secrets.* We're working our way through the series."

"I love Harry Potty," Sherri declared passionately. She'd taken position next to Richard, settling snugly against his leg.

Suddenly all the children began talking at once, anxious to share their enthusiasm for the popular narrative. One particularly zealous boy explained their progress. "We're up to the part where Harry goes to Nearly Headless Nick's one hundredth's death-day party and all the headless horsemen come in on the ghost horses and Sir Patrick jumps up and his head falls off and everyone laughs," he recounted all in one breath, accentuating the grisly scene by galloping on an imaginary horse around the palm tree and letting out a series of hair-raising screeches.

"I can't wait until we read *The Prisoner of Azkaban,*" chimed in another, struggling to make himself heard over the loud chatter, and added braggingly, "I've watched the DVD three times."

Richard found himself suddenly out of his depth. What little he knew about J. K. Rowlings' popular series could be summed up in the dusters of the volumes he'd seen abundantly displayed in bookstore windows and on movie billboards. He'd never been into goblins and wizards, not even at their gullible age. Gulliver, he could relate to—a colleague, albeit in a primitive and legendary way.

The children's attention quickly pivoted away from him as they engaged in a heated debate on whether Nearly Headless Nick should have been allowed to join the headless hunt, and he was grateful for the respite. Even Sherri lost interest in the adults and strutted off to join her peers.

Clare removed the glasses and placed them on top of the book next to her. "You don't have much experience around children, do you?" she asked bluntly.

"That obvious, huh?"

"If I didn't know you're a surgeon used to handling difficult situations, I'd think they put the fear of God in you," she replied.

Not just any children, but hers and what they symbolized, he wanted to explain, but that would mean having to bring up his own troubled childhood, which he didn't want to do.

"You would, too, if you'd narrowly missed being mobbed by a gang of miniature goblins," he said.

Her spontaneous laughter erupted, permeating his soul with its fresh, natural resonance. He liked how her face lit up when she laughed—or even just hinted at a smile, or how her eyes crinkled at the corners. Everything about her fascinated him. Stirrings of a deep physical yearning caught him unawares, jerking him back to reality.

Damn, this wasn't supposed to happen. It had to be a natural consequence of his emotional setback, he told himself. She was distracting, as well as refreshing. His was a perfectly normal biological reaction—and totally innocent.

If only he could make himself believe it.

Courtney's disquieting revelation reechoed in his head, putting a damper on his spirits. He attempted to see beyond Clare's external façade, trying to associate her with the emotionally fragile individual her sister had hinted at, and found that he couldn't. She was blatantly normal, so . . . together.

Clare was suddenly on her feet. "Tommy, Elsie, out of the water, now," she called to the children who tried to sneak into the lagoon. She ignored their mournful moans of protest, and added in a firm, no-nonsense tone, "Sister Adelia will be here soon to take you up."

Richard noticed not everyone was taking advantage of their teacher's momentary distraction to get into mischief. One of them hung back, not straying far from where he and Clare sat.

"Hey, buddy," he said to the small bristly-haired boy from the glass house portrait. The boy reacted by inching closer to Clare and regarding him circumspectly from under thick blond lashes.

"Joey, isn't it? I don't think he likes me."

"Joey's naturally distrustful of grownups," Clare said. "It's nothing personal."

A rustling of leaves behind him made him turn around. The young woman emerging from the shrubs wasn't wearing the traditional garb of nuns, but her austerely cut attire and the large silver crucifix hanging from a black cord around her neck indicated she had to be at least a postulant or a novice.

He stood up awkwardly, suddenly aware all he wore was a pair of wet swim trunks and a guilty look. Despite all their alleged frolicking on the beach, the nuns of the Humility of the Blessed Virgin Mary were obviously very protective of their privacy and he doubted they walked in on near-naked male trespassers every day.

Clare rose and made the introductions. "Sister Adelia, the houseparent aide. She has recently transferred to the monastery from Spain. Adelia, this is Richard Kelly, a guest at Serena."

"How do you do, Mr. Kelly?" the nun asked in a very precise but markedly accented English. "Welcome to St. Isabel. You are enjoying your stay, yes?"

"Yes, ma'm—sister. Thank you for asking," he replied, feeling a little uncomfortable as the woman's blatantly curious gaze swept over him.

He was relieved when her attention turned to the children. "Come along, now," she called out, clapping her hands together in a sharp rap. "Time for dinner."

"If you need to go . . ." Richard began when the young woman and the children started walking away.

"No, I'm done for the day—and I mean literally," Clare said with a wry smile.

She eased down on the mat again and leaned against the tree trunk, signs of fatigue discernible around her eyes. "So, tell me, what brought you over to Monks' Cove this time?"

"The truth? I was curious to know how the nuns make use of their secret beach. Maybe, you know, catch a few sunbathing."

She had the grace to laugh at his sorry excuse for a joke. "And here I thought it was the cove's irresistible appeal that finally lured you back," she said with an exaggerated sigh.

He tried not to dwell on the word "finally," which may or may not have implied she'd been waiting for him to make another appearance.

"So, it's true. I didn't imagine it?"

"What?" Clare asked, appearing confused.

"The magic of this place. You said the cove has an irresistible appeal. It would explain why I didn't see the sign the first time."

She tilted her head, giving him an amused look. "Nice try. But yes, Monks' Cove does have a compelling effect on people. Its peaceful, untamed beauty has been known to inspire many artists and poets in their work."

"You get a lot of return trespassers?"

"Not really. You're the first repeat offender."

He chuckled at her joke, but the thought she could consider him arrogant for thinking he could come and go as he pleased niggled at him. "I don't want you to think because I got off scot-free the first time I feel I have the right to drop by any time I want to," he said. "I wouldn't have come if . . ."

"If?" she urged, amused at his obvious discomfort.

"If it hadn't felt right the first time."

It wasn't what he had meant to say, but it was the truth. Something had begun to unravel inside him that first day, something that had been coiled so tightly it had robbed him of the power to feel.

Her gaze burned through his, sympathetic and understanding. "You've been hurt," she said softly, as if she could see right through the solid walls of his reserve. He looked away from eyes that contained such heartfelt compassion, it made him feel vulnerable and exposed.

"So, you're clairvoyant, are you?" he said.

She smiled. "Just intuitive, I guess."

He didn't find her response reassuring. He felt the mesmerizing pull on his defenses, the force with which she threatened to shatter them with only the power of her compelling eyes.

"You and your mother have the same soul-scrutinizing abilities, the same dissecting power. Is it a hereditary thing or do you come from a long line of witches?" he asked, barely reining in his frustration.

She smiled. "Neither. I prefer to think of myself as an elf—a mischievous albeit benevolent one."

"Mischievous, huh? Should I be on the lookout for magic spells and mind-stealing potions?"

She waved her hand dismissively. "That stuff's overrated. I prefer more organic methods of infiltrating a person's mind, ones that don't require the use of amulets or powders."

He eyed her warily, not sure he liked the idea of her messing with his mind—organically or otherwise.

"Why am I inclined to believe you?"

She smiled. "Because it's true. You just haven't seen me in action yet."

"These deep, ugly furrows, for instance . . ." She leaned toward him and lifted a hand to his face. With a feather-light brush of her fingertips she smoothed the space between his eyes. Everything in him went still, including his heart. A heady combination of sweet female scent and body heat permeated his senses, throwing his mind off-kilter. "I can make them go away," she snapped her fingers in front of his eyes, "just like magic."

The abrupt gesture jerked him out of his dangerously floundering thoughts. He grunted his skepticism. "Sounds like some form of Botox treatment."

She laughed and shook her head at him. "Trust a doctor to attribute a scientific interpretation to a purely figurative observation. I was talking about separating mind and body. Letting go of emotional restraints. Laughter is a great healing power, did you know that?"

Without waiting for his answer, she sprang to her feet and motioned him to follow her. The sly come-hither smile she gave him made her look every bit the alluring mermaid of his daytime fantasy. Intrigued by the air of roguish mystery in her eyes, he stood and did as she asked.

She took both his hands and backed away toward the edge of the lagoon, tugging him along until they were knee deep in water. Not for a moment did he suspect what she had in mind. Of course, had he not been so completely bewitched by her mystifying presence he'd have been prepared for the shock of the cool ocean spray on his overheated body as she threw her arms backward and spun them in a rotating movement.

Jet after jet of water hit him square in the face, and for a moment he was stunned into inertia. Then he ducked his head and lunged for her. "You cheat. That was an underhanded trick," he said.

She laughed. "Don't be too sure of yourself, city boy," she said, and swam quickly out of reach, clothes and all.

Diving in after her, he tried to grab her feet, but she was too quick for him and slithered away, disappearing into the depths of the lagoon. Mere seconds later, he was tackled from behind in a surprisingly strong grip and plunged backward into the water. As he resurfaced, he heard her triumphant laughter. He clenched his jaw, teetering between conflicting emotions of annoyance and amusement.

Shaking the water from his eyes, he perused the area, but she was nowhere in sight. The only sign of life around the lagoon was an osprey perched on top of a rock, pecking at the pilchard it had just captured. Below the surface, only the seagrass moved, undulating gently in the undercurrents, while the sand, disturbed by the occasional small fish, billowed and settled onto the seabed.

He treaded water for a while, becoming frustrated in the enveloping silence that seemed to mock his gullibility. Finally, ducking underwater he swam toward the rock formations that hugged the cove, the only spot likely to offer plenty of hiding places. He guessed Clare could find her way through the intricate maze of rocks as effortlessly as a fish.

Shards of light penetrated the translucent water, highlighting the limestone's multitude of colors. He explored the area for a while, at intervals coming up for air. He was beginning to get an uneasy feeling about this. As he debated what to do, he spotted a flash of white slither behind a rock. Relieved, he smirked to himself.

She didn't see him when he came up behind her. When he seized her hips, she jerked and kicked outward hitting him squarely in the belly with the heel of her foot. The blow knocked the air from his lungs, causing him to relinquish his hold.

Desperate for air, he swam to the surface, replenished his oxygen, then set off in pursuit again. When he caught up with her, she was clambering among the rocks. She was probably planning to outwit him with her natural-born islander's agility, but he hadn't grown up on the streets of a concrete jungle without developing a few survival skills of his own.

He waded around to the other side, keeping his head below water. When he emerged, he saw she was crouched on the edge of the rock, on the lookout for him. Slowly, he hoisted himself out of the water and noiselessly crept up behind her.

"Looking for me?"

Clare swung around, startled. This time, though, he didn't give her a chance to escape. He scooped her up and lifted her effortlessly over his shoulder in a fireman's grip, ignoring her pleas for mercy. With his arms locked around her legs he clambered higher onto the rocks then dumped her unceremoniously over the side.

He was still laughing when she came up coughing and sputtering. "That was unfair. You crept up on me!"

"You didn't give me fair warning either, so we're even," he said. He held out a hand to help her up, but she gave him a circumspect look. "Come on. I promise to behave."

She succumbed, and he lifted her up onto the rock. She stumbled on the flat slippery surface and he gripped her arms to steady her. "Are you all right?" he asked.

She nodded but her eyes told him otherwise. Under the wet sleeves of her shirt, he felt the tremors in her tense muscles.

He ran his fingers along her arms. "You're trembling," he said, searching her gaze. It was much too warm for her to be cold.

"You took me by surprise, that's all. I guess you're better at the game than I gave you credit for." Though her tone was light, her words were strangely stilted, betraying a nervousness that surprised him.

Even if in her innocent and spontaneous way she'd made it her business to show him a good time, he was still little more than a stranger to her. Naturally she'd be on her guard.

"It's been a while since I had this much fun. Seems you really are a witch," he said, giving the wet tie still dangling from her neck a playful tug.

"Elf," she rectified, smiling smugly.

Witch or elf, it had felt incredibly good, even if only for a few minutes, to immerse himself in her wonderfully ordinary, carefree world.

She broke the contact and raised her hands to smooth her wet hair away from her face—and then he saw it. A tiny crescent-shaped scar on her left temple just below her hairline. His heart stopped for what seemed like an unnatural amount of time.

Misty! It was her! He was sure of it.

He almost blurted out her name, but he caught himself, a sixth sense telling him he shouldn't.

Trying to disguise his shock, he slid back into the water. "I'd best be on my way and you need to get some dry clothes on," he said.

CHAPTER 13

Manhattan, seventeen years earlier

It had finally come. The day when Misty's destiny would be determined. The bandages had come off and she had been declared strong enough to be discharged. Richard hadn't dwelled over the thought of Misty eventually leaving the hospital; he'd just accepted it as a natural and inevitable outcome. Now, seeing her tiny form huddled on the armchair next to her bed, her pitifully scarred cheeks streaked with tears, it just tore at his insides. It was a feeling he wasn't used to. "Whoa, what's up with the waterworks?"

Misty wrapped her arms around her legs. "They want to take me away," she sobbed onto her knees.

The muscles in his abdomen clenched. "Who?" he asked.

"The people. The ones that keep coming."

"How do you know?"

"I heard Nurse Roberts talking to Nurse Rodriguez last night. They thought I was sleeping but I wasn't."

While his anger mounted, Richard told himself to be rational. Misty had been in the hospital for almost six weeks, more than reasonably justifiable. Although the search for anyone connected to her was still ongoing, she couldn't stay here indefinitely. Her care was now up to Child Protective Services.

The idea of Misty becoming a "client" of the same system he'd resisted for most of his childhood was nauseating. Of course, it'd be different for her than it had been for him, he told himself. Even before the age of ten he'd been a rebel and a troublemaker and never lasted long in the foster homes he'd stayed in. A smart, sweet kid like her must have family somewhere. In the meantime, she would have no problem finding a temporary home she could easily fit into. She'd be well-cared for. Protected. As a ward of the state, she'd be properly provided for and have top-notch medical care.

He discovered it was one thing to reason with himself, another to make Misty herself see the logic in the arrangement. "You have to understand, they can't keep you here now that you're healed," he said.

She raised her head and, as usual, he couldn't help wincing internally at seeing the unflattering scars on her face. "I don't want to go with those people."

"They'll place you with a nice family, possibly with other children of their own. You'll be well-cared for. Besides, sooner or later your own family will find you, you'll see."

On the other hand, he thought, there'd be no Molly to sneak in and play with her, no one to soothe her worries away and tell her how cute she'd look once those scars were dealt with. There'd be no secret late-night visits from friends and cartons of French fries shared on top of the bed covers.

"I'll let you in on a little secret," he told her, sitting on the bed facing her. "For a time I was raised by foster parents. You see, I was an orphan—not that we know you're actually one yourself," he hastened to add.

Her eyes clouded over with empathy. "You were?"

"Yes, until I met Dr. Mallory, that is. He found me when I was twelve after I ran away from a foster home and he took me in. He helped me become the person I am today."

"Dr. Mallory raised you?" she asked, clearly astonished.

"Yeah, I guess you could say that. He's the closest thing I've ever had to a father. I was a bit older than you, back then, and as a single man living alone he couldn't get legal custody, so I had to stay in a group home. He became my legal guardian. He watched over me, bought me clothes, paid for my education. He taught me a lot of things."

"Does he still do that? Raise you?"

Richard thought about the restrained and unobtrusive ways Maxwell Mallory still managed to stay involved in his personal life, even now he was no longer legally responsible for him and smiled. "I guess in a way he still does," he admitted.

Two moist pupils fixed themselves on him. "Richard, can I come live with you?"

His initial reaction was one of shock. Then he almost burst out laughing. That would go over real well with social services. Two penniless students, a struggling musician, a cat and a not-so-tame primate. All they needed was an abandoned minor to complement the domestic tableau.

"I'm afraid that's out of the question," he said, maybe a trifle too gruffly.

She started to cry again. "I wouldn't be any trouble, I promise," she said.

He sighed. It was his fault if she was taking things too much for granted. He shouldn't have gotten so involved. "Look, kiddo, what you're suggesting is impossible. The authorities would never even consider housing you with a bunch of guys. It's just not done."

"Could Dr. Mallory watch over me, like he did with you?"

"It was different with me. I was older and didn't require much supervision. Besides, until last year, when I turned eighteen, the government was still very much in control of my life."

"I don't want to lose my friends. I don't want to lose you."

Her last statement rocked him. He managed to work up an insulted front. "Lose me? Come on, do I look like the type who'd just walk away from a friend? Who's been sneaking inside this dull, antiseptic-smelling room at all hours of the day playing babysitter to a lonely kid and getting under the skin of the nursing staff? Who's been neglecting more pressing duties in an effort to keep a certain insatiable little girl entertained? I'll have you know it'll be your fault if I don't make it to senior level this year."

Not only wasn't Misty amused by his argument, but she wasn't the least bit reassured. "If I go away, will you still be my friend? Will you come visit me?" she asked.

The desperate plea in her voice tore him apart. She looked so lonely and lost curled up in the chair, her chest still heaving from the crying spell. He knew, suddenly, if he had to dedicate his whole damn life to the cause, he'd make sure this kid didn't suffer any of the loneliness and deprivation he had suffered as a child. "You bet, funny face," he replied.

Her eyes brightened up to let in a tentative ray of hope. "Pro . . . promise?"

"Promise."

THE DAY RICHARD had turned eighteen he'd signed a mountain of documents, shaken his last caseworker's hand, and permanently severed all ties with the Department of Social Services. Reveling in his new emancipated status, he'd moved in with Tony Valenti, a former roommate at the group home and a year older than himself. Tony studied piano jazz at Juilliard on a full scholarship and dreamed of becoming the next Bill Evans. Together they shared a dark, ramshackle studio in a modified warehouse in Chelsea. Richard knew the next several years would be tough without the state grants. Though the generous scholarship he'd been awarded would go a long way toward covering his tuition bills, he'd have to hold onto his biweekly paychecks if he wanted to make it on his own. He refused to accept more financial help from Dr. Max. His guardian had gone over and beyond the call of duty by supporting him all these years. The least he could do to pay him back for his kindness and generosity was to study hard and make something of himself, and he was determined to do so, even if it took him a lifetime to pay off his student debt. Jake had joined them a few months later, after he, too, had "graduated" from the group home. By then, however, the studio had become too cramped, and when Mrs. Butler had offered to lease them her newly renovated East Village first-floor apartment at a bargain price, they'd readily accepted.

Mrs. Butler—or Mrs. B, as he and his mates had taken to calling her, was a retired widow. She was Dr. Mallory's former nurse, and a kindly soul.

"She could shack up with Mrs. Butler—at least for a while," he told Dr. Max. "Then she wouldn't be among strangers."

The older man looked at Richard as if he had proposed she be placed with Cruella de Vil's real-life twin. "Mrs. Butler?" he echoed.

Mary Butler was more than just a former employee to Dr. Max. She was a friend. A good friend. Richard suspected the doctor had always nurtured secret feelings for her even when her husband still lived, and that those feelings weren't quite one-sided. He'd always wondered if it was the reason Dr. Max had never married. Maybe Misty was just the catalyst they needed to finally bring them together.

Maxwell Mallory's eyebrows were drawn together in a thoughtful frown. "Assuming such a preposterous arrangement were feasible—which, knowing the system like you do you'd agree it's highly unlikely—what makes you think Mary—Mrs. Butler would be willing to take a ten-year-old into her home?"

Richard didn't know, but he sincerely hoped his instincts were correct. His landlady was a kind and caring person, and he hoped she'd show the same compassion for Misty she'd shown him when Dr. Max had brought him home—a half-starved, emotionally-deprived twelve-year-old street waif—and taken him under her wing.

CHAPTER 14

Mrs. B took one look at Misty and fell in love. Thanks to Dr. Max's intervention, the probate state granted her temporary legal guardianship of Misty until her family was found or until the court decided otherwise.

While it appeared clear to everyone concerned her stay in Mrs. Butler's townhouse on Myrtle Place would only be a short-term arrangement, Misty, on the other hand, settled in as if for the long haul. She adored Mrs. Butler, whom she, too, had taken to calling Mrs. B, and the woman doted on her from the first moment the child arrived. To Richard's relief, Dr. Mallory continued to be involved in the child's personal affairs. He'd taken it upon himself to ensure she was rightfully compensated for the physical and psychological injuries she'd sustained and had initiated court proceedings against Lancey's Superstore on behalf of the minor, suing the owners for negligence and reckless endangerment. He also found Misty a tutor so she could be homeschooled until the worst of her scars could heal. For now, at least, Misty was in good hands.

It wasn't until a couple of months later that Richard realized he'd been ignoring the possibility of Misty leaving one day, especially since his former guardian and Mrs. B had finally dropped all pretense of coyness and tied the knot, applying for temporary co-guardianship of the child. No one was happier than Misty when after the wedding, Dr. Mallory moved into Mrs. B's townhouse on Myrtle Place.

It had been one evening when at the end of his shift at his new workplace he'd found her waiting for him at the service entrance.

"Misty, how did you get here?" he asked in alarm, as gruesome scenes of serial killers, gang rapists, and other possible dangers lurking in the shadows of the big city flashed through his mind.

"By cab," she replied casually.

"All by yourself?"

She giggled. "Of course not, silly. Dr. Max brought me."

Just then a large figure stepped out of the shadows, into the glow of the streetlights. Richard breathed a sigh of relief. He'd been so surprised to see Misty, the distinct aroma of Max's pipe tobacco hadn't registered.

"We went inside Lancey's," Misty informed him excitedly.

"I thought Misty should visit the store again. It's been three months," Dr. Max explained. "If I recall, you'd promised to take her."

Heat rushed to Richard's face. Misty's counselor had suggested Misty be taken to the site of the accident in the hope it would help trigger her memory, and Dr. Max thought Richard should be the one to do it. While Richard had grudgingly agreed, he'd conveniently avoided the issue, hoping his "forgetfulness" would go unnoticed. He didn't see the point in submitting the child to unnecessary trauma. Misty was happy and she didn't appear to be experiencing pangs of nostalgia. Why try to fix something that didn't need fixing?

"Yeah, well, my schedule's kind of tight right now. Between work and finals . . ." he mumbled, avoiding Dr. Max's stern look.

"We went up the whole three floors," Misty said, eager to share her experience. She showed him the doll Dr. Max had bought her. "Dr. Max says she looks just like me. I think I'm too old for dolls, but Dr. Max doesn't think so. Isn't she pretty?"

He threw a distracted glance in the doll's direction. "Yeah . . . sure."

He dug his hands in the pockets of his worn leather jacket, which was beginning to fit a little too tightly around the shoulders. Money was tight, too, which meant he couldn't get a new one for a few years at least.

"So, um, how'd it go?"

Richard didn't need to hear the older man's answer. It was plainly reflected in the grim expression on his face. His shoulders relaxed. "It was a long shot, anyway," he said trying not to sound smug.

"Perhaps. But it was well worth the try, don't you think? I believe no stone should be left unturned, no matter how slim the chances of success. We owe it to her."

Richard turned up the collar of his jacket against the chill. "Want to join me for a sandwich? There's a great new place around the corner. Cheap, too."

Dr. Mallory shook his head. "Thanks, but I'm going to have to pass. I was paged a few minutes ago; there's been a nasty accident on the FDR and they need me at the hospital. I was hoping you could take Misty home, but first I think she'd appreciate a snack after all that gallivanting."

"I'm starving!" Misty said clutching her belly in an exaggerated gesture. "Can we go to McDonald's? *Please*?"

Max laughed and tugged at the pom-pom on her woolen hat. "Thank you for the company. It's been a while since I've had so much fun."

"Can we do it again another day?"

"You bet, Princess."

Richard helped him hail a cab, then he and Misty waited while Max gave the driver the directions and the vehicle sped away.

"I like Lancey's," Misty said, skipping alongside Richard. "Why aren't you working there anymore?"

"I got tired of rearranging stuff little devils like you scatter all over the place."

He saw her expression had dimmed. "Is it because of me that you left? Because of what happened? I heard Tony say you quarreled with that awful Mr. Murphy, that it was his fault I got hurt."

"Of course not," he replied quickly. "And anyway, I like working in a shoe store," he added, making it sound as if he were having a jolly time of it.

But Misty's downcast expression told him he hadn't been very convincing. "I'm sorry to have caused you so much trouble," she said in a small voice, and surprised him by curling her small, gloved hand around his. Reflexively, he squeezed her fingers and immediately a warm, tingly sensation shot up his arm and spread like a comforting blanket around his heart. It was the first time in his nineteen years he experienced this kind of feeling. It was soothing and alien at the same time. "It wasn't your fault. Don't ever think that," he said.

"Thank you for saving me," she said, smiling shyly.

He was humbled by her words. He didn't deserve her gratitude. Her damaged face was a constant reminder he hadn't done nearly enough for her, and he'd always carry the guilt around with him.

He shook his head. "Sometimes I can't help but think you're an alien being from another world," he said, almost to himself.

He heard her giggle and looked down at her. The streetlights reflected in her eyes, making them twinkle. "Like from another planet, you mean?"

He grinned. "Yeah, like from another planet in some faraway galaxy, somewhere in the far recesses of the universe."

"What's recesses?" she asked.

"A place so far out into space it would take us earthlings thousands and thousands of years to travel there."

She glanced up at the sky. "Or maybe from a star," she said playing along with his game. "Did you know Sirius is the biggest and brightest star in the sky? Dr. Max showed it to me when we went to the top of the Empire State Building. But how did I get here? It's billions and billions of miles away."

"On a superfast spaceship, how else? You were sent out here on a secret mission, to embark in the most important extraterrestrial covert operation ever to be experimented by any population from outer space," he said assuming a strong theatrical baritone, "but you were sidetracked by Molly the Terrible and her viciously villainous act and brutally attacked by a herd of ferocious deer, leaving you stranded on Earth."

Misty's giggle rippled musically in the quiet street, sounding, Richard thought, like water rushing over stepping-stones. "But what happened to the spaceship?"

"It vanished into thin air, after abandoning you on Lancey's rooftop."

Misty's eyes were round and danced with merriment. "You mean, forever and ever?"

"Of course. Remember, it'd take thousands of years for another spaceship to come for you. Now," he said eager to change the subject, "did I hear McDonald's before?"

CHAPTER 15

"How did you and Dr. Max meet?" It was Misty's fourth month in Greenwich Village. She and Richard had left the subway and were strolling southbound on Sixth Avenue, past tired-looking buildings and fast-food joints, a Dean & Deluca shopping bag swinging between them. These days he rarely saw her. He was graduating college this year, thanks to the advanced placement courses he'd taken in high school. He had put in hours of study, as well as juggling two part-time jobs, and he didn't have much time for anything else. When he'd asked her to accompany him to the popular gourmet store to pick up some fresh mozzarella for Mrs. B, she'd been so euphoric you'd have thought he'd offered to take her to Disney World.

"Again? I've already told you the story."

"Tell me once more," she begged.

He suppressed a sigh and proceeded to give her the abbreviated version. "I'd just turned twelve and was on the run from a foster home, when a bunch of thugs attacked me in Washington Square Park. They beat me up and stole my money. Dr. Max happened to be passing by, and when the guys saw him, they ran away. I had a bad gash on my knee and he took me to his private practice to stitch me up. When he heard I was a runaway, he decided to help me."

"How did he help you?"

"He gave me an after-school job in his practice and saw to my education."

"Is that why you decided to become a doctor?"

"That's right."

"Dr. Max says you're quick and smart, that you know way more than most of his interns."

Richard grinned. "He said that?"

Misty nodded vigorously. "He said you've come a long way from the wild and unruly youngster you used to be."

This was information he wished Dr. Max had kept to himself. "Good to know," he mumbled.

"What happened to your parents?"

He stumbled at the unexpected question and almost lost his footing. It was one thing to poke into the positives in his life, another to dig into a past he'd rather obliterate from his memory. He looked away, pretending to be interested in an expired poster of an off-Broadway show. "My mother died when I was little," he replied, and picked up the pace.

Misty latched onto the handle of the shopping bag in her struggle to keep up with his long strides. "What about your father?" she asked.

He kicked irritably at a soda can that had fallen from an overflowing trash basket. It rolled across the sidewalk and landed with a loud clatter under a UPS van parked curbside. "Never knew him."

"Did he die before you were born?"

He pretended not to hear. They were nearing home; a few more steps now and he could hustle her off to the Mallory's quarters and barricade himself in his own apartment.

Once inside, she trailed in right after him.

"I'm busy, so scram," he said, shoving the shopping bag into her hands. "Mrs. B will be waiting for the cheese."

She stood looking at him with her transparently honest gaze.

"Would you rather not talk about it now?"

"For the record, I *never* talk about it."

"My therapist says it's bad to keep things locked up inside, that we should talk about the things that bother us."

"Yeah, well, thanks for the unsolicited advice." If it were up to him, he'd fire her therapist, for all the good it was doing her.

"I asked Dr. Max why you never talk about your family and he said that sometimes it's painful for people who didn't have a happy childhood to look back on the past. He said that before he met you, you were living in the streets and stealing from the tourists to survive, and that you weren't very sociable on account of you having been all alone, but that underneath you're really a nice person."

He gritted his teeth. He must remember to thank Dr. Max for the nonsense he put in his charge's head. The man obviously didn't take other people's private business as seriously as he took the Hippocratic Oath.

"If you ever want to talk about it, I won't mind listening," Misty offered charitably.

"Thanks, but I feel a lot better already. Goodbye, Misty."

He didn't see her again until a few days later coming home from the hospital. She was sitting on Mrs. B's front steps, sketching. It was her favorite pastime, and she had a real knack for it.

"That's pretty cool," he said looking at the half-finished drawing of Mrs. B's potted azaleas. It was the last weekend of April; the days were getting longer and the afternoons milder, so Misty had taken to sitting there with her inseparable pencils and drawing pad until almost sundown.

"Thank you. Mrs. B's house has the prettiest flowers on all of Myrtle Place, don't you think?" she asked him. She had on denim overalls and a red-and-white checkered blouse. A navy Yankees baseball cap sat backward on her head in imitation of Jake's favorite style. She could easily pass for a naughty tomboy, until she turned those killer blue eyes on you and mesmerized you with their guilelessness. His gut still wrenched every time he looked at her. While significantly improved, the scars were still glaringly visible on her face, and she insisted on wearing a cap most of the time.

He sat next to her on the steps and cleared his throat. "Remember when you asked me about my parents?"

She nodded but didn't say anything. With her pencil poised over the sketch, she waited for him to continue. "I told you I never got to meet my father. The truth is, I didn't know my mother very well, either. She left when I was three. My grandmother used to say she was a social butterfly."

"What's that?" Misty asked.

"Someone who has a lot of friends, who likes to party and have fun." She watched him expectantly, as if sensing there was more to come. "There wasn't much money to squander in social activities, so she chose rich friends with nice cars, people who made her forget she was dirt poor."

It was the first time he talked about his childhood and it was harder than he'd expected. As much as he tried to repress them, his treacherous mind evoked unwelcome memories of a shabby third-floor apartment over the elevated subway tracks he'd once fervently believed would eventually bring his mother home. "My father was one of those friends."

He decided not to point out his mother didn't know which one. No need to explain the dangers of promiscuity to a ten-year-old. "She took off for Los Angeles with her aspiring actor boyfriend, leaving me with my grandmother."

The pencil dropped from Misty's fingers and rolled off the board. She made no move to pick it up. "She left you?" Her face was the picture of horror as she failed to remember she herself had been touched by a similar fate. "But . . . you said she died."

"She did. A few years later, in a car accident." He omitted the fact she'd been found—or what was left of her charred remains—next to her boyfriend's, more booze and pot in their veins than plasma. Grandma hadn't bothered to send him out of the room when the police officer had come to give her the gruesome news, and he remembered with sickening clarity his feelings of shock and numbness.

Misty set aside the drawing board and scooted closer to him. "Perhaps she meant to come get you, except she never got to do it because of the accident," she suggested.

"Yeah. You're probably right," he said, trying to focus on anything but the somber, sympathetic look in her eyes.

She placed a gentle hand on his arm. "Does it hurt to talk about it?"

"Some," he replied, surprised at the effort it took to utter that simple word.

In one fluid motion she had both her arms around him, enveloping him in her sweet little-girl scent. "I promise I'll never leave you, Richard. I'll stay with you and take care of you forever," she said in a solemn tone.

Richard couldn't think of a single thing to say, which was just fine, because he wouldn't have been able to get the words past the gigantic lump in his throat.

CHAPTER 16

Someone was ringing the Mallory's doorbell insistently, grating on Richard's nerves. The Mallorys, he knew, were out. Dr. Max was at the hospital and Mrs. B had taken Misty to the dentist for a loose tooth. But the ringer, apparently, had no intention of giving up.

"Dumb-ass," he growled under his breath. He pulled away from his desk and stalked to the door, jerking it open.

He stared at the stranger standing on the doorstep, poised to ring again. He was tall and distinguished, in a suit and tie. "If you're looking for Mrs. Butler, she's not home," he said.

"When will she be back?" the man asked.

"Are you a reporter?" Richard asked, ready to send him packing. He'd had to fend off several of them when Misty was in the hospital. Dr. Max was all in favor of media interest, saying it could help trace Misty's family, but Richard found them intrusive and annoying.

"No. My name is James Morgan," the man said. He dug in the inside pocket of his jacket and pulled out a business card. "I would like to speak with Doctor and Mrs. Mallory. If you would be so kind as to give them this and ask them to give me a call. It's important."

Richard got a bad feeling in the pit of his stomach. "Important, how?" he asked bluntly.

The man gave him an appraising look, as if trying to determine Richard's relationship to the couple. "Are you a family member?"

"Yes," Richard replied without hesitation, offering no further explanation.

"I have information about the child currently in their care. It's imperative that I speak to them as soon as possible."

It was a few seconds before Richard could speak. "Oh, uh . . . I'll make sure they get it."

"Thank you," the man said, and with a brief nod descended the steps. Only then did Richard notice the sleek black sedan parked at the curbside, the driver standing tall and straight next to the open passenger door.

The name on the card said James D. Morgan of Williamson, Wolff & Morgan, LLP with a Park Avenue address.

An attorney, he thought, and an expensive one, with offices in New York, London, and Paris.

He wanted to rip the card into little pieces and flush them down the toilet, but it would be stupid as well as selfish.

But what if the man's a fraud, an opportunist? Richard asked himself. A reward had been offered to anyone who could provide relevant information on any person connected to Misty. In the eight months since the accident in Lancey's, there'd been lots of false reports from people claiming either that they knew the girl or they knew someone who knew her. Head cases, wackos. But none of them had come in expensive lawyer suits.

He wasn't ready for Misty to go. She was happy with the Mallorys. She'd overcome the trauma of the accident and come to terms with her amnesia. What if in her previous life she was mistreated by her family? What if she had run away to get away from one of them?

It wasn't until late the next evening, upon his return from work, that he got all the answers to his questions, none of which were good.

"What do you mean she's gone?" he asked, staring at Tony and Jake.

"She's gone, man. She's gone back to her family," Tony said, looking as if he'd just been told he had a terminal illness.

"That guy you told us about came back with Social Services. They took her," Jake said.

Richard spun around and bounded up the stairs. Mrs. B opened the door before he could knock, tears streaming down her face.

"Oh, Richard," she said flinging her arms around him. "She's gone. She's back with her family. I should be happy for her, but I can't help feeling like a part of me's gone. I loved having her around," she sobbed.

"Come, sweetheart," Dr. Max said, putting a comforting arm around his wife's shoulders, and motioned Richard inside.

Richard's eyes darted around the room, almost expecting Misty to spring out from behind a piece of furniture and shout "Ha ha, we tricked you!" except April Fool's had been four months ago.

"When?" he asked.

"Earlier this afternoon. That lawyer . . . Mr. Morgan, he came with the caseworker. He said he suspected it could be her from reading about it in the papers. He's a friend of the family," Mrs. Butler said. "Theirs is such an astonishing story I still can't wrap my head around it."

"Apparently Misty was believed to have drowned," Dr. Max intervened. "The family's from up in Maine— somewhere near Portland. That's where she was when she disappeared," Max Mallory continued. "They thought she'd fallen from a cliff into the ocean after things of hers were found on the premises. It looked like an accident. No one suspected she'd been abducted. Someone had to have snatched her up and driven with her to New York, though I can't imagine why he or she would go to the trouble of driving hundreds of miles, then abandon her in a department store."

"Abducted," Richard repeated in a rush of breath. He sank onto the armrest of a stuffed chair, emotions swirling through his head. He thought of the little girl who'd stared at him and Molly across the floor that night in Lancey's, looking a little lost, and damned his lack of insight. He hadn't suspected foul play.

Channeling his anger made him momentarily numb to the pain. "Their kid disappeared and they just gave her up for dead? Based on what evidence—a few items they found? What kind of parents are they? Why weren't they taking better care of their daughter?"

"A good family, I was told, of good standing. The husband had a bad heart and passed away a month after the child's disappearance. They've been through a rough period."

Richard scoffed. "Who was he . . . the man who came here?" he asked.

"A long-time friend of the family. He and his wife recently returned from a business trip in Europe and heard of the child's alleged death. When he read about Misty in the papers and saw her picture, even with the bandages he noticed a strong resemblance to his friends' daughter. Apparently, the child disappeared the same day she was found in Lancey's."

Maxwell Mallory must have seen something on Richard's face because he looked at him with sympathy. "I'm sorry, son. It all happened so quickly we barely had time to say goodbye."

"Poor child," Mary said sniffling. "She looked so disoriented, so lost."

An invisible hand clutched Richard's chest until he thought his lungs would explode.

She couldn't be gone, he thought. He'd promised to take her boating in Central Park on Sunday now all of the bandages were off. He'd just spent a fortune on tickets.

He looked at Dr. Max. "How could you let her go? How can you be sure these people are who they say they are? Did you check their credentials? People with money will go to great lengths to snatch up a cute kid like Misty, even lie."

"Of course, I checked," Max said. "Do you think I'd hand her over to just any stranger? It wasn't just the Children's Bureau; the FBI got involved—a special unit called the Evidence Response Team. The governor of Maine herself assured me the girl is the daughter of a prominent family, well-respected and liked in their community. Their name wasn't released, to protect the child's privacy."

Richard didn't need to know her real name. To him she would always be Misty.

CHAPTER 17

St. Isabel Island, present day

Sweat ran in rivulets down Richard's body as he pushed himself to cover the last stretch of beach, punishing his atrophied muscles until they ached. At seven in the morning the sun was already a fireball skimming the oily horizon, promising another scorching day. Out of the corner of his eye he followed the course of a great white heron as it took off from an outcropping of rocks, sailed in an elegant arch across the wide expanse of water, and dipped into its surface to secure its morning meal. It reminded him of his own breakfast waiting on the deck, as it had every morning since his arrival at Serena, while he worked off his stress and tried to build up a modest appetite. The exertion made him realize how gravely out of shape he was. Weeks of inertia had weakened not only his brain but the rest of him as well, and the loss of sleep didn't help.

He finally slowed down to a cooling pace until he reached the spot where he'd left his towel. Then he pulled off his sweat-drenched T-shirt and dove into the cool water. One hundred strokes later he emerged and lay face down on the terrycloth sheet, allowing his body to go limp and letting the light breeze and peacefulness of the surroundings wash over him.

But nothing seemed to soothe his restless mind. Other than for his daily workout routine, he hadn't left the cabin since his last trip to Monks' Cove. Discovering Clare was

Misty had thrown his emotions off kilter again, but for entirely different reasons than what had brought him here.

What were the odds of finding her here after all these years? he asked himself. Could I have recognized something in the SoHo painting without realizing it? Could I have sensed it was tied to her? And why didn't she recognize me?

She hadn't shown any sign of knowing who he was when he'd told her his name. Yet, she'd slipped into an easy camaraderie with him as effortlessly as if she'd known him for years. He'd have thought he'd changed a lot physically, but the Misty he knew would have never forgotten his name. Something wasn't right.

Strange things had been happening since he'd seen the painting in SoHo. He hadn't thought of Misty, then, but since his first night at Serena when he'd looked up at the sky and saw that special star, he'd sensed her presence.

Misty's star. That's how he'd started to think of it. A guiding light of some sort.

He'd promised to protect her, to keep her safe, but he hadn't been there for her when they'd taken her away. Often, he wondered if she'd been scared, torn away from the only family she was cognizant of having. Had she recovered her memory? Most importantly, was she happy?

His chest contracted as the memories took him back to the aftermath of Misty's abrupt departure. He never heard from her again and neither did the Mallorys. According to sources, after her family took her back to Maine, they kept a low profile to protect the child's privacy, and it wasn't long before the media sensation that had surged around the case died down.

The Myrtle Place home was never quite the same after Misty was gone. It was as if she had taken the light with her. He'd spent a lot of time out of the house, as had Tony and Jake. Even Molly became depressed and morose, rarely emerging from her cage. They had been dismal times for all of them.

He'd immersed himself in his studies, pushing impatiently through medical school, eager to get to the good stuff. He'd joined Doctors Without Borders and spent a good portion of his internship doing humanitarian work, providing medical aid where it was most needed—Iraq, Somalia, Sudan. It had turned out to be an all-absorbing, harrowing challenge, but one he'd poured his heart and soul into. He'd faced all kinds of dangerous situations, seen and done things most people couldn't even imagine. It had helped dull the ache and fill the void Misty had left in his heart, until all that remained was a vague memory of the child who had put all her trust in him.

CHAPTER 18

He wasn't surprised when Sonia showed up at his door, not when he hadn't bothered to return the dozen messages she'd left on his voicemail.

"Good heavens, you're a mess," was the first thing she said.

He knew, even without her telling him so concisely, the state he was in. His bathroom mirror hadn't been kind to him either. His beard had long surpassed the stubbled stage, his eyes were bloodshot and sunken from lack of sleep, and he was in dire need of a shower and a fresh change of clothes.

Without waiting to be invited, she whisked briskly past him and flung the shutters wide open. "What are—" He let out a groan and shut his eyes against the blinding light. "Why did you have to do that?"

Her eyes zeroed in on the half-empty bottle of single-malt whiskey on the bedside table and scrunched up her nose in disgust. "And here I was worrying about you when you've been holding fraternity parties behind my back."

He stalked over to the bed and grabbed his shirt. "Sorry, wasn't expecting company," he said. He slipped his arms through the sleeves, not bothering to button it up. Even the simple act of dressing required too much energy.

"Why haven't you returned my calls?"

He shrugged. "Too busy working."

Her eyes slid to the desk, where his laptop lay buried under a stack of papers, a glaring testament it hadn't been touched in days.

This time there was concern in her eyes when she looked at him. "I'm being told you barely touch your meals and even refuse to allow the cleaning staff in."

"I can do my own cleaning, thank you very much, and I haven't had much of an appetite lately."

His churlish attitude didn't deter her from speaking her mind. "It's not surprising, seeing you insist on staying cooped up in this place. You need to be out and about . . . a change of air."

What I need is a shrink, Richard thought.

He sank onto the bed and covered his head with his hands. It felt as if there was someone in there swinging a spiked club. He rubbed his hands over his face, wishing she'd go away. Then maybe he could finally drink himself into a comatose state, preferably with a quick painless death to follow.

"What is it, Richard? It isn't bad news from home, is it?"

He almost laughed at the idea. How much worse could things at home get? "No, it isn't bad news," he replied.

"Are you having difficulty with the book?"

"The book's coming along fine. Just can't seem to work up enough interest, that's all."

It wasn't the whole truth, but it was certainly better than, 'Your younger daughter sent my nerves haywire just when I thought I had a handle on them.'

He tamped down on his anger, suddenly reminded this was the woman who had whisked Misty away from the Mallory's home seventeen years ago without so much as a "thank you for keeping my daughter safe while we gave her up for dead," as if the Mallorys were no better than the thug who had kidnapped their child.

"Look, I really appreciate your concern. I'm just going through a bad phase and I need to ride it out. I'll be okay once I get a shower and some sleep."

"Good, because it hurts my pride to see one of my guests reduced to this state. It kind of defeats Serena's mission, if you know what I mean. Speaking of that, we're hosting a beach barbeque tonight, near the marina. I'd like it if you came."

Before he could respond she held up her hand. "Call me arrogant—call me what you will, but I refuse to take no for an answer. Now, get some sleep, take a shower, do whatever it takes to pull yourself together. We begin at seven."

He didn't want to like her, but he couldn't help it. "I don't think you're arrogant—just pushy."

"I'll take that as a compliment. Now, promise me you'll come."

"I'll think about it."

"Good. I'll have some aspirin and a fresh pot of strong coffee brought down. And, for heaven's sake, don't harass the staff when I send them up to air the cabin."

JOSEPHINE STRAND

PART 2

Clare and Richard

JOSEPHINE STRAND

CHAPTER 19

CLARE

Clare's bare feet sank into the soft sand still warm from the day's sun. The sound of music and laughter drifted up from the clearing reserved for the party on Serena's private beach. There was nothing like food, music, and the sound of crackling fire to liven up a crowd, she thought. It seemed half the island had shown up tonight. Serena was famous for its beach parties, especially because, on principle, no one was ever turned away.

As she advanced toward the sounds, the tantalizing aroma of meat roasting on the barbecue enveloped her, reminding her she hadn't eaten anything since breakfast.

Sonia spotted her almost immediately. "There you are, sweetheart," she said when Clare joined her and the middle-aged couple with her. "Brian and Lydia were just asking me about you."

Clare smiled at the two. "It's so nice to see you."

Brian Haynes, the mayor of St. Isabel and the island's most prominent figure lifted his mojito drink in greeting. "Clare. We sure don't see much of you these days. How are things on the Hill?"

"Splendid," she replied. "The construction of the new arts center annex is coming along nicely."

"Glad to hear it."

His wife Lydia hugged her, enshrouding her in an intoxicating cloud of Chanel N° 5. "Honey, I'm so glad to see you. Paul went off looking for you—Oh, here he comes now."

Before Clare could turn around a strong pair of arms grasped her from behind and spun her wildly in a circle. She yelped. "Paul . . . Put me down!"

As soon as her feet touched the ground again, she glared at her aggressor. The Haynes' son and Clare's best friend since childhood, was the eternal prankster and treated her as if they were still five years old chasing each other on the school playground.

"You scared the daylights out of me."

"Sorry," he said with a smirk that showed no remorse. Then, on a more sober note, "I haven't seen you around town anymore. Where have you been hiding?"

"I haven't been hiding. I've been working—as you well know. I don't get much time now that I've taken over the after-school cultural program."

Her mother seized the opportunity to voice her concerns. "Are you sure you aren't taking on too much? All this extra work sounds stressful, and I have the impression you're not getting enough rest."

"I'm fine, really, and I enjoy the extra work," she said, not able to meet her mother's eyes.

A sleepless night, one in a long series in the last few months, had left dark shadows under Clare's eyes that no amount of concealer had been able to disguise.

"Who's that?" Lydia asked, her gaze directed toward Serena's grounds.

Glad for the interruption, Clare followed the direction of Lydia's gaze, and her heart skipped a beat. Richard had emerged from the path leading from the cabin to the beach. He was dressed appropriately for the event in beige linen pants and buttoned-up print shirt but wore the air of wanting to be anywhere but there. Clare hadn't seen him in several days. He hadn't returned to Monks' Cove since their playful interlude in the lagoon, and she was afraid she might be the cause. She'd acted like a jittery schoolgirl when he'd held her close that day, and she'd probably frightened him away.

"That's my newest guest. He's lodging in the cabin," Sonia said, and signaled to Richard.

"I'm so glad you could make it," she said when he joined them. She introduced him. "This is Richard Kelly, from New York. Richard, meet the most dynamic couple on the island, Brian and Lydia Haynes. And this is their son, Paul. Brian is our esteemed mayor. His beautiful wife chairs the St. Isabel Island Preservation Society."

Richard shook hands with each of Sonia's guests, then nodded to Clare. "Good to see you, Clare." His smile was friendly but curt.

"You've met?" Her mother's wide-eyed glance shifted from her to Richard.

Clare hoped the glow from the lanterns strung along the perimeter of the space was subdued enough to hide her flush. "He dropped by Monks' Cove, while sailing," she said.

"I didn't know it was a private beach and missed the sign," Richard explained.

"I see," her mother said.

"I thought you looked familiar. You're Dr. Richard Kelly, the neurosurgeon." All eyes turned to Paul. Clare hadn't realized how silent Paul had been through the introductions, until he spoke.

She glanced at Richard and noticed the instant tightening of his jaw. "Have we met?" he asked Paul.

"Not exactly," Paul replied. "I attended one of your lectures at Stanford a couple of years ago. Not that I'd expect you to remember me from an auditorium close to overflowing," he added with a chuckle. "Your books on spinal cord injury and spinal kinetics proved instrumental in shaping my career path."

"Glad to have been of help. You're aiming for a career in neuroscience?"

"Orthopedics. I'm a junior resident at the local ER and working toward a specialization in sports medicine," Paul explained. "I figured home was as good a place as any to get a head start, although I hope to move on eventually."

"Smart choice," Richard said.

Paul addressed the other members of the group. "Dr. Kelly is a celebrity in his field and a pioneer in brain and spinal surgery," he explained.

"A neurosurgeon, eh?" Brian said. "Well, Dr. Kelly, as the mayor of this humble little island, let me welcome you and tell you it's an honor to have you here."

"It's an honor to be here. Please, call me Richard."

"And is there a Mrs. Kelly somewhere around here or are you traveling alone?" Lydia asked.

Clare cringed inwardly. Lydia Haynes was charming and gregarious but had a tendency to be too inquisitive, a privilege she thought came with her First Lady status.

"No Mrs.—just me," Richard replied.

"You must come to dinner one of these days. We'd be delighted to have you over at our house. We were just telling Clare we don't get to see her often enough since she set up house on Monastery Hill. Perhaps we can arrange an informal get-together just for the few of us."

Richard's smile appeared forced. "Thank you, but I'm actually here to work on a medical textbook and won't have much time for socializing."

"Oh, nonsense," said Lydia with a dismissive wave. "You don't come to St. Isabel and not find time to mingle. We islanders are a friendly, outgoing bunch and love to entertain visitors."

"It's settled, then," Paul said. He slipped an arm around Clare's shoulders. "As Clare knows, my mother never takes no for an answer."

Clare was acutely aware of Richard's intense gaze on her, and when Courtney chose that moment to join the group, she was thankful for the diversion.

"Here you all are. The singing has started down by the fire. Why don't you get something to eat and join everyone else there?"

"Good idea," Paul said. "How about you, professor?" he asked Richard. "Care to join us for a good old-fashioned sing-along?"

"No, thanks, I'll pass. Do me a favor, though. Save the 'professor' for the lecture halls."

Courtney's gaze narrowed as it shifted from Paul to Richard. "Lecture hall? Did I miss something?" she asked.

Before Paul could respond, Sonia intervened. "Courtney, why don't you introduce Richard around to the other guests? We've been monopolizing his attention far too long."

"Gladly," Courtney said. She slipped an arm through Richard's. "But first, I believe the *professor* and I have some catching up to do."

CHAPTER 20

CLARE

Clare loved Paul dearly. Their families had been close friends since before she was born. He was the caring brother she had never had and her best friend. Their relationship had never progressed beyond that of a close friendship, but tonight Paul was being unusually watchful and overly attentive, more like a devoted boyfriend than an old friend.

In the quiet spot where they sat watching the musicians play and roasting marshmallows over the dying embers, his fingers gently massaged her skin beneath her waist-length blouse. She'd spent the last few minutes telling herself not to make a big deal of an essentially harmless gesture, and she wouldn't have, if his roaming fingers hadn't strayed beyond the boundaries of propriety.

"What are you doing?" she asked, jerking away from him.

He withdrew his hand, grinning sheepishly. "Nothing. I like touching you. I didn't mean anything by it."

It wasn't "nothing." She was pretty sure his thumb had grazed the underside of her breast.

She pulled away again. "I'd rather you didn't. It feels . . . wrong."

He snorted. "Come on, it's not the first time I've touched you. It hasn't bothered you before."

She wanted to remind him the closest they'd come to touching was to hold hands, and they'd stopped doing that a long time ago, when it had started to feel awkward. When she saw where his gaze was focused, she froze.

Richard stood beyond the row of lanterns, his gaze on them. She realized immediately what Paul's intent was.

"What's wrong with you?" she hissed.

Paul took a swig of his beer, then gave her an innocent look. "What do you mean?"

"You've been acting strange since meeting Richard Kelly. I thought you liked him."

"I do. That doesn't mean I like you making puppy eyes at him."

"Puppy eyes?"

Heat rushed to her face. Had she been staring at Richard so blatantly? She was mortified at the thought she may have inadvertently sent him the wrong message. "I don't know what you're talking about. I only saw him a couple of times." Well, three, if you counted tonight. "I hardly know him." Technically it was true, though each time she was with him she felt as though they'd always known each other.

She scrambled to her feet. "Anyway, I don't need to justify myself to you. It's none of your business which way I look at a man."

"Where are you going?" he asked.

"Somewhere where I can breathe, and where I don't have unwanted bodyguards breathing down my neck," she said.

She walked blindly toward the palm grove, away from the activities zone.

Since when did Paul have anything to say about my love life? she thought.

Then again, she didn't have one, and Paul knew it. Most likely her new acquaintance with an attractive, intelligent, older male had caused his protective instincts to surface.

"Lovers' spat?"

She looked up, startled. Richard stood on the wooden walkway in front of her.

"You . . . you scared me," she said.

"Sorry, I didn't mean to. I was in the vicinity and saw you running away from your boyfriend in a huff."

His words caught her off guard. "Paul is not my boyfriend," she said.

He raised an eyebrow. "Could have fooled me."

His obvious skepticism lit a spark of anger inside her. "I don't know what you think you saw, but Paul and I are just friends."

A corner of his lips kicked up sardonically. "Really? The man had his hands all over you all night. I doubt that's code for 'friendship,' even in this gregarious slice of paradise."

His sarcasm hurt and confused her as much as Paul's earlier accusation. This was a side of Richard she hadn't seen before, and she didn't like it. She tried to get past him but he held her wrist, preventing her escape. His fingers bit into her flesh, but the pain they inflicted was nothing compared to the ache blooming in her chest.

She blamed the accumulation of stress and disappointment for the tears suddenly filling her eyes. "Let go of me, you're hurting me," she said.

He abruptly released her arm, as if startled by his own action.

"Excuse me," she said starting to move away from him.

"Wait," he said.

He took her elbow, gently this time, and urged her to turn around. "I'm so sorry. I was way out of line."

She hated that she had no control over her emotions. That this man—this stranger had the power to make her feel so vulnerable was a new and terrifying experience.

He turned her hand to examine her wrist, his fingers brushing over the imprints he'd left on her skin. "I didn't mean to hurt you."

The sincerity in his voice was soothing on her nerves, and a different type of emotion spread around her heart. "I know," she said. She didn't need his apology to know it hadn't been him saying those hurtful words. It had been the irate stranger inside him. She'd caught a glimpse of him that first day on the nuns' beach, when he'd mentioned going through some personal issues. The mix of repressed anger and sorrow she'd perceived in him had shaken her profoundly. "I know," she repeated softly, and without knowing why, she reached out to touch her palm to his cheek. It was smooth and clean-shaven, hard with tension. She closed her eyes. He smelled so good. Like pine wood and fresh laundry. Before she realized what she was doing, she raised herself on her toes and touched her lips to his lightly.

His quick intake of breath jerked her back from whatever foolish fantasy was going through her mind, and she stepped back.

"I . . ." Mortification prevented any coherent words from forming in her throat. Face burning, she swung around and fled.

CHAPTER 21

CLARE

Clare sat on the edge of the jetty, away from the crowded area. Her heart was still racing, as much in mortification as with the realization of being attracted to a man she'd barely met.

What was I thinking, she thought, to have acted that way? He must think her a tease or at the very least a weirdo. He was a famous neurosurgeon, by Paul's account, a worldly man with a multitude of noble accomplishments tagged onto his name. For all she knew he had hordes of sophisticated women in tow, maybe even a classy wife or lover waiting for him in New York. She knew nothing about him, save something had gone seriously wrong in his life, something that had left him emotionally scarred.

Something about him was off tonight. She'd noticed it immediately when he'd arrived, and Paul revealing his real identity certainly hadn't made things better.

The sound of footsteps on the wooden planks interrupted her thoughts and she glanced up sharply. She relaxed when she saw it was Courtney.

"So this is where you're hiding."

"I'm not hiding, just taking a break from the crowd," Clare said.

Courtney sat next to her. "I saw you with Mom's secretive guest a few minutes ago. I didn't know you were already on such intimate terms," she said.

Clare stiffened. "What makes you say that? We were just talking."

"That wasn't what it looked like from where I was standing." Courtney eyed her intently. "Don't tell me you're developing feelings for him."

"What? No."

She started to protest but knew it would be useless. Like their mother, Courtney had a special radar where Clare was concerned.

"He lied to Mom—to all of us, claiming he was here to work on a mystery novel. Why keep his real identity a secret unless he's hiding something?"

"You make it sound so covert. Last I checked, protecting one's privacy wasn't a crime."

Surprise flashed in Courtney's eyes. "You knew?"

Clare bit her lip, wishing she hadn't made the comment. "Yes."

Courtney pressed her lips together, silent for a heartbeat. "Did he also tell you he was recently divorced?"

Divorced. He had a wife. An ex-wife, Clare thought. She tucked her hands under her legs to prevent them from shaking.

"It seems he walked out on his wife after she lost the baby she was carrying. What decent man would do that?"

"What . . . How do you know all this?"

"I heard it from Lydia who heard it from her son. Paul texted a former colleague in New York to tell him about his encounter with the famous Dr. Kelly and received some interesting feedback. Apparently, there are voices circulating in the field about Richard's inability to practice surgery since the loss of the baby."

Thoughts assaulted Clare's mind as if by storm. Not only an ex-wife but a baby as well. Was the baby the cause of the dark despair reflected in his eyes?

Despite the turmoil inside her, she felt the need to defend Richard. "Paul and Lydia have no business going around spreading such rumors, especially about one of Serena's guests, and neither should you. Mom would be furious if she knew. You know how she feels about her guests' privacy," she said.

Courtney shrugged. "You know Lydia—she loves a juicy story. Anyway, I just wanted you to know Richard may not be the person you think he is."

"Thank you for the heads-up. Rest assured I have no romantic designs on Richard Kelly, if that's what you're afraid of."

Courtney raised a skeptical eyebrow. "I saw the way you looked at him. Richard is a complicated man and falling for him is a certified way of getting hurt."

Clare leveled her gaze with Courtney's. "Is that how you keep from getting hurt—by staying away from anyone or anything that threatens to make you feel the least bit happy or even just remotely satisfied?"

Even in the semidarkness surrounding the jetty she saw Courtney's cheeks had paled, which was as much emotion she could ever hope to squeeze out of her sister's arid heart. She doubted she even had one. Very little seemed to touch Courtney. She loved and admired her sister, but she missed not having the kind of close-knit relationship most female siblings shared.

"Don't attempt to change the subject. It's you we're talking about," Courtney said. "You and the mysterious Dr. Kelly."

Clare sprang to her feet, unable to listen to another word her sister said. She stalked back toward the beach.

Philippe stood at the end of the pier. "What's wrong?" he asked immediately, reading Clare's taut expression.

"Nothing." She tried to push past him, but his tall muscular frame blocked her passage.

He glanced at Courtney just as she caught up to them. "What damage has your sharp tongue done this time?" he asked her suspiciously.

"Get lost, Girard. I'm in no mood for a fight tonight," Courtney replied.

"I asked you a question."

"I was just carrying out my older sibling duty, that's all. I warned Clare to stay away from Richard Kelly. He's a devious, cold-hearted jerk who left his wife of three years after she lost their baby."

Philippe laughed incredulously. "Whoa, where did you come up with that story, in some cheap supermarket tabloid?"

Courtney smiled smugly. "Who needs those when we have Lydia Haynes doing the honors? It seems my mother's newest guest isn't an aspiring writer after all, but a neurosurgeon down on his luck. Paul met him in one of his courses and knows people who are acquainted with him."

Philippe flashed her a sardonic smirk. "Wait, don't tell me the handsome New Yorker failed to fall for your wily charm," he drawled.

Clare held her breath, knowing the sting of Philippe's words would likely draw a violent reaction from her sister. She'd been witness to their heated arguments too many times to count, and they almost always ended with Courtney having the upper hand.

"You bastard," Courtney hissed, turning on him like an enraged tigress.

Philippe didn't lose his calm. "Watch it, Courtney, I'm beginning to dislike you."

His tone was icy, determined.

"Good, because I certainly don't like *you*, Philippe Girard. As a matter of fact, I detest you. I rue the day you came to this island."

Clare gasped, but Philippe merely continued to smirk.

"That long, eh? Better hatred than indifference. It means you have feelings for me, one way or another."

They were still arguing when Clare slipped quietly away.

CHAPTER 22

RICHARD

Richard had followed the altercation between Courtney and Philippe from a discreet distance with a mixture of curiosity and amusement. It was becoming more apparent that between the attractive air-freight executive and her part-time pilot, there was more than just an informal employer-employee relationship. The ostensibly good-natured Canadian, when provoked, could bring the woman's haughtiness down a peg or two, if the watery eyes and trembling lips he'd noticed when she'd careened blindly past him in her haste to escape were any evidence.

He stepped out into the stream of artificial light just as Philippe reached the outskirt of the gathering area.

"Congratulations. You seem to have the rare gift for getting the boss-lady's dander up," he said.

Philippe's scowl was instantly replaced by a cocky grin. "She'll get over it. She always does. She has a short fuse, that one."

"In general, or only where you're concerned?"

Philippe made a face. "Good question. I'll tell you the answer when I finally figure it out."

He took a cigarette from a pack he drew from the inside pocket of his linen jacket, then hesitated in the act of lighting it. "You don't mind if I smoke, do you . . . doctor?"

Richard threw him a swift glance. News was spreading faster than an oil spill from an upturned tanker, he realized with a stab of annoyance. Courtesy of Paul Haynes, no doubt.

The female laughter ringing out from a short distance away sounded like Clare's, and he instinctively turned. But it wasn't her. He hadn't seen Clare since she'd disappeared into the palm grove, leaving him in a paralyzing state of confusion. Given his deplorable behavior, a kiss—as chaste as it had been—was the last thing he'd expected from her. Her taste still lingered on his lips. He'd had no idea marshmallows could taste so good.

He didn't know what had prompted him to act the way he had. Seeing her and the mayor's son locked in an intimate embrace had set off an adverse reaction in him, making him lose all rationality. The memory of her watery eyes still tugged at his conscience.

"They're very different. The Elliot sisters, I mean."

Philippe slanted his eyes at him. "You don't know?"

"Know what?"

"Courtney and Clare are not biological sisters."

Richard was surprised yet knowing he shouldn't be. The two couldn't be less alike, and the differences weren't only on the surface.

"Courtney was a year old when Eddie and Sonia adopted her. Clare came as a surprise four years later, when the couple had lost all hope of conceiving a child of their own. She was their miracle baby—kind of stole the limelight away from Courtney, if you know what I mean."

Philippe took one last draw of his cigarette, then stubbed it out in the sand with the heel of his loafer. At least the man had the decency to pick up the spent butt and slip it in his pants pocket, Richard noted.

Philippe gave Richard a calculating look. "Clare is a very special person—but then, you already know that, no?"

Richard recognized a loaded question when he heard one, though he found it odd. "I do," he replied evenly.

"She's a kind, caring person, honest to a fault," Philippe continued. "I'd hate it if she were to get hurt."

Richard narrowed his eyes. "Do I detect a warning here?"

"Should it be?" Philippe countered with a challenging question of his own.

Richard clenched his jaw. Philippe was the second person, after Courtney, to warn him off Clare. "I'm not in the market for new attachments, if that's what you're worried about," he said.

Philippe regaled him with a smile that was anything but friendly. "*Bien.* I'm glad we understand each other. Now, can I get you interested in a drink?"

CHAPTER 23

CLARE

Clare gathered up her hair and twisted it into a haphazard knot on top of her head, contemplating her handiwork. Dusk was fast approaching; it was time to pack up. A few minor touch-ups tomorrow and it'd be finished.

"Nice work."

She jumped at the sound of Richard's voice behind her. Telling herself not to overreact, she slowly swiveled around to face him. "Thank you. It's a bromeliad, or air plant, of the pineapple family," she said with as much confidence as she could muster.

He stepped closer and leaned forward to study the painting. "Funny how it grows out of a tree trunk rather than from the soil."

His nearness kicked up her heart rate. "That's because this particular one isn't of the terrestrial kind. It's attached to the tree trunk by special roots—just like that one," she said, pointing to the live specimen she'd used as a model. "In its natural habitat it derives its moisture from the air and from the rain."

"Interesting."

She couldn't tell whether he was being polite or sarcastic. She decided to give him the benefit of the doubt. "It's a gift for the South Florida Bromeliad Society—that's an organization dedicated to protecting wild bromeliad species from the pest weevil, which threatens to destroy its population," she explained, for no reason other than to disguise the turmoil going on inside her.

"Sister Adelia said I'd find you in the monastery garden."

She'd suspected he might come, if anything because she hadn't given him the chance to justify his actions the previous night. She decided to spare him the trouble of apologizing first.

"I'm sorry for last night. I'm not in the habit of hitting on my mother's guests," she said in a rush.

His lips twitched slightly, though he maintained a serious front. "It was my fault. I upset you. I deserved to be slapped, let alone kissed."

Heat rushed up to her face. "I . . . I don't know what got into me. It won't happen again," she said. She began gathering up her tools.

"Are you saying you're sorry you kissed me?"

There was no mistaking the hint of humor in his tone, which only served to make her more flustered.

"No . . . Yes." She exhaled. "Let's just pretend it didn't happen, all right?"

"Only if you promise to forgive me for the way I insulted you. There's no justification for my behavior."

"Consider yourself forgiven."

She finished putting her equipment into the canvas tote she used for her painting paraphernalia and hitched it over her shoulder.

"That looks heavy. I have my rental car parked outside the gates. I could give you a ride home." he said.

"That won't be necessary. I live just a short walk away. I'll come back for the rest."

He ignored her refusal and reached for the folded easel and stool. He tucked one under each armpit. "Lead the way."

They cut through the garden past the monastery church, toward the gates of the complex. "The church is known for its unique mosaics and beautiful frescoes," Clare told him when he mentioned seeing the tower from the cove. "Some say the stained-glass windows were designed by Louis Comfort Tiffany, but no one knows for sure."

"Frescoes, huh? The kind with angels on the ceiling?"

She laughed. "Of course. Have you ever seen a church fresco without angels?" she teased.

She thought she saw him wince slightly, but she wasn't sure. Perhaps he just wasn't a man of faith.

When they passed the busy construction site where the new cultural center was well on the way to completion, she was excited to introduce him to her pet project.

"This is Rainbow's End, the future site of St. Isabel's Creative Arts and Cultural Center," she said. "It's scheduled to be opened in the fall."

Richard's gaze took in the excavators, cement mixers, and pallets of bricks scattered throughout the area then glanced at the sign affixed to the retaining fence.

"You're listed as the principal sponsor."

It embarrassed her that he'd notice that. "I'm not filthy rich, if that's what you're thinking," she said. "I came into some money from a trust fund when I turned twenty-five, and I was able to realize the dream I'd been cultivating since I came to teach at the monastery."

He appeared impressed. "Which is?"

"To create a spacious, well-outfitted facility where the monastery children can channel their creativity through art and music, as well as engage in a variety of sports. The monastery doesn't have the capacity for this type of extracurricular activities." She grinned. "There's only so much creativity one can elicit on a small, secluded beach."

The liquid warmth in his eyes touched something deep inside her in a way that felt eerily familiar. "Why Rainbow's End?" he asked.

She found she could talk to him of things she didn't normally discuss with strangers. "Rainbows are a symbol of purity and joy, things some of these children haven't experienced in a long time—perhaps never. I like to think of their being here as the start of a new beginning, a preparation stage for what lies ahead." When they reached her house she said, "Welcome to my humble abode."

He contemplated her small, sadly-in-need-of-TLC country cottage with knitted brows. "You live here?"

She rolled her eyes. "You needn't look so impressed," she said wryly.

"I didn't mean to sound disparaging. I just hadn't expected an Elliot—least of all one who's inherited a sizeable trust fund—to live in a real-life replica of the Seven Dwarfs' cottage," he said.

"Oh, and just what did you expect, Cinderella's castle?"

"No. Something a little less . . . needy."

Needy was a kind way to put it. She'd always loved this little cottage, and when it had come up for sale, she hadn't been able to resist putting in an offer. The thought someone less caring would snatch it up only to tear it down and build a luxury home in its place was the only incentive she'd needed. The place needed a complete overhaul. The exterior paint was faded and chipped, the gutters rusted and dangling precariously in some parts, and the sagging roof had more plywood patches than shingles.

She sighed. "I keep telling myself to hire a contractor, but somehow there's always something more urgent to take care of."

A film of sweat had formed on Richard's brow. "Come on in. Looks like you could use a drink."

"Thank you."

She dropped her tote in the hallway and immediately activated the ceiling fan. She threw him a contrite look. "The air conditioning unit's on the blink and I haven't gotten around to getting it fixed."

She led him to her studio and opened the door. "You can drop everything in here."

He did as instructed, then glanced at the half-finished painting standing on the easel.

"A work in progress?" he asked.

She nodded, quickly closing the door behind them. "Make yourself at home while I get you that drink. Lemonade or beer?"

"Lemonade, please."

She quickly changed into something more presentable than a paint-smeared smock, then took two cans of lemon soda from the refrigerator. When she returned to the living room, she noticed he'd undone a few buttons on the front of his shirt and was frowning at the Carrier wall unit. The ancient air conditioner was grunting noisily, emitting a stingy trickle of air.

"Do you have a screwdriver?" he asked.

His question stopped her in midstep. "A what?" she asked, not sure she'd heard correctly.

"A screwdriver—one of those Phillips things."

"Oh . . . sure." Intrigued, she added, "I also have a hammer, pliers, and a wrench. Of course, it depends on the kind of project you have in mind."

"A screwdriver will do," he replied, giving her a mock scowl.

Clare went to the kitchen and returned with the tool. He took it from her and promptly went to work on the malfunctioning unit. He unscrewed the front panel and peered inside the dusty interior. "Uhmm . . . just as I thought. Bring me a vacuum cleaner, will you? I assume you have one of those, too?"

Bossy, too she thought. I wonder if this is the same commanding attitude he adopts in the operating room.

She retrieved the hand-operated Dirt Devil from the broom closet and handed it to him. Five minutes later the unit was humming merrily and pumping a steady stream of refrigerated air into the room.

Clare stared at him. "You fixed it."

"There was nothing wrong with it. All I did was remove some dust around the coils and fan and now it's as good as new."

She shook her head in bewilderment. "I don't know what to say."

"Thank you?" he suggested with a quick grin.

"Of course—thank you. I just didn't expect a surgeon to be this handy around the house."

He took a long swig from his drink, then set the can on the coffee table. "I should go," he said. "I've taken up enough of your time."

She realized she didn't want him to leave just yet. There was so much she didn't know about him. "Please, stay a while and cool off. It's the least I can do after you fixed my air conditioner."

He hesitated a moment, then lowered himself on the sofa.

"I'm sorry Paul blew your cover last night," she said, settling down on the seat next to him.

He shrugged. "It was bound to happen sooner or later."

"He admires you very much. He paints you as some kind of miracle worker."

His lips twisted ironically. "There was a time when I used to think so myself—thought I had the gift, I mean."

"What made you change your mind?"

He hesitated, clearly not at ease with the subject. "I discovered I wasn't God after all."

She decided not to push him further on the subject. "May I ask you a question?"

His lips twitched. "Just one?"

She ignored his dig at her obvious curiosity. "Why did you ask if there were angels on the ceiling of the church?"

The swiftness with which the humor faded from his eyes proved this was something else he didn't like to talk about. "It goes back to when I was a kid," he said after a brief silence. "The church I attended with my grandmother had figures of angels painted on its ceiling. I'd sit through

Sunday Mass staring up at them—talking to them in my head. My mother had run off with a man and I had this crazy notion they could help bring her back."

She wasn't sure what she had expected, but it wasn't anything quite so heart-wrenching. "Did she? Come back, I mean."

He shook his head. "She died in a car accident somewhere off the coast of California. I was six. I never looked at those angels again."

She was suddenly filled with sadness. "I'm so sorry. I didn't mean to bring back painful memories."

He made a dismissive gesture. "Lots of water under the bridge."

The words were said offhandedly, but his closed-off demeanor was a clear sign all that water hadn't managed to wash away the pain.

"Did you have a father in your life?"

"No. I was raised by my grandmother. She died when I was eight. After that I was taken into foster care, but I had a hard time following rules and didn't last long in any of the homes. I took to running. At ten I was living out of dumpsters and sleeping underneath park benches, determined not to depend on others for survival."

This last statement took her breath away. "You were just a child. Weren't you scared?" she asked.

He hesitated but didn't shift his gaze from hers like he had before. In fact, he appeared to be studying her, which felt strangely uncomfortable. "All the time, but my hunger for freedom was stronger. Conning the system was a cinch, but survival on the streets was a different matter altogether. I'd rough it out for a few days, then when it got too cold to sleep under the bridges, or the pangs of hunger became unbearable, I'd pretend to get careless and make it easy for them to catch up with me."

She had heard many stories of neglect and abandonment since working with the monastery children, but none had impacted her emotions as much as Richard's. The words could barely make it past the tightness in her throat. "How did you . . . I mean, you obviously turned out all right. You got an education, made a name for yourself."

"I got lucky. I met Dr. Maxwell Mallory."

He was looking at her strangely, as if the name was supposed to tell her something. "Was he someone important?" she asked.

"He was chief of surgery at Mercy General. If not for him I'd have ended up in a juvenile correctional facility. He took pity on me and took me in his charge. He turned my life around." Not only his tone but his eyes spoke of a deep affection for the man.

"I'm sure you've repaid him tenfold," Clare said. "You made him proud by becoming a good surgeon."

Instead of acknowledging her comment he said, "You were very young, too, when you lost your father."

She was surprised he knew. "Lots of water under the bridge for me, as well," she said.

When he got up to leave, she said, "Thank you for fixing the air conditioning."

"Thank you for the drink . . . and for listening."

"Listening is what friends do."

She didn't know what had prompted her to say that, but it was the truth. Since the first moment, she'd sensed a special connection with him, one she had never felt with any man before.

She read surprise in his eyes. "I'm honored to be considered your friend, Clare Elliot." His lips curved into a rare smile. "Walk me to the car?"

Night had fallen like a star-studded mantle over the hushed countryside when they left the house. A light breeze rustled the skirt of Clare's dress as she walked beside him.

"Tell me about Joey," he said.

She was surprised he'd ask about Joey. She'd sensed his uneasiness around the monastery children and didn't expect him to take an interest in them.

"Seven months ago he suffered a terrible trauma. His mother's boyfriend murdered her right before his eyes. It wasn't the first time the monster beat her, but the final time she wasn't able to get up. She died of a massive brain hemorrhage. Joey was barely three years old when it happened. He hasn't spoken a word since."

She heard Richard hiss under his breath. "How did he end up here?"

"He has no living relative who can take care of him. They tried placing him with a foster family, but he wasn't getting any better. His caseworker had heard about the nuns' program and reached out to them."

The expression on his face was hard. "What about the man—the boyfriend. I hope he got the punishment he deserved."

"He's behind bars, awaiting sentence for voluntary manslaughter and aggravated assault. With his history of violence, he's looking at a minimum of thirty years to life." She sighed. "Regardless, no sentence will be harsh enough to compensate for Joey's loss."

"No, it won't."

They stopped where he'd left his rental car and stood in the pool of light from a lamppost.

She shook her head. "Sometimes I fear he'll never recover. He's always so subdued, so closed off."

There was a soft smile on his lips. "You really do take these children's well-being to heart, don't you, Mother Clare?"

She scrunched up her nose. "You make me sound so . . . nunnish."

"Nunnish. Is that even a word?"

"Probably not," she said.

She held her breath as his hand lingered on the door handle for what seemed a disproportionate amount of time. Finally, he said, "I was wondering if you'd like to go sailing with me. You probably know your way around these coasts better than I do, and I could do with an experienced guide."

The unexpected invitation filled her with both delight and trepidation. "Sure."

"Does Saturday work for you? You could bring Joey along. It would do the kid good to get away for a change."

"I'm sure he'd love that."

"Need a ride?"

She shook her head. "I'll meet you at the marina at ten."

CHAPTER 24

CLARE

Philippe was coaching a family of four preparing to set off on a self-guided cruise, alerting them on the dos and don'ts of diving in the coral reefs, when Clare arrived at the marina.

His strong, authoritative voice carried over the distance that separated her from the slip. "Watch out for deceptively shallow water zones; you don't want to wander too close to the reefs on this baby. Try to avoid contact with the corals, and whatever you do, don't drop anchor on them."

His stern gaze was focused on the younger members of the group, two impatient-looking teenage boys. "And don't even think of bringing home an original souvenir to impress your buddies at home. You wouldn't want to destroy something that's taken thousands of centuries to form, now, would you?" he asked, eliciting a paltry smile from the youngsters.

Clare waited until the craft left the dockside, then approached Philippe. She smiled at him from under the visor of her blue Marlins cap. "Ahoy, there, Captain. Still your usual charming self with the tourists, I see."

"Hey," he said in greeting, delight brightening his ruggedly handsome face. He wrapped his big arms around her and gave her a crushing hug. "*Mon petit chou*, about time you came to see your old friend."

She wrinkled her nose at his old pet name for her. Little cabbage was not what a normal twenty-seven-year-old woman wanted to be likened to by a charming and handsome bachelor, but no matter how many times she brought up that particular argument, the vegan moniker stuck.

"And who do we have here?" Philippe asked, only then noticing the surly little boy at her side.

"This is Joey. Say hello to Philippe, Joey. He's the captain in charge of all these boats," she said to the small boy, knowing better than to expect a vocal reaction from him. "Joey is one of my students. We're going sailing."

Philippe's eyebrows drew together. "You are? I don't have a boat in your name. Did you call for one?"

"I'm not going out alone. I'm meeting a friend."

"A friend," he drawled. The narrowing of his eyes told her he had a good idea who her friend might be. "So, it takes a famous surgeon from New York to tear you away from the selfish nuns," he said, heavy on the sarcasm.

Clare took umbrage at his tone. "Please don't bad-mouth the nuns, especially in front of Joey."

His lips pulled into a tight line. "Sorry, *chérie*, but you and this doctor . . . I can't say I like the idea of you going anywhere with him."

She stared at him disbelievingly. "It's only a boat ride, not an elopement," she pointed out.

"He's too old for you."

"No, he's not."

"Ah-ha," he said catching her defensive slip. "So, I am right. Something is going on between you and the secretive doctor."

Clare was sure the shade of red on her face rivaled that of Joey's Spiderman hat, but it was mostly anger-related. "Nothing is *going on*, as you succinctly put it. Stop acting like you're my father."

He gave her a stubborn glare. "Since you don't have one to watch over you, that responsibility falls on me by default. I watched you grow up."

She snorted. "Hardly."

What was wrong with the men in her life, lately? They were all under the impression they had control rights over her. First Paul with his clumsy proprietary attitude, then Richard with his irrational insinuations. She didn't need Philippe turning big brother on her.

"I'm touched by your concern, truly I am, but I can take care of myself. I'm not a child anymore."

He stuck a finger under his bandanna and scratched his head. "Not a child anymore? My Clare de Lune?" he asked, tagging her with another favorite of his. "Damn, when did that happen?"

At her threatening glare, he held up his hands. "All right, all right." Slightly pacified, he added, "It won't be easy, but I will try to remember that."

"It seems every time I see you with a guy, he has his hands all over you," another voice said.

Clare jumped guiltily. Neither she nor Philippe had seen Richard arriving.

Philippe stood up straighter. "Where I choose to put my hands is none of your business, *mon ami.*"

The hostile expression on Richard's face reminded Clare of the night of the beach party. "You don't consider me a friend any more than I consider you one, so drop the French sweet-talk, Girard."

"I thought we had an understanding," the other man said curtly.

Richard didn't flinch. "I wasn't aware I had to ask your permission to take a friend out on a boat."

"What understanding?" Clare asked.

Philippe took a step forward, ignoring Clare completely.

Clamping a steely hand on Richard's shoulder, he said with exaggerated politeness, "Don't take this personally, Mr.

Kelly or whatever the hell they call you, but I can't help but be a little suspicious of a man who comes to our island under false pretenses."

Richard flexed his shoulder, shrugging off Philippe's hand. "I didn't lie to anyone. I chose not to divulge my personal business," he specified.

Clare had enough. "In case you hadn't noticed, I'm standing right here, and I don't appreciate being discussed about as if I were invisible. What understanding?" she repeated.

Philippe's belligerence sagged a little. "Nothing you should be concerned about," he said. With a last glacial glance at Richard, he said briskly. "Let's get you a boat."

"I thought we were going for the dinghy?" Richard asked, when Philippe led them to a stately twenty-two-feet sloop.

"The wind's a little high. The dinghy might be too bumpy and make the kid sick. The *Camèlie* is better equipped to handle the currents."

The *Camèlie*, Clare thought, stunned.

Since when did Philippe trust anyone, let alone a man he obviously considered dishonest, with his pride and joy?

Richard helped her get Joey onto the boat. "Hey, little guy," he said, tapping the brim of the boy's hat. "Gonna be my second in command today?"

Joey furrowed his brow and shrank away from him. Clare held back a sigh. So far the day had pretty much sucked. She wondered if accepting Richard's invitation hadn't been a colossal mistake.

Philippe snickered. "Even the kid knows better than to trust you," he said, and threw three personal flotation devices in Richard's direction.

Richard caught them promptly. To his credit, he ignored Philippe's deliberate jab.

Clare was still fuming when Richard powered up the boat's motor and pointed it toward the row of small islets that made up Dolphin's End, the southern-most part of the Mermaid Point Keys.

Thankfully Richard was too busy to notice. He was juggling the tiller and mainsail, his attention focused on steadying the boat as it caught a particularly robust gust of wind. She kept a firm grip on Joey who was kneeling on the bench leaning over the side, fascinated by the foaming wake. She raised her face to the wind, allowing the cooling effect of the salty spray to soothe her both physically and mentally. It had been a long time since she'd been on a boat, not since she'd graduated and returned to work at the monastery.

"Everything all right?"

She blinked, realizing she'd been wrapped up in her own thoughts and hadn't noticed they were cruising on a more even keel. "Yes. I haven't been on the water in a long time, and it brings back a lot of memories," she said. "I didn't realize how much I missed it. My father used to take me and Courtney out sailing when we were kids. Later we'd go with Philippe. He taught us to sail."

"Do you want to steer a while?" he asked.

Excitement coursed through her at the thought of standing at the helm of a boat once again, of experiencing the rush of adrenaline as it cut through wind and ocean. They switched positions, and before long Clare was manning both the tiller and mainsail like Philippe had taught her.

As they drew closer to their destination, the wind picked up speed. The boat heeled sharply to port and a wall of spray flew over the teak deck, catching them by surprise.

Richard sprung up to ease the mainsail back out, and the boat flattened. "Good work, skipper," he said to Clare. "Would you mind keeping an eye on the mainsheet while Joey and I steer this fine lady to our final destination?" He winked at Joey. "How about giving me a hand here?"

Joey looked hesitant at first, then slid off the bench and crossed to Richard's side. Richard retrieved an old wooden crate for Joey to stand on. "You have to hold on real fast to the tiller or the force of the wind will snatch it right out of your hands," he cautioned as he guided Joey's hands on the instrument while keeping his own over the boy's. Clare doubted the child understood everything that was being explained to him, but at least Richard had his attention.

It was a short wade to shore, but Joey flatly refused to walk, terrified of the life flashing visibly on the seabed. In the end Richard carried him piggyback to dry land, then went back for the thermal bag Serena's cook had filled for them. By the time Clare had rolled out the bamboo mats under the canopy of trees, Joey had slipped back into his cranky self. He refused to take off his life jacket and sat broodingly in a puddle of seawater, digging craters with his heels.

Her mounting frustration didn't go unnoticed. "He's just being a kid. I'm convinced under that implacable mask of indifference, he's actually enjoying himself," Richard said.

She appreciated his effort to boost her morale. He had shown remarkable patience with Joey despite the boy's despondency, and she was grateful to him. It was the first time she'd seen Joey warm up to anyone outside of the monastery.

"I apologize for Philippe's boorish behavior, earlier. Since my father passed away, he feels duty-bound to protect Courtney and me."

"I can't say I blame him," he said. "In his place I'd do the same."

Flattered, she smiled at him. "You up for a swim? I promise, no spraying or dunking this time," she said with a teasing grin.

CHAPTER 25

RICHARD

Clare had fallen asleep. Joey's tantrums had finally worn her out. Dealing with these children on a daily basis had to be exhausting, as well as mentally draining, he thought. Richard was living proof of that, having been on the giving end of much of that stress in his childhood.

He wondered how her life had been after reuniting with her family. Had she remembered them—her previous life? Had she been happy growing up? It rankled that she didn't seem to have a clue who he was. Yesterday she hadn't even blinked at the mention of Dr. Max's name. It was as if the eight months she'd spent with the Mallorys hadn't happened. Could time have erased all of that from her mind?

Her honey-colored hair was spread out on the mat and he reached out to touch it, testing its texture between his fingers. It was as silky and soft as he remembered it, even still damp from the seawater. She was so young . . . a young woman with a big heart. Nearing thirty-six he felt ancient in comparison, but the raw yearning inside him was one he hadn't experienced since his days as a gawking pubescent teen.

He stifled a groan. How had he gone from being instinctively drawn to an anonymous painting, to being utterly obsessed with the woman whose hands had crafted it? What was it about Clare that fascinated him so—aside from the obvious fact she was extremely desirable, as well as kind and smart and funny? She had a narcotic effect on his brain, like an anesthetizing drug that pervaded his bloodstream. It was more than hard liquor had ever accomplished, except to make him feel wretched. His rational side warned him Clare was a potential addiction, one far more detrimental to his healing process than any good whiskey, which made him wonder where his rational side had been when he'd decided to invite her on a boat outing.

He caught Joey stealing furtive glances at him. Richard couldn't tell whether the boy was curious or just vigilant. He'd hate if it were the latter. The child had seen a grown man at his worst and could perceive him as a potential threat.

"She's not real, you know," he said, unable to resist taunting him. "She looks like a real person but she's actually a fairy. A good fairy."

For once Joey looked at him in earnest, and Richard experienced a sense of triumph. There was nothing like good old jealousy to make a male pay attention.

"See this?" he whispered, balancing the lock of hair on his fingers. "It's not real hair; they're fine threads spun from pure gold." He beckoned him to get closer. "Here, feel for yourself."

When he was beginning to think the child wouldn't budge, Joey let go of the pail and shovel he'd been playing with and crawled over to his side.

"There, feel how soft it is?" Richard said, guiding Joey's fingers around the soft strands. "She has wings, too, only we can't see them 'cause they're invisible."

Joey let go of the hair. His eyes were glued to Clare's back, as if expecting a pair of gossamer wings to sprout from between her shoulder blades. His fingers kept twitching and flexing, as if itching to touch and explore, to validate such an extraordinary phenomenon for himself.

"Careful now, you might wake her," Richard warned.

Joey retreated, and Richard felt a pang of remorse. "I have an idea," he said getting to his feet. "Why don't we build a nice castle for our fairy princess?"

CHAPTER 26

CLARE

Clare sprang to a sitting position, glancing frantically around for Joey. She couldn't believe she'd fallen asleep. What would Richard think of her, and what if something had happened to Joey? Then she saw them. Both Joey and Richard were asleep in a shaded spot. A few feet away, the surf was lapping at the edges of a lopsided sandcastle, nibbling away at its outer walls.

They were curled up next to each other, with Richard's arm thrown protectively around the boy. The picture they made warmed her heart. Just when she thought she'd seen all facets of Richard's character, he managed to surprise her. Nothing she'd detected so far came close to the cold and insensitive person the rumors made him out to be.

She allowed herself a moment to study him, noticing how his thick dark hair fell onto his brow, the way it grew a little long and curled up at the nape of his neck. The artist in her itched to paint him, to immortalize his face in oils—then she'd have something of him to keep after he left.

The rush of panic that coursed through her at the thought of his leaving left her breathless. She hadn't expected to develop such strong feelings for him and in such a short period of time. Courtney was right; she knew nothing about him. Besides, he was way out of her league—a world-renowned neurosurgeon, practically a legend in his field. For all she knew he could still be in love with his wife despite the rumors of a recent divorce.

As if sensing her watching him, Richard opened his eyes. The indolent smile that spread over his face made her instantly self-conscious. She reached for her T-shirt and pulled it over her bathing suit.

"I'm sorry, I didn't mean to fall asleep. It must have been the Chardonnay," she said, threading her fingers through her sleep tousled hair.

Richard removed his arm from around Joey, careful not to wake him, and took two cans of soda from the small cooler. Sitting next to Clare, he handed one to her.

She drank from it gratefully. The shade from the trees brought little relief from the early afternoon heat, and she realized she was parched.

"Or you probably just needed the nap."

That too, she thought, but kept it to herself. She'd have to tell him about the strange dreams that kept her up at night, and she'd hate to spoil the mood.

"I'm sorry I left you to deal with Joey," she said.

He shrugged. "I didn't mind. Besides, it gave us a chance to get acquainted."

She arched her eyebrows. "I would have liked to have seen that. He's not exactly the loquacious type."

"Sometimes words are not essential to communication," he said.

His philosophical rationale made her even more curious to know what had really happened while she was asleep. "How did you . . . uh . . . communicate?" she asked.

A hint of a grin glanced his lips. "Nothing slated to develop into a bromance any time soon. We got off to a rocky start, but we decided to call a truce, in the spirit of . . . mutual interests."

She wondered what he meant by that cryptic remark, but the sound of it filled her with a pleasant warmth. He may be reserved, but he was a good person, one who had suffered deeply, and she was convinced there was more to his story than the so-called rumors implied.

She didn't realize she'd sighed audibly until he looked at her strangely. "What?"

"I was thinking how little I know about you. You've told me a little about your past but nothing of the Richard Kelly of today."

She caught the almost imperceptible tensing of his jaw. "And here I thought after beach night my life was pretty much an open book."

"I meant the real you. The one you left behind in New York."

His expression clouded over, and she could almost hear the bolts of his protective shield sliding all the way home. "I don't even know who the real me is anymore."

The hollowness of his tone shook her profoundly. "Is it because of your divorce that you left New York?"

His stunned expression told her he hadn't expected her to know.

She decided he had a right to know his personal business had become public domain, and that thanks to Paul and Lydia, he had become a hot topic of conversation in St. Isabel.

She explained how Paul had gotten wind of the voices circulating in the medical field on Richard's account. "It's being said you abandoned your career after your divorce. That you . . . That you left your wife after she—"

"After she what? After she killed my child?"

The chilling words sent cold shivers down her spine. "Killed?"

"Terminated, disposed of, as if it was nothing more than a benign tumor," he said through clenched teeth. "I didn't know Erica was pregnant, not until after the divorce proceedings had begun. By the time I found out, it was too late."

Clare had to fight back a wave of nausea. "But . . . why did she do it?"

His fingers contracted spasmodically in the powdery sand, causing the veins in his biceps to bulge. "She never wanted a child, never planned for it. It had to have been an accident, and she used it against me, to punish me."

"Punish you. For what?"

"For not having the same high standards as hers. We were worlds apart, Erica and me. Financial success and social stature were everything to her. I just wanted to be free to do the work I love, to be a surgeon. It took me three years to realize we were going in different directions."

His expression was hard, inscrutable, but the shadows in his eyes betrayed his inner turmoil. She wanted to reach out and touch him, to smooth out the deep lines etched on his brow. "What happened?" she asked gently.

"I got greedy, me, a hoodlum from the Bronx." He scoffed. "I thought I could beat the odds and have it all—a family, money, a successful career. I was wrong. Where I come from you can't raise your stakes too high. I'll always be the kid from the wrong side of the tracks."

"That's not true. Who we are, whatever our roots, shouldn't determine what is rightfully human to desire," she said, "and you've clearly worked hard to deserve all of those things." He gave her a distracted look as if to say she couldn't possibly understand. "Perhaps this break is exactly what you need to get you to start fresh. "Your job—"

"I can't go back to doing my job," he said cutting her off. "I haven't performed surgery in over three months because I can't trust my hands to function properly."

"What's wrong with them?" she asked, shaken by his violent reaction.

He pulled them from the sand, holding them out in front of him. "They're unsteady. They've been this way since I found out about the abortion. Just the thought of stepping inside an OR gives me panic attacks."

Clare stared at his hands. Aside from a slight tremor, which could easily be attributed to nervous tension, she didn't notice anything overly concerning.

His voice took on a flat, hollow tone. "I'd never given much thought to having a child. I was convinced I wasn't wired to be a father. But there was a fleeting moment when I envisioned that tiny life growing inside Erica's womb and I . . ." He quickly glanced away, but not before she saw the moisture glistening in his eyes. "She didn't even pretend to be upset. She lied, claiming it had come about naturally. 'Mother Nature's way of taking care of things when conditions are not favorable' were her exact words."

To see this big, strong man in so much agony, tore at Clare. She understood, now, about the anger always simmering beneath the surface. "How did you find out?" she asked.

"I was returning from a medical conference when I decided to take a ride out to the Hamptons to pick up the last of my stuff. I still had my keys and purposefully picked a time when I knew Erica wouldn't be home, so I'd be spared another of her cold confrontations. Her mail was stacked on top of the console, some of it opened. That was when I saw the hospital bill; it was a notice of payment due for a D&C—dilation and curettage of the uterus—from a well-known Manhattan clinic. The words 'elective termination of pregnancy' stood out from the paper like a neon light. That's when I knew I'd been played for a fool, and in the worst possible way."

Clare shook her head disbelievingly. "What did you do?"

He raised his shoulders. "There was nothing I could do except confront her and demand an explanation. Apparently, there's no law requiring a partner's consent if a woman seeks to terminate her pregnancy. Her general practitioner was an old college friend of hers. I'm convinced he helped arrange everything at Erica's request. I wanted to confront the bastard who'd conspired with her to butcher my child and force him to admit the truth, if I didn't kill him first. Fortunately, I came to my senses before I could do anything stupid. I convinced myself it wasn't worth it. The baby was gone and so was my marriage. There was nothing to salvage, nothing worth fighting for."

"I'm sorry," she said. She couldn't imagine anything more painful than losing a child, but to lose it in such a cruel, senseless way had to be devastating.

He didn't acknowledge her sympathy but got to his feet and stepped away toward the water. He crouched on the compact sand and began to toss bits of shell into the surf. She saw the suppressed anger in every movement, in the knotted muscles of his back, in the stiff posture of his neck and shoulders, and she ached for him.

An impulse more compelling than her desire to give him the space he so obviously sought prompted her to join him. She placed her hands on the smooth planes of his back and his muscles jerked slightly at the contact. She rubbed gently, feeling the rigidity beneath her fingers, the wiry tension as they flexed. Her throat tight with emotion, she mourned the tragedy of the losses he'd endured, beginning with his mother's abandonment and now that of his unborn child.

She lost track of how long they sat like that, each absorbed in their own turbulent thoughts.

"Clare?"

She blinked, his face suddenly swimming before her eyes. She had let her emotions rise so close to the surface when she should have been the strong one, the one to offer comfort. Some friend she'd turned out to be. Then the truth hit her. She was in love with this man. How had it happened so soon?

His laser-sharp eyes bore into hers, holding her captive. Gently, he wiped the moisture from her cheek with his thumb then, just as gently traced the outline of her face. With a soft moan he lowered his head and brushed his lips over hers. Clare felt herself go limp, weightless. His arms slid around her, sweeping her up against his body. His kiss became deeper, more demanding. All at once she was caught up in an exquisite dream from which she never wanted to wake up.

All too soon she did wake up, and it was when he let her go, holding her at arm's length. "Clare . . . no. We can't do this."

"Why not?" she asked, not understanding.

"Because it's wrong. It's my fault. I shouldn't have unburdened on you."

If he'd slapped her, it couldn't have stung more. He thought of their kiss as a mistake, nothing more than a chemical reaction sparked by emotional overload. Suddenly, the magic vanished and all that was left was a deep, humiliating shame.

Trembling from the aftershocks of his reaction, she turned away.

"We should head back. I'll wake Joey," she said quickly, and began to gather their belongings.

CHAPTER 27

CLARE

Her mother's call didn't come as a surprise. With the St. Isabel grapevine in full action mode, she'd known it wouldn't be long before Sonia heard of her sailing trip with Richard. News of Clare's liaison with Serena's newly divorced guest was sure to have set off all kinds of alarms in her mother's head. Under normal circumstances Clare would have been happy to tell her all about her day with Richard and Joey, but after what had happened on Dolphin's End the previous day, things were far from normal.

She decided to get straight to the point and skip the small talk.

"I assume you're calling to ask about my outing with Richard yesterday."

"I was calling because we didn't get a chance to talk the night of the beach party," her mother said, sounding a little defensive.

"Mom," Clare warned.

Sonia released an audible sigh. "All right, I was curious," she admitted.

And most likely concerned out of your mind, Clare thought.

"I didn't realize you were on such friendly terms."

"We met a couple of times on Monks' Beach and he asked me to show him around the Mermaid Keys. We brought little

165

Joey along. Richard suggested the child might benefit from a day away from the monastery."

"That was very considerate of him. I'm glad you were out and about for a change, but I can't deny I'm surprised. He seems such a loner, always keeping to himself."

Though her mother's tone sounded genuinely pleased, Clare sensed the underlying apprehension behind it. "It wasn't a date, if that's what you think," she said. "I was just being helpful. He's . . . going through some bad stuff."

"And you being you, feel a moral obligation to take every suffering creature on the planet under your wing," Sonia said, with a sigh.

Clare wasn't surprised her mother was aware of Richard's emotional issues. Island gossip aside, Sonia had an uncanny perception when it came to intercepting people's innermost feelings. People were naturally drawn to her, which was the reason Serena had so many return guests.

"He's a good man, but an emotionally crippled one, and I'm not sure it's healthy for you to be seeing him."

"It's not like that with Richard," Clare said, implying he wasn't another destitute child she wanted to help, though in some respect he was. As a child, he hadn't fared any better than most of the children she worked with at the monastery, and it saddened her to know he'd suffered so much.

"All I'm saying is, be careful," her mother said gently, before they ended the call, leaving Clare with a feeling of frustration.

Her family's oppressive preoccupation with her well-being was one of the reasons Clare had decided to move out of Serena. She'd needed to assert herself, to gain her independence, and she couldn't do that without getting away from her mother and sister's obsessive vigilance. Having a place all her own meant being her own person and not having to justify her every action, especially to her sister.

It hadn't been an easy decision for her. Serena was the home she'd grown up in, where the memories of her father still lived, and she missed it, just as she missed her mother, but she didn't regret moving to Monastery Hill. There was nothing more gratifying than the laughter of the children that rang down from the top of the rise when the windows were open or the hourly toll of the church bells. Contrary to her mother's belief, she was never alone up here. Someone was always dropping by, whether one of the children or a friend bringing over a meal to share or to watch a movie with her. Even Paul had visited a few times.

Thinking of Paul, it occurred to her she hadn't seen him since the night of the beach party. It wasn't like him to avoid her. She wondered if he was still smarting from her rejection.

She was debating whether to give him a call when her cell phone rang again. It was Serena's main number again. Had her mother forgotten to tell her something?

"Mom?"

There was a brief silence on the other end of the line. "I've been called many names in my lifetime but Mom is definitely not one of them," said a deep, amused voice.

Her breath caught in her throat. How had Richard gotten her number?

"Did I catch you at a bad time?" he asked when she didn't respond immediately.

"No, not at all," she replied a little too quickly. She sucked in a deep breath, willing her frantic nerves to settle down. "I just finished talking with my mother and I thought she had forgotten to tell me something."

"I had to twist Juan's arm for your number. I hope you don't mind."

"No. I . . ." Suddenly at a loss for words, she wondered how he'd managed that. Juan wasn't easily manipulated.

"I've been told there's this little Italian place in town I should check out. *Canzone del Mare*. Philippe swears they make the best linguini this side of the Pond. Are you familiar with it?"

He'd discussed Italian cuisine with Philippe? After that bizarre exchange at the marina, she was surprised the two were even on speaking terms.

She recovered enough to apply some irony to her response. "Asking an islander if she's familiar with Tommaso's *trattoria* is like asking someone who lives in Rome if they've ever seen the Colosseum. Philippe wasn't overstating its merits. They do make excellent linguini, among other delicious things."

"Good to know. I admit I was a little skeptical, him being a frog-eating Frenchman and all."

She had to smile at that. "He's French Canadian."

She envisioned his careless shrug.

"A minor geographical detail," he said.

"Well, enjoy your dinner," she said, disappointed the reason for his call was to get a restaurant recommendation.

"I will, but only if you come with me."

"What?" she asked, choking out the word.

"It's not a date, mind you," he said, as if he had some telepathic ability to read her mind. "Just a test drive of our friendship, to make sure you haven't written me off completely after my deplorable behavior yesterday. While we're at it, you could show me around town."

Moments away from her legs giving from underneath her, Clare lowered herself onto the nearest chair. They'd barely exchanged a word during their return to the marina yesterday, except for a perfunctory "thank you" before she and Joey had driven off in her car. If anyone had expected to be "written off," it was her. She opened her mouth to reassure him, but the only thing that emerged was, "I'd love to."

CHAPTER 28

RICHARD

He'd known, coming into this, he'd be taking a big risk, but he had to see Clare one last time. It was getting harder and harder to ignore his attraction to her, and it was abundantly clear she was developing feelings for him. He had to leave the island before the situation got any worse, and she deserved to know.

His optimistic expectations of a stress-free evening floundered the moment he saw her. The shorts and T-shirt-clad woman he'd become accustomed to was gone. Her lacy off-the-shoulder top and calf-length flouncy skirt gave her a bohemian look, as did the mass of honey-blond hair she had gathered on top of her head in a loose knot. For some bizarre reason she made him think of cream puffs and warm, frothy cappuccinos, among other, more prohibitive things.

"Come on in," she said waving him inside as if he were a lifelong friend accustomed to stopping by from time to time. "I'll just get my purse."

He'd wrestled with the idea of bringing a gift. He didn't want her to read more into the gesture than he intended it to be, a sort of peace offering. In the end he'd relented, though finding the right one had turned out to be more of a challenge than he'd expected. St. Isabel's main hub, he'd discovered on his first trip into town, didn't offer much in the way of shopping venues.

He handed her the package, and said, "Unfortunately they were all out of fairy dust."

She laughed, then her eyes widened as she unwrapped the gift. "It's a vintage copy of Dr. Seuss . . ." She gazed up at him. "It must have cost a fortune."

"Nothing that would break the bank," he reassured her. "I thought the children might enjoy having you read it to them."

"Thank you. It will be a precious addition to my storybook library."

The glint of genuine pleasure in her eyes convinced him he'd made the right choice.

ST. ISABEL VILLAGE was the quintessential southern town. With its picturesque Victorian houses and well-tended gardens, it exuded the same kind of laid-back, old-world charm of a middle-class southern neighborhood. What distinguished it from the other towns of the barrier was the almost total lack of tourist activity. There were no upscale boutiques sporting glitzy designer names nor trendy restaurants and noisy sidewalk cafes, while an unobtrusively sited McDonald's and a Starbucks off Main Street appeared to embody the entire fast-food franchise concession to the town. Aside from a handful of B&Bs, he hadn't come across a single hotel.

"The island is part of Florida's Coastal Conservancy and is state protected," Clare explained when he remarked on the island's scant commercial development. "It adopts a form of controlled tourism to reduce the impact on the environment thus preventing the island from becoming the stereotypical mainstream attraction."

"Controlled tourism, huh? I suppose there's something to be said about not being ambushed by time-share vultures at every turn."

She gave a little shrug. "The islanders have no interest in turning St. Isabel into another popular vacation destination and curbing the influx of visitors is the only way we're able to keep real estate developers away."

This explained the lack of commercial flights to the island and limited ferry service. "That's taking the term 'insular' to a whole new level," he said.

"I prefer the term 'conservative,'" she said coolly.

He parked on a quiet side street and together they headed for the waterfront. Fishing vessels and pleasure boats were tethered alongside the slips, their lights reflecting on the gleaming surface of the water.

He noticed she'd become defensive since the subject of the island's unconventional practices had come up, and he felt an irresistible urge to needle her.

"Do the St. Isabellians—is that what you call yourselves?—ever feel the call of the mainland? Or do you fear something terrible will happen to you when you leave your safe haven—you know, like age rapidly and disintegrate into dust?"

She glared at him. "Very funny. And it's 'St. Isabellites.' We're protective, not reclusive. The same way most people on the mainland own a car, most islanders own or rent powerboats and make regular trips to the mainland to shop for necessities that can't be had locally—or even just for fun. I lived in Miami for four years when I was attending UM."

She leaned over the railing to watch a large fishing boat mooring for the night with its bounty of twitching silverfish. She waved at someone on board, who promptly waved back. "That's Jeff, a former boarder at the monastery," she explained. "He just turned eighteen and is emancipated."

Richard eyed the strappy, suntanned youth exchanging an easy smile with Clare, telling himself the sudden surge of irritability wasn't jealousy.

"And tell me, are all New Yorkers as cynical as you?" she asked with a defiant glint in her eyes.

He grimaced. "Ouch. I guess I deserved that."

The feeling of Americana vanished the minute they entered the bustling Italian restaurant on the pier and were met with noisy chatter and mouthwatering aromas. Here, the sensation of geographic transport, rather than a historical one, prevailed. *Canzone del Mare*, Song of the Sea, was a family-friendly Italian *trattoria*, complete with checkered red-and-white vinyl tablecloths and cheerful servers exchanging jokes with the customers. A brawny salt-and-pepper haired man in a white apron came to greet them, his red face lighting up like a Chinese lantern upon seeing Clare.

"Clare! What a pleasure to see you again. You don't come see old Tommaso no more. Too busy being the little schoolteacher, eh?" He caught Clare in a vigorous bear hug.

"Hello, Tommaso. It's good to see you, too," Clare said. Then in response to the host's question she said, "Things are a little different now that I live on Monastery Hill. I seldom get the opportunity to drive into town, unless it's to grab a few supplies on the fly."

"Ah, you keep too much company with the nuns," Tommaso said, wagging a stern finger at her. "It is a great loss for us common mortals, who live only to see your beautiful smile once in a while."

Clare laughed. "I bet you say that to all your female patrons. How is Marisa?"

"As well as can be. She has her hands full with the little ones."

"What is it now, eight grandchildren?"

"Nine, with Rita's last," Tommaso said, his eyes shining with pride. "Soon I will have enough to form my very own soccer team." He swept his arm in a wide arch simulating an imaginary banner. "Tommaso's Island Devils." His bellow of a laugh made the glasses on the table rattle precariously.

"This is Richard Kelly. He's my mother's guest from New York," Clare said, drawing the host's attention toward Richard.

The older man straightened, assuming a more dignified stance. "Kelly . . . Of course. You called for reservations. Table for two, right?" Richard nodded, finding the host's handshake to be as overpowering as his personality. "It's very kind of you to grace my modest restaurant."

Suddenly all business, Tommaso guided them to their table in a discreet corner next to a window overlooking the small harbor. The host left them momentarily to return with folded menus. "Now, I hope you both brought along a healthy appetite because tonight we have our special fettuccine with artichokes and fresh porcini mushrooms. But of course, you are free to choose whatever you like from our wide selection of entrees," he added graciously. "If I may make a suggestion, the marinated grilled swordfish is an excellent choice." He brought the tips of his fingers to his lips and kissed them in an eloquent gesture of rapture. "Simply irresistible! Of course, all watered down with dry Lambrusco, or if you prefer, a good California Chardonnay." He pulled a pen from behind his ear and notebook in hand, stood poised to take their orders.

"The swordfish sounds delicious, thank you," Clare said, then leaned toward Richard, saying in a low tone, "Feel free to order anything you like, but I should warn you when Tommaso makes his recommendations, he expects people to humor him."

"I'll have the same," Richard said.

The host's laughter rumbled above the lulling music. "Ah, Clare, she likes to make fun of old Tommaso. Used to do it since she was little and came in with her father, my dear friend Eddie."

A melancholic haze dimmed the man's eyes. "How I have missed your impudent little mouth," he said shaking his head. He leaned over toward Richard. "She is a little—how do you say? Cheeky. But she has a heart of gold, this little one. When she comes here, she brightens up the place. I am convinced she is *una fata*. A magical fairy."

Finally, something we can agree on, Richard thought.

He looked at Clare, but it was a mistake. The memory of her droopy eyes after a couple of glasses of Celeste's Chardonnay brought back all the disturbing memories of Dolphin's End, and he quickly pulled his gaze away.

Tommaso scribbled down their orders on his notepad. When he was finished, he turned to Richard. "You are a long way from New York, Mr. Kelly, are you not?"

It was obviously a rhetorical question because he didn't pause to wait for a response. "People come to St. Isabel Island and then they leave, never to come back again. Too quiet, they say, and they go back to their noisy cities." He edged a little toward Clare, placing a proprietary hand on her shoulder. "Clare, she is like a niece to me. She was raised on this island. Her heart is on this island," he added, placing particular emphasis on the word 'heart.' "It would make the people of St. Isabel very sad if one day she were to give it away to some inconsiderate stranger from the city. *Buon appetito!*" Wishing them a pleasant meal, he headed for the kitchen shouting out their orders to the chef.

Several moments passed before Richard finally remembered how to breathe again. "That was . . . intense," he murmured, unable to find a more suitable term to define the host's cryptic monologue.

Clare appeared mortified. "I'm sorry. He isn't usually like this. I don't know what got into him."

He caught the frustration in her tone and realized it wasn't just embarrassment that had turned her face several shades of pink. He had a feeling Tommaso's rant hadn't been the product of good old island conservatism but of something much more profound and personal. "I'm curious to know what it is that makes everyone so protective of you," he said studying her.

"It's a small island. We all look out for each other," she said, but her airy, too-quick response didn't fool him.

CHAPTER 29

CLARE

They decided to skip dessert. Instead, they took a walk on the pier making a stop at the Scoop-A-Licious, St. Isabel's most popular ice-cream place. To her delight, Clare discovered he was as much a glutton for ice cream as she was. Neither seemed eager for the evening to end, and almost without realizing it, they wandered away from the town center toward the water.

They strolled along the dark and deserted beach, guided by the waterfront lights and a hazy full moon. She didn't object when he took her sandals from her hands and slipped one in each pocket of his jacket. Afterward he removed the jacket, flinging it negligently—sandals and all—over one shoulder.

There was a soothing, almost sensual pleasure to be derived from walking barefoot on the beach under a clear, star-studded sky, Clare thought, relishing the feel of the warm dry sand oozing between her toes. She realized she hadn't felt this lighthearted and content in a long time.

If not for the brief awkwardness after Tommaso's unanticipated and totally inappropriate lecture, every moment she spent with Richard had felt relaxed and natural. She was determined not to dwell on how they had left off the previous day but to enjoy this time with him for what it was, a rekindling of their friendship, and he seemed to be doing the same.

When he wasn't so closed-off, he was a great conversationalist. He exuded an aura of confidence that held her enthralled. She could easily envision him in scrubs leading a team of surgeons through complex surgeries or holding an entire lecture hall spellbound with his charisma and intellect. It was mystifying how a man could appear so self-possessed and together and at the same time hide a vulnerable core, one which had almost destroyed him.

He caught her staring at him and eyed her with a mixture of amusement and wariness.

"What—do I have chocolate ice cream on my chin or something?"

Her face became warm. She hadn't realized her thoughts had strayed and laughed guiltily. "I'm sorry, I didn't realize I was staring."

"It was more like frowning."

"Frowning?"

"Right after I agreed with you *Casablanca* is by far one of the greatest movies of all time."

"Oh." As usual, he'd managed to throw her off-balance. "I admit I lost my train of thought for a moment."

"I'm curious to know what you find so distracting about me it messes with your concentration," he said, openly amused.

"I was trying to envision you in your everyday work environment," she said.

"And?"

"And somehow you don't fit the bill."

His brow knitted. "I don't?"

"I imagined all high-profile surgeons to be cold, insensitive, egotistical individuals."

"Oh? And how do you see me?" he asked, cocking an eyebrow at her.

"Kind, considerate, unstylishly chivalrous . . ."

"Thank you . . . I think."

"And you like ice cream."

This time he smiled. "Well, you're nothing like I expected, either. Who'd have thought, a few weeks ago, I'd be nursing my emotional wounds on an isolated island, with the help of a pretty, generous, soft-hearted kindergarten teacher?"

She told herself he was just being nice, which didn't stop her heart from doing a hopeful little dance in her chest. "Be careful, doctor, or I might think you're flirting with me," she said, pretending to be unaffected by the compliment.

"I mean it," he said, all traces of amusement gone. He stopped walking and faced her, his tall frame backlit by the moon. "I apologize for sounding cynical about the islanders' conservative sentiment. I appreciate the fact there are people who put their communities and the preservation of their environment ahead of financial gain. I would hate the idea of leaving the island thinking I made a bad impression on you."

His words sounded sincere and genuinely heartfelt, though she could only focus on the latter part of his speech. "You're leaving?"

He nodded. "That's why I wanted to see you." The grim set of his mouth caused a terrible contraction in her belly. "This is the last night I will be spending in St. Isabel. I'm taking the ferry first thing tomorrow morning and flying back to New York."

All the mellowness and good feelings she'd been experiencing drained out of her. She took a step back and folded her arms in front of her. "This is . . . unexpected," she said.

"I've been meaning to tell you, but I'm enjoying our time together and was reluctant to spoil it," he said.

So, this is what his invitation has been about, she thought, an excuse to say a proper goodbye. She never should have encouraged that kiss, and now he couldn't get away from her fast enough.

She said the first thing that came to her mind. "But what about your book?"

He smiled. "You know as well as I do the book was just a pretext to get away. Anyway, it's almost completed. Minor stuff, nothing that can't be accomplished from home."

"I see," she said, her mouth so dry the words were almost inaudible.

His expression softened as he looked at her with regret. "Coming out to the island was an expedient to escape the ugliness of what my life had become. I didn't have many expectations, other than to gain some measure of serenity. And you gave me that, in a totally selfless way." He grazed his knuckles over her cheek smiling melancholically. "You've been a healthy distraction, Clare Elliot, a much-needed one, and I'll always be grateful to you for that."

Then why are you so set on leaving so soon? she wanted to ask. She tried not to show how hurt she was by pasting a buoyant smile on her face. "Glad I could be of help. Feel free to come back any time urban life gets to be a little too much for you," she said, her tone sounding more brittle than she'd intended.

"I'd like that," he said, but there was a hint of uncertainty in his eyes.

"We should be getting back. I'm sure you'll want to grab a few hours of sleep if you're planning an early departure," she said. She didn't wait for his response. "Race you back to the pier!" she shouted over her shoulder and set off at a run.

"Clare."

She heard his call but continued to run. She couldn't allow him to see the devastation. He caught up with her and swung her around to face him. His face was so close she could see flecks of silver dancing in his irises.

"I didn't mean to offend you. I've really enjoyed our time together. You're . . . you're so much like someone I used to know. Someone I lost."

It was the last thing she expected him to say. Something told her he wasn't talking about his wife. "A woman?"

"A young girl—a child, really."

The tenderness in his smile almost made her regret asking. She wasn't sure she wanted to know someone else other than his ex-wife had held a special place in his heart.

"Her name was Misty. She was sweet and generous and kind. Loyal to a fault. I used to tell her she couldn't be human, that she was a benevolent creature from another world."

Misty . . . a benevolent creature from another world. Without any reason, her pulse quickened. She heard the beats of her heart pulsating in her ears. Why was he telling her this?

She tried to talk but her mouth was dry. Her breathing came in short, fast gasps, just like when she woke up from one of her nightmares.

His voice cut through the fog in her brain. "Are you all right? You're shaking like a leaf."

"I . . . yes. I'm . . . just a bit dizzy," she said.

Before she realized his intentions, he'd lifted her in his arms and carried her closer to the water's edge, where he made her sit on the sand. Seconds later she felt something cool and wet against her temples. Richard was crouched next to her. He had removed his shoes and socks and obtained a makeshift compress from a strip torn off his shirt.

"I'm better now," she said. "Probably too much food and wine, and to top it off, that huge ice cream."

Her paltry excuse failed to assuage the worry in his eyes. "That didn't look like indigestion to me. Have you experienced this sort of thing before?"

She managed a smile. "No, Dr. Kelly," she lied. She could have told him about her nightly anxiety, how she'd be yanked from her sleep by restless, convoluted dreams she couldn't understand, but she was afraid he'd add "mentally unbalanced" to his already poor estimation of her. "I'm sorry, I didn't mean to ruin your last evening in St. Isabel," she added.

He pressed his lips together. "If anyone here is responsible for ruining anything, it's me. It's wrong for me to even be here, with you. I should never have come to St. Isabel."

She was shocked, confused as to why he thought coming to St. Isabel was a mistake. "No, it isn't wrong. I know it will sound crazy to you, but I knew from the first moment I saw you on Monks' Beach that you were meant to come."

For a moment he looked startled, then he turned his gaze away. "That's bogus, it's stuff that belongs in romance novels and fairy tales, and God knows I'm no Prince Charming."

A spark of rebellion igniting within her bolstered her sense of pride. "I haven't led a charmed life, if that's what you think, but I'm not a gullible small-town girl."

"That's not how I think of you," he said. His expression softened. "I don't know a lot about you, but I do know there's more to you than just an island girl with an obsessive dedication to her work."

She scrambled to her feet. "I'm tired of everyone wanting to protect me. Ever since I can remember I've been surrounded by family and friends whose primary mission in life is to make sure I'm safeguarded and protected."

"From what?" Richard asked.

She hesitated, doubting she could ever explain it, even to herself. "From myself, I suppose."

CHAPTER 30

RICHARD

S he stood ankle-deep in the water, oblivious to the rising surf swirling around the hem of her skirt and the intermittent gusts of wind playing havoc with her hair, now irremediably loose from the knot.

He covered her shoulders with his jacket. "Want to talk about it?" he asked gently.

She lowered her eyes. "I can't," she said in a hoarse whisper.

The painful note in those two simple words were a jarring reminder of the desolate, frightened little girl in a hospital room he'd known all those years ago.

What happened to you, Misty?

Had the memory of her abduction returned? Did she have some lasting effects of PTSD, he asked himself, or was it something else?

His pants legs were soaked up to his knees and clamping to his skin, but he didn't care. He found himself unable to resist wrapping his arms around her and holding her. He had thought of little else the entire evening. For all his cocky criticism of her army of guardian angels, he was feeling pretty protective himself, and maybe a little in love.

He'd scoffed at her claim his coming to St. Isabel was fated, but she wasn't that far off. He wondered how she would react if he were to tell her about the SoHo painting. How to explain the strange pull it had exerted over him without revealing the role he'd played in a particularly delicate part of her past?

He decided he was better off not knowing. His life was complicated enough, and he didn't want to risk complicating hers.

"Thank you for this."

"This?"

"For being here. For holding me."

"Isn't this what friends do . . . be there for each other?" He hoped, by underscoring the platonic nature of their relationship, to more effectively defuse any romantic notions she might still be harboring.

"You're different from any man I've ever known, you know that?"

He stiffened, not liking the direction this was going, but he felt a compulsion to ask, "How so?"

"For one, you're a brain surgeon, and a compassionate one, at that. That's rare."

She twisted around to face him and he saw the teasing glimmer in her eyes. "There's always Haynes, if it's the medical profession that tickles your fancy," he said.

She gave a disdainful sniff. "He's into orthopedics, not near as fascinating as delving inside a human brain. Besides, he doesn't like ice cream."

"Now, there's a serious turn-off."

"Not to mention he'd never sacrifice an expensive shirt to make a wet compress, let alone get his hand-tailored suit wet in the surf."

It was a Hugo Boss, but that was beside the point. He sighed, then held her away from him.

"Don't try to make me into some kind of ill-fated hero, a wretched soul you can coerce into redemption with your sweet talk and those perceptive eyes of yours. I'm not worth it."

"Is that what you think? That the reason I care for you is because I feel sorry for you?"

She cared for him. Though her admission hardly came as a surprise, it hit him hard.

"Clare . . ." he began, but she didn't give him the chance to continue.

She removed his jacket and handed it back to him. "Never mind. It's getting late and I have school tomorrow," she said, starting up the beach.

It was his fault, he thought. It never should have gone this far. He should've taken her home right after their dinner, as had been his initial plan, not indulge in romantic moonlit walks with a woman he had no right being with. He'd gone about it all wrong, sending off all the wrong vibes.

"Are you sure you don't want me to take you up to Monastery Hill?" he asked, when she asked him to drop her off at Serena.

"There's no need," she replied. "I plan on spending the night at the house. I'll get a ride from one of the staff in the morning."

"Then take my car." He handed her his key fob. "I'll have someone pick it up later in the day and return it to the rental place."

She hesitated for a few brief seconds, then took the key fob from him. "Thank you."

CHAPTER 31

RICHARD

When Richard set off for the mansion the next morning, drops of rain peppered the tiled courtyard, permeating the air with the scent of damp earth. He had woken up to a pewter sky and an even darker mood. All through the night, he hadn't dozed off for more than a few minutes at a time, unable to blot out the image of Clare standing on the steps of Serena with her shattered heart mirrored in her eyes.

No "goodbye" or "it's been nice knowing you," not even a vague nod that may or may not have left him with less of an empty feeling in his gut. But then, what had he expected? He'd hurt her feelings. He'd encouraged their friendship to keep his mind off his own troubles, disregarding the fact it could easily be misconstrued as something deeper, more personal. He should have ended it on Dolphin's End, made up some excuse—an emergency situation at home, an unexpected work-related commitment—something, but he'd wanted to bask in her special aura one last time, and he'd ended up tainting it. He'd bruised her spirit.

He stopped in midstride, surprised to see the Range Rover still parked where he'd left it the night before, the keys on the dashboard.

Clare must have decided to sleep in, he thought, a complication he hadn't anticipated.

He found Sonia serving breakfast in the solarium. She glanced up in surprise. "Richard, what brings you up so early? Will you be joining us for breakfast?" she asked.

"No, I had the usual from room service," he replied. He nodded to the other guests in greeting. Clare was nowhere in sight.

"That's too bad," Louise Van Patten said, looking disappointed. "We get to see so little of you around here I sometimes wonder if you're actually real or a figment of my imagination."

General Morris snickered from behind his morning paper, then mumbled something that sounded like, "Fancy Manhattan brain surgeons too hoity-toity to mix with a bunch of decrepit seniors."

"Now, James, there's no call to be rude," Rosemary Hathaway said to the older man.

"It's all right. The general is perfectly justified in feeling snubbed, considering my obvious lack of socialization skills. Besides, I owe you all an apology for not having been completely honest with you from the beginning."

Louise was quick to rise to his defense. "My dear young man, you have nothing to apologize for. There's nothing wrong with wanting to safeguard your privacy," she said.

He gave her a grateful smile. "Thank you,"

As if sensing there was a specific reason for his visit, Sonia gestured him to follow her into the hall. "Is everything all right?" she asked with patent apprehension.

"Everything's fine. I came to inform you I'm returning to New York today. I apologize for the short notice, but it was a last-minute decision."

"You're leaving? But . . . you're booked until the end of the month," Sonia said, obviously taken aback.

"I intend to settle the bill to cover the entire term of the agreement, of course."

She appeared a little affronted. "That won't be necessary. I'm just surprised you're cutting your visit short. Not bad news, I hope?"

"No, nothing like that, just some business to take care of."

"I understand. That's too bad. Next week I'm hosting the annual Preservation Society Gala Dinner at Serena and I was looking forward to having you along with the other guests. It's the island's most exciting and prestigious event of the year."

"I'm sorry to be missing such an important occasion," he said politely. In truth, he couldn't be more relieved he'd be spared just the kind of tedious affair he preferred to avoid.

Sonia placed a hand on his arm. "I hope you found what you came looking for in St. Isabel."

He stared into her perceptive blue eyes. "Let's just say it's . . . a work in progress," he replied.

"I'm glad to hear it. I wish you well wherever the next leg of your journey may take you."

He was touched by the genuine sympathy in her words. "Thank you. Also for talking some sense into me. If it weren't for you, I'd probably still be holed up in the cabin draining the resort's liquor reserves."

"You're welcome," she said smiling.

"I'd like to have a word with you in private before I go," he said.

She looked surprised. "Of course. Why don't we go into my office?"

He instinctively gazed toward the landing at the top of the grand staircase, almost expecting Clare to appear from one of the upstairs rooms. "Is Clare up? I'd rather she not hear what I have to say."

His host gave him a curious glance. "Clare doesn't live at Serena. I thought you knew that," she said.

It occurred to him she may not have been aware of her daughter's plan to stay overnight at the mansion. Clare hadn't gotten inside until well past midnight, probably long after her mother's bedtime.

He told her about his dinner with Clare and his suggestion she take his rental car to drive herself home the next day. "It was late when we got back from town and she probably didn't want to wake you."

Sonia gestured to a passing maid. "Lyla, have you seen Clare? Did she sleep in her old room last night?" she asked.

"No, ma'am. The room hasn't been slept in. I know because I was just in to vacuum," the maid replied.

"Please check if any of the property vehicles are missing," she instructed the maid. "Although, I can't imagine her borrowing one without telling me."

"Could she have called a cab?" Richard asked.

"Not likely. In St. Isabel only a life-threatening emergency or a natural catastrophe would drag a cabby from his bed in the middle of the night." Her tone was droll but something in the way she kept twisting the ring at her finger told him she was more troubled than she wanted to let on.

Just then the phone on her desk rang, and she rushed to pick it up. When she returned her face was waxy. "That was the monastery. They say Clare didn't show up for class and she's not answering her phone. They thought she might be here."

Every member of the household, houseguests included, was interrogated. No one, it seemed, had seen Clare since Saturday, when she'd left with Joey. Juan, the Cuban Jack-of-All-Trades, returned to confirm all the vehicles on the premises were accounted for.

By then Sonia wasn't even pretending to mask her agitation. He was beginning to feel a little uneasy himself, remembering how utterly dejected Clare had looked when they'd separated the previous night. "Is there anyone else she could have stayed with—a friend, perhaps?" he asked.

Sonia shook her head. "No, at least not in the immediate vicinity of Serena. Besides, she would have notified the monastery if she were going to be late. It's not like her to be careless."

"I'm sure there's no cause for concern," he tried to reassure her while ignoring the prickly feeling at the base of his skull. "She's probably still somewhere on Serena's grounds and lost track of time."

As if a switch had been flipped in front of her, Sonia's eyes lit up. "Of course—the studio. Heavens, why didn't I think of it before?"

Less than sixty seconds later, Richard dashed through the pavilion doors several strides ahead of Sonia. He was immediately assaulted by the odor of mildew and oil paint he'd come to associate with Clare's work environment. Sure enough, there she was, just as Sonia had predicted. She lay stretched out on the sofa, still wearing the clothes she'd worn the night before, seemingly fast asleep. Her hair cascaded in adorable disarray over the armrest, while a book rested open on her gently heaving chest, indicating she'd fallen asleep while reading. Prior to that she had been drawing, as evidenced by the sketchpad abandoned on the rug next to the sofa. It was a charcoal sketch of him, one so surprisingly accurate it caused him to do a mental double take. It was a rather unkempt rendition of him, he had to admit, with his disheveled appearance, windblown hair, and jacket flung over one shoulder, but what kept him staring was the look on his face, one he wasn't used to seeing in the mirror. It was the face of a happy man, one without a care in the world.

Sonia barged into the pavilion almost knocking the door off its hinges in her eagerness to reach her daughter. The noise startled Clare awake, and her eyes sprang open.

"Mom . . . Richard?" she murmured, sitting up.

"Clare, honey, you gave us all such a scare," her mother said, one hand splayed over her heart, the other clutching a dripping umbrella, still opened. "What are you doing sleeping out here? Did you forget your keys? You could have rung even if it was late. You know I wouldn't have minded."

"Keys?" Clare sat upright, still looking groggy and disoriented. The book slid off her chest tumbling onto the rug with a soft thud. She checked her wristwatch. "Oh, no, I'm late for school."

Richard automatically stepped forward to pick the book off the floor. For a moment he remained there, his gaze fixed on the object that had slipped from the pages of the book.

A fake sprig of Christmas holly. It was the one he had given her that long-ago Christmas Eve. She had kept it all this time.

CHAPTER 32

RICHARD

Sonia held the photograph of Misty in front of her, her expression shocked, confused. "How did you get this?" she asked Richard.

"I've been carrying it around for seventeen years. It was taken when Misty—Clare was staying with the Mallorys before you found her."

She removed her reading glasses and placed them on the desk. Her face was unnaturally pale, her lips trembling slightly. "The Mallorys. Yes, I remember. The doctor who followed Clare's case when she was in the hospital. He and his wife had her in their custody."

Oh, and by the way, they made sure she didn't lack for anything she most likely was lacking before, he was tempted to say, but he held his tongue.

"But . . ." Her eyes were clouded with suspicion when she raised them to his. "Why do you have it?"

"I was one of three students renting an apartment in the Mallorys' building. I was the one who saw Clare for the first time in Lancey's Superstore, before the accident occurred. Dr. Mallory was my former guardian. We were all very close to Misty."

But he knew it wasn't what she was asking. "Clare isn't the reason I'm here. That is, she is—indirectly . . ."

"I don't understand."

He told her about the painting he'd come across in New York and his spur-of-the-moment decision to trace it back to the island. "I didn't know it was hers until I saw similar ones in her studio. When I met Clare for the first time, I immediately noticed a resemblance to Misty, but I didn't realize it was her until I saw the scar on her temple. She was very self-conscious about that scar. What I find bewildering," he continued looking probingly into her confused eyes, "is that she doesn't remember me at all."

Sonia's expression tensed. "I can't say it surprises me. Clare remembers nothing after she was taken from us. At first, she didn't even remember us—her family. Her memory returned gradually, and even then, much of it was missing. We were told it was most likely psychological, her brain's way of dealing with the trauma, and that it would eventually come back. But so far it hasn't."

"Did she ever remember the details of her abduction?"

"No, not a single thing. It was frustrating to say the least. The slightest detail would have gone a long way in helping the police track down her kidnapper. Nothing was ever found, and it was filed away as a cold case." Her lips pressed down into a thin line. "It scares me to know that monster is still out there, perhaps still preying on other young victims."

"I'm sorry for what you and your family went through," he said. "I meant to tell you as soon as I realized who Clare was, but I didn't know how you'd take it. I wasn't sure I should even be here."

It was clear the fear and anxiety still plagued her, even after all this time. "No, I'm glad you came, and thank you for being sincere. Does . . . Does Clare know?"

"No."

He thought she'd ask why he hadn't told her, but she didn't. He wouldn't have known what to say. Instinct? Self-preservation?

"Tell me more about Clare's paintings. I wasn't aware she was doing abstracts. It's not her usual style."

"They're certainly unusual. They obviously represent something, but the message is unclear. I can only describe them as images as they would appear in a dream, perhaps, or in the mind of someone who can't quite put the broken pieces of a memory together."

"Do you think she may be experiencing flashbacks after all this time?"

"It's possible. Some lost memories can take years to return. Some never do," he replied.

"She's never said anything to me."

"Most likely she doesn't want you to worry," he suggested. He remembered something about the paintings that had stood out to him. "Has Clare ever owned a dog, perhaps even before her disappearance?"

"A dog?" Sonia repeated puzzled. "No. Why do you ask?"

"The vague characteristics of the images reproduced in those paintings all differ, except for one common element. The silhouette of a dog."

"How peculiar," she said.

When she grew quiet, he asked, "Do you feel like telling me what happened in Maine?"

For several seconds he thought she'd refuse. She rose from the chair and went to open the patio doors. It had stopped raining and the sun was pushing through the receding clouds. She stared out into the garden, as if the beads of rainwater shimmering off the leaves of the flowering bushes hid the secrets of the past.

"We were spending Christmas with my sister in Floralport, the small town in Maine where I grew up. Edward, my husband, stayed behind in St. Isabel to take care of business. Elizabeth—Lizzie, as we called her—had been fighting a long battle with lymphoblastic leukemia and was finally starting to show signs of remission."

She resumed her place at her desk, her gaze murky with the pain of remembering. "On Christmas Eve, on our way back from the hospital where Lizzie had undergone her final chemotherapy session, Courtney called me on my cell phone to tell me she couldn't find Clare. She sounded frantic, almost incoherent. She and Clare had been playing near the lighthouse not far from my sister's home, an area known as Puffin Top, but they got into a squabble and Clare ran off. When Courtney returned home, Clare wasn't there."

She rubbed her hands over her arms, as if feeling the chill of that long-ago winter. "We searched everywhere for her, until finally we called 9-1-1. The police's response was immediate. They initiated an extensive search of the area, interrogating the town people in the hope someone had seen her. No one had caught so much as a glimpse of Clare after she ran away from Courtney. There were no signs of a struggle up on the bluff or around the house, no clues indicating she'd been taken away forcibly. My husband rushed to Floralport, and with the help of volunteers we organized our own search party. For an entire day and night we combed the area inch by inch but found no clue. The next morning search dogs found her parka, the one she'd been wearing the day she disappeared. It had caught on some saplings growing out of the cliff wall, a few feet below the ledge. The discovery pointed to the fact she had ventured too close to the edge of the cliff and had fallen over. They said my baby . . ." Her voice faltered and cracked, ". . . my miracle child had fallen into the cold ocean and that her body had most likely been washed away by the currents."

The chilling verdict produced a shiver along Richard's spine.

Sonia bit her lip in an apparent struggle to regain composure, then continued. "Still, we refused to lose hope. We latched onto the possibility, however slim, that the parka being in such an odd location was simply a coincidence, and that she could still be out there somewhere, perhaps lost. Also, her favorite doll was missing, the one she never separated herself from. It was quite possible she had ventured too far inland and lost her way in the woods, but less than forty-eight hours later even that last hope was shattered. They retrieved the doll. It had washed up on a rocky stretch of beach miles down shore."

Her voice faded to a raspy whisper, and her shoulders sagged a little more. "They told us there was absolutely no way a child could have plummeted from a height of seventy-five feet and not be crushed on the shallow rocks. That's when they abandoned the search on land and sent divers into the water to find her body. But of course, they never did."

Richard slowly released the breath he wasn't aware he'd been holding. They'd stopped looking for Misty, all because of a few personal items they'd retrieved.

"I remember asking myself over and over why it couldn't have been Clare's body instead of that silly rag doll. Then at least we'd have some closure, a grave to weep on, and perhaps Ed would still be alive today. My husband never recovered from the pain of losing Clare. He had a weak heart and passed away less than a month after she disappeared, never knowing his daughter was alive. Even then, I couldn't bring myself to go back home. I couldn't tear myself away from Floralport. It was as if something kept me there, hoping, for what I didn't know. When I received the call from James Morgan about the possible link with a girl found in Manhattan, I realized that deep down in my heart I'd known all along she was still alive."

"I'm sorry," was all Richard could say. The woman had suffered too deeply for him to feel any residual anger toward her.

She looked at him. "You said you were the first one to notice her in the department store." He nodded. "How did she look? Did she appear frightened? I read the report but at the time I was too concerned with Clare's wellbeing to think about anything else."

"Not particularly. I remember thinking she looked a little out of place, bundled up in a heavy blue coat. She seemed overdressed for the warmth of a crowded store."

"Did you say blue?"

"Yes, one of those downy things, with white fur around the edges. Why?" he asked.

She was silent for a moment, deep in thought. "I just thought . . . Her jacket was found on the cliff. Whoever took her must have provided her with a new one."

Richard hadn't thought of that. In retrospect, it had been a little too large on her. He didn't know what had happened to it after she was rushed to the hospital.

"Did she . . . While she was with the Mallorys, did she ever show signs of missing her family?"

He couldn't help thinking her concern was past overdue. "No, not that she let on." He stared at her squarely. "Clare was never unhappy while in their care, if that's what you're implying. They couldn't have loved her more if she were their own flesh and blood."

Her chin went up. "She was living as someone else's child, with strangers who weren't related to her."

"People who came to her rescue, whom she learned to trust," he couldn't help rebutting. "A surrogate family who gave her an identity when she didn't have one, and a safe haven when the only other alternative would have been staying with strangers."

He realized his mistake when he saw the flash of anger in her eyes. "She was hardly abandoned. She had a family, a real family who believed she'd died and who mourned her loss. For heaven's sake, we had a *funeral*."

Her words broke on a choked sob, and all at once Richard understood. It wasn't just sorrow and anger at the core of Sonia's emotional outburst. It was also guilt, guilt for believing her ten-year-old daughter had died in a tragic accident, for having given up on her. Dredging up old memories he'd long kept buried had reawakened his old resentment toward Misty's absentee family, and for a moment he'd been a nineteen-year-old again, angry at the injustices of life.

"Forgive me, I didn't mean to judge you," he said.

Sonia recomposed herself. "No, I should be the one apologizing. It was wrong of me to disregard your former guardian and his wife after Clare was returned to me. They must think me so ungrateful, so unappreciative of their generosity, but it couldn't be farther from the truth. You see, I wasn't very rational at the time. My only focus was getting Clare away from the place where it had all happened and back to St. Isabel, away from the media frenzy that had developed around the case. I should have at least thanked them for taking care of Clare and for making sure she was rightly compensated for the store owners' negligence. The settlement from the lawsuit enabled me to set up a sizeable trust fund in Clare's name, and it was possible thanks to Dr. Mallory's timely intervention."

She blinked the moisture from her eyes. "The first few months were difficult for her as well as for us. She seemed to have lost touch with all memory related to her disappearance. She plunged into a state of depression, retreating deeper and deeper into herself. She was always so shuttered, so disconnected from everything and everyone, it broke my heart. Some experts believed it might help if her memory of the kidnapping returned, but it never did, no matter what they tried."

"What about psychotherapy? Excellent results have been obtained with hypnosis and drugs," he said.

She made a dismissive gesture with her hand. "Hypnosis, psychodynamic therapy, stress-management sessions, you name it—we tried them all. She hated all the poking and prodding and it only served to cause her more distress. I couldn't bear to see her suffer, so I finally put a stop to all the treatments. There was no point in trying to resuscitate memories she obviously had no desire to reacquaint herself with. It was time to put the past behind us and allow her to adjust naturally, and eventually she did."

"Did she?" he asked. "She's painting strange portraits she doesn't want anyone to see. Do you really believe she's gotten over it?"

Her expression tensed. "What are you saying?" she asked.

"I'm saying she wants to remember. Perhaps it's what she needs to get closure. I happen to agree with the experts you hired. Talk to her, have her confide in you."

"I'm afraid to reawaken her old fears. I hate that whoever did that to her got away with it, but what if remembering her abductor's face causes a setback? I couldn't handle it, not again."

"Clare isn't ten years old anymore. She can handle it," he said.

She reached to clutch his arm. "You won't tell her, will you?"

"No, not if you don't want me to. But I can't keep it from the Mallorys. They haven't stopped thinking about her and often wonder how she is. They, too, deserve to get closure."

"Of course, I understand. Would you consider staying a little longer? You and Clare seem to have developed a good friendship, which can only mean that deep down she still feels the connection and knows she can trust you. Perhaps your being here is just what Clare needs to find the missing parts."

She suddenly appeared more animated. "Better yet, invite Dr. and Mrs. Mallory to come to Serena. A little reunion might help shake things up inside her head, in which case I'll be grateful for your support. They can stay here as my guests, and I'll make sure they have plenty of opportunity to get to know Clare."

Richard hadn't quite expected that. "You want Max and Mary to come here?"

A definite glow of anticipation had replaced the angst in Sonia's eyes, as she warmed up to her own idea. He could tell her mind was already working out the logistics. "Is there any reason they can't travel?" she asked.

"Not that I'm aware of."

"Well, then, it's settled. I'll have Clare's old rooms converted into a guest suite. I'll make sure they're very comfortable here."

She chuckled with girlish enthusiasm. "I know I'm getting ahead of myself, but I look forward to making their acquaintance. I'd like to have the opportunity to make amends and thank them in person for keeping Clare safe." She leaned forward to squeeze his arm. "You will stay a while longer, won't you? At least for a few days?"

Suddenly, everything he'd been feeling prior to finding Clare in the pavilion rushed back, yanking him back to the thorny reality of his situation. Clare was the reason he'd decided to cut his stay short in the first place, the reason he needed to get away. As happy as he was to have found Misty, he wasn't sure he could face Clare again.

"Please, Richard, I couldn't do it without your support." He felt cornered. Even knowing he was going to regret his decision he said, "Fine, I'll stay, but only for a few days."

CHAPTER 33

RICHARD

The day had turned out nothing like Richard had planned. He should have been back in Manhattan. Instead, he was still here, still running off his stress on the beach.

He'd walked right into his host's trap. If only he'd had the guts to confess having severed all ties with her younger daughter, he might have avoided it, but her heartfelt plea had rendered him powerless to resist. On the upside, Max and Mary had been ecstatic when he'd conveyed the news to them. He doubted they'd fully understood how he'd discovered her whereabouts, but they'd been delighted to accept Sonia's invitation to spend a week at Serena. Where his benefactor was concerned, he hadn't exactly been a model of appreciation, these past months. Reuniting him and Mary with Misty was the best way he could make it up to them. The couple hadn't seemed overly put out by the secrecy caveat Sonia had imposed on them. The prospect of seeing Misty again and knowing she was happy in her little island alcove was enough reassurance for them.

It's going to be a long week, he thought, as he entered the cabin.

A shower and some aspirin might do him good. The lingering exhaustion and gritty eyes reminded him he hadn't gotten much rest last night.

Peeling off his sweat-drenched T-shirt, he stepped into the cool interior. Ready to strip, he froze with his fingers hooked on the elastic band of his trunks. Courtney Elliot was sprawled nonchalantly on his bed, arms folded behind her head.

"Please, don't stop now. The fun was only just beginning," she drawled, observing him unabashedly from beneath her long black lashes.

"What the—how did you get in here?"

"The door was open," she replied. She stretched languorously rubbing her cheek on the pillow. "Uhmm . . . I'm guessing Dolce & Gabbana's. Very manly."

She sat up, stifling a yawn with the back of her hand. "I thought all New Yorkers lock their doors as a habit when they leave the house."

Since his first days at Serena, he'd gotten into the habit of not paying attention to basic urban precautions such as personal security. Now he regretted his negligence.

He didn't bother to mask his annoyance. "I was under the impression the resort was real big on privacy. Obviously I was mistaken."

She swung her legs over the side of the bed and undulated over to him in a cat-like gait. "You disappoint me, Dr. Kelly," she chided. "I thought you'd appreciate the warm welcome."

The healthy male in him focused on the tight white top she wore, the bottom edge of which didn't quite meet the belt of her low-riding skirt.

She arched toward him and trailed her cool fingers lightly over his bare chest, looking at him with indolent eyes. "I came to deliver a message and when I realized the door was unlocked I decided to wait for you inside where it's cooler," she explained casually, as if crashing guests' lodgings was a normal everyday practice for her.

His gaze fell on the half-full glass of amber liquid on the bedside table. "Seems you didn't have a problem making yourself at home in my absence," he said wryly.

She made a face. "Don't you have anything stronger than ginger ale in this place?"

"No," he replied curtly, and angled away. He went to the compact refrigerator where he took out a can of the soft drink for himself. After taking a long swig, he asked, "To what do I owe this unexpected visit?"

"My mother would like you to dine at the house tonight. The newlyweds are leaving tomorrow, and she thought it would be nice if everyone was there for their last dinner with us."

"No point in going out of your way to convey a message when there's a state-of-the-art phone system complete with voicemail in here intended for that purpose," he pointed out.

"True, but I had some time to kill so I decided to do the honors in person. Besides, it was time well spent. Amazing what you can pick up about a man's habits just from studying his living environment."

The brittleness in her tone made the back of his neck tingle. "What, did I forget to pick up my dirty laundry off the floor?" he asked mockingly.

"On the contrary. Everything is in perfect order," she said, making a sweeping gesture with her arm to encompass the tidy interior. "Clothes neatly folded, personal items perfectly organized. Not a thing out of place."

She strolled over to open the wall closet, displaying his scant wardrobe. "You also have a good sense of color coordination, besides having an excellent taste in fine clothing and shoes. I usually find neat-freaks boring, but I have a weakness for men who know how to dress. I could easily pass over a neatness flaw for sense of style," she added, throwing him a meaningful glance.

He wondered where she was going with this little charade of hers, but he wasn't amused. Knowing she'd been through his personal things irritated the heck out of him.

"You're a regular Nancy Drew," he drawled, intentionally making metaphorical use of the fictional teenage sleuth to highlight Courtney's very juvenile conduct, one unbefitting the head of a multimillion-dollar corporation.

He'd noticed her attitude toward him had cooled off considerably since beach night, whether due to his having lied about his profession or his liaison with Clare.

She simply smirked and walked over to the desk, riffling idly through his work papers. "I may be nosy but you're a complete disaster when it comes to guarding your precious space. You should be more vigilant. You never know who might come rummaging through your things and uncover your dirty little secrets," she said.

He curled his fingers around the empty soda can and squeezed, feeling a powerful urge to do the same with Courtney's graceful neck. He tossed the can into the wastebasket. "That's why I'm paying top dollar, so I can enjoy the solitary freedom I was promised. I'm seriously considering placing a complaint with the management."

She laughed. "That would be a little awkward, don't you think, since I *am* the management? A minor constituent, perhaps, nonetheless with some leverage."

"Why are you really here, Courtney?" he asked.

"I told you. To invite you to the house for dinner. But then I found this."

She held up some of the papers from the pile next to his laptop. She wasn't smiling anymore. "For one who places so much value on personal space, you don't seem to have any regard for that of other people's."

He glanced sharply at her. "Excuse me?"

In response she began to read from one of the pages.

"*Severe retrograde amnesia for autobiographical events caused by sudden trauma to the brain is comparatively rare, though over the past two decades several cases have been reported. In contrast to disease-related RA, as, for example, in—*"

"I know what it says. What's your point?"

Her expression made it clear she wasn't playing anymore. "My point, *Professor*, is you're a fraud. You may think you have everyone fooled, my mother included, but you don't fool me."

He stared at her in bafflement. "What on earth are you talking about?"

"I'm talking about your research on amnesia. The long overdue textbook you finally set out to finish? It seems my sister caused quite a stir this morning, when everyone thought she'd made another disappearing act. When I heard from the other guests how my mother was conferring with you privately in her office, I knew it had to do with what happened to Clare as a child." She lasered him with a cold stare. "Tell me, is my mother in on this little scheme of yours or did you plan it out all on your own?"

He realized she thought he was here for Clare, to do research on her condition. "You're obviously under a grave misconception," he said. "My book deals with the cognitive behavior of the brain. You happened to read a reference to memory loss caused by physical damage to the brain. Clare has nothing to do with it."

Clare, perhaps, but not Misty. Misty had everything to do with it. It was because of her he'd specialized in traumatic brain injury, but Courtney was accusing him of something entirely different, and he wouldn't let it get to him.

She raised her chin. "Oh, please, don't expect me to believe you don't have a vested interest in her case, that you didn't leap at the opportunity to get a firsthand shot at studying a condition as rare as hers."

"Frankly, I don't care what you believe," he said.

"Admit it, you came to St. Isabel hoping to learn more about what happened to Clare. She was the missing chapter in your book. Everything else was just a cover up, wasn't it?"

It occurred to him to tell her the truth, just to set the record straight. But his gut told him it wouldn't be a wise move, regardless of his promise to Sonia.

He stared at her stonily. "I repeat, Clare has nothing to do with my coming to St. Isabel, and neither has Sonia. I had no knowledge of Clare's memory loss until earlier today, when your mother happened to mention it."

"Happened to mention it, did she? How perfectly convenient," she said.

Her cold attitude went up a notch. "I warned you before, my sister isn't as strong as she appears to be. That phase of her life was very traumatic for her, and she's had a hard time putting it all behind her. Your meddling will only hurt her."

Something stirred inside him, something resembling the vengeful force that had provoked him to lash out at Sonia earlier that day. "My, my, is that concern I detect in your warning?"

Fury flashed in Courtney's eyes. "She's my sister. I care about her."

"Really? Weren't you perhaps a little disappointed when she suddenly turned up again after you thought she'd died?"

He didn't see the hand coming, though he should have expected it. His question was intended to provoke but its implication was beyond insulting, and he almost welcomed the hot sting that brought him to his senses. "I'm sorry. That was a cruel thing to say," he said, seeing her tear-filled eyes.

It was the first time he noticed any display of emotion from Courtney and it made him feel lousy. "Damn it, I said I'm sorry," he repeated as a tear spilled onto her cheek. Out of sheer remorse he brushed it away with his thumb. Immediately she mistook his gesture for a weakening of his resolve to keep her at a distance, and she leaned toward him. Something hard and brutal took hold of him, and before he could stop himself, he pulled her up against him and crushed his mouth down hard on hers.

It was a knee-jerk reaction, but something else as well. It was a desperate hunger he hadn't been able to appease when he'd left Clare standing on Serena's doorstep, a hunger so consuming he could, for just a moment, imagine they were Clare's lips beneath his, willing and pliant, Clare's warm skin he touched as his hands curled around her naked midriff. The illusion lasted only a few heartbeats of pure insanity, and he quickly released her, filled with self-disgust.

Courtney staggered a little, then regained her footing. "Well, that was . . . nice," she said breathlessly, once again dry-eyed and glowing with triumph.

Ignoring her he went to the door and held it open. "I'd like to take my shower, now, if you don't mind."

The scorn was back in her eyes as she brushed past him. "I'm warning you, Kelly, if you do anything to upset either my mother or Clare, I'll make sure your already shaky reputation is ruined for good. In the meantime," she added flashing him a falsely sweet smile, "think about that invitation to dinner."

205

CHAPTER 34

RICHARD

He watched Clare from beyond the white picket fence. She stood in the middle of a vegetable patch, set against a backdrop of ripening pear tomatoes, lush zucchini vines, and fat green beans, looking adorably disheveled, as if the task she'd been engrossed in had been long and arduous.

His hand froze on the latch that held the gate closed.

"Hi," he said.

"Hi," she echoed, dusting dirt off her hands. "I didn't expect to see you again."

He couldn't tell from her expression if she was pleased to see him. "There's been a last-minute change of plans. My former guardian and his wife have decided to take a long-overdue vacation and I thought a few days at Serena might do them good. They've asked me to stay a little longer to be with them."

He felt like a jerk for lying. It seemed all he did since coming to St. Isabel was lie.

"How nice," she said, appearing genuinely pleased.

He pointed his gaze over her shoulder. "Planning on opening a produce stand?"

"No, just eating healthier. Besides, the nuns never refuse the odd basket of tomatoes or squash."

She eyed his hand still glued to the gate post. "It's unlocked. All you have to do is lift the latch and push. Don't worry, I promise not to attempt at your virtue."

To his annoyance, he flushed. She always managed to knock the breath out of him with her random directness.

He tried to conjure up the little girl whose spontaneity and innocence had captured his heart, but the woman whose lingering gaze taunted him across the walkway had nothing of Misty. As she pushed at some loose tendrils of hair with her forearm, the instinctive, uncalculated movement caused her blouse to stretch suggestively across her breasts, a brutal reminder of the soft mature curves he'd held in his arms just hours ago. He didn't know which was stronger, the urge to blurt out the truth and recapture the familiarity so brusquely interrupted all those years ago, or the desire to take her in his arms and kiss that smirk off her face. Both would go a long way in tempering his urges, but neither was an option.

She tipped her chin in the direction of the road. "Was that the general's Lincoln that just drove away?"

He removed his sunglasses and slipped them inside his shirt pocket. "It was." He'd almost had to strong-arm the man into giving him a ride. The old codger was still sore about his posing as a mystery writer. "I helped him change a flat tire and he repaid the favor by dropping me off."

She dropped her gaze. "About last night . . . I'm not usually that bold around men."

He suppressed a smile. "I didn't think you were."

She reached for a wayward branch of wisteria and tucked it among the tangle of green and purple vines lining the latticed arbor. "I'm sorry about this morning. I hadn't planned on falling asleep in the pavilion, but I started drawing and time got away from me."

He guessed the intense rosy shade of her cheeks wasn't entirely a product of the activity she had been engaged in. "I imagine my mother told you the whole wretched story of my abduction."

"Yes," he said, relieved she'd broached the subject first.

Her lips tightened. "I figured as much when I saw you follow her in her office."

"She confided in me as a friend, something I'd have expected you to do. You may be a good hand at getting people to open up—maybe throwing in a little back rub as a bonus, but when it comes to disclosing your personal demons, you're pretty much a closed book."

She paled visibly at his deliberate allusion to what had happened on Dolphin's End. "Did you think the fact there's a blank spot in your memory would make me think less of you?" he asked more gently.

"No, of course not."

"Then talk to me about it."

Not surprisingly, she closed up. "What's the point? I'm sure my mother pretty much covered all the basics."

He decided to be brutally honest. "I'd be lying if I said learning about your background didn't arouse my professional interest. I'm a trauma specialist, after all, and sometimes a head injury can lead to memory loss. But this has nothing to do with my credentials. I thought we'd come far enough in our friendship to warrant your trust."

She laughed shortly. "What friendship, the one you were so nonchalantly turning your back on only last night?"

He flinched as if she had slapped him. "Clare . . ."

She dug a hand in the pocket of her shorts and pulled out a key fob. "Thank you for letting me borrow the car," she said, handing it to him.

He hesitated, reluctant to take his cue and leave. Suddenly there was so much he wanted to tell her, like how sorry he was for not dedicating more time to her seventeen years ago, for not having expressed all the little ways she'd filled his life with meaning while he'd had the opportunity, but he just nodded and turned away.

CHAPTER 35

CLARE

S he had just finished applying a second coat of base paint to a terra-cotta planter when she heard the sound of an approaching vehicle. She carefully set the paintbrush aside and turned just in time to see Courtney's silver Miata pull up to the curb and stop with a squeal of tires. In the six months since Clare had moved to the Hill, her sister had visited only once, and it was to help her with the move. As far as Courtney was concerned, this part of the island was the boondocks and rarely ventured far from town, unless it was to visit the mainland. Suddenly, the little flowering corner of paradise Clare had so proudly managed to restore to its original glory seemed dull and ordinary.

"Well, isn't this something," Courtney said with what sounded like genuine appreciation. "This garden has certainly come a long way since poor Mrs. Parsons stopped taking care of it."

In another occasion Clare would have reminded her sister "poor Mrs. Parsons" had been unable to take care of her beloved garden due to her advanced arthritis, but she was left momentarily speechless. She couldn't remember the last time her sister had said anything remotely flattering to her. She appeared not to notice the sad and battered cherub with the broken wing she'd salvaged from the wreckage left by last fall's devastating hurricane or the rusted wrought-iron bench she hadn't yet found the time to revamp.

"And this little fishpond is just darling," Courtney said, admiring the showpiece of the entire garden and Clare's pride and joy. "I just love the pebble-stone design all around the perimeter. Did you put it in yourself?"

"Yes, though the pond was already there," Clare said, trying to sound blasé. "It was in a sad state of neglect, practically buried in dead leaves and brambles. I cleaned it up and spruced it up a bit. The monastery's maintenance crew helped out with the heavy part."

Her sister was, as usual, impeccably dressed in a cream-colored silk business suit and elegant pumps, causing her to feel shabby and unkempt. She slipped off her work gloves and tossed them aside, then smoothed her hands over her shorts. "Why don't we go inside? It's suffocating out here," she said.

Not waiting for a response, she led the way into the cottage. With its old creaky floors and garage sales furnishings, it wasn't the ultra-modern apartment her sister kept in Miami for when she tired of island life. Clare loved her little house in the country and wouldn't have traded places with her. It was quaint and cozy, and most importantly, exclusively hers.

Courtney's expression was impassive as her gaze swept the ambiance. She studied the vintage lace runner on the antique sideboard Clare had bid for and won on eBay. "You have a knack for finding the most extraordinary things," Courtney said. "I couldn't tell a nineteenth century Victorian doily from a dollar-store variety placemat."

Clare wasn't sure whether to consider it a compliment but murmured her thanks all the same. "Can I get you something? Iced tea, lemonade?" she asked.

"No, thank you. I can't stay long. I haven't seen you since the beach party, and I wanted to apologize for being so hard on you. I tend to forget you're a mature, self-sufficient adult."

Something told Clare there was more to the impromptu visit than a belated attack of remorse. Courtney had never felt the need to apologize to her. "Apology accepted," she said, hoping they could put the issue at rest.

But her sister refused to drop the subject. "To be completely honest, I was a tad jealous," she admitted, having the grace to look sheepish. "After all, we don't get too many handsome bachelors at Serena."

Clare stiffened. This wasn't a social call at all, she realized. Courtney hadn't come here to apologize; she'd come to talk about Richard.

"Richard Kelly is hardly a bachelor," she said.

"He's divorced, and as such, available—a fact he didn't waste any time using to his advantage," Courtney said. Softening, she reached out and took her hand. "I don't want you to think I'm being meddlesome. I'm just looking out for you. I can tell you have a soft spot for him, but what do you really know about him?"

"I know he's a good man, a highly respected one," Clare said. She wasn't about to discuss Richard's private matters, especially not with Courtney.

Courtney sighed, her expression pained. "I wish it didn't have to come to this, but under the circumstances, it's only right I tell you."

"Tell me what?" Clare asked.

Courtney's fingers tightened around hers. "Sweetie, the man's a fraud. An impostor."

Clare stared at her. "What? If this is about—"

"I'm not referring to his hiding his identity. Think about it. A prominent brain surgeon in the prime of his life—a neuroscience professor, for heaven's sake, who suddenly drops everything to hole up on an obscure little island, allegedly to work on a medical book. Doesn't it sound a little bit strange to you?"

Clare cut her a searing glance. "Are you implying the book is a lie? That it doesn't really exist?"

"Oh, the book exists," Courtney said, "and, believe me, it says a lot about our illustrious guest."

"What do you mean?" Clare asked, not liking the ominous tone of her sister's words.

"It's a study of the cognitive behavior of the brain—which incorporates, of all things, a very informative well-referenced section on amnesia."

Clare's heart ceased to beat. She had to grip the armrests to steady herself because the room had suddenly started spinning all around her. "Amnesia . . ."

Courtney's eyes filled with sympathy. "Oh, honey, don't you see? You're the reason he came to St. Isabel. He made up a story just so he could come here and study your case from up close."

Clare fought for breath. "Does . . . does Mom know?" she asked, forcing the words through the painful knot in her throat.

"I don't know, but it wouldn't surprise me if she did. He may have charmed his way into her head and somehow managed to get her to back him up in this unscrupulous scheme of his."

Clare's mind flashed back to the previous weeks, trying to remember if she'd missed something. Had he been studying her all this time, gauging her behavior, observing how someone who'd lost a piece of her life went about her daily routine? Had everything else been a lie?

She told herself there was absolutely no way Richard could have faked his grief that day on Dolphin's End, when he'd told her about the unborn child his ex-wife had cruelly disposed of. Someone with his unshakable reserve could never forge that deep an emotion, but suddenly she wasn't sure of anything.

She felt hollow inside, as if something in her had shriveled and died. "How did you find out?" she asked.

Courtney looked genuinely uncomfortable for the first time as she told Clare about the papers she'd found on Richard's desk.

"You mean you broke into his cabin?" Clare asked aghast.

"No . . . well, not exactly. The door was open, so technically it wasn't a break in. I was delivering a message and when I saw he wasn't there, I decided to do a little snooping around. He never would have known if he'd turned out clean as a whistle."

"You actually confronted him about it?"

"You bet, I did. Gave him a piece of my mind, too. If it were up to me, he'd be packing his bags and leaving right now. I don't know what kind of hold he has over our mother, but I intend to find out. I just thought you deserved to know the truth before you did something stupid like fall for him."

If only she knew just how incredibly stupid I am, Clare thought.

"Thank you," she said, not sure whether she was thanking her for opening her eyes or for exposing Richard as a fraud.

"Just doing my sisterly duty," Courtney said with a smile.

Clare followed her to the door like an automaton, rigid with pain and disappointment. "I wouldn't worry Mom with this just yet," Courtney said. "She'd be very upset if she were to find out I've been poking around one of her guests' private quarters. She wouldn't understand, even if I were to swear it was for a good cause."

"Don't worry, I have no intention of telling her or anyone else," Clare reassured her.

She stood numbly as Courtney gave her a parting hug. "Don't look so glum. The man's not worth losing sleep over. Turns out he's not only a fraud but a bit of a player, too." Her lashes fluttered dreamily as she let out a mournful sigh. "Darn shame, though, for such a great kisser."

CHAPTER 36

RICHARD

If someone had told him he'd one day be sitting with an amateur psychic while she told him something he already knew—like how screwed up his life was—he'd have thought they were crazy. He needed a shrink, not a palm reader.

"A dominant hand—as a surgeon's hands should be," Rosemary Hathaway said, studying Richard's palm with such fervent anticipation, as if she was about to uncover the secrets of the universe. "But then, a hand that has performed medical miracles can only be a strong and capable one."

She traced her thumb over the pronounced line that from the curve formed by his thumb and index finger stretched across the palm almost to the opposite edge. "You have a long and well defined 'head' line, which indicates a tendency to think things through very carefully before making an important decision. You always weigh your options and want to know what you're up against. That's a very important trait, for one in your line of work."

He held back a snort. He certainly hadn't lived up to his remarkable head line last night, when he'd decided to take a trip to Monastery Hill after the two messages he'd left on Clare's voicemail had gone unanswered. He couldn't shake off the feeling something was wrong.

"I see many cross-hatch lines here, between those representing your life and your work," Rosemary was saying. "Marks like these typically conceal a long-lasting desire for something visceral—an unfulfilled passion, perhaps?"

She chuckled when she caught the dismay on his face. "Never mind, that was a rhetorical question," she reassured him, and returned to scrutinizing his hand. "Your success line, on the other hand, is more distinctive. It appears remarkably strong, but ending as it does at the head line, it suggests you'll probably lose your way somewhere between thirty and forty years old." Her face darkened with consternation. "Oh, dear, I believe we've already come to that difficult crossroads, haven't we, love?"

Her allusion to his recent downfall wasn't lost on him, but it wasn't his failed career he was concerned about right now. It was discovering a vulnerability he didn't know he had.

He'd recognized the man the instant he'd stepped out of the sleek sports vehicle parked in front of Clare's house. It was Paul Haynes, the mayor's son. From the cover of darkness, he'd watched Paul walk around to the passenger side and open the door for Clare—a happy, laughing Clare. Then the two had disappeared inside the house, closing the door behind them.

The memory still hounded him. He hadn't recognized it at first, this bitter-sweet ache in his gut that wouldn't let up. This *neediness*. His entire life he'd only known the need to survive, to learn, to succeed. The need to rise above all things negative. But this . . . this raw, gut-wrenching craving was something completely new to him, and it scared him.

"Oh, dear, your hand has turned ice cold, and no wonder. Men don't like it when their weaker traits are brought out into the open, do they? And do stop fidgeting, for heaven's sake, we're almost done."

"Give it up, Rosemary," the general grumbled from the far end of the solarium. "Brains, not hands, are what interest the man. At least that's what he claims," he added with marked sarcasm, as if to imply he still had some reservations about Richard's credibility.

Courtney snickered from the gently rocking glider. "Dr. Kelly isn't so much concerned with his future as with the past—other people's past, that is."

Before Richard could come up with the proper comeback, Sonia intervened. "Why, what do you mean?" she asked, looking up sharply from her needlepoint.

Courtney shrugged and studied her nails. "Why don't you ask the good doctor himself?"

Sonia stared at Richard, a puzzled frown on her face as the other guests present assisted with curiosity. Even the general had shifted his attention from the financial section of the *Miami Herald* to stare at him over the top of his reading glasses.

"Your daughter suspects me of having come to Serena under false pretenses," Richard told her without shifting his gaze from Courtney's. He refrained from saying she'd accused him outright.

The general emitted a throaty laugh. "No kidding."

Sonia's expression hardened. "Courtney? What is this about?"

Courtney's cool composure didn't waver under her mother's sharp scrutiny. "It appears Dr. Kelly, as well as being an affirmed neurosurgeon, is no stranger to memory disorders," she informed her. "Apparently he's written numerous books and articles in which he cites amnesia-related case studies. Not to mention—"

"I'm aware of Dr. Kelly's accomplishments," her mother interrupted, "but what does that have to do with anything?"

"It has everything to do with it. Don't you think his presence at Serena is a bit too coincidental considering . . . well, considering our family history?"

The angry flush on Sonia's face indicated she didn't appreciate Courtney discussing family matters in the presence of her guests. "Courtney, this is completely inappropriate," she said.

"No, it's fine," Richard interjected. "Your daughter's right. The book I'm working on does indeed include a synopsis on memory disorders, though it focuses on the organic aspect of the condition rather than the psychogenic, usually when there's brain damage involved, as do all my previous works. I'm a trauma specialist, not a psychologist," he specified with a pointed look at Courtney. "If you'd been more thorough in your . . . research you'd have come to that conclusion yourself."

Anger flashed in Courtney's eyes but she kept her mouth shut this time. Sonia picked up her embroidery and gave Richard an apologetic expression. "Please excuse my daughter. She has a penchant for drama and can be a little presumptuous at times."

"No harm done," he reassured her, and had the perverse satisfaction of seeing Courtney's cheeks flush.

Then he smiled apologetically at Rosemary. "I'm sorry for my lack of attentiveness. I'll try to be more cooperative. Please, by all means, continue."

The woman patted his hand sympathetically. "Another time, perhaps, when you're in a more receptive mood," she said. "Besides, I promised Sonia I'd finish writing the place cards for tomorrow night's event." She peered at him from under her overly made-up lashes. "I assume you will attend the annual Preservation Society Gala?"

"Of course, Richard will attend," Sonia said before Richard could answer. "As well as Dr. and Mrs. Mallory, his dearest friends from New York who will arrive tomorrow morning. No member of my household is excused from the gala, not even my own daughters." She gave Richard a meaningful look no doubt intended to reassure him she'd make sure her younger daughter didn't miss a perfect opportunity for her grand reunion with the Mallorys.

"I wouldn't dream of missing it," he replied.

CHAPTER 37

CLARE

Clare examined the work in front of her. The runny watercolor displayed a tentacled yellow blob floating randomly against a soggy blue backdrop. "How very colorful," she said, careful to sound properly impressed.

"The sun is smiling, see? It has a mouf," Sherri said, pointing to a gash on the blob. The "mouf" was crosshatched by tiny jagged marks resembling teeth.

Clare smiled, reminded of the reason she loved her job so much. Her children never ceased to delight her with their unique creativity and boundless imagination.

"This is an excellent interpretation of 'happiness,'" she said, referring to the theme of the day's art project. "Just looking at it brightens me up." She handed it back. "Run along and put it up on the board with the others," she said to the little girl.

Sherri had barely run off to hang up her handiwork when another completed project was thrust in front of her. It was an impressively accurate sketch of a bird's-eye view of St. Isabel Island. The shell-shaped island was interspersed with little green dots representing the dense vegetation and was surrounded by scalloped blue waves. "Excellent work, Michael," she said, praising the little boy with a perennially grim expression and somber eyes.

"You're supposed to draw something happy, not a dumb island," Davy, one of his classmates pointed out, flaunting his own contribution, the sketch of a smiling father, mother, and son matchstick trio holding hands.

"St. Isabel's not dumb," Michael retorted, glowering at Davy.

"Of course not," Clare interjected before the argument could spiral out of control. "Michael's drawing is in perfect harmony with our theme because we're happy to live here. Right, children?"

The response was a chorus of "Yes, m'am!"

Clare had a soft spot for the little ebony-skinned boy. Of all the wards of the monastery, he came from perhaps the most tragic of circumstances, having been rescued from an underground ring specializing in pedophilia and child prostitution. It was still unclear whether he'd been kidnapped or "bought" by the organization in question, as was the fate of many little innocent victims like him. He was extremely diffident and withdrawn and, like Joey, rarely smiled.

She glanced around. "Who else has finished?"

A wrinkled sheet of paper crept over the edge of the desk. Clare sucked in her breath when she saw what—or, rather, who the crayon matchstick figure represented, the long yellow tresses being a dead giveaway. The asymmetrical, slightly crossed blue eyes would have made her smile if not for the telling dots running down the gaunt cheeks. Joey would never grow up to be a Van Gogh but his sketch, in deliberate contrast with the day's assignment, managed to convey his message quite effectively. His teacher was unhappy, and it hadn't escaped his notice.

She swallowed, pushing back a knot of emotion. "This is good, Joey, but I wanted you to draw something happy." She handed him a blank sheet of paper, "Why don't you give it another try? This time, make sure you draw her with a nice big smiley face." She lifted the corners of her mouth upward with the pads of her forefingers. "Like this."

All except Joey giggled at her funny pose. "Five more minutes," she announced to the rest of the class. "Make sure all of you hand in your work and wash your hands at the sink before the bell sounds."

Instead of the usual scatter of feet, an unnatural stillness fell on the room. It took her a moment to realize everyone's attention was riveted on the door.

She glanced up and froze. Richard stood on the other side, his hooded eyes watching her through the narrow glass panel.

"What are you doing here?" she asked in a whisper, opening the door a fraction.

"Nice to see you, too," he said with a smirk.

"In case you haven't noticed, I'm in the middle of class."

"Only for another five minutes or so. I checked with the sister at the front desk."

Before Clare could respond, Sherri squeezed through the narrow opening. "Richard, you came!" she squealed.

His disgruntled look immediately softened, and he stooped to scoop up the little redhead. The child threw her arms around his neck with her usual exuberance and plunked a kiss on his cheek.

"Now, this is what I call a warm welcome," he drawled.

"I drawd a picture of a happy sun, 'cause the sun is a happy thing. You wanna see it?" the child offered eagerly.

"Sure," he replied, and set her down.

Sherri scampered back inside, eager to show off her work. Before Clare could stop him, Richard swept past her and sauntered into the room.

"What are you doing? You can't be here," she said.

"Why haven't you returned my calls?"

Her belly fluttered nervously. His larger-than-life presence inside the small classroom, with its miniature furnishings and rows of toy storage boxes, made her as jittery as a student called up to the principal. "I've been busy," she lied.

He scoffed. "Of course you have, with Lover-Boy Haynes, no doubt."

Her mouth dropped open. Before she could come up with an appropriate answer, Sherri claimed his attention once more.

"Look! Look at my painting!"

Richard glanced at the watercolor and whistled his admiration. "That's an awesome sun," he said, and the child beamed.

"You want to see Joey's?" the little girl asked, waving her classmate's original drawing in front of him. "It's Ms. Elliot, see? She has blond hair and blue eyes. Joey got it wrong 'cause he was supposed to draw something happy."

Clare snatched the sheet out of Sherri's hand and placed it face-down on her desk. "That's enough, Sherri. Don't bother Dr. Kelly."

Richard's gaze wandered over to Joey. The boy was hard at work on a new matchstick figure, his head bowed resolutely over the paper. "Hey, buddy, what are you working on?" Richard asked, approaching the desk.

Joey ignored him, continuing to rub the crayon over the paper with renewed purpose.

"Please go. You're distracting the children," Clare said, hoping he'd take the hint and leave.

He gave her a look that said he wasn't quite finished with her. "Fine. I'll wait in the hallway until you're finished," he said and strode out of the room.

At the sound of the bell he was waiting in the hall. Resigned, she handed the children over to Sister Adelia and invited him back inside.

"What's going on, Clare?"

She wasn't prepared for the change she saw in him. His eyes had lost their hard veneer, the chill replaced by deep concern. "What do you mean?"

"I didn't need to see a four-year-old's matchstick drawing of you to know something is wrong. You seem . . . angry."

221

The reference to Joey's drawing made the heat rise to her cheeks.

"I'm not angry. I'm . . . disappointed."

"Disappointed?"

"I thought I could trust you."

He narrowed his eyes. "What are you talking about?"

She bristled. "I'm talking about the real reason you came to St. Isabel. Did you really tell me the truth, or was I going to have to purchase your book to find out how you'd used me? Were you planning on sending me an autographed copy?"

Understanding dawned in his eyes. "Let me guess, you've been talking to Courtney."

When she didn't deny it, he made a disgusted sound. "*Used* you. Is that what you think?"

He rounded the desk and came to stand with his feet inches from hers, causing her to back up against the blackboard. "Do you honestly believe my coming to St. Isabel was all an act, that I befriended you for the sole purpose of securing material for my research?"

More than affronted he seemed hurt. She cowered under the heat of his gaze and she touched the tip of her tongue to her dry lips.

"Do you?" he asked again, his voice huskier.

"I don't know what to believe," she said, feeling her stoic resolve sliding. She didn't trust him but try as she might, she couldn't bring herself to hate him.

He moved so close to her she had to crane her neck to look at him. "Then believe this." His hand came up to cup her cheek, and something in his expression started a tremor deep within her. "I could never hurt you, Clare. You're the first person who's ever made me feel the least bit salvageable, that I'm not beyond repair. That's more than I ever expected to gain coming here."

She sucked in a breath and held it as his thumb grazed her lips, his eyes never leaving hers.

Darn shame, though, for such a great kisser. The memory of Courtney's parting shot cut through the fog of sensuality in her brain, turning off the flames as quickly as he'd ignited them.

"You kissed Courtney."

He froze, then closed his eyes momentarily. "That was a stupid mistake. It didn't mean anything."

For once she wished he had lied, told her it wasn't true, that Courtney had made it up. She stepped away from him. "Please go away."

She tried to slide past him, but his fingers locked around her wrist, impeding her escape.

"Let me go," she said, feeling close to tears. She refused to break down in front of him again. She'd withstood enough humiliation already.

"Go 'way! You're bad!"

Startled, they jumped apart. Joey had materialized seemingly out of nowhere. The little boy charged Richard, his fists pummeling him with the force of a miniature street fighter. "Go 'way! Go 'way!" he cried over and over, tears of outrage streaming down his face.

Clare was too stunned to react. Her mind was unable to process any thought other than that Joey had spoken. It was the first time she heard his voice.

Sister Adelia rushed into the room, then skidded to a stop when she saw Clare wasn't alone. "I'm so sorry, he ran away before I could stop him," she said, mortified. Then her eyes went wide, as if just realizing something more momentous had occurred than thirty-five pounds of pure rage pounding mercilessly on a grown man. "*Madre de Dios*, he talked," she said.

Clare fell onto her knees in front of the child. "Yes. Yes, he talked," she said laughing and crying at the same time. She managed to pry Joey away from Richard, holding him in her arms. "It's all right," she whispered reassuringly. "Dr. Kelly didn't mean any harm. We were just talking."

Silently she rocked him back and forth while he continued to sob against her chest as if his heart was breaking.

"Let me speak to him," Richard said.

She kept her gaze averted. "I don't think this is the right moment."

"Please, I need to do this."

Something in his tone made her look up at him. There was an expression on his face she'd only seen once before, on Dolphin's End. She relaxed her hold on the recalcitrant boy, allowing Richard to take control.

"I'm sorry," she heard him say in a gentle tone. "I didn't mean to scare you. I wasn't trying to hurt Ms. Elliot, I swear."

Joey scowled at him. His wiry little body was still convulsing with hiccups. "Remember what I said the other day, about Ms. Elliot being like a good fairy? Would anyone hurt a fairy?"

Joey turned his teary gaze to Clare. For a moment he just looked at her, then with his index fingers touched the corners of her mouth. "Fairy," he said in a small croaky voice, then added, "Happy."

Clare laughed. "Yes. Yes, I'm happy," she said, hugging him.

"It's a miracle. We must inform Sister Ursula right away," Sister Adelia cried.

"Yes," Clare said, and urged the child toward the woman. "Please, go with Joey and give Mother Superior the wonderful news."

Clare could have hugged Richard at that moment, but she settled on a simple "Thank you."

He gave her a rueful grin. "You mean, for getting under Joey's skin?"

She shook her head. "Whatever that was, it worked."

His expression clouded over. "Yeah," he said, but there was no triumph in his tone.

Clare knew what he was thinking. She'd seen it, too, the unbridled fury on Joey's little face, the animal fear in his eyes.

He exhaled, long and hard. "He was protecting you. He was afraid I'd jump you and beat the crap out of you, just like that scumbag did to his mother."

She realized he was more shaken than he wanted to let on. "Don't take it personally. He suffered a terrible trauma, and he's not likely to forget it any time soon."

She wondered what he had meant about her being like a fairy. "I really don't know what to make of you," she said, before realizing she'd said it aloud.

He gave her a half smile. "Let me know when you figure it out," he said, and walked out.

CHAPTER 38

RICHARD

"Nervous?"

Standing by the open doorway of the ballroom, Sonia made a striking picture in an elegant but understated floor-length black gown as she greeted the arriving guests. Glints of golden light from the chandeliers reflected off the translucent stones at her throat as she smiled at him, the same stones her restless fingers had been tormenting for the past fifteen minutes.

"A little," she admitted. "Years hosting the gala dinner and it still feels a little unnerving." She squinted her eyes at him. "If you breathe a word of this to anyone, I'll have to kill you."

He grinned, guessing her insecurity had very little to do with ensuring the success of St. Isabel's most important event of the year. It was Clare's impending encounter with the Mallorys that had her on edge. The upsurge of nerves had been increasingly evident since the early afternoon, when the elderly couple had finally arrived at Serena.

He'd spent most of the week telling her everything he remembered about Clare's brief time in New York, details Sonia couldn't seem to get enough of, but whenever he attempted to advise her against keeping the truth from Clare, he was met with fierce resistance. He was beginning to suspect it was Sonia who was afraid of Clare recovering her memory more than Clare herself.

When his former guardian and his wife made their appearance, he smiled. The couple seemed to have shed twenty years since the last time Richard had seen them, no doubt due to the joyous prospect of seeing Misty again.

"It was thoughtful of you to insist we attend the gala," Max said graciously to their host.

"I wouldn't have had it any other way," Sonia reassured him. "Besides, having you here makes this occasion all the more special."

Mary was awestruck by the rich elegance of their surroundings. "Oh, my, I feel as if I've walked into a bygone era," she said.

As much as Richard detested black-tie affairs, he had to admit he was impressed. The crew of experts Sonia had hired had done an outstanding job transforming Serena's main parlor and the adjoining terrace into an elegant neoclassic grand ballroom. It was clear the Elliots were held in very high esteem, not only on the island but in the entire state of Florida. He'd already been introduced to an impressive number of state politicians, environmental lobbyists, and prominent business figures. He'd even recognized a few famous icons from the entertainment world as people stopped to be greeted by the hostess.

Mary clasped her hands together. "I still can't believe we'll soon be seeing Misty after all these years. The anticipation is simply killing me," she said.

"Just remember, honey, her real name is Clare," Max reminded his wife. From the momentary cloud that crossed the older man's eyes, Richard assumed his former guardian wasn't any happier than he about having to carry on this unnecessary farce.

"Why, there you are, darling," he heard Sonia say.

He wasn't prepared for the jolt of electricity that ran through him at the sight of Clare. She was gliding toward them looking like a water nymph, a dazzling and sophisticated sea creature emerging from the waters of her lagoon.

"You look lovely, darling," Sonia said, brushing her daughter's cheek with her lips.

"Thank you, though not near as dazzling as the hostess," Clare said.

Richard's mouth went dry. The necktie that went with the black formal ensemble Mary had picked up from his apartment for the occasion suddenly felt like a noose around his neck. Clare, on the other hand, appeared cool and unperturbed, even if the nod of acknowledgment she sent his way was formal. Her floor-length gown the same color as the water in her little cove brushed his side, and he caught a whiff of a scent, something fresh and outdoorsy that reminded him of ocean spray and a moonlit walk along the beach. She'd done something different to her hair, something soft and bouncy that made his fingers want to touch it.

"Darling, I'd like you to meet my new guests. They've just arrived from New York," Sonia said.

Something sharp dug into Richard's palm, and he realized it was Sonia's fingernails. The pain galvanized him into action.

"Clare, meet my former guardian, Dr. Maxwell Mallory, and this beautiful lady is his wife, Mary," he said. "Max, Mary—this is Clare, Sonia's younger daughter."

Clare smiled engagingly at the couple. Nothing in her expression showed anything other than friendly curiosity. "It's such a pleasure to meet you," she said. "I'm glad you decided to join Richard in St. Isabel."

Mary hid her nervousness well, though her eyes looked a little dewy. "I'm so glad to meet you, my dear. You're just as pretty as Richard described."

Richard gritted his teeth. He could have done without Mary's candor for once, although he had to admit it was worth it just to see the instant rush of color inflame Clare's cheeks.

Clare appeared a little taken aback when the older woman enveloped her in a warm hug. "Thank you. He's told me a little about you, as well."

Max bounced back from his momentary daze and cleared his throat. "He has, has he? Being away from home must have softened him up," he said with a chuckle. Anyone who wasn't privy to the truth about Clare's ordeal would have taken the slight tremor in his voice as a natural consequence of the aging process, but Richard knew better.

"Richard spoke so enthusiastically of St. Isabel—and particularly of Serena—we decided it was the perfect occasion for an overdue vacation," his wife elaborated, reveling in her new role. "He said we should visit the monastery. Apparently, it has quite a fascinating history."

The brief, slightly bemused smile Clare shot him made Richard a little hot under the collar. "It certainly does," she said. "Let Mother know when you'd like to come for a tour and I'll arrange it with the Mother Superior."

"That would be wonderful," Mary said with too much ardor.

"I've made some last-minute changes to the seating arrangements and placed you with Richard and the Mallorys and the rest of the Serena crowd," Sonia told her daughter. "Seeing as I'll be at the honorary committee table, I'd like at least one member of the family to make sure our guests feel at home."

"Of course," Clare said.

"Good. Now, if you'll all excuse me, I see Mayor Haynes and his family have just arrived."

Clare escorted Richard and the Mallorys to their table, then set off to find the rest of their fellow guests.

"Good heavens, if I hadn't known it was Misty I'd most likely not have recognized her," Mary said not bothering to hide her excitement now that Clare was out of earshot. "She's so . . . well, mature."

"She's turned into a darn fine young woman," Max agreed with a distinctive note of pride.

"Indeed," Mary said, then sighed. "How frustrating she doesn't have the least inkling of who we are."

"I warned you not to expect some sort of miracle," Max reminded his wife. "After all, she was just a child the last time she saw us."

"Well, you can't fault me for hoping," Mary retorted. She pulled out a tissue from her purse and dabbed at the corner of her eyes.

Richard caught sight of General Morris looking dapper in full army regalia, complete with decorations. Draped playfully to his arm was Courtney, stunning and regal as usual. The daringly low back of her gown, not surprisingly, seemed to be drawing quite a bit of male attention. As she turned her head, their gazes clashed briefly.

He felt Mary's eyes on him. "What's wrong?" she asked.

"Nothing. Why do you ask?"

"You've turned moody all of a sudden."

He forced a laugh. "This is me, the king of moody, remember?"

Her worried frown said she wasn't fooled by his paltry attempt at disguising his crankiness. "How have you been . . . with everything?" she asked gently.

"Great," he replied, unable to meet her gaze. "Nothing like connecting with a ghost from the past to gain a new perspective on life."

His irony seemed lost on Mary, who patted his arm affectionately. "I believe your coming across that painting was God's way of guiding you to Misty. It's a true miracle."

A miracle that is starting to feel like bad karma, he thought.

"You ready to get back to work?" Max asked, butting in on the conversation with characteristic bluntness.

Mary launched her husband a censorious glance. "Now, Maxwell, you promised not to harass Richard. He'll go back when he's good and ready."

"I'm thinking of taking it slow for a while, explore different avenues," Richard said. He didn't know if he'd ever be ready.

The older man grunted. "As long as these, uh, avenues don't lead to some other hoity-toity establishment like Minerva. You know how I always felt about you teaming up with that bunch of self-serving, money-grabbing academics in fancy suits. A damn waste of talent, if you ask me. Of course, not that you ever did."

Richard suppressed a grin. It was as close to an expression of empathy as he'd ever get from Max, but it was more than he deserved.

CHAPTER 39

CLARE

Clare kicked off her shoes, sinking her aching toes into the cool grass still damp from the nightly watering, and groaned in relief. She'd been waiting for the right moment to make a quick getaway, and when the mayor had claimed Paul's attention to introduce him to an old college friend, she'd quietly slipped away. She didn't think her feet could have survived another minute of dancing in the too-tight, stiletto-heeled Manolos Courtney had insisted she borrow, claiming they matched perfectly with her dress.

As she made her way through the garden, the music and laughter from the ballroom grew more faint, outmatched by the shrill chirping of the cicadas hiding in the bushes. She had an inkling Richard was somewhere out here. He'd barely said a word to her all through dinner, and when he'd excused himself and disappeared from sight, she'd had the impression he'd wanted to get away from her. He was still angry with her, and she couldn't fault him for that after she'd outright accused him of having a hidden agenda.

Since the day he'd shown up in her classroom, all she'd been able to think about was how skillfully he'd handled Joey's emotional meltdown, how tactfully and gently he'd gotten the boy to settle down and to trust him. Someone with his sensibility couldn't have only his own interests at heart. Tonight, the pride and affection she'd seen in the Mallorys' eyes when they looked at him gave her more reason to believe he couldn't be the unscrupulous villain Courtney had painted him to be. It was clear they thought the world of him, and not even his staunch reserve had been able to hide his love for the couple.

I could never hurt you, he'd told her, and in her heart she believed him.

If not for the dim lighting flooding the deserted pool area, she wouldn't have seen him. He was stretched out on a lounger, legs crossed at the ankles, arms folded beneath his head as if he didn't have a care in the world. Only, she realized as she came closer, he looked anything but carefree. Even in the semidarkness she could make out the tense, haggard lines of his face. His bow tie hung loose around his neck and he'd undone the top buttons of his shirt.

His eyes were closed, but she could tell by the imperceptible stiffening of his features he had perceived her presence.

"What are you doing out here?" he asked, sounding vaguely annoyed.

Suddenly she wasn't feeling quite so confident as when she'd set out to find him. She took shallow breaths to calm the accelerated drumming of her heart. "I wanted to apologize," she said.

As he turned his head, the silvery light glancing off the pool reflected in his eyes, making them glint like liquid metal. "Apologize," he mimicked in a lazy drawl.

She had expected a chilly reception, and she was determined to not let it intimidate her. She lowered herself on the lounger next to his, arranging the skirt of her gown around her. Taking a deep breath, she filled her lungs with the scent of flowers and freshly mowed grass. "For thinking the worst of you. I'm particularly sensitive when it comes to . . . that difficult part of my past, and I let my feelings cloud my judgment," she admitted.

He returned to stare at the darkened sky, his expression inscrutable. "Why the change of heart?"

She winced at the sardonic bite in his tone. "I know you're a good person and you wouldn't lie about something like that."

He sat up and brought his feet to the ground. Up close he looked even worse than she'd initially thought. His hair was tousled, as if he'd run his fingers through it multiple times. The look gave him a vulnerable, almost boyish appearance that tugged at her heart.

"Maybe you shouldn't have been so quick to exonerate me. Turns out you weren't too far off the mark."

She stared at him in confusion. "What do you mean?"

"You were partly right. My decision to come to St. Isabel wasn't quite as random as I led you to believe."

His words hit her with the force of a lightning bolt. Had she been justified in her suspicions, after all?

"It wasn't planned. It was something of yours that led me here." She stared at him and he continued. "I was going through a rough time. I was a wreck after Erica pulled the rug from under me with her cruel stunt. I wasn't able to work or sleep, I drank too much. I'd hit rock-bottom. I'd spend my days either holed up in my apartment or wandering aimlessly around the city. It was during one of these outings I came across a painting in a backstreet gallery. It was signed with the initials C.E."

Her hands clutched the edge of the lounger. She signed those paintings with her initials because she couldn't bear to see her name on something that evoked such disturbing sensations.

"How . . . how did you know it was mine?" she asked.

"I didn't. It was only after I met you that I realized Clare Elliot and C.E. were the same person."

She didn't know if she was more stupefied by his story or the fact that one of those hideous paintings had been displayed in a Manhattan art store. She hadn't expected any of them to make it further than a local charity sale.

"I don't understand. How did my painting lead you here?"

"The label on the dust cover had the address of an art supplies store on the island. Before then I had never heard of St. Isabel. I followed a whim. I needed an escape route from the rut I was stuck in and that address handed it to me. I didn't expect to find more paintings like that on Serena's property."

What a hopeless romantic I am, conjuring up all sorts of idealistic fantasies, she thought. She had been foolish to believe they'd been brought together by some mystical force, something beyond their control.

She disguised her disappointment with an attempt at humor. "And for a moment I thought you'd been so deeply moved by my unique artistry, you absolutely had to meet me," she said, with an exaggerated sigh.

She was surprised when she didn't get the reaction she'd expected. "Tell me about the C.E. paintings," he said.

Everything in her screamed "no." She had never told anyone about her dreams, not even her mother or her closest friends. Somehow, she found herself opening her heart to Richard. "I call them my *Dreams* paintings," she said. "It all started several months ago, after I moved to the Hill. I have these strange, convoluted dreams where everything feels oddly familiar. Sometimes I wake up with foggy images in my head, and I feel the urge to reproduce them on canvas hoping to make sense of them. So far, it hasn't worked."

His eyes narrowed slightly. "What kind of images?" he asked.

"Places, people, but mostly just . . . feelings of déjà-vu," she tried to explain.

"You mean, things related to the time you were taken from your family."

She couldn't repress a shudder. "I think so. Except, it's all so fleeting, so vague. It's like looking at moving objects through frosted glass. I see shapes, colors, but nothing I can actually put my finger on."

"The day I helped carry your painting gear to your house, was that one of them, in your studio?"

She winced. "Yes, the last in a long series of nonsensical puzzles," she admitted. "I don't know why I bother. As if it's possible to bring back memories with a few brush strokes. I should be destroying them, making a huge bonfire and burning them to cinders."

"Instead, you take them to the art shop in town," he said with a faint smile.

She nodded. "The owner's been buying my stuff for years. I told him I was trying my hand at a new technique. When he told me he'd sold a few to some out-of-state reseller, I thought he was making it up, that he was just being kind."

"They're not all that bad," he said, and she laughed.

Drawn by his intense, sympathetic gaze, she found herself asking, "I don't understand why this is happening. Why after all this time?"

He shrugged. "It's hard to understand why the brain behaves the way it does. My guess is you're experiencing flashbacks. Bits of memory gradually returning. Your brain is struggling to bring them back to the surface, but they've been stowed away for far too long to make sense of them."

It wasn't an answer she liked, but it was something she'd always suspected. "Do you think I'll ever get it back?" she asked.

"It's highly improbable, though it's been known to happen. In extreme cases, certain amnesiacs can go for years not remembering and then suddenly, for no apparent reason, it all comes back."

The moon had sunk lower behind the trees, and what little light from the pool area seeped through the thick vegetation wasn't enough for her to make out the features of his face as clearly as she'd have liked. His warm, husky voice reached her like a warm caress over her skin. "I've been meaning to tell you all night how exceptionally lovely you look."

The compliment made her giddy with pleasure. "Thank you, though I'd never have guessed," she joked.

She wanted to tell him he was looking pretty good himself, but with the memory of their walk on the beach still fresh in her mind, she was afraid of sounding too brazen.

The mayor's deep, authoritative voice boomed from the speakers as he began to deliver his closing speech, and she realized how much time had lapsed since she'd left the party.

She got to her feet. "I should get back. My mother will be wondering where I am."

"I'm surprised lover-boy isn't scouring the grounds searching for you."

She decided to ignore the snide comment. "Are you doing anything tomorrow?" she asked.

He unfolded his long frame and stood, slipping his hands into the pockets of his trousers. "Depends. What do you have in mind?"

"I'm taking a few of the children hiking in the nature reserve, and I was wondering if you'd like to come. Unless you're not into that sort of thing."

Immediately she regretted her sudden impulse. "It was just a thought. You've probably made plans with Max and Mary."

"I am. Into hiking, I mean. And I don't have anything planned."

She tried not to smile too enthusiastically. "Great. Meet us in the monastery courtyard tomorrow morning, nine o' clock sharp."

CHAPTER 40

CLARE

*C*lare huddled inside her heavy coat. Gusts of wind whipped against her face, filling her nostrils with the scent of winter. She knew this snow-bordered path; she'd walked here before, inhaled these same smells, felt the same bone-chilling cold. Even the sounds were familiar. People were waiting for her at home. But where was home?

She stopped in her tracks as a storm of pigeons burst out of a tree. They circled over her head, squawking and flapping their wings in a mad frenzy, then swarmed down on her. Fear gripped her, and she shielded her face with her arms. She was trapped—hounded, like a character in a classic horror movie. Then the pigeons were gone, as if they'd never been there. She was alone again, walking along the solitary path. No, not walking, but gliding, as if on winged skates.

The calm was brief, fleeting. It was soon shattered by another sound, a strange rumble, a growl, like that of a large animal, only more . . .metallic. She heard it coming toward her, moving closer—faster, its terrifying growls becoming louder, scarier. She tried to run, but her legs wouldn't move fast enough. It was as if she were wading through a wall of thick molasses.

All the time the sound grew louder, the thump . . .thump . . . thump of the huge paws pounding the ground sounding

dangerously close—too close. There was no time. It was coming at her! It was going to mow her down!
She screamed.

RICHARD ARRIVED SHORTLY before nine. Clare had just finished strapping the children into the back seat of the school minivan and was loading the last items into the trunk.

"Good morning," he said giving her one of his rare bone-melting smiles. His eyes lingered on her face a moment too long, as if he could see right through her sleep-deprived eyes.

"Good morning," she replied.

He stuck his head in the van to ruffle Sherri's curls and exchange high-fives with the boys. "We're going to the ninja park to see the wild animals," Sherri promptly informed him.

"*Nature* park, silly." Tommy scoffed at the little girl, and erupted into hysterical laughter. Sherri glared at the older boy, her expression darkening ominously.

"Everything all right?" Richard asked.

Clare tucked imaginary loose tendrils of hair inside her cap. "Sure," she replied in what she hoped was a lighthearted tone. She gave him an appraising look, taking in his chambray shirt and too-new jeans, the hems of which were tucked into a sturdy pair of military issue boots.

His expression turned wary. "Overkill?"

She was unable to suppress a grin. "Not at all—for an expedition in the Amazon jungle."

"It's the boots, isn't it? I borrowed them from Juan. It's the best I could do on a few hours' notice."

"They'll do," she said. "It doesn't hurt to play it safe. You never know what dangers might be lurking on the forest floor."

"There's that," he said.

"Where's the rest of your gear?" she asked, trying her best not to laugh.

"In my backpack. I don't have much. Sunscreen, bug spray and plenty of water. I figured you'd bring the chow."

She patted the insulated bag she'd just stored in the trunk. "There's PB and J sandwiches. And juice, of course."

"PB—?" He looked like he'd swallowed an ice cube. "You're kidding, right?"

"It's a kid's outing. What did you expect, pâté and burgundy?"

He sighed resignedly and climbed into the passenger seat.

Twenty minutes later they were parked in front of the sprawling log cabin that housed the park's visitors' center. With schools still in session, few vehicles were parked on the premises, all with out-of-state number plates, with the exception of a yellow school bus, the occupants of which were already filing out of the building on their way to the trails.

Clare stopped at the reception desk to register their group, while Richard and the children explored the various specimens of mummified local wildlife and historic exhibits of Indian pottery displayed along the walls. When she returned, Richard was studying the bronze bust of Edward John Elliot, Senior standing on the marble pedestal in the center of the foyer.

"My grandfather was the founder of the nature reserve," she told him.

She was proud of her grandfather's legacy and the influence he'd had on St. Isabel's demographic and economic development. She told him the story her parents had related countless times. "He came to this island because he loved to surround himself with nature. His dream was to create a sanctuary where people from all over the world could learn and care about the plight of the world's rainforests and the creatures that inhabit them. Sadly, he didn't live long enough to enjoy the fruits of his labor. He died not too long after it became a reality. It's been a federally protected marine preserve for several years now and attracts a fair amount of nature enthusiasts—mostly day trippers from the mainland, as well as biologists and study groups."

It wasn't long before Clare realized she had underestimated the amount of energy a healthy preschooler accumulates after a week of being cooped up in class. Multiply that by four and what she had hoped would be a stress-free hike along one of the easier walking trails the park had to offer turned out to be a real chore. Trouble began almost as soon as they hit the trail, with Michael tripping on a tree root and scraping his knee. The incident opened the floodgates to more incidents, in a sort of domino effect, which made Clare wonder if she hadn't placed too much faith in her own ability to muddle through a day-long excursion with four small children in tow, while struggling to disguise the lingering effects of another bad night.

While Richard tended to Michael's scrape with the help of her first aid kit, she tried to keep the other three from wandering too close to the bank of a bubbling stream.

"I wanna swim. Can we swim, Miss Elliot?" Sherri pleaded. Without waiting for permission, the child kicked off her sneakers and got started on her socks.

"No, sweetie, you may not. You can dip your feet when we get to the waterfall," Clare said.

Richard dropped the lunch bag on the forest floor to pluck Tommy off a tree branch and set him on his feet.

"I can't walk," Tommy's classmate Michael wailed, limping and dragging his leg stiffly. "My knee hurts."

Clare felt the stirrings of an impending headache. "All right, then, you'll have to wait here while the rest of us complete the tour," she said, and began to gather up their belongings.

Obviously not comfortable with the thought of being left stranded in a forest surrounded by the screeching of unidentified creatures, Michael forgot his aching knee and trudged along sulkily.

A wooden bridge across the stream led them to a magnificent three-tiered waterfall. Clare suggested they stop to rest a while and freshen up. She allowed the children to take off their shoes and socks and splash around at the foot of the waterfall. While they played, she and Richard sat watching them and admiring the hundreds of colored macaws that populated the area.

She sensed his eyes on her from time to time, studying her.

"Nightly demons?" he asked, with astounding perceptiveness.

"That obvious, huh?"

"So much so, I'm starting to feel left out."

Remorse bit at her conscience. "I'm sorry. Wrong timing, I suppose. Usually my work keeps me distracted, and I don't think about it too much."

He looked into her eyes with such unmitigated tenderness it made her weak. "Anything I can do to help?"

"You're already helping, just by being here," she said, meaning it.

Fortunately, he didn't probe. The last thing she wanted was to have to relate the all-too realistic moments of terror she'd experienced before she'd woken up screaming to find it was just another dream.

She was relieved when he didn't bring up the subject again. Not that they had much opportunity for leisurely talk after that incident. As the day progressed, the children grew increasingly cranky and restless, absorbing all her attention and energy. Keeping them from straying off the trail and getting into more trouble was a constant test of her patience, and she was grateful for Richard's support. For one with no experience with children outside of his professional capacity, he showed surprising sportsmanship and endurance in dealing with the constant skirmishes and histrionics. He was quick-thinking and resourceful, often volunteering piggyback rides when the children were too tired to walk and even improvising a bug scavenger hunt. What ultimately put the man on equal ground with a superhero were the simple tricks he showed them involving camouflage and basic survival skills.

"I owe you an apology," she said.

One corner of his mouth tipped upward. "What, another one?"

"For not realizing you are, among other things, a skilled outdoorsman."

He shrugged. "I've had my fair share of exposure to the perils of life in the wilderness," he said.

She wondered whether he alluded to his experience as a fugitive minor on the streets of New York or to something more literal.

By the time they returned to the visitors' center, the parking grounds had almost emptied out. Young boys and girls were filing into the school bus, preparing for their return trip.

"You're tired. Let me do the driving," Richard said taking the keys from her hand.

She was so exhausted she didn't have the strength to refuse. For a while he drove in silence while she kept the children distracted by singing camp songs with them. It wasn't long, however, before all four fell asleep.

She settled back against her seat and glanced at Richard's profile. "Thank you for being such a good sport today," she said. "And for making me feel better."

He took his eyes briefly off the road to give her a concerned glance. "Have you ever thought of getting help? I can recommend a good therapist, the best in the field."

She clamped her jaw. "No," she said tersely. The thought of repeating the experience she'd gone through years ago made her ill.

"So, you'll just—what—continue to paint your creepy dreams and stress over what makes them come in the first place?"

She winced at his candidness. "I don't stress. Anyway, I don't see how that would matter to you. In a few days you'll be gone, and I'll be just a brief parenthesis in your life, one you'll scarcely remember."

The old van gave an angry growl as Richard's foot exercised a little more pressure than was necessary on the gas. "Don't. It's not like that," he said.

She bit her lip, blaming a combination of leftover misery and frustration for saying things she hadn't meant to say out loud. Her tight throat made it difficult to speak. "Then how is it? Explain it to me, Richard."

The vehicle slowed down brusquely, and she was jerked forward in her seat. Before she realized his intentions, he'd swerved to the right and pulled over onto the shoulder of the road, bringing the minivan to an abrupt stop.

He grasped her by her shoulders, forcing her to face him as far as the seat belt would allow. The fiery intensity of his gaze caused a tremor of anxiety to run through her. "You will never be just a parenthesis, Clare. You're far, far more than that."

His words triggered an emotional storm inside her. It was as close as he'd ever come to admitting he cared for her.

The pad of his thumb brushed lightly over her burning cheek, and she closed her eyes, savoring the moment, storing it away in her memory for when she would need to tap into it just to survive the agony of not knowing when or if she'd ever see him again. When she opened them again, new tension lines had formed around his mouth and eyes.

"I keep telling myself I should stay away, but the truth is, the more time I spend with you, the harder it is to not want to," he said.

How could words have the power to both melt my heart and hurt me at the same time? she asked herself. "You say that like it's a bad thing."

He whispered something unintelligible that sounded like a prayer or perhaps a curse. "Not bad, but wrong. You make me want things I shouldn't be wanting." He tucked a stray lock of her hair behind her ear, but his eyes were centered on her mouth. "Such as this . . ."

She stopped breathing when he bent over her and pressed his lips to one corner of her mouth. ". . . and this," he said, brushing them gently over her cheek with exasperating slowness all the way up to her earlobe, making her discover sensations she never even knew were possible to feel. Too soon he eased back with a drawn-out breath, leaving her desperately wanting more. "And if there weren't four preschoolers sitting back there," he added in a rough whisper, "I don't know if I'd be able to stop."

Her heart beat so fast she felt it bouncing off the wall of his chest in unison with his. She wondered if the children were merely an excuse. Something about him was off. From that day when he'd found her asleep in the pavilion, he'd been tiptoeing around her as if she were a rare artifact that could shatter at the merest touch.

"Is it because I remind you of the girl you once knew?" she asked, her voice sounding almost unnatural as it pushed through the tightness around her throat.

He flinched as if she'd slapped him. "What?"

"Are you afraid of hurting me like you hurt her?"

He was suddenly staring straight ahead. "I don't know where you get that crazy idea."

She sensed a conflict in him and feared there was more going on in his head than he wanted to let on.

The loud honking of a vehicle startled her out of her troubling thoughts as the school bus they'd seen at the visitors' center sped past them on the solitary road. She caught sight of youngsters waving at them, their smiling faces pressed up against the windows. When she glanced at Richard again, he'd already pulled back, physically and emotionally.

Without another word, he set the car in motion. They continued their journey in silence, while she tried to understand what had happened to make him change mood. Moments later a jolting sound split the tranquility of the countryside.

One glance at Richard's tense expression and she knew they were thinking the same thing. It was the unmistakable sound of tires skidding on asphalt. It was followed almost immediately by the sickening sound of crunching metal.

Richard yanked the minivan into gear and swerved back onto the roadway, stepping on the gas. A few hundred yards farther along the road he slammed on the brakes. They stared in shock at the horrific scene up ahead.

CHAPTER 41

RICHARD

"Help! Please, help us!"

The yellow school bus was flipped over on its left flank, its nose pressed against the mangled guardrail bordering a steep ravine. Children were climbing out of the emergency exit looking scared and in shock. A few were favoring an injured limb, others had bleeding wounds.

"Wait here," Richard said to Clare, and rushed out of the van.

The young woman calling for help had an arm around a child's shoulders while holding a handkerchief to a bleeding gash on her own forehead. The unnatural angle with which the girl was holding her arm indicated the limb was broken.

"The driver . . . I think he passed out. Several of the children are injured, fortunately not seriously. One of them is still in there," she said, pointing toward the capsized bus.

The woman's cut appeared to be superficial, but the little girl was crying as much from shock as from pain. "Easy, now. I'm a doctor," he said. "Keep that bandanna firmly pressed to the wound. I'll be right back."

He jogged back to the minivan to find Clare had placed a collapsible emergency cone on the side of the road and had already called the emergency line.

"They've dispatched the ambulances," she said. Then she asked, "How bad is it?"

"Not sure. One of the children is still trapped in the bus. Give me your first aid kit. It's not much but it's better than nothing." He put a hand on her shoulder. "Why don't you go on to the monastery, I'll find a way to get back," he told her.

She made to object then appeared to change her mind. "All right. I'll drop off the children then I'm coming straight back here."

He nodded and jogged back to the bus. The boy's feet jutted out onto the aisle all the way up front. To get to him he had to clamber over rows of overturned seats, a few of which had been ripped clear out of the paneling. His head was caught between the metal frame on the underside of the front passenger seat and the divider panel that separated it from the driver's seat. He was unconscious but alive.

The driver hadn't been as lucky. He was slumped over the side of his seat, still in his seat belt. Blood was seeping from his head, flush with the pavement. Richard noticed immediately he wasn't breathing.

He returned to the chaperone, who had the situation under control. "The boy is unconscious and needs immediate attention. I'm afraid there's nothing I can do for the driver."

The woman pressed her fingers to her trembling lips. "I don't know what happened. One minute he was singing along with the rest of us, the next he was slumped over the wheel. We couldn't even get to him because the bus was swerving in all directions and we were holding on for dear life," she said in a quivering voice.

Most likely a massive coronary, Richard thought. He recalled the bus overtaking them shortly before the crash, but he hadn't had the impression it was going over the speed limit.

"What's your name?" he asked the young woman.

"Sandy."

"Sandy, I'm going to need you to be brave. I'll need a hand with the boy. Do you think you can manage?"

The woman nodded. Minutes later, with the chaperone's help and that of a motorist who'd stopped to lend a hand, Richard had the boy distended on a patch of grass, his head bandaged with strips of fabric and immobilized with a makeshift splint.

By the time the paramedics arrived escorted by the police, the more serious wounds had been disinfected and dressed, if somewhat rudimentarily due to the shortage of first aid supplies, the broken arm splintered and most of the wailing and sobbing had subsided. While the medics took over, Richard gave the officers a detailed report of the victims' condition.

Clare reappeared just as the two ambulances were pulling out, sirens on full blast. She walked toward him still dressed in the same jeans and T-shirt she'd worn earlier.

A sensation of déjà vu sent a chill running through his veins as a vision of another unconscious child laying underneath a pile of rubble, her face bleeding and torn, flashed in his mind. Suddenly the horror of that day at Lancey's came rushing back, as vividly as if it had just occurred.

He bent over, bracing his hands on his knees, waiting for the shockwaves to subside.

"Are you all right?" Clare asked.

He straightened and nodded. "Poor kid got his head crushed between steel bars. He's critical but stable. The driver didn't make it; looks like he lost control of the wheel. Most likely a heart attack."

She glanced at the mangled bus where the police were studying the dynamics of the accident. "What about the other children?" she asked.

"Mostly minor injuries and abrasions. They're from a parochial school in the Miami-Dade area. I guess not all will be taking that ferry home tonight."

"I want to go to the hospital," Clare said starting back toward the van.

Richard caught her by the arm. "Wait. There's no reason to, it's all under control. There's nothing more either of us can do."

There was a grim determination in her vivid blue eyes reminiscent of the obstinate and headstrong Misty he remembered. "I have to make sure those children are going to be all right," she said. She gave him a sympathetic look, as if sensing his reluctance. "It's all right if you don't want to go. I'll drop you off at the monastery so you can pick up your car."

He shook his head. "No, I'll come with you. I'll pick up my car later," he said.

THE EMERGENCY ROOM was a flurry of activity when Clare and Richard arrived, as the accident victims were triaged and tended to. It was a while before anyone could give them any information. It was Paul Haynes who finally came to apprise them of the situation, looking unusually tousled and somber.

"The paramedics said you called in the accident," he said to Clare, and gave Richard a circumspect look, no doubt wondering why he was with her.

Clare explained how they'd been returning from the nature reserve and come upon the scene of the accident moments after it had occurred.

"A fortunate coincidence," Paul said a little too animatedly not to sound forced. "It seems the driver suffered a heart attack. The medical examiner thinks he went into cardiac arrest almost instantly. Fortunately, the rest were injuries. Of course, it could have been a lot worse had the bus driven into the ravine."

"What about the boy with the head injury?" Clare asked.

Paul shook his head, his expression grim. "Not good, I'm afraid. I've seen the scans; aside from a minor skull fracture, the CT revealed a large epidural hematoma. Emergency surgery will be required to remove it. We're having him transported to Ryder Trauma Center in Miami. Dr. Sullivan, the chief surgeon, thinks he stands a better chance of making it there."

A middle-aged man in green scrubs and a scruffy gray beard came out of the intensive care unit, his surgical mask still dangling around his neck, a somber expression on his face.

"Dr. John Sullivan, chief surgeon of this hospital," Paul said as the man approached them. "Chief, meet Dr. Richard Kelly. He's a well-known neurosurgeon in New York. You may have heard of him."

"Yes, of course," the surgeon said in instant recognition. "It's indeed an honor to meet you, Dr. Kelly."

Richard stiffened, already regretting his decision to come. "Pleasure to meet you, Dr. Sullivan," he said, accepting the surgeon's hand.

Paul introduced Clare as Sonia Elliot's younger daughter.

Dr. Sullivan smiled at her. "How are you, Ms. Elliot? You may not know me, but your mother and I both serve on the hospital board."

"Nice to meet you," Clare said.

"Dr. Kelly was a first responder at the scene of the accident and was able to help before the medics arrived," Paul explained to his boss.

"I'm sorry the boy is in critical condition," Clare said.

The surgeon's expression was grim. "Unfortunately, there's not much we can do for him here but provide stabilization while we arrange for him to be transferred to a Level 1 trauma facility. Every minute counts in situations like these, and I'm afraid we're not equipped to handle a cranial injury of such severe proportions, nor do we have the training." he explained.

"We don't, but there's someone here who does," Paul said, his eyes on Richard. "Dr. Kelly may be just the man for the job. That is, if he's willing to volunteer his services."

Every muscle in Richard's body tensed. His shaky, useless hands, now clammy with sweat, twitched with nervous tension, reminding him of something he'd conveniently forgotten in the last couple of days. He shoved them into the back pockets of his jeans.

"Of course," Dr. Sullivan said, instantly animated. "If memory serves me well, you made quite a name for yourself very early in your career operating in military camps, often under precarious conditions. At St. Isabel Hospital we may not be equipped with today's cutting-edge technology like some of the places you've worked in, but there's no shortage of surgical instruments."

"I'm afraid that's impossible," Richard said.

Dr. Sullivan misinterpreted his response. "I understand you're on vacation, but I hope you will make an exception given the severity of the situation. Delaying the surgery could result in more severe complications. You could save the boy's life."

"Dr. Kelly is on long-term leave," Clare explained, trying to be helpful.

"I no longer practice surgery—for personal reasons," Richard clarified, deciding to put an end to any misconception about where he stood on the matter.

The older man gave an embarrassed cough. "I apologize, I didn't intend to put you in a difficult situation," he said.

"No apology necessary," Richard said.

"Would you at least consider taking a look at the scans? I'd like to get your expert opinion before I determine the best course of action. In light of your personal involvement as a concerned bystander, of course."

Richard hesitated, then not wanting to appear overly rude he said, "I'd be happy to."

CHAPTER 42

CLARE

The instant Richard and Dr. Sullivan disappeared from sight, Clare confronted Paul. "What's wrong with you?" she asked through gritted teeth.

"What do you mean?"

"How could you put Richard on the spot like that? It was unfair."

"He's the best in his field and he's available. What could be more fair—and ethical, I should add—than him helping out in a situation of extreme emergency?"

"Don't pretend not to know what I'm talking about. Your well-informed sources did a fine job of bringing you up to speed on the medical community's latest gossip."

Paul had the grace to look embarrassed. "I wasn't trying to provoke him. I did it because I believe he's the best chance we have to save the boy's life."

Clare believed him. She suspected he was jealous of her friendship with Richard, but he hadn't mentioned anything since their awkward exchange the night of the beach party.

"Surgeons are trained to perform in high-stress environments, and he's had more than his fair share. He can do it, Clare."

"You heard him. He won't."

Paul gave her a knowing smirk. "I wouldn't be too sure about that."

When Richard came out of Dr. Sullivan's office, a deep V of concern was carved into the area between his brows.

"Dr. Kelly has confirmed my fears," the chief surgeon informed them somberly. "The situation is dire. The boy needs an immediate left temporal craniotomy. The CT scans show a swelling of the brain tissue that, added to the pressure exercised by the hematoma, makes the situation more dangerous with every passing minute, increasing the risk of brain damage."

"Then there's no time to be wasted," Paul said resolutely. "We can't afford to medevac him. We have to do it here."

The older doctor shook his head. "I've never performed a craniotomy, let alone an EDH evacuation. I'd be flying blindly, so to speak, without any real direction but God's and my own instinct. I'm afraid we don't have a choice."

Just then Dr. Sullivan's beeper went off. He made a humming sound as he glanced at it. "I left instructions to alert me when the helicopter is ready to leave Miami," he told them.

He rubbed his beard pensively. "Perhaps there is another solution," he said to Richard. "You could scrub in with me and walk me through the procedure."

Clare saw the conflict in Richard's eyes.

It was her fault, she thought. He wouldn't have been in this situation if she hadn't been so set on coming.

"Fine," she heard Richard say. The tension in his voice made her realize how much the decision cost him. "Pray we're not both making a terrible mistake."

The look on Sullivan's face underscored the extent of his relief. "Of course, the boy's parents will have to authorize the procedure, but I have a gut feeling once I've explained the urgency of the situation, they'll elect not to waste any more precious time." He gave Richard a smile of profound gratitude. "You won't regret your decision," he said, before rushing off to make the necessary arrangements.

Clare noticed Paul watching Richard, but it wasn't triumph or smugness reflected in his eyes. It was respect.

MUCH LATER, A NURSE tapped Clare lightly on the shoulder. "Ms. Elliot?"

She woke up with a start, realizing she was still in the private waiting room reserved for family members. She looked into the nurse's kindly eyes. "The boy . . . how is he?" she asked.

The nurse smiled reassuringly. "Jimmy is fine. Dr. Sullivan will fill you in just as soon as he's finished talking with Mr. and Mrs. Serrano, the boy's parents."

She stood, smoothing out her rumpled clothing. The clock on the wall above the door showed it was past midnight. The surgery had lasted over five hours.

"Where's Dr. Kelly?" she asked the nurse.

"He's in Dr. Sullivan's office," the woman replied. She smiled and squeezed Clare's hand with surprising gentleness, as if she sensed the fate of the young patient wasn't Clare's only concern. "I'm sure he'll be out soon."

Just then, a young couple entered the waiting room, accompanied by Dr. Sullivan. The couple had been flown in by an ElliotAir plane and had arrived at the hospital just in time to see their son being rolled into the operating room.

The petite olive-skinned woman in her early thirties was crying softly. Her face brightened when she saw Clare. "He's fine. My Jimmy is going to be fine," she told her in a heavily accented English.

Clare had talked at length with the couple during their long wait, reassuring them their son was under the supervision of one of the best brain surgeons in the world, but it was also herself she'd been trying to reassure. The memory of Richard's taut features when he'd finally succumbed to Dr. Sullivan's plea still haunted her, and she worried about how the experience might have affected him.

"Jimmy is in a medically induced coma but should be waking up soon," Dr. Sullivan informed Clare.

"Thank you for saving my boy's life," the husband said to the doctor. "Who knows what would have happened to him if he had been taken away on the helicopter."

The surgeon's satisfied smile failed to disguise the stress of the night-long ordeal. "It's not me you should thank, but Dr. Kelly. We owe it to him if we were able to intervene in a timely manner. Dr. Kelly was able to remove the blood clot quickly and efficiently, thus preventing the brain tissue from suffering any permanent damage."

Clare stared at the surgeon, certain she'd misunderstood.

The doctor gave her a quick smile and a wink. "In the end, sense of duty prevailed," he said, "but then, I never knew a surgeon of his caliber who didn't rise to a challenge."

Clare was weak with relief. Not only had the surgery been a success, but Richard had performed most of it.

"It will take some time, but with the help of physical therapy Jimmy will be able to make a full recovery and resume his normal activities within a few months," Dr. Sullivan was saying to the Serranos. "You should go and get some rest, now. I've arranged for a vacant room to accommodate you for the night. What's left of it, anyway. The nurse will escort you there."

Mrs. Serrano seemed hesitant to leave. "What if he wakes up?"

"He won't, not for several hours at least, and when he does," the doctor added with a smile, "you're not going to be of much use to him in the state you're in."

CLARE FOUND RICHARD half sprawled on a black leather sofa, his forearm shielding his eyes. He turned his head when she entered the room. "Still here?" he asked in a flat, disembodied tone.

"I decided to wait with the boy's parents."

"You should be home. Tomorrow's a school day."

"I'll go home as soon as I make sure you're all right."

He sat up and glowered at her. "I'm fine. I don't need a damn babysitter."

She flinched inwardly at his crude remark, but given the trying ordeal he'd come out of, she decided to ignore it. She also knew it wasn't sympathy he needed right now.

"Come, let's go home," she said.

This time he really looked at her. His lips were pulled back in a wicked grin. "Now, that's an interesting proposition. Shall we make it mine or yours?"

She didn't dignify him with an answer but waited at the door, expecting him to follow her. Instead, he hurried past her.

"Give me a minute," he mumbled, and disappeared along the corridor.

She found him leaning on the hood of the minivan in the almost deserted parking lot. Something about his posture sent a quiver of alarm through her.

"Are you all right?" she asked, then realized how stupid the question sounded. Everything about the slight tremor in the taut muscles of his arms, in his harsh, shallow breathing, and in the wild look about him spoke of some delayed psychological reaction.

She placed a hand on his shoulder, half expecting him to recoil, but he stood motionless, wrestling with whatever troubled thoughts were going through his mind.

"I don't know how I pulled it off. All it would have taken was one tiny misstep and we'd have lost him."

His tone was labored, as if he'd been running. He stared down at his hands for a long time, as if he couldn't believe what they'd been capable of. "I was terrified I'd lose my nerve. I don't know how I held it together. Sullivan was on a roll. I thought he had it handled. He pulled off the craniotomy like a pro and was able to get the arterial laceration under control . . ." He closed his eyes as if envisioning the tense moment, and she felt a powerful shudder ripple through his body. ". . . but when it was time to suck out the blood clot, he froze. That late in the game, time and precision were of the essence. One slight hesitation, a wrong move and it would have been the end. I just couldn't let it happen . . ."

She increased the pressure on his shoulder but said nothing. She understood his need to let it all out, to face the enormity of what he'd been up against.

"It was touch and go for a while. We'd wasted too much time; his vitals were plummeting. We were losing him. I had no choice but to take over."

Paul's words came back to Clare. "You did what you had to do to save a life. It's what you're trained to do, and because of that, a ten-year-old boy will live to see the daylight tomorrow and for a lifetime after that," she said.

"I hesitated, and that in itself is a grave error. I almost lost him. I've never lost a patient for an EDH evacuation."

"You need to rest," she said.

The reflection from the parking lot lights danced around the silver in his irises, making them sparkle like embers from a burning fire. He gave a slight shake of the head, a faintly sardonic grin playing on his lips. "You haven't changed a bit, still bossy and controlling as ever."

The strange comment surprised her, but it sounded more natural and intimate than anything he'd ever said to her, leaving her with a warm, tingly feeling inside.

CHAPTER 43

CLARE

The beach was steeped in darkness, so that it was impossible to see where the ocean ended and the sky began. The air was saturated with the scents of an oncoming storm. She could smell it in the strong gusts of wind that made the palms sway riotously, and in the salt-encrusted spray that clung to her skin. A flash of lightning crackled in the distance, revealing for a few brief seconds the faint outline of a half-moon through ominously low clouds, followed almost immediately by a rumble of thunder.

"Stay and walk with me for a while," he said, taking her by surprise. She'd expected him to say it was late, that she should leave before the rain came, but perhaps he didn't feel like being alone just yet.

They walked in silence side by side, accompanied by the sound of the palms rustling in the wind and the rhythmic percussion of waves pounding the sand. She loved the beach at night, especially in an incipient storm. She enjoyed listening to the sounds, to feel the wind in her face and hair. It relaxed her, and she hoped it was doing the same for Richard. After his adrenaline-driven release in the hospital parking grounds, he'd closed himself off again.

"I hope you don't harbor hard feelings toward Paul for putting you in a tight spot. He's not a bad person," she said, more as a means to draw him out of his shell than because she was feeling particularly magnanimous toward Paul.

His lips twitched slightly in a faint smirk. "No hard feelings. I don't doubt his motivations were honorable—from an ethical standpoint, anyway. On a personal level, I'm not so sure."

"What do you mean?"

He gave her a skeptical look, as if the answer should have been obvious. "Do you think I don't see he's jealous of you—of us?"

She was thankful for the semidarkness that hid her embarrassment. He, too, had noticed the blatant suspicion on Paul's face in seeing them together in the ER. Before she could come up with a plausible explanation for Paul's behavior, he said, "I saw you with him one night, in front of your house."

His admission took her by surprise. "You came to Monastery Hill?"

He stood with his hands jammed in the back pockets of his jeans. "I wanted to know why you were avoiding me, but you weren't home. Then you showed up in golden boy's fancy car," he said. He sounded blasé, as if making light of the incident rather than confessing to a momentary weakness.

She tried to recall when she'd last seen Paul. "It must have been the time he drove me home from town, after I dropped off the minivan in the repair shop for a tune-up."

"Mighty chivalrous of him," he said.

She heard the marked sarcasm in his tone and couldn't tell if he disliked Paul or if he was jealous of him.

When the first drops of rain fell, the cabin was far behind them, discernible only by the porch light blinking through the branches of the trees. A not-too-distant flash of lightning split the sky in half, culminating in a powerful explosion of thunder that sent a ripple of shockwaves across the wide stretch of beach. What had started off as a light drizzle soon morphed into a torrential downpour.

"We'd better head back," Richard said.

She had kicked off her shoes at the cabin, but he still wore his borrowed boots. "What's the hurry?" she said, laughing as he struggled to maintain a steady pace. "There's nothing more fun and invigorating than walking in a tropical thunderstorm."

"Or more dangerous," he muttered, but he was chuckling. He shook the rain from his face and hair. "And this is no thunderstorm, it's a typhoon."

A devilish impulse propelled her to taunt him. "Come on, city boy, live a little."

She spread out her arms letting the rain soak through her hair and clothes. She'd forgotten how good it felt. When she caught his eye, his expression was somber again.

Back at his cabin they stood on the porch, watching intermittent flashes of lightning send electrically charged currents into the atmosphere.

"Isn't it spectacular?" she asked, trying to keep her teeth from chattering, either from the chill of the wind against her wet skin or her acute perception of his proximity.

He gave a low chuckle and shook his head. "You're crazy, you know that?"

Her teetering confidence began to vacillate.

Great, she thought, not only does he think I'm unrefined, but crazy as well.

"Because I enjoy the rain so much?" she asked.

"And because you think risking being electrocuted by lightning is exciting and fun."

She scoffed. "And you're just a jaded urbanite with little or no imagination. People in your world seek distraction in luxury and material comforts when it's the simple things that make life interesting."

He didn't respond; instead, he continued to look at her with an intensity she desperately wanted to believe was longing. "I'm beginning to believe you're right," he said softly. "And this is what scares me, missing the simplicity . . . Missing you."

Though the words were almost smothered by the raging storm, her heart made them out clearly. She raised her hand to smooth back a dripping lock of hair from his forehead. "It doesn't have to be like that, you know."

There was a sad smile on his face as he caught her hand and kissed it almost with reverence. She read the conflict in his eyes, saw the restraint in the deep vertical creases crossing his forehead. In one swift movement he lifted her and pushed her up against the wall of the cabin, pinning her with his warm, wet body. Then he bent his head and kissed her, a hot, hungry kiss that stole her breath. It all happened so fast, and before she could fully savor the moment, it was over. With a low grunt that came from deep inside his chest, he tore his mouth from hers and leaned his forehead against her temple. His breath came in short gasps.

Sensing he was about to pull away, she fisted her hands on his wet shirt and clung to him. "I love you," she whispered.

She felt warm air on her face as his breath rushed out, then suddenly, her bare feet were touching the wooden deck again.

"You need to get home. It's late," he said gruffly. He turned his back to her, leaning on the railing. "There are towels inside if you want to dry off."

His abrupt release left her hurting, so that it was unbearably painful to form the words. "I . . . If you don't mind, I'd like to use the shower to wash off some of this sand."

"Take all the time you need," he said, still staring out into the blackness. "I'll hang out here a bit longer."

CHAPTER 44

RICHARD

Richard sat sprawled on an Adirondack chair. Behind his closed eyelids, visions of Clare in his shower, rivulets of soapy water sliding down her soft, sun-kissed body exercised exquisite torture on his senses.

He'd almost lost it this time. Every time he looked at her he wanted her, and in his vulnerable state, he'd been defenseless against her disarming beauty. It had taken every ounce of strength to pull away. The image of her, twirling and laughing up at the storm, so fearless and bold, was imprinted in his brain. Even when she was being adorably quirky and cute, he saw a smart and beautiful woman, with a zest for life like no other person he knew. He'd fallen for her hard, in a way he didn't think was possible, and the timing and circumstances were all wrong. She deserved more than what he could give her. She deserved a lifetime of love, with someone stable and dependable, a man whose life wasn't rife with complications. Someone like Paul Haynes.

He pushed aside the niggling voice inside his brain telling him Clare would be wasted on the mayor's son.

Who am I to judge? he asked himself. I'm no expert on romantic relationships, as my track record clearly indicates.

He was suddenly aware of the silence around him. He'd been so focused on self-recriminating, his brain hadn't registered that both the rain and the bathroom shower had ceased. Even the wind had abated, and a narrow clearing in the clouds allowed a glimmer of moonlight to shine through. Wondering what was taking Clare so long, he got up and pushed the cabin door open.

It took a moment for his vision to adjust to the glare from the floor lamp in a corner of the room. Clare sat on the floor next to the dresser, her hair still damp from the shower. She was wearing a white T-shirt—one of his. She must have rummaged through his drawers for something dry to wear.

She was holding something, and then he realized what it was—the photo of Misty.

He held his breath for the interminable amount of time it took her to finally sense his presence.

"This girl . . . It's me," she said in a quivering voice.

He took a tentative step inside, but she scuttled back against the wall holding her knees up against her chest. "Don't. Don't come near me."

The animal fear in her eyes shocked him. "I can explain," he said.

"You lied to me. Courtney was right, you've been lying the entire time."

The suspicion and accusation in her frightened eyes hurt more than the words. "I didn't lie to you. I didn't know who you were until the second time I saw you in Monks' Cove, until I saw the scar."

"Scar?" she repeated, while reflexively bringing a hand to her temple. "How . . . how did you know?"

"Because I know you, Clare. I knew you a long time ago when you were just ten. Your name was Misty, then."

Her mouth dropped open. "You knew me?"

"You don't remember, but you were staying with Max and Mary in their Manhattan home. They were your guardians until your family found you."

She shook her head as if she was still having difficulty believing him. "But why didn't you tell me?" she asked.

"I wanted to, but your mother wanted to wait. She asked me to stay a while longer, hoping my presence and that of the Mallorys would help jog your memory. She's afraid you could suffer a setback after what you went through years ago and thinks a spontaneous recovery would be easier on you."

Her eyes were unfocused, as if her mind were lost in time. "They told me I'd had a terrible accident, that I'd been left alone inside a store and things from the ceiling fell on me. Someone . . . Santa Claus . . . pulled me out of the rubble and saved me."

"You really don't remember, do you?" he asked, and at her vacuous expression explained, "That Santa was me. I was working my shift in the toy department that Christmas Eve. You got hurt trying to push me out of harm's way."

"You?"

Her eyes drilled into his, as if wanting to extract his image from her buried memories with the sheer force of will.

"I had a second job at Mercy General at the time. I kept tabs on you while you were recovering. When you woke up from the coma your mind was a blank slate. You looked so scared, so helpless in a strange new world. We named you Misty, short for mysterious."

Her brow creased again. "Misty . . . the girl you told me about the night we went to Tommaso's."

She looked at him. "You really didn't know who I was when you came to St. Isabel?"

He was relieved when he saw the doubt begin to clear from her eyes. "No. I was being sincere when I told you about seeing the painting in Manhattan. Something about it had to have resonated in my memory. It was the painting that led me here—to you. It sounds crazy, but it's true."

She looked down at the photo then at him. "You kept the photo all this time—why?"

"It was the only thing of you I had left. Parting with it would have seemed . . . like you'd never been there."

A tear rolled down Clare's cheek. "I knew there was something . . . that special connection. I wasn't imagining it."

"No, you weren't."

"Ever since I can remember there's been this . . . comforting presence shadowing me." She looked at him as if she were seeing him for the first time. "That shadow was you."

CHAPTER 45

CLARE

Tears blurring her vision, Clare picked up the old photograph of herself with the little monkey perched on her shoulder. Her name was Molly, Richard had told her. She and Clare had been best friends. Clare looked happy in the picture.

She had listened avidly while Richard related anecdotes of the months she had spent with the Mallorys, of the people she'd known, details that left her with a bittersweet sensation for not remembering any of it—of them. She had only a vague memory of when she had returned to Maine, of being terribly confused. She'd only wanted to sleep, at the time. When they'd returned to St. Isabel, it had gotten better, and after a while it had been as if she had never left. Her mother had never mentioned New York again, and she hadn't wanted to know.

They'd never talked about the abduction, or the eight months she had been away from home. Only once she recalled asking her sister what had happened to her, why she couldn't remember, and Courtney had told her about the accident that had taken away her memory, and how lucky she had been that James Morgan had found her.

She often wondered if it was her conscience blocking out the memories. Her family had believed she'd died. While they were grieving for her, she was living in someone else's home. She had become a daughter to people who weren't her parents and forgotten all about her real ones.

The sobs she had been fighting tore out from deep inside her chest. "My parents thought I'd fallen from the cliff. If I hadn't forgotten them, they wouldn't have stopped looking for me and my father would still be alive. It all happened because of me."

Richard crouched next to her, and the scent of rain and damp cotton filled her nostrils, reminding her of their kiss on the porch. "You didn't forget them. Your memories were misplaced. You were a child who had just escaped a terrible fate, only to sustain a serious brain injury. You can't blame yourself for what happened."

"But if I wasn't unhappy in New York, why did I forget all of it? Why did I forget you—the Mallorys?"

"Because your brain can't distinguish the good memories from the bad ones. It's why they call it selective amnesia. Sometimes it's safer for our subconscious to delete entire events rather than risk remembering the bad parts."

Was this what my dreams have been about? she asked herself. My brain's need to fill in the blanks? If so, why after all this time?

His gaze was tender when he said, "A few missing pieces of memory aren't what's important. What's important is that you turned out fine, that you were never in any danger after the accident." He put his arms around her and pulled her to him. "You were right, after all. I was meant to be here. I'm so glad I found you, Misty-Clare. Gladder still that you're all grown up."

His next words sucked the breath from her lungs. "I love you. I tried convincing myself I didn't deserve you, but my heart won't listen. Maybe it's right and maybe it's not, but I'm done fighting it. I don't want to lose you, Clare."

Joy warred with panic inside her. He loved her. How she'd longed to hear him say those words. She heard the quiver in his voice, saw the raw, unchecked emotion mirrored in his eyes, and the promise of things to come.

Suddenly, she couldn't breathe.

"What's wrong?" he asked, when she pulled away.

All at once the world seemed caught up in a vortex, and she was spinning within it. An awful rumbling started inside her head, and flashes of color attacked her brain like flying ping-pong balls. A flash of gray . . . a huge beast, its glossy coat rippling with energy, coming for her, like in her dreams. It was happening again, only this time she was wide awake.

Her sweaty palms pushed against him. "I . . . I can't," she gasped, and backed away from him. "I have to find them. The missing pieces. It's the only way I can get them to stop," she said.

"Stop what?"

She hadn't realized she had spoken her fears out loud. She needed to think, to sort the upheaval inside her head. "I have to go," she said.

CHAPTER 46

RICHARD

Richard jerked awake to the jarring ring of the telephone on the nightstand. Conscious of a dull ache pulsating in his head, he raised himself onto his elbows and reached to answer it.

"Good morning. You'll be happy to know our young patient is awake and talking up a storm," Dr. Sullivan's energetic voice said. "He's all fired up about having had a hole drilled into his skull and can't wait to brag about it to his friends."

It took a moment for the surgeon's words to register. Then he remembered the surgery. Last night's incident with Clare had pushed the school bus accident and all related thoughts from his mind. He had to have passed out from exhaustion sometime around dawn because he distinctly remembered a grayish glow filtering through the slats in the blinds.

He rubbed a hand over his eyes. "Good to hear."

"I was hoping you'd come by the hospital before he's moved to Ryder. The Serranos are anxious to meet the surgeon responsible for saving their boy's life," Dr. Sullivan said.

"I'm sorry, but that won't be possible. I'm leaving today."

He was going to break the news to Sonia and the Mallorys first thing this morning, deciding there was no point in hanging around. It was what he should have done in the first place. Instead, he'd made things worse. He thought he'd have learned the lesson by now that everything he coveted, everything he took he destroyed.

"Had enough of the quiet island life?" the surgeon asked with a chuckle.

"Something like that."

"Can't say I'm surprised. Not much action around these parts—certainly not the type you're used to."

Sullivan paused, then cleared his throat. "I hope you weren't serious about quitting your job. What you did in the OR yesterday was phenomenal. Pure artistry. To let all that talent go to waste would be, with all due respect, almost a disservice to humanity."

Richard would have laughed if he weren't feeling so miserable. Sullivan had to have guessed his decision to give up his surgical career wasn't the byproduct of occupational burnout but of something more personal.

"You give me too much credit but thank you all the same."

"Well," the doctor said, "should you change your mind, at St. Isabel's we could really do with someone of your inestimable skill and experience."

Richard was taken aback, both by the offer and his own reaction. In his previous life he would have been insulted by such a bold proposition. Now, he was humbled.

"Thanks, I'll keep that in mind."

When he came out of the shower minutes later, the red light on the phone was blinking. He'd had the water jet running full blast and he hadn't heard it ring.

He pressed the play-back button and was surprised to hear Sonia's voice. "Come up to the house. We need to talk."

HE FOUND SERENA'S hostess and the other guests congregated around the breakfast table in the solarium. Max and Mary were also there.

When he saw Louise Van Patten heading toward him, it was all he could do not to execute a U-turn and retreat into the palmettos. Despite the knot of anxiety twisting in his gut, his mouth watered with the aroma of coffee and freshly baked pastries.

"We read all about that horrible school bus accident. It's in the *St. Isabel Chronicle*," Louise said. "How fortunate that you were at the site to lend a hand."

The maid placed a fragrant cup in front of him but suddenly he wasn't quite hungry anymore. He had hoped his involvement in the rescue wouldn't become public knowledge. All he needed was some overzealous reporter digging a little deeper into the case and his whole life would be out in the open.

Rosemary passed him a copy of the local newspaper with a front-page photo of the yellow bus, under the title: "Tragic School Bus Accident Leaves One Fatality and One Badly Injured Boy."

"Those poor children. They must have been so frightened," she said.

For once General Morris didn't stare down his nose at him. "Heard your timely intervention saved that kid's life," he said with what sounded like respect.

Richard coughed as he scalded his palate with the hot coffee. "That was in the *Chronicle*, too?"

"Not exactly," Louise said, an amused twinkle in her eye. "Lydia Haynes called earlier telling us all about how you rolled up your sleeves and took matters into your own hands."

Hardly, he thought.

"I just happened to be in the wrong spot at the right time," he said.

His irony was lost on the crotchety old gentleman. "Nonsense. You were doing your job, which is precisely what you should be doing, not wasting time writing doctor books."

"Couldn't have said it better myself," Max said.

Just what I need, Richard thought, two crotchety old men to remind me of my failures.

"Good morning to you, too," he said to his old mentor.

Maxwell grunted. "Your sarcasm is wasted on me, boy. I always say what I think, and I think it's high time you went back to doing what you do best. Being a damn surgeon."

Richard gritted his teeth. Gala night's Mr. Softy was gone and the Grinch was back in character, unapologetically blunt and grumpy as ever. He couldn't believe he'd actually missed the old geezer.

"Maxwell, stop harassing Richard," Mary chastised her husband, then turned to Richard with an apprehensive smile. "How are you, dear?"

He translated her question to mean, "How are you holding up after being strong-armed into facing the monster inside you?" She had always been able to read him better than anybody else.

As she leaned toward him, her familiar powdery scent made him realize how much he had missed her warm, comforting presence. "Fine," he replied, giving her a reassuring smile.

He stole a glance at Sonia, but she seemed distracted, as if her mind were somewhere else. She had barely touched her toast. He looked from Max to Mary, but their blank expressions indicated they were clueless, too. He suspected it might have something to do with Clare and what had happened last night. Whatever it was, he was prepared to take full responsibility for it.

"You wanted to talk to me?" he asked her, anxious to get whatever it was over with.

"Yes, and with Maxwell and Mary, as well. Why don't I have fresh coffee brought to my office where it's more private?"

To Louise and Rosemary she said, "You and the general go on down to the pool. I will join you in a short while."

The minute she closed the door of her studio behind them, Sonia said, "Clare's gone."

Those two simple words were like a one-two punch to Richard's solar plexus. "What do you mean, gone?" he managed.

Seeing Max's and Mary's shocked expressions, she said, "It's not as bad as it sounds. She's . . . decided to take a brief vacation."

Mary lowered herself onto a seat, disappointment clouding her face. Max and Richard remained standing.

"She texted me a message early this morning. By the time I saw it and tried to call her, she had turned off her phone," Sonia said.

She handed Richard her phone showing him the message.

"*Have to leave the island for a couple of days. Don't worry, I just need a change of air. I'll call you when I get back. Love you,*" he read aloud.

"Any idea where's she's headed?" Max asked.

Sonia shook her head. "It isn't the first time she's taken a trip on her own, but she's never been so secretive about it."

"Could she have gone to stay with a friend?" Mary asked.

"I doubt it. She would have had no reason to keep it from me."

"It's my fault." Richard said. "It's because of me she left."

Three sets of eyes stared at him in astonishment. "Why would you say that?" Mary asked.

He looked at Sonia. "She found the photo I had of her as a child. I had to tell her."

"What do you mean 'found'? Where?" Mary asked.

Richard exhaled. He wasn't ready to get into the specifics of his and Clare's complicated relationship quite yet. "I had it with me in the cabin. I didn't mean for her to find it. I'm sorry, Sonia, I'm afraid I messed up."

Even in his wretched mental state, he didn't miss the glint of excitement in Mary's eyes. "Oh, dear," she murmured sounding anything but dismayed.

Sonia lowered herself onto the sofa, as if in need of support. "No, if anyone is to blame, it's me. I was the one who insisted you not say anything to her."

Mary reached out to squeeze her hand. "My dear, you did what any good mother would do to protect her daughter," she said.

Sonia looked apprehensively at Richard. "How did she react?"

"Let's say she wasn't happy at discovering we'd lied to her. It brought back feelings of guilt and remorse."

"It wasn't her fault she got into that horrible accident," Mary protested.

"Now, now, being reminded of that time has made her understandably upset and confused. She just needs some time to process it all," Max said with his usual pragmatism.

"Please forgive me," Sonia said. "It was unfair of me to ask you to withhold the truth, especially considering everything you did for Clare. It was foolish of me to want to put off the inevitable."

Richard wasn't so sure Sonia's concern wasn't justified. Something about Clare's hasty getaway bothered him. It had to do with the desperate resolve he'd seen in her eyes as she distanced herself from him.

I have to find them. The missing pieces. It's the only way I can get them to stop. It had taken him a while to understand that by "them" she meant her dreams.

"I think I know where she might have gone."

They all stared at him. "Where?" Sonia asked.

"To find the missing pieces of her memory—to search for clues."

Sonia's face drained of all color. In a surprisingly swift move, Max relieved her of the cup she was holding a second before it tumbled to the rug and placed it back onto the coffee table.

"You think she's gone to Floralport?" she asked. She read the affirmative answer on Richard's face and flattened her palm on her chest. "Of course. Where it all started," she said in a rush of breath.

Mary brushed a tear from the corner of her eye with her napkin. "We should never have come. We should leave."

"Nonsense," Sonia protested. "None of this is your fault and it doesn't change anything. You and Richard are welcome to stay for as long as you like."

"That's very kind of you, but Mary is right," Max said. "We should leave the past alone and let Clare get on with her life."

Richard couldn't agree more. The thought of Clare, alone and defenseless in the town that could potentially hold the key to the mysterious events that had torn her young life apart made him want to take the first plane to Maine and bring her right back where she belonged, but he knew she needed to do this alone.

Mary didn't bother to hide her emotion. "Please let her know we love her very much, and that we hope to see her again one day soon," she said in a teary voice.

"Of course," Sonia said. "Please know you'll always be welcome in this house. All of you," she added, looking at Richard.

Her words made him realize she understood far more than he gave her credit for. All he could do was nod in acknowledgment because he didn't trust his voice to remain steady.

"As you in ours," Mary said. "Seeing Misty—Oh, dear, I still tend to forget her real name—reuniting with her and getting to know the beautiful woman she's become has been more than we could ever wish for. We didn't think we would ever see her again."

"See who?"

All heads turned toward the door. Courtney stared suspiciously from one to the other. None of them had heard the door opening.

Sonia moved to her daughter's side and urged her all the way inside. "Come sit, dear, there's something you need to know."

CHAPTER 47

CLARE

Clare stood on the bluff, facing the wind. The wooden guardrail hadn't been there the year she was ten. Her mother had told her the town had it installed after the "accident" they'd initially believed had taken Clare's life. She had never returned in seventeen years.

She stared out over the vast ocean and breathed in the pungent air that had become as pleasantly familiar to her as the rugged coastline. Today the water was an iridescent sapphire blue for as far as the eye could see. Seagrass and wildflowers grew profusely along the pathways leading to the cliff and around the lighthouse. It was her sixth trip to the bluff in as many days, and the landscape was always the same, vibrant with color and breathtakingly serene. The area was always mostly deserted, though occasionally a few tourists would stop by to admire the view or watch the colonies of the colorful birds for which the area had been named sunning on the rocks below. The last time she had been on Puffin Top as a child, there had been no sign of the iconic puffins, but it had been late December then, and the birds had already departed for warmer climates. The ground had been bare and frozen, and the gloomy, mottled gray of the sky was mirrored on the ocean's surface.

Funny how such trivial details like that were clear in her memory while everything else lay buried deep, she thought.

She had been lucky to find a room at a small bed and breakfast close to the bluff this time of the year, when occupancy was at its peak. She hadn't planned to stay this long—a day or two at most, but something had compelled her to return, day after day, in the hope something—a shape, a sound, a familiar fragrance carried by the gentle breeze— would break through the obstinate barrier in her brain, but so far nothing seemed to resonate. Something told her the key to the mystery of her disappearance was here, on this tranquil rise where she had enjoyed hanging out with her sister whenever they'd come to Floralport to visit their aunt.

The texts Clare had received from her mother in response to her brief, reassuring ones had failed to disguise Sonia's anxiety, no matter how upbeat they sounded, and she felt guilty for running off without an explanation. She hadn't been surprised to learn Richard and the Mallorys had left. She often thought about him, how he'd opened his heart to her, made himself vulnerable like he never did easily. She had hurt him badly, but she hadn't been able to help herself. After what she had experienced that night in his cabin, she knew this big empty space inside her head would always come between them.

Her aunt's house now belonged to someone else, and she hadn't wanted to ask the desk clerk at the B&B who the new owners were. The girl didn't look old enough to remember the story of the missing ten-year-old who had come home eight months after her family had given her up for dead, and she preferred it stay that way.

Only once she had ventured into town, just to take a break from her fruitless mind-searching. It hadn't changed much from the way she remembered it. It was still the quintessential New England fishing village, with its snug harbor filled with lobster boats and its narrow streets lined with quaint buildings, except it had become busier and more touristy. Several new restaurants, souvenir shops, and trendy cafes lined the pretty town square, but the white steepled church was still the same, towering over the other buildings.

Where a diner once stood was now a fancy pet spa. Occasionally a customer would enter or exit the building holding an animal carrying case or leading a dog on a leash. One of the dogs, in particular, had caught her attention. It had been a young Whippet, perhaps, or a Great Dane—she wasn't sure of the breed. Its sleek dark coat and supple musculature had made the hairs at the back of her neck stand on end and her heart flutter nervously. It reminded her strongly of the canine figure that was the centerpiece of all her Dreams paintings. It had been the only time since arriving in Floralport that she had experienced such an unsettling feeling. She hadn't returned to the village after that.

CHAPTER 48

RICHARD

"Well, now, look what the tide's dragged in. I didn't expect to see you here again."

Richard met Philippe's unveiled hostility with cool composure. "You're just sore because I chose public transportation over Serena's exclusive shuttle service."

Philippe repaid him with an evil snicker. "Too much turbulence for you?"

"Just playing it safe."

"Just as well. A few hours later and you'd have had to wait out the storm in Miami. All flights were canceled at seven p.m." He said it grudgingly, as if disappointed it had worked out for Richard.

Richard's gaze scoured his surroundings, noticing most of the boats had been placed on trailers and jack stands and hoisted ashore ahead of the storm, their booms and masts unstopped. The area was littered with ripped tarps, sailing paraphernalia and tangled cables as a result of the gales that had swept the island overnight.

"Looks like the hurricane wreaked havoc in your marina," he said, deliberately shifting away from the barbed gibing that seemed to characterize their conversations.

Philippe tugged one last time on the tie-down rope of a power boat, secured it tightly to the bulwark, then jumped onto the jetty. The squint lines around his eyes deepened as he surveyed the damage. "A real bitch, if you ask me, though we were lucky to have been spared the brunt of it."

He dragged an arm across his sweat-drenched brow, then adjusted his bandanna. "So, you're back," he said with a suspicious glint in his green eyes.

"I am."

"Writing another book?"

Again, Richard ignored the sarcasm. "No. Just tending to some unfinished business," he replied.

Philippe snorted. "If this so-called business centers around Monastery Hill, you're two months overdue."

The man's insolence knew no boundaries, Richard thought. "Not by choice. Not that it's any of your business."

"Anything that concerns the Elliot women's well-being is my business."

"Such loyalty warms my heart."

Philippe ignored the jibe but continued to stare at him, his expression stony.

"Look, Girard," Richard said, deciding he'd had enough of the man's flippant attitude, "I don't know what you were told about my involvement in Clare's past but I assure you I'm not the villain here."

For a moment Philippe seemed a little less cocksure. "It's not your past association with Clare I have a problem with. It's the present that concerns me."

"I'm just here to see her, to make sure she's all right."

"And then what? You have your fancy medical career in New York, your glamorous city lifestyle. Clare is just a simple island girl with a big heart. St. Isabel is the only real home she has ever known, the only one that matters to her. She doesn't fit into your world."

Philippe's words stung because there was some measure of truth in them. "I'll cross that bridge if and when I get to it," he replied.

"And now I suppose you want one of my boats," Philippe concluded reluctantly, albeit with the spirit of one who is resigned to the inevitable.

"That's right, *mon ami*. Possibly with the fastest motor you have."

CHAPTER 49

CLARE

Clare knew it was him even before her brain perceived the nearing sound as that of an outboard motor. She felt his physical presence as acutely as if he were standing next to her. Nothing had changed in the two months since she'd last seen him; that intense, almost tangible connection they shared was still there, not weakened by the long separation. She hadn't expected to see him, not after all this time.

Her fingers shook as she laid down her paintbrush and turned toward the water. From under the wide brim of her hat, she saw the boat glide into the cove, its captain standing tall and straight at the center of the pit.

Her heart pulsed erratically as she watched him descend into the water and wade the short distance to shore. She could tell immediately he'd lost some weight, though his body was still firm and muscular. He'd also lost most of the tan he'd acquired while staying at the cabin.

As he approached, he peeled off his polarized sunglasses, giving her a full view of his achingly familiar eyes. A corner of his lips was tilted upward in a faint smile.

"You look good, Misty," he said.

The sound of his deep, modulated voice caused a lump to form in her throat. "I'm Clare, now. Misty's in the past."

His mouth tightened. "Is that your new mantra? Ignore the past and hope it goes away?"

She winced inwardly at the chill in his tone. "That's not what I meant."

"What did you mean, *Clare*?"

Heat burned her cheeks, and she blinked back the tears that quickly sprung to her eyes. She'd become quite adept at that lately.

Ignoring his question, she asked, "Why did you come?"

"Hell if I know. Maybe I just wanted to see for myself how well you're going about this business of recuperating your lost memories. So far it doesn't seem like you've made much headway."

"I'm managing just fine," she said, telling herself she wasn't going to break down in front of him.

He looked past her shoulder to the painting she'd been working on. It was a house by the sea; a fictitious and empty house, the beach on which it stood as sad and desolate as the house itself. Everything she painted these days was drab and lifeless, just as she felt inside.

"That's not the vibe I'm getting."

She shifted her gaze away from his. "I'm glad you started practicing again," she said, deliberately changing the subject. His eyebrows rose, but before he could ask, she said, "My mother told me. She's kept in touch with the Mallorys." Seeing his blank expression, she realized he hadn't known. "They must think I'm a terrible, ungrateful person."

"They could never think that of you," he said.

She did know, of course, but it would serve her right if they did. "You're not the enemy in all of this, Richard, and neither are Max and Mary. I never wanted you to think that."

"Didn't you? I have to say you're making a hell of a job proving otherwise," he said. "I think you're too afraid to remember."

His statement shook her because he was right. She was afraid, but her desire to remember what it had been like knowing him seventeen years ago was stronger.

Her lips were dry, and she moistened them with her tongue. "It's not just about bridging the gap. It's about finding what I lost. I fell in love with Max and Mary on gala night, and now I know why. I didn't realize until you told me about it how incredibly fortunate I was to have survived the ordeal and to have ended up in a good home, surrounded by generous, loving people. I want to wake up one day and be transported back seventeen years. I want to recall all the moments we shared, I want to be able to feel it all, the same way Misty felt it, even if it means reliving the trauma of whatever got me there in the first place."

She shivered at the thought of seeing the face of her kidnapper again and to confront the terror she must have felt as she was being taken away.

A sudden gust of wind lifted her hat off her head and whipped it away into the mangroves. Neither of them made a move to retrieve it.

She could see a pulse beat rapidly in his neck. In his gaze was an assortment of emotions she couldn't decipher. How she'd missed those eyes, the ironic twist of his lips meant to pass as a smile. The memory of his last kiss was still vivid in her mind. Whenever dejection set in, that memory gave her the strength to pick herself up and not lose sight of the goal she had set for herself.

"Then let me help you find them," he said, his tone gentler. "Come back to New York with me. We'll retrace every step we took together, visit the places we liked to see, do the fun things we did. Together we'll fill up that empty space, I promise you."

She stared at him with longing in her heart. As much as she ached to say yes, the thought of facing another disappointment like she'd experienced in Floralport held her back.

"I can't," she said.

His smile now verged on a sneer. "Not can't. Won't. Girard is right. You're just an island girl at heart, safe and protected in your snug cocoon. The Misty I knew was fearless. She was a fighter."

Her first thought was, What does Philippe have to do with this?

But it was the accusatory words that struck her most, hitting her like a slap to the face. She'd always thought of herself as a survivor. She'd overcome one of the most traumatic experiences a child can ever go through, but perhaps it was just a delusion. What had she done all her life but shut out the past pretending it never happened?

"I'm sorry," she whispered.

He raised his hand then let it drop again, as if he'd been about to touch her then changed his mind. "Yeah, me too," he said.

When he turned back toward the lagoon, she didn't make any move to stop him. Heartsick, she watched him swim to the boat and board it. He didn't look her way.

CHAPTER 50

CLARE

Later that evening Clare answered the door to find Sister Adelia and Joey standing on her porch.

"What a surprise," she said, thinking it was late for the child to be up and about.

"We can't stay long, we need to get Joey tucked in," Sister Adelia said. "He's had quite an eventful day."

"Is that right?" Clare asked Joey.

"We went to the Scoop-A-Licious for ice cream," Joey said, bouncing restlessly on the balls of his feet. She couldn't believe the progress the child had made since he'd started talking again.

"Who's we?" Clare asked.

"Me an' Tommy an' Michael an' Richard. Sister Adelia came, too."

The nun gave Joey a meaningful nudge. "I mean, Dr. Kelly," the boy amended quickly with a bashful glance at the housemother.

Clare cut Adelia a glance, not sure she'd heard correctly. "That's right," her friend said. "Dr. Kelly asked Mother Ursula permission to take the boys into town for ice cream, which she granted, provided I went along to chaperone."

Clare was flabbergasted. Richard had gone to see the reverend mother? "That's . . . awfully thoughtful of him," was all she could say.

"He felt bad for leaving the island so suddenly the last time and wanted to do something nice for the children before he went back to New York." Clare was surprised to see a film of moisture in her friend's eyes. "When I told him Sherri had been adopted by a nice couple from Illinois, he seemed genuinely disappointed."

Clare felt thoroughly confused. She had imagined him back in New York, not entertaining three orphaned little boys with a trip into town. Besides, the monastery had a strict rule against entrusting its wards to anyone who wasn't either staff or an authorized person. He must have made quite an impression on the reverend mother to convince her to break protocol.

"That must have been fun," she said to Joey.

The boy nodded vigorously, vibrating with nervous energy. She hadn't noticed he had one hand hidden behind his back until he brought it out. "I have something for you," he said.

Clare looked at the oddly shaped package he held and recognized the nature reserve's signature gift wrap.

"He insisted he wasn't going to bed until he delivered it to you personally," Sister Adelia said, sounding more amused than exasperated.

"Open it," Joey said.

Clare smiled, flattered Joey had thought to get her a gift. She removed the paper and pulled out a small stuffed monkey. It wasn't just an ordinary toy animal; it was a life-size reproduction of the capuchin in the photo she had found in Richard's cabin.

She stood clutching the toy in her hands, unable to say anything.

"Oh, did I forget to mention the outing included an unscheduled stop at the nature reserve's gift shop?" Adelia said, a teasing glint in her eyes.

"Do you like it?" Joey asked expectantly. "Her name is Molly. Rich . . . Dr. Kelly said he used to have a real one just like this one. Me, Tommy an' Michael got toys, too."

"I love it," Clare said, pressing the stuffed animal to her chest.

"And that's not all Joey has for you. Isn't that right?"

On the housemother's cue, the child extracted a folded, half-crumpled, chocolate-stained paper napkin from inside the pocket of his shorts.

"Open it."

Clare did as he asked and barely suppressed a gasp when she saw the bold doctor's scrawl that could only belong to Richard. Her eyes darted quickly to Adelia's, but her friend's face appeared suspiciously blank.

An angel once said to me, "I promise I'll never leave you, Richard. I'll take care of you forever." And again, I believed.

"What's it say?"

Joey's impatient question broke through her tumultuous thoughts.

"It says . . ." She licked her dry lips. "It says he had a great time with you boys at the Scoop-A-Licious."

Sister Adelia's shrewd gaze bore into hers, then she said, "Come along, now, Joey, we should get back to the monastery."

"But I wanna—"

"Not now," the nun said more firmly, and taking the boy by the hand, she began to pull him toward the door.

Clare leaned down to give him a hug. "Thank you so much for the present," she said.

To her surprise, the boy's scrawny little body trembled in her arms. When she looked at him, his eyes were brimming with tears.

"I don't want Richard to go away," he said in a small quivering voice.

Her heart wrenched at the desolation etched on his little face. "I don't either, sweetie," she said, "but he can't stay.

He has to go back to New York, to his work." She forced a smile. "Go with Sister Adelia, now. We'll talk more tomorrow."

Adelia looked at her with an expression that said, "Oh, yes, we'll certainly talk tomorrow," and walked off pulling a reluctant Joey along with her.

After she'd closed the door behind them, Clare walked blindly into her studio where she'd been working before their arrival, the napkin still clutched in her hand.

An angel once said to me, "I promise I'll never leave you, Richard. I'll take care of you forever. And again, I believed.

The nuance of disappointment in those three simple words couldn't have been clearer. She was the angel who had promised to stay and take care of him, and he'd believed her, the same way he'd once believed the angels he'd spoken to in his head as a child would bring his runaway mother home. Now, she was turning her back on him.

He was right. She wasn't anything like the girl in the picture. Misty had been strong despite all that had befallen her. She'd never dwelt on a past she couldn't remember, which seemed all Clare was capable of these days.

She turned to look at the last of her Dreams paintings and felt a powerful jolt of electricity course through her. It wasn't as she had last seen it. Something had changed. It was as if a veil had lifted, allowing her to see more clearly through the frosted glass. Her eyes singled out one scrambled piece of the puzzle, then another, and another, starting to shuffle them around, mentally placing them in the right place. With mixed feelings of trepidation and excitement, she picked up her paintbrush and got to work, rapidly retouching, outlining, and giving body and meaning to the shapes. By the time she was done, it was as if a cleaning solution had been sprayed over an old oil painting to bring out the original image.

It wasn't just a collection of vague silhouettes anymore; it was a patchwork of actual images, pieces of her past life. Out of her paintbrush, tall buildings had emerged, and cars lined up on busy streets. People walked the sidewalks, each figure alive and vibrant with color. Her artistic imagination had added elements of its own; a yellow taxicab at the curb, letting a man off, a young girl walking her small dog, a dark-faced musician playing his saxophone on a street corner while people gathered around to watch and listen. At the center of it all, two figures sat on the edge of a fountain, a small monkey perched on the shoulder of the taller one. Only the big gray dog seemed oddly out of place, as if it were a stray piece belonging to a different puzzle.

An angel once said . . .

She swayed dizzily as more images flashed behind her closed eyelids. This wasn't her imagination working overtime, she thought. The vision of a younger Richard had been real. He was walking by her side as she struggled to keep up with him on her much shorter legs, just as she hadn't imagined the old house on a quiet cul-de-sac. She heard sounds, the distant wail of sirens, the rumble of an underground subway train, the soft mew of a cat . . .

She gasped for air.

CHAPTER 51

CLARE

The beach cabin appeared deserted. Not a sliver of light seeped through the blinds at the windows, no sounds escaped from inside. It looked as solitary and uninhabited as it had for the past two months. As Clare reached the porch, the motion sensor set off the security beam. She rapped lightly on the door on the off-chance he was in there sleeping. She waited, but nothing stirred inside. She knocked again, this time with a little more purpose, but again, the result was an ominous, hollow silence that left a gaping hole inside her.

"Looking for someone?"

She jumped at the sound of Richard's voice. He was standing at the base of the steps, his figure cast in shadow. Only his metallic blue eyes were discernible, lancing the darkness like two sinister laser beams. A few yards behind him, the macramé hammock creaked as it undulated idly on its posts. He'd been lying there the entire time, hidden from view by the shrubs growing profusely on the beach.

"I . . . didn't see you there. I thought you'd already left the island," she said.

He slowly cleared the few steps and joined her on the porch. His sardonic gaze lingered briefly on the stuffed capuchin she held clutched to her chest. "To what do I owe this unexpected visit? If it's to return the gift you needn't have bothered coming all the way out here. You could have left it with Joey."

She flinched inwardly at the barb of his tone. "That's not why I'm here," she said, refusing to be intimidated. "I love the monkey. It looks so much like the real Molly."

She thought she saw a flash of remorse cross his eyes, even as he gave a noncommittal shrug. "It was the least I could do, seeing I can't give you back the real thing. In many ways Molly was more your pet than mine." The tight line of his lips eased. "It used to baffle me how attuned you two were. But then, I didn't know you came from similar habitats. Like Molly, you're a true creature of the wild."

Clare didn't like being described in those terms, but she knew there was some truth to it. "Molly loved being outdoors, except when there were pigeons around. The pesky creatures annoyed her to no end even when they were innocently going about their business."

He went deathly still, as if he'd stopped breathing. "You remember," he murmured. She nodded, smiling. "When? Why didn't you say anything this morning?"

"I didn't realize it was happening. After my trip to Maine, I began to experience some random flashbacks of being somewhere other than Floralport, but nothing that fully resonated. I wasn't even sure they were actual memories or if they were merely fantasies conjured up by my over-stimulated brain receptors. Then tonight, all the pieces suddenly came together. It was as if a veil had been pulled aside and everything became clear. It was your note that did it, I think."

She was unnerved by his silence as he continued to stare at her, but she took it as an incentive to continue. "At first I didn't understand. It was like viewing someone else's life, the life of someone I once knew. It took a while for me to realize it was me in those images, me inside a home filled with soft-colored brocades and chenilles and tasseled throw pillows, in a warm kitchen smelling of freshly baked cookies. A lot of it's fuzzy, but I have glimpses of Dr. Max sitting at the kitchen table reading his morning paper and Mrs. B hovering over him, reprimanding him for allowing his coffee to get cold. I recognized parts of the neighborhood—the newsstand on the corner of Myrtle and Broadway where we'd stop to buy peanuts for Molly, just down the road from the church I used to attend on Sunday with the Mallorys . . ." She swallowed to ease the tension in her vocal cords. "I saw *you*, Richard. A different, younger version of you, and suddenly I knew what it was, that void I'd been carrying inside me for years, that elusive something that was always missing from my life."

A goofy smile appeared on his face. "You're back. You're really back," he said with a strange, throaty laugh.

His pleasure quickly faded from his face, overshadowed by apprehension. "Did you remember everything? Even . . ."

She shook her head. "No, not everything. I don't remember being in the hospital . . . or even before that, you know . . ." She felt an inevitable shiver, like every time she thought about being snatched away on that cliff and dragged away from her aunt's hometown.

He took a step toward her. Without a moment's hesitation she let go of the stuffed monkey and flew into his waiting arms. The comforting strength of his body enveloped her all at once, and it was like coming home.

He held her close, brushing his hand over her hair. "You were such a needy little thing, yet so brave. I couldn't believe you'd chosen me, a surly, bad-tempered recovering reprobate, as your guardian angel. The day I came home and discovered you were gone . . . it was as if a part of me went with you."

"I'm so sorry," she said with a catch in her voice.

"You have nothing to be sorry about," he said. He tipped up her chin, staring into her eyes. "But I don't want to think of you as Misty anymore. I want to think of you as Clare."

"I think that's a good idea."

His eyelids drooped as his gaze perused her face. "The truth is, you stopped being Misty on Gala Night when you showed up in that lacy thing looking like the real-life version of the Little Mermaid."

She pretended his words didn't have an electrifying effect on her. "One would have never suspected it, the way you ignored me most of the evening."

He brushed a strand of hair from her face, tucking it behind her ear in the gentlest of caresses. "If you only knew how much it cost me, to pretend you didn't affect me," he said, "to turn my back on you so as not to watch you dance with Haynes. I kept reminding myself of the little girl who used to shadow me, but each time I looked at you all chaste thoughts flew out the window."

Hearing the vulnerability in his confession made her giddy with happiness. It was the first time she felt truly complete. "I love you. I don't want to be apart from you anymore."

His frown failed to disguise the emotion in his eyes. "You'd better not be messing with me, Misty-Clare. A man can only endure so much soul-baring without losing his dignity entirely."

Then he kissed her.

A few giddy moments later he released her. "Come back to New York with me. Now. Tomorrow. School doesn't reopen for another week and Max and Mary would welcome you with open arms. They're anxious to see you again."

A wave of euphoria hit Clare, until she remembered who he was. An important career man, one with important commitments. All sorts of doubts flooded her mind. Would she even fit in his kind of world? Would he, in hers? She hadn't asked herself any of these questions. She just knew she wanted to be with him.

"Yes," she said.

They jumped apart when a sharp voice asked, "What is going on here?"

CHAPTER 52

CLARE

"Courtney. What are you doing here?"

Her sister ignored her question and pointed her index finger at Richard. "More to the point, what is *he* doing here?"

"I see you haven't lost your habit of barging in on your guests," Richard said wryly.

"Why did you come back? Haven't you done enough harm already?"

"He's staying at Serena," Clare said. "Not that it's any business of yours."

"Everything that goes on at Serena is also my business," Courtney said.

Her attention reverted to Richard. "I don't know what lame excuse you gave my mother this time, but you have no right to come here and disrupt Clare's life all over again. She hasn't been the same since you showed up the first time."

Clare gasped at her sister's audacity. "Richard is a friend—someone I cared a lot about when I was a lonely and defenseless child. I remember, now."

Courtney looked as if she'd swallowed a stone. "You remembered?"

"Yes. It all came back . . . me staying with the Mallorys, and Mom coming to pick me up. Bits and pieces, anyway."

Her sister bounced back from her momentary stupor and enveloped her in a smothering hug. "Oh, Clare. Was it bad? Are you all right?" she asked.

Clare froze, the gesture throwing her off guard. She hadn't been prepared for such an outpouring of empathy and concern from Courtney. She hadn't expected anything but scorn and ridicule.

"Why do you always have to follow me?"

"Why are you always so mean? Sisters are supposed to hang out together."

"We aren't blood sisters. We aren't even friends."

"Mary Kate is my friend, and she loves me."

"Mary Kate's gone. She moved to New York with her parents, remember?"

The voices resonated unexpectedly inside her head, words that had mortified and hurt her all those years ago.

She pushed them aside and lifted her chin, determined not to show weakness. "I didn't faint or succumb to fits of hysteria, if that's what you're afraid of," she said.

Courtney let go of her, almost as if embarrassed by her impetuous gesture. "Oh, thank God," she said.

She wanted to believe her sister's concern was sincere, that she really cared about her. Maybe Clare had judged her too harshly for wanting to protect her.

"We have to tell Mom right away. She's been so worried about you," Courtney was saying, but Clare heard her as if from afar, as remnants of the past kept popping up inside her head. The wheels of time were on a reverse spiral, and she was powerless to stop them.

"Look what you've done to my new boots. They're splattered with mud. I told you not to jump in that puddle."

"I'm sorry. I'll tell Mom it was my fault, then she won't get mad at you."

"Right, as if her little golden girl could ever do anything wrong."

"We'll say it was an accident, that—"

"Better yet, just stay away from me. Stop following me everywhere I go, you and that stupid rag doll. You're nothing but trouble. I wish you were never born!"

"I wish I were never born, too. I hate you!"

Richard's voice invaded her thoughts, as if from afar. "Perhaps we should give Clare some time to adjust. It's been a harrowing day for her."

And Courtney's immediate response. "You stay out of this. Stay out of my family's life."

A sickening feeling clutched Clare's insides as flashes of a moving vehicle exploded in her brain. She heard the familiar, rumbling noise of the engine, smelled the stuffy interior. She saw herself curled up in a tight, dark place, so frightened she could hardly breathe, in her nostrils the odor of stale air freshener mixed with exhaust fumes.

I wish you were never born . . . I wish you were never born . . .

A hand touched her shoulder and Richard's warm breath feathered her temple. "You've had a long day. Why don't I take you home?"

"That sounds like a good plan."

All three turned toward the voice. Her mother stood in the halo of the porch light, Philippe close behind her.

Courtney was first to recover. "Mom . . . Philippe. What are you doing here?"

"Damage control, by the look of things." It was Philippe who responded. He wore a hard expression as he stared at Courtney.

The concern in her mother's eyes told Clare she had heard enough of their conversation to understand something was amiss.

"Are you all right, darling?" Sonia asked, moving closer to Clare.

Clare couldn't stop the shaking that had taken control of every part of her body. "Yes . . . I'm fine," she said.

Sonia looked at Richard. "I'm sorry. My eldest daughter can be a little controlling at times."

Courtney's temper was quick to ignite, even under her mother's stern scrutiny. "I'm only looking out for Clare," she said, her tone clearly implying, *since you're obviously not doing it.*

"I think you should leave," Sonia said.

"But . . ."

"Do as I say," Sonia insisted, in a sharp tone.

Courtney's face turned bright red, but she refrained from pronouncing whatever scathing retort had been about to spew from her mouth. It had been years since Clare had heard her mother speak to Courtney in that tone, and just as the voices inside her head had done, its sound catapulted her back to a dark and lonely time in her life when her fourteen-year-old sister had the power to make her feel as small and fragile as butterfly wings, and just as easily crushed.

Fighting the persistent queasiness roiling in her stomach she took in a deep breath. "No, let her stay. I remember, now. All of it. I . . . I wasn't abducted that day in Floralport. I ran away."

CHAPTER 53

CLARE

Floralport, Seventeen Years Earlier

*C*lare *brushed angry tears from her eyes and pulled the hood of the jacket lower over her head. It was Courtney's, the blue one with the white fur trim she had always admired. Her sister would be furious when she discovered she had taken it.*

Serves Courtney right for being so mean to me, she thought.

It was Courtney's fault she had run away. She would stay in town until her sister grew so concerned, she'd have no choice but to come looking for her.

If only it wasn't this cold, she thought, and sank her hands deep inside the jacket pockets to keep them from freezing. She wished she had thought to bring gloves and a scarf before rushing out of the house.

The park was deserted, but it was Christmas Eve and most people would be home helping with the Christmas preparations. They had planned to do that, too, after her mother and Aunt Lizzie returned from the hospital later that afternoon, but her row with Courtney had taken all the excitement out of her.

A bus pulled up in front of Marcy's Drugstore. It was the one that took people across five states all the way to New York City every week. They called it the Greyhound because of the big leaping dog painted on its sides. She'd often wondered, during her summer visits with Aunt Lizzie, what it would be like to travel to the big city in one of these. Mary Kate's last letter had been full of her plans for her family's first Christmas in Manhattan, and Clare had been envious. She'd give anything to be in Mary Kate's shoes just once and see the decorated windows of the store she called Saks, to walk in the snow in Central Park and munch hot dogs. She'd love to do all the fun things Mary Kate had promised to do with her when she finally visited her friend in New York.

She saw the driver step off the bus, zip up his windbreaker and cross the street, then disappear inside the Finer Diner.

He must be taking a lunch break before setting off for New York with his busload of passengers, she thought, though he couldn't be planning on staying away long, since he hadn't closed the passenger door.

The open door beckoned to her, making strange ideas pop into her head. What if she just took a peek inside? She could sit in one of the seats and look out the window, pretending she was going on a vacation to visit Mary Kate. How exciting it would be to imagine for a while to be headed to the big glittering city of Manhattan, even if it would only be make-believe.

"You wouldn't dare," her sister would say. "You're too chicken."

She blinked back fresh tears. She wasn't a coward. She was none of the bad things her sister accused her of being.

It was so quiet around her. It would be so easy to run across the street and pop inside the bus. No one would see her, not if she was quick. Before she could change her mind, she scurried across the street.

The interior of the bus smelled funny, like on an airplane, but it was warmer than being outside. There were seats on either side of the aisle, waiting to be filled with happy, excited travelers. She made her way toward the back, brushing her hands over the velvety upholstery, imagining all sorts of wonderful things. Her mom always said she had an overactive imagination, which Courtney said was pure silliness.

She slid into one of the seats all the way in the back and stared out the tinted window. The clock on the corner of the park said 2:15.

Is Courtney missing me yet, she wondered?

Her eyelids felt heavy, and she sank against the backrest, yawning. All that crying had tired her out, but she felt better now. At least she wasn't so angry anymore.

She closed her eyes and imagined going to see Mary Kate and spending Christmas with her. Of course, it was only a fantasy. Who knew if her dream would ever come true? Not until Aunt Lizzie got better, anyway. She pictured brightly lit store windows filled with the beautiful things Mary Kate had described, and it wasn't made up, either. She had watched Miracle on 34th Street *a hundred times on TV, and it was just as her friend had described it. Manhattan was like a magical wonderland during the holidays, so bright and colorful, with Christmas jingles playing everywhere. Mary Kate had ice skated in Rockefeller Center, below the huge decorated tree. It sounded like the most exciting thing ever. Mary Kate probably had a tree just like that one in her own house. She said their new apartment was humongous.*

Her eyelids fluttered as she envisioned herself riding in Santa's sleigh, like in The Christmas Rescue, *the movie she'd watched with Mom earlier that week. She imagined she was the little girl who helped Santa deliver all the gifts after his sleigh had been damaged. Like the character in the movie, she saw herself soaring up, up, high above the rooftops of the buildings, over that magical wonderland. It was the best feeling ever!*

Something soft under her cheek prickled her skin, but she was too lazy to open her eyes. She was having the best dream and she wanted it to go on forever. But the sleigh was no longer sailing smoothly across the sky like a sailboat. It was jerking and rocking from side to side and making a funny noise.

Clare's eyes flew open. It wasn't the sleigh moving. It was the bus.

CHAPTER 54

RICHARD

As she recalled the astonishing events of that day, Clare retreated into her frightened ten-year-old self, looking small and fragile. There was a distressed look in her eyes, unlike what he had witnessed that night in Lancey's. Could he have been so wrapped up in his own grievances at the time he'd missed it?

"I didn't understand right away what was happening. I thought it was all part of the dream that was transporting me to New York, to where Mary Kate lived. I was so caught up in my fantasies, I didn't realize I'd fallen asleep."

"Good Lord."

Sonia's softly uttered words resonated with the same degree of shock and disbelief Richard himself was feeling. He kept his attention focused on Clare while trying to make sense of the staggering facts. Clare's mysterious disappearance from her aunt's hometown hadn't been the result of a criminal misdeed but of a childish fantasy gone bad. A fluke. Just as the dog featured in her paintings wasn't an actual dog but the distorted memory of the Greyhound logo emblazoned on the motor coaches owned by the renowned intercity bus line. In her warped fragments of memory it impersonated the 'monster' that had taken her away from her family.

"How long were you asleep?" he asked her.

"I don't know for sure, but when I woke up it was dark outside. I couldn't make out the landscape. I stayed hunkered down where no one could see me. I was afraid that if I got caught, I'd get in trouble, that the driver would call the police and I'd end up in a home for runaway children or even in jail."

"In jail. You were a child. It was an accident, an innocent mistake," Courtney said.

Richard saw Clare's startled reaction, as if she'd momentarily forgotten Courtney was there.

"Are you all right?" he asked, edging closer to her.

She nodded but didn't take her eyes off her sister.

"I don't get it," Sonia said. "How can anyone overlook a child sitting all alone on an interstate bus?"

"There weren't many passengers, and most were sitting upfront. The lighting was dim, and I was too scared even to move."

Philippe muttered what sounded like a string of Québécois expletives. "You were on the road for what, three-four hours?" he asked.

"Closer to five, in holiday traffic," Richard guessed.

"It seemed like an awful long time," Clare said. "The few times I was brave enough to peek out the window I saw road signs, names I didn't recognize. I didn't know where we were until I heard the driver call out 'New York' and . . . and some kind of port . . ."

"Port Authority," Richard guessed.

"Yes. Yes, that's it. I remember thinking I could find Mary Kate. I had memorized her address, hoping I'd go there someday. The Morgans lived in a high-rise near Central Park. Mary Kate's parents would know what to do. They'd help me get back home."

Richard took one of her hands and laced his fingers with hers, not caring how it would look. "Go on," he said gently.

She took a shuddering breath, then proceeded. "The bus rode into some sort of underground station. I waited until all the passengers had disembarked. From the window I could see the driver retrieving the passengers' baggage from the hold. No one saw me get out."

She rubbed her arms, as if reliving the anxiety of those frightful moments. "I don't recall much from that point on, except that I had an urgent need to use the restroom. I hadn't dared use the one on the bus for fear of being discovered. Outside everything seemed big and noisy. It was my first time in a big city, and I remember feeling overwhelmed. People crowded the sidewalks. Everyone seemed to be in a hurry to get somewhere. I have a vague recollection of being inside a crowded place, somewhere animated and festive . . . a sort of noisy and chaotic winter wonderland, filled with decorations and music."

"Lancey's," Richard said. It was close enough to the Port Authority bus terminal for her to have found her way there, perhaps hoping to find a restroom.

She looked at him, her brow creased. "I can't recall anything after that. I'm sorry."

He squeezed her hand, letting her know it didn't matter.

Turning to her mother, Clare said, "I did something really stupid by running off like that. I let you and Dad down. He died believing I was killed falling off the cliff. I broke his heart."

"Oh, sweetheart, his heart was already broken. It wasn't your fault he died," Sonia rushed to say.

But Clare didn't appear to have heard her. Her attention had shifted to Courtney. When she spoke, it was in a sad, broken little-girl voice that made the hairs on Richard's skin stand on end.

"Why? Why did you never tell?"

Courtney shrunk back as if Clare had slapped her. "What are you talking about?"

"Why didn't you tell the truth about what happened that day on Puffin Top, that I had threatened to run away, to find Mary Kate in New York?"

Sonia gasped.

"I said it in anger. I was never going to do it. I ran off to town so that you would worry. I wanted to get back at you."

Sonia stared horror-struck at her older daughter. "You knew Clare had gone into town that day?"

"No," Courtney replied, immediately defensive. "I don't know what she's talking about. She's obviously distraught and doesn't know what she's saying."

Clare appeared strangely calm, as if a heavy weight had been lifted off her shoulders with her confession. "I remember what you said to me when Mom brought me back to Floralport. You said not to worry, that you'd never tell a soul what had really happened the day I disappeared. You said it would be our secret. I was confused. I didn't know what you meant, because I couldn't remember what really happened. As far as I knew, I had been kidnapped, taken against my will."

Her mother's face was ashen. "Please tell me it isn't true," she said to Courtney.

"I thought she was making it up," Courtney lashed out angrily, "that she was throwing a tantrum. It never occurred to me she'd do it. She said herself it was an accident."

Philippe sprung away from the balustrade and stood in front of Courtney. "That's not the point. Don't you see what you did? You withheld information that could have helped find Clare sooner and spared your family eight months of mourning."

Richard flexed his fingers. For once he felt empathy for the man, except he wouldn't have stopped at yelling. It was only for Clare's sake he was able to hold onto his temper.

"I thought she had died," Courtney threw back. "When they found her jacket and doll, I believed she'd fallen from the cliff, just like everyone else."

No one, including Richard, had noticed Sonia's quiet withdrawal until she spoke. "But if Clare wasn't a victim of foul play, how did her jacket and doll end up over the side of the cliff?" She turned a horrified look at Courtney. "It was you, wasn't it? You threw them over the side to make everyone believe she'd fallen."

"What?" Courtney's shocked reaction seemed genuine. "How could you think I'd do something so terrible? I was jealous, I admit it, even spiteful at times, but I'd never stoop so low as to stage my own sister's death. You have to believe me," Courtney said.

"It's true," Clare said calmly. "Courtney didn't throw my jacket and doll over the cliff. I did."

CHAPTER 55

RICHARD

Richard's mind did another double take. He was beginning to see a different Clare emerge, one her own sister's hostility and vile nature had helped shape.

"Courtney didn't see me do it," Clare said. "I hid behind the lighthouse, and when she wasn't looking, I flung them over the edge. Afterward I raced home. I remembered seeing her blue windbreaker lying on the porch swing. Courtney had left it there claiming it was too heavy for such a sunny day. I snatched it up and started running toward town."

He studied her, trying to reconcile the rash and rebellious youngster she was describing with the poised, wise-beyond-her-years little girl who had shadowed him. Just how far had her sister pushed her to have provoked such a defiant reaction from her?

As if in answer to his question, Clare said, "Courtney had said some bad things. I was hurt and angry." Her chest rose and fell rapidly, as if she had trouble breathing. "She said . . . she said she wished I'd never been born."

Richard exhaled slowly, struggling to hold on to his temper. It had been clear to him early on Clare and her sister had never been on good terms, but he had believed Courtney when she had claimed she had Clare's well-being at heart. She had him fooled. Underneath the concerned big sister façade, she was a cold and manipulative woman.

Philippe looked at her in disgust. "I was fourteen—" Courtney said in self-defense.

"—and selfish," Philippe finished. "You drove her to the brink with your insane jealousy and egocentricity. *Bon Dieu*, she was just a child."

Courtney flinched as if he'd struck her, but she was quick to recover. Defiance flashed in unblinking green eyes. "All right, fine, I was jealous. Jealous because she was our parents' blood-child, the adored baby they'd waited so long to have, while I was an adoptee, someone who had been brought into the world by mistake and not because she was wanted, yearned for. I thought I was that long-desired child for them, then she came along, and everything changed."

Only Richard heard Clare's soft whimper as Sonia hastened to contradict her older daughter. "That's not true. Your father and I fell in love with you the first moment we laid eyes on you. Not for a moment did Clare's arrival take away from that love. But you never gave it a chance." She pressed her lips together in obvious disappointment. "The pains we took to soften the impact of the changes that took place in our family, but you were such a stubborn child. It was either all or nothing with you."

"But I—"

Her mother held up a hand. "Don't. No more excuses. No more lies."

"Lies?"

"Yes, like the one about your blue jacket. You claimed it had been stolen after you left it on Lizzie's porch. I had a hunch you weren't being completely sincere, but I was too preoccupied with losing Clare to dwell on it. Afterward, it just didn't matter anymore, and I forgot all about it."

"It was the truth," Courtney said. "I did leave it on the porch, but when I got home it was gone. How could I have known Clare had taken it?"

Sonia just turned her head away, as if she couldn't bear to look at her. "What I couldn't forget," she continued as if each word were being ripped from her heart, "was the horrible suspicion I had to live with until Clare was returned to us. Because, you see, when I still thought she had fallen from that cliff, I couldn't bring myself to believe it had been accidental. Clare had always been a sensible, levelheaded child. She never would have ventured too close to the cliff's edge, not intentionally."

She looked at Courtney again. "You told me you had had an argument, one of your usual squabbles, and I kept thinking, what if things had gotten bad? What if . . . what if you did something to put Clare in harm's way?"

Courtney uttered a strangled sound. "You thought I'd pushed her? You thought I'd *killed* Clare?"

Sonia's stoop became more pronounced, her face more pinched. "All I could think was how hostile you'd always been toward Clare, how bitter for such a young girl. Your father, bless his soul, didn't harbor any such feeling—not that he ever said, anyway, and I made sure he never knew mine."

Courtney's disbelief morphed into painful outrage. "How could you? How could you have thought me capable of such a heinous act?"

"Oh, Mom," Clare murmured.

"I know, but at the time . . ." Sonia shook her head. "It was a feeling I couldn't shake off. When Clare was found it was as if a weight had been lifted off my shoulders, on all fronts. Clare was safe. I had both my daughters with me again. Our family was reunited, and it was all that mattered. So I filed my qualms away with the past and never thought about it again."

Her eyes were red and puffy when she finally looked at Clare. "Forgive me for not understanding, for not realizing how you really felt. I should have paid more attention, done more to prevent things from getting out of hand."

"Oh, Mom, there's nothing to forgive. You did what you thought was best for me and for our family."

"No. I did what was best for me. Because it was easier to pretend things weren't all that bad."

Finally, her tired gaze met Courtney's. "I hope you, too, can find it in your heart to forgive me for thinking the worst. I should have confronted you, laid it all out in the open, but I was too afraid I'd lose you, too. I realize, now, my silence did more harm than good. Instead of helping you and your sister grow closer, I caused the rift to widen."

The Courtney that emerged after Sonia's revelation was an entirely different person. There was no trace of the polished, self-possessed career woman Richard had come to know. Her makeup was smudged, giving her an owlish look, her face puffy and damp with sweat. She had become a broken version of herself.

When she spoke, there was a dull resignation in her tone. "No, you have nothing to forgive. How can I fault you for suspecting? I wasn't exactly the loving sister you'd hoped I'd be for Clare. All I can say in my defense is I truly believed she had died falling off the cliff. It was only after she turned up alive that I realized it was quite possible she'd run away like she'd threatened to do, and that she'd somehow fallen into the wrong hands. But by then it was too late to come clean."

She turned to Clare. "When I learned you'd lost your memory, I was profoundly relieved. I was terrified Mom would discover the truth about our argument that day on Puffin Top and hold me responsible for your disappearance. I was convinced she'd never forgive me." She gave a short, humorless laugh. "So much for my sense of self-preservation."

"I'm sorry," Clare said.

Courtney gave a careless shrug. "Don't be. I'm glad it's finally out in the open. It's been a constant struggle to ignore my part of responsibility in what happened to you. Your amnesia was a constant reminder of that, and I resented you for it. At least, that's what I told myself. The truth is, it was me I hated. I understand that now, and I'm sorry for the way I treated you. If I could, I'd go back and undo all the wrong I did to you, but I can't."

When she finally turned to the silent man standing off to the side, it was with a sad smile. Philippe had retreated into himself after his last outburst. Discovering a dark side to the woman he was clearly in love with had left him morally bruised and beaten.

"I'm sorry you had to find out about my shameful past this way. All these years I've done everything in my power to convince you I'm not the right woman for you, that you're better off pursuing someone else, someone worthy of the honest, upstanding man you are. But you just wouldn't listen."

When she turned to leave, Philippe didn't make a move to stop her. Richard sympathized with him. Having experienced a woman's betrayal firsthand, he knew how it felt to be blindsided.

Sonia caught Philippe's arm. "Go to her, make sure she's all right," she pleaded.

Philippe appeared conflicted. Something that sounded like French invective hissed from his lips, then he spun on his heels and took off after Courtney.

Clare sprung forward, ready to go after them. "Let them be," Richard said taking her arm.

It was more than concern on her face, it was panic. "Oh, Richard, what if Courtney hates me even more now?"

"She doesn't hate you, nor did she ever. It was fear all along. Fear you'd always hold first place in your parents' hearts. That's what drove her to behave with you the way she did."

"Richard's right," her mother said. "The question is whether she can forgive herself."

"It's my fault. I shouldn't have confronted her like this, but after everything came back to me, I couldn't stop myself."

"Hush, darling," her mother said. "None of this is your fault. Let's just be thankful it's over. It's time we all put the past behind us and got on with our lives."

Richard slid his arm around Clare's waist. "Your mother's right. No more recriminations, what ifs. No more strange dreams, for that matter."

She smiled up at him, eyes full of hope and promise.

"Well, then," Sonia said, pretending to be oblivious to the sparks of intimacy flying between him and her daughter. "I'm sure you two have a lot of catching up to do, so I'd best be on my way."

"It will be all right," he said to Clare after her mother had left, sensing her lingering concern.

She sighed heavily, leaning against him. "I hope you're right. I'd never forgive myself if I spoiled Courtney's chances with Philippe."

"I don't think you have anything to worry about. The man doesn't strike me as being the type to give up. And neither am I."

She swung around to face him. "I should think not."

Her serious tone filled him with hope. "Does that mean you'll marry me, Misty-Clare?"

Her mouth dropped open. "Marry you?"

"I thought we were working our way up to that before we were so rudely interrupted."

Suddenly he was nervous, worried he was going too fast. "I didn't think I'd ever want to propose to another woman, but you changed that . . . me. Being away from you made me understand how important you are to me. You're the only woman I can see a future with. The only one I want to share it with. I can't risk losing you again."

Her slow, guileless smile was the sweetest thing he had seen in a long time. "What makes you think I'm going anywhere, Dr. Kelly, unless it's with you? Of course, I'll marry you. It's time I make good on my promise to take care of you forever."

"Damn right." He cupped her face with his hands and pulled her in for a long, smoldering kiss. "Because I'm going to need lots and lots of . . . care," he said afterwards.

EPILOGUE

CLARE

The park was practically deserted, which was just as well, given they were about to commit an act of vandalism. Richard had told Clare how years ago he'd risked a hefty fine and possibly jail time to bury Molly in this very spot, in the heart of Washington Square Park, Molly's favorite place to be. But he hadn't been a prominent neurosurgeon with a hard-earned reputation to defend at the time. Only a pair of elderly men sat a few benches down, but they were deeply engrossed in a game of chess and weren't paying them any mind.

She went down on her knees on the hard-packed earth and brushed some dry leaves from the flat stone marker, then she tore open the plastic bag she carried with her. Before she could prevent it, a full pound of prime quality sunflower seeds poured out onto the stone with the rudimentarily engraved name "Molly" on its crude surface. Molly had been a glutton for sunflower seeds.

"Oops. Too much?" she asked looking up at Richard.

"Only enough to lure the entire park's population of squirrels out of their cozy dens," he said grinning.

He held out his hand to pull her up and into his arms. "Hey, you did good," he said kissing the tip of her nose. "And you know Molly wouldn't have appreciated flowers as much."

She smiled, remembering how flowers had made the primate sneeze. Every time she remembered something new it gave her a thrill of joy.

Hand in hand, they walked toward the nearby fountain, now emptied of its water in preparation of the winter season. The entire park was a lot different than she remembered it. It had been completely redesigned, and several of the larger, older trees had been removed to make space for green areas. Even the fountain had been relocated to a different spot, strategically aligned with the arch, but the place was still reminiscent of the many happy hours she'd spent there.

From the moment she had stepped back into the bustling old neighborhood, Clare had experienced a persistent feeling of familiarity, like the reawakening of a different part of herself she was only just beginning to discover. Not many new memories had made it to the surface, but then, she had been too young for them not to have faded naturally with time.

Richard reached out and gently brushed away a tear she didn't even know was there. Something in that tender gesture brought about a feeling of déjà vu.

"Let's go someplace more private," he said.

"Where?"

"How about Charlie's Bar and Grill? It's not exactly private but at least it'll be warm."

She still struggled with remembering things, but she remembered the guys' old stomping ground well, though she had never set foot inside. The place was off-limits to her whenever they went there in their spare time.

"All right," she said.

It was past the morning rush, so the place wasn't crowded. A young couple sat at a table chatting over coffee, while two men in suits occupied the stools at the oak-paneled counter. They were nursing an early beer and prognosticating animatedly the upcoming Rangers' versus Predators' game.

The server directed them to a booth and stood by for their orders. Clare had already had breakfast at Mrs. B's and asked for a latte while Richard ordered black coffee.

The smugness she was feeling must have been showing on her face because he asked, "What?"

"Why didn't you ever want to bring me here?"

He frowned. "Because. It wasn't a place for kids. It was always teeming with raunchy college dudes."

"Does this mean I'm a big girl now and can defend myself from lurking perverts?"

His face darkened menacingly. "It means God help any smart-ass guy that thinks he can hit on you."

She almost laughed until she realized he was serious.

"I'm so happy Tony and Jake will be spending Christmas with us at Mrs. B's," she said, deeming it wise to change the subject.

Richard had told her Tony was a successful concert pianist with the New York Philharmonic, and that he'd married and had two boys. Jake was now living in Seattle and had done well for himself with his software consulting business. He and his girlfriend would be flying in just before Christmas to join them.

He shifted in his chair. "Speaking of which . . ." He dug a hand inside the back pocket of his jeans and produced a folded piece of paper. He placed it in front of her.

She gazed at it with curiosity. "What is it?" she asked.

"Your Christmas present."

"Christmas present? But it's not even Thanksgiving yet."

He looked slightly embarrassed. "It's . . . time sensitive."

Intrigued, she unfolded the sheet of paper. It was an electronic receipt for a boat ride for two in Central Park. It was for the day after tomorrow, November 10.

"It's the last day before the boathouse closes for the winter. Seventeen years ago I made you a promise, and I pride myself on being a man of my word."

His image swam as moisture pooled in her eyes. "Oh, Richard . . . I love you so much," was all she could say.

A bemused expression lingered in his gaze, as it always did whenever she expressed her feelings for him, as if he couldn't quite believe anyone could love him so deeply.

"I love you, too," he said, linking his fingers with hers.

The magical aura of intimacy that enveloped them was brusquely shattered when the door opened and a group of boisterous youngsters strode in, letting in a rush of cold air. They made straight for the bar where they slid noisily onto the barstools, talking and laughing among themselves.

"So much for cozy and private," Richard said under his breath.

There was a hint of frustration in his tone, prompting her to ask, "What's wrong?"

He snapped out of his surliness. "Nothing. It's just . . . Well, there's something I've been meaning to talk to you about."

"All right," she said, suddenly nervous.

"This morning I got a call from John Sullivan."

"The chief of St. Isabel Hospital?"

He nodded. "Right after Jimmy Serrano's surgery, he asked me if I'd be interested in becoming part of his team. I didn't take his proposal seriously at the time, thinking it was the adrenaline talking. Turns out he meant it. They're expanding the facility to include a state-of-the-art neurosurgical unit, and the board of directors want me to head it. They plan to partner with Miami's Ryder Trauma Center to handle some of their more serious cases involving patients with traumatic brain and spinal cord injuries." He gauged her expression. "The joint venture would be contingent on my acceptance."

The news surprised Clare. They'd never broached the subject of where they'd live after they were married, and she'd assumed she'd follow him to New York.

She took a sip of her latte to give herself time to absorb the details.

"What did you tell him?" she asked.

"I said I'd think about it. It's an enticing offer but it's not something one can decide on the spur of the moment."

He's doing it for me, she thought. He's willing to sacrifice everything he's worked for, to ensure I don't have to leave St. Isabel and the life he knows I love.

"And have you? Thought about it, I mean."

"Some, but I wanted to run it by you first."

She tried to curb her excitement. "But what about your practice—your hard-earned career? Why would you give it all up to work in an obscure little island?"

The gaze holding hers softened. "Perhaps because there's something more valuable to me on that island no amount of success or notoriety could substitute for, something I've been unwittingly yearning for all my life," he replied.

His words took her breath away for the unmitigated love that transpired from them.

"Besides, I wouldn't have to give up my practice. I was thinking I could take on a partner or two to take care of business on this end and fly in a couple of times a month for consults and surgical procedures. St. Isabel's may be a small operation, but I know I can make a difference there, too."

She swallowed the lump in her throat. It sounded as if he had it all planned out. She had to admit his reasoning made perfect sense, but she couldn't shake the feeling he was putting her needs and happiness before his own.

As if seeing through her hesitation, he took her hands in his. "Do you think I'd ask you to marry me if I didn't think I could build a life with you in St. Isabel? You belong there. Rainbow's End is your dream, what you've worked so hard to achieve. I'd never expect you to walk away from that."

Richard was right. She loved New York, loved being with Max and Mary, but St. Isabel was her real home, where she'd always wanted to be, even if she'd gladly follow him anywhere. As for Rainbow's End, she hadn't allowed herself to think that far ahead, but deep in her heart she knew she wanted to see its completion through, to have an active part in its management. The settlement money from the Lancey's lawsuit had enabled her not only to fulfill her dream, but to expand it beyond anything she had ever hoped for. It was now to incorporate The Misty Rehabilitation Center, an educational facility for children from troubled backgrounds with psychic trauma and behavioral issues. The idea had come to her after recovering her memory of her own traumatic experience, and she knew she wanted to do something to help children like her, to make everything she and her family had gone through count for something.

Only one thing was missing for her life to be perfect. Guilt still gnawed at her for having exposed her sister's secret, although she knew she had done the right thing. She hadn't seen Courtney since that harrowing night at the cabin and had left her several messages on her phone in Miami. When Courtney had finally responded, it had been with a brief text, congratulating her on her engagement to Richard and promising she and Philippe would be at their wedding. She had taken it as a positive sign her sister had finally given up fighting her love for Philippe, and it had given her hope for a full reconciliation.

Richard's touch on the inside of her wrist was gentle, caressing. "But that's only half the truth. The other half is that it's what I want to do. Granted, there've been some gratifying moments in my career, but things have changed. *I've* changed. This is the chance for me to do what I really like doing, and that's dealing with critical situations and treating trauma victims." The gleam of anticipation in his eyes left no doubt as to the depth of his feelings on the matter. "Opportunities like this don't come around very often in life, and I've overlooked one too many."

"Well, when you put it that way . . ."

His eyes crinkled at the corners. He smiled a lot, these days, so much so it was difficult to picture him as the distant and closed-off man she'd first met on Monks' Beach.

"I went to visit Mother Superior the day before we left."

The abrupt change in subject came as a surprise.

"You did?" She wondered why he hadn't mentioned it before.

"I decided it was time to properly introduce myself, you know, seeing as I'll be a frequent visitor of the abbey for the foreseeable future."

"Makes sense," she said, trying not to grin.

"She told me some of the kids had moved on, placed in good homes," he added, and she thought she detected a touch of the old cynicism in his comment.

"Yes, Michael and Sherri have both been adopted. I was sad to see them go."

"Joey will be the next one to go, I feel it," he said.

She was touched to see the consternation on his face. It was clear he'd developed a soft spot for the child.

"I sincerely hope so. He's made a lot of progress in the past few months. It won't be long before he's a viable candidate himself," she said.

Richard scrunched his napkin into a ball and tossed it into his empty cup. "So that some well-meaning couple can snatch him up, have a cute trophy they can parade around to their high-society friends? What if no one wants him? He could end up being bounced around the foster care system, or worse, be neglected or abused—become a child delinquent."

The heated diatribe left Clare speechless. She hadn't realized how strongly he felt about Joey, but she understood. He was afraid Joey would experience the same fate he had, the same he'd fought to ensure Clare didn't meet with.

She was about to argue nothing like that was likely to befall Joey, that authorities these days had strict standards and policies in place to protect children like him, when his next words stopped her.

"What do you say we throw in our lot?"

She stared open-mouthed at him, for a moment wondering if she'd misunderstood.

"You mean . . . adopt Joey?"

He leaned in and took her hands in his. "I've watched you with him. There's something special there that you don't have with any of the others. Face it, you've become emotionally attached to him. And the kid's crazy about you. He may even be starting to like me."

The chatter around them and the noise of clinking glasses receded into the background. Clare was aware only of the two of them, as if they were caught in a soundproof bubble. It was true, she loved Joey. She'd always known sooner or later he'd be gone, like all the children before him, but she'd been powerless to prevent her heart from succumbing to his innocent charm. The possibility the boy could become a permanent fixture in her life was almost too good to contemplate.

"Sister Ursula thinks we stand a good chance. As a married couple, I mean," Richard said.

She blinked. "You talked to Mother Ursula about it?"

"Actually, it was her idea. She must have seen something me and you had yet to see."

He mistook her shock for hesitation, and he pulled back. "I must be crazy. I don't know what I was thinking dropping this on you."

"No, I think it's a wonderful idea," she said, her smile so wide her jaw hurt.

"Really?"

"Really. I just need a moment to absorb it all."

His expression relaxed. "Good, but I don't want you to get your hopes up yet. The odds may be in our favor, but the final decision is up to the courts, and there's always a chance our application is rejected."

The thought they might not pass muster was sobering, but it was worth the try. Richard was right. What if Joey ended up with an unsuitable family? What if they didn't love him enough or weren't sensitive enough to his special needs?

She straightened. "I know, but Joey's worth fighting for, and I'm all up for the battle."

He chuckled. "That's my girl. I'm confident we're going to beat this, even if I have to call in the big guns. Max's done this before and won't hesitate to get involved if I ask him to. Besides, it's what's best for Joey that counts."

Joy bubbled up inside Clare. In the space of a few minutes her entire future had been reshaped, and it was even better than any she had envisioned before.

She exhaled slowly. "Could you perhaps give me some time to regain my breath before you spring any more surprises on me?" she asked.

His smile was slow and suspiciously sultry. "I have one more I was saving for later, one that requires a much more private venue, a comfortable sofa in front of the fireplace, soft music playing in the background, and lots of cuddling."

His soft, seductive tone sent a shiver of anticipation through her body. "Well, what are we waiting for?"

He cupped the back of her neck and pulled her face to his for a swift passionate kiss. Then he sprang to his feet, threw some bills on the table, and took her hand in a firm grip. "Let's get out of here," he said.

It was snowing when the door of Charlie's swung closed behind them, big, fat snowflakes that melted on Clare's open lips as she looked up at the leaden sky. Snow in November, she thought delighted. Could it get any better than this?

She cocked an eyebrow at Richard. "Tell me you didn't arrange for this to happen."

He winked at her. "Of course. It's all part of the plan."

THE END

Kijimea IBS

ABOUT THE AUTHOR

Josephine Strand was born in Italy, grew up in South Africa, and is a long-time resident of the United States. Her travels between the three continents have strengthened her love for the sea and the outdoors. When not writing or absorbed in the latest gripping page-turner, she loves to cook and enjoys long nature walks. *Misty Dreams* is her first novel. Visit her at josephinestrand.com.